Also by Tarah Benner

The Defectors
Enemy Inside

The Last Uprising

Book three in the Defectors Trilogy

By
Tarah Benner

Copyright 2014 Tarah Benner

All rights reserved

Printed in the United States of America

First Edition

Cover design by Adrijus Guscia

This book is a work of fiction. Names, characters, places, and incidents either are the product of the author's imagination or are used fictitiously, and any resemblance to actual persons, living or dead, is entirely coincidental.

No part of this book may be reproduced, scanned, or distributed in any printed or electronic form without permission. Please do not participate in or encourage piracy of copyrighted materials in violation of the author's rights. Purchase only authorized editions.

ISBN 978-1500609290
www.tarahbenner.com

To my earliest readers. You are the ones who kept me going and made the rest of this series possible.

Chapter One

The only thing worse than fear is uncertainty.

In the simulation room, familiar images flashed before my eyes. The pictures still made my stomach clench with nausea, but it was getting better.

Now, I could look at the twisted, bloody remains of men strewn across the battlefield. I could look at the melting skin of the children in the pictures. I remembered those pictures from a documentary I had seen about Hiroshima. Crime scene photos were mixed in with the images of war. The blood and the peeling, burnt, broken, and twisted human beings blended with the images of destruction. I'd seen these pictures over and over again so many times that I had the order memorized.

What bothered me more than the images themselves was the nagging feeling of déjà vu. Yes, I'd seen this sequence twelve times a day every day for thirty-five days, but I felt as though I'd seen it more than that. Where had I seen it before?

Such a dangerous world requires a new generation of soldiers . . . a force for good to keep ordinary citizens safe from evildoers . . . safe from the violence of rebellion and the abominations created by the modern age.

A carrier appeared, and something in the back of my mind — an old fear — made me recoil.

The Private Military Company of the United States is always working to protect and serve, and World Corp International is

The Last Uprising

committed to rebuilding a future from the ashes in this the New Northern Territory, where brothers and sisters work side by side for the common good.

Order. Compliance. Progress. This is our credo.

There are those who seek to disrupt our harmony and destroy our world. These menaces don't deserve your sympathy. They are the true plague upon our world, and they must be defeated.

Go forth and do your duty, citizen. The New Republic needs you.

The sequence ended, and a robotic feminine tone sounded.

End of simulation.

The screen went black, and that feeling of boredom mixed with relief began to sink in. As awful as the simulations were, the strange dread that I was missing something important tormented me more.

Reluctantly, I got up to exit the theater, knocking one of the hundred identical white chairs out of place. There were exactly one hundred. I'd counted every day that first week. It seemed odd that there should be a hundred chairs when there was only one of me.

"Now, Haven . . ." taunted a familiar voice.

I jumped when I saw the man sitting in the back row. He was so tan he was practically orange, and he wore crisply pleated white pants and a blazer. His hair and goatee were the lightest silver, and he had cold, steely eyes like a shark.

"That's a little . . . passive aggressive, don't you think?" His thin lips curved into a smile I didn't like.

"Just stumbled a little," I said lightly, hoping he didn't register the fear that lifted my voice an octave too high.

This man had visited me before during my first behavioral adjustment. He had stood and watched me through the clear, cold water in my hallucination, flashing that same smile as I cried out in anguish.

"I doubt that very much. You're determined, that's for sure. It's taken us a long time to get here. But you've made tremendous progress."

My nostrils flared, but I didn't say anything. Yes, I had made progress, but it had been painful. Within the first two weeks here, I'd learned that I could avoid trips to that horrible room with the cold metal table if I stayed within the boundaries, ate my meals, and "responded" to the simulations. I'd gotten sixteen new HALLO burns for my trouble. They stood out more sharply than my old ones. For some reason, I couldn't remember where I'd gotten those.

I was used to the HALLO tags by now — so used to them in fact that they'd had to go up to five on the last session before I passed out. The worst part about adjustments was that they increased the settings on my CID. Although I'd memorized the boundaries of the atrium — how far I could go before the pain started — occasionally, I would still look away from the screen during my sessions in the theater and receive a sharp shock to the back of my skull.

They wanted me to look.

"You could be a great asset, you know," the man continued lazily. "Probably my greatest achievement."

For some reason, that made my chest swell with pride. Despite the pain, the horror, and the silence that stretched the hours of each day, I desperately wanted to be useful to the Republic.

Sensing my receptiveness, he stood up, stepped around the chairs without touching them, and stopped just inches away from me. "If I can take the Republic's most defiant and turn her into a force for good, then others will see it is pointless to resist. You and I . . . we could fix all this."

The Last Uprising

"All of what?" I breathed, trying not to cringe as the sharp tang of ginseng lozenges reached my nostrils.

The man turned away, seemingly lost in thought. "When I was a child, we lived out in the country. Fresh air, good exercise . . . it was a great place to grow up, as a young boy. My family lived so far out that we weren't on city water. We drank well water. It didn't taste very good, but what we didn't know, of course, was that the water was tainted."

I swallowed, willing myself to nod.

"Until, when I was twelve, my mother was diagnosed with cancer."

He gripped the back of one of the chairs, and I watched his tan knuckles whiten. "A chemical company was dumping toxic waste illegally, and there was nothing we could do about it. We couldn't afford to take the company to *court*. We could barely afford to keep our house."

"That's awful," I said, just so he would know I was still listening. I wasn't really sure why he was telling me this.

"The world is a terrible place, Haven. It always has been."

"Unless we change things," I said slowly, echoing what he had told me before, just wishing he would leave.

"Exactly, Haven! Exactly!" he said, clapping his hands together in delight. "When I was younger, I told myself I would never be so powerless again. I wanted to be richer than God himself so no one — no one — could ever ignore me again. I thought I could make them listen if I had wealth and power . . . if I created an American dynasty."

He turned to face me. "But that's not the solution, is it? There will always be people who get *shit* on. Maybe not me, but someone. The key to change isn't money; it's control. People need the Republic to tell them what to do — to tell them what's right. Otherwise, given half the chance, humanity will destroy everything we have worked for."

The Last Uprising

I nodded numbly.

"We're doing it, Haven. You and me."

I closed my eyes, fighting the nausea that was churning in my stomach. I hated this man with every fiber of my being, yet I had no idea why. Everything he said sent a ripple of sickness and wrongness through my body, and his voice filled me with a sense of dread.

When I opened my eyes, I was alone in the simulation room — alone as always. I dragged myself into the main atrium and headed for the dining room. I'd memorized where all the white doors went, and they no longer had to send a nurse to escort me. I knew what would happen if I tried to run.

Everything here was white: the walls, the chairs, the floor, my scrubs. Even the room where I slept and the room where I was allowed to eat was white. I hated it.

The food wasn't supposed to be white, but the bland, muted vegetables turned to ash in my mouth. I'd lost a lot of weight in the first two weeks I was here, and they forced the white, flavorless food down my throat with a tube. I didn't like that.

Now I ate on my own.

When I entered the dining room, my meal was waiting on a flimsy white silicon tray just as always. No one had to come serve my meals. The table was pushed up against the wall at just the right height to receive my tray through a tiny slot in the wall. Sometimes I waited by the slot to see the little window open up and catch a glimpse of the person on the other side, but it was completely dark.

By now, I knew there *was* no person on the other side — just a conveyer belt that ran the frozen meal through an oven, through the slot, and onto my table.

Today, dinner was a tofu brick with sweet potatoes and

The Last Uprising

dark gray green beans. That meant it was day five. I had no idea what day of the week I first came here, so I considered my first day number one. I noticed they used the same seven breakfasts, the same seven lunches, and the same seven dinners on a repeated rotation, so that was how I remembered how many days I'd been here. I suspected that day seven was Sunday, because that was the only day I got actual meat: a lukewarm cube of meatloaf with bits of confetti inside masquerading as dehydrated onions.

    I didn't mind. The only thing that really bothered me was how my entire meal had to be either hot or cold, confirming my suspicions that a machine ran the entire frozen meal through an oven.

    I glared at the clear, round pill sitting in its own little indentation on my tray — so harmless looking. They'd been giving it to me since I'd arrived. I couldn't remember what they had drugged me with when I was in the hospital. It had been an endless parade of doctors poking and prodding, horrible sweating fevers, and nausea. I'd thought I was dying, but then they had cured me.

    This little clear pill was almost worse. It made me tired and careless and foggy, but if I did not take it, they would send in a nurse with a syringe, and I would be sent to the adjustment room. I picked it up between my thumb and index finger, made eye contact with the camera pointed at my table, and dry-swallowed the smooth tablet dramatically. I could almost feel my willpower draining.

    Just as I was about to stick my fork into the sharp corner of my tofu brick, I heard the bang of a door. I sat up straight.

    Why were they sending a nurse? I'd been on good behavior today. It didn't seem fair that they would haul me off for an adjustment when I hadn't done anything to warrant it. I bent my head over my tofu, hoping that if she saw me contentedly eating as I was supposed to, maybe she would see that I didn't need to be adjusted.

My back tightened as the quick footsteps echoed off the high walls of the atrium. They weren't nurses' shoes. Those made a squeaky noise on the shiny white tile. These steps were loud and angry.

"Haven!"

I jerked my head up at the familiar hiss. There, poking his head around the corner of the doorway, was a young man about my age with clean-cut dark hair and bright, sharp gray eyes.

"Amory," I whispered. Without thinking, the name had slipped out of my mouth. Somehow I knew him — at least I knew his name.

"You're alive!" He wore a look so beautiful and happy it took my breath away.

"How do I —"

"Come on! There isn't much time."

My mind was working furiously, but I couldn't remember how I knew him. It was the same odd sense of déjà vu I got during the simulations.

"How do I . . . know you?"

The relief drained from his face to be replaced by hurt and confusion.

"Haven. It's me. We have to go! Now!"

Something tugged at the edges of my memory, but it was like feeling my way through a dark room. "I don't understand."

"What?"

His eyes crinkled in distress, and he crossed the room to me and put his hands on my arms. I jumped at his touch, and a look of fear flashed through his eyes.

"You don't remember me?"

"No. Not really . . ."

"What did they do to you, Haven?"

"Stop saying my name!" I was starting to panic. He knew who I was, and I knew his name, but I didn't *know* him.

"What did they *do* to you?" he asked louder.

"Who?"

"Aryus Edric. World Corp International."

"What do you mean?"

"We have to get out of here."

"I can't leave."

"I know. It's going to be hard, but I've done it. You helped me. Remember?"

Something stirred in the back of my mind. I pictured Amory in my white scrubs, and a memory flickered in the back of my mind.

"Yes," I stammered in surprise. "I-I did. Why did I do that?"

"Because you don't want to be here. These are bad people."

"What? Where do you want me to go?"

Amory was shaking his head now, thinking hard.

"Just come on. I'll explain when we get out of here."

In the back of my mind, I knew I shouldn't, but something about the way he talked ignited a feeling of excitement in my chest. *So what if it would end in an adjustment?* It might be worth it just to see what he was talking about.

The Last Uprising

I'd been trying to get through the door that led out beyond the atrium for weeks, but every time, it had ended in a very painful, humiliating shock to the back of the head.

"All right," I said, hesitating slightly.

He grabbed my hand, pulling me out of the dining room. I wanted to protest, but his warm hand felt nice holding mine. Something about it was familiar. In fact, everything about him screamed familiarity, but I couldn't quite access the part of my brain that knew him. It was all very strange.

My white, no-slip soles squeaked against the tile as we crossed the atrium. Watching Amory pull me along, I took in the black jacket that stretched across his broad shoulders and olive-colored pants tucked over dirty black boots. He didn't look as if he belonged, and I liked it. Everyone here wore white scrubs and lab coats.

Under the cleanly shaven line of hair on the back of his neck, I could just make out a square scar that looked the way mine felt, but it was cut across the middle in a shaky line. By the looks of it, we had the same CID. Or we *had*. Somehow, I remembered he didn't have his anymore.

He pushed open the white door that the nurses used to enter the atrium and pulled me across the threshold.

Instantly, a sharp, familiar pain cracked across the back of my skull. It pulsated through my head, splitting me in two between the eyes and down the bridge of my nose. I tried to get back into the safe boundaries, but my legs wouldn't move.

"Haven!" Amory's voice sounded oddly fuzzy.

Blinking through the mist, I forced myself to focus on his face. His eyes were filled with apprehension. He remembered how it felt when it had happened to him. He pulled on my hand, dragging my feet incrementally over the floor. The pain intensified, and black spots erupted in my vision.

A sharp shriek echoed down the corridor, and I covered my ears. The sound reverberated, and I thought for a moment that I could see the waves of sound disturbing the air and rocking back toward me. The scream sounded again, stronger this time. Then I realized it belonged to me.

Someone was yanking me away from the safety of the atrium into the blinding white corridor. I didn't want to go. Every step I took intensified the pain in the back of my head.

"Haven! Haven!" I squinted through the black fog unfurling around my eyes.

Amory.

"Haven! Come on. It's all an illusion. It isn't real."

His face was fuzzy, but I could still make out the resolve in those gray eyes. They shone through the mist like two beacons of light.

As I concentrated, the mist lifted enough for me to discern the crinkles around Amory's eyes and his distressed grimace as he watched me scream.

Why was he putting me through this? Every step I took just caused me pain.

I backed away, pulling out of Amory's grip to return to the atrium. He grabbed both of my wrists, pulling me in the other direction. But it hurt too much.

I felt the hard shock to my knees as they hit the cold tile, and the pain reverberated up to my thighs. I couldn't let him take me any farther. I screamed again, and a pair of strong arms wrapped around me and lifted me up against my will.

He was carrying me — strangling me — and every step he took caused me more pain. My whole body felt as though it were being stabbed all over by a thousand knives, but the wounds did not bleed. They merely punctured the skin enough to leave tracks of angry skids and burns, occasionally hitting with such force that they bruised me down to the bone.

Why did he not understand that he was hurting me? Why hadn't I passed out?

The pain was too much — worse than I'd ever experienced. It was nothing the HALLO tags could have prepared me for. The hallucinations the HALLO tags produced were tangible: flames that charred you, chemical ice that froze and blistered the skin, or water that filled your lungs and drowned you. This was just pain in its rawest, most basic form. There was no way out — no way to fight it — because it had no source. It was everywhere at once, breaking me down with every step Amory took.

I became aware of soreness in my hands and wrists. Beating my fists against his back, kicking and screaming and crying, I tried to tell him to stop.

The light pulsating sensation in my head had escalated to a constant throttling, as though I were experiencing repeated whiplash in the middle seat of a car.

I thought I might be sick. I retched, but my stomach was empty. I continued to dry heave, and the spasms escalated.

Shaking uncontrollably, I tried to yell out.

He was killing me. Amory was killing me. Something deep in the recesses of my brain shut off, and I felt myself losing the fight.

Why was he taking me from the atrium in the first place?

I didn't understand. I didn't understand why he would take me away from my bed and the food and the routine of it all. Twelve times a day, I experienced the joyful moment of déjà vu — a whispered clue to something I used to know. That was all I needed.

The Last Uprising

    I didn't care. I didn't want to go back, and I didn't want to leave with him. I just wanted it to stop.

    And then it did.

Chapter Two

The voices started as no more than a faraway rumble of activity I couldn't discern — a theater of excited people waiting for the show to start. Then, little by little, the voices pulled apart like drips of honey. The spatters of conversation began to take shape.

"It was terrible. I've never seen her like that. I've never seen anybody like that."

"Yours was pretty bad."

"I don't remember it being that terrible. She was almost . . . a different person."

"She's been there a lot longer."

"Only two months."

"That's all the time they need, I guess."

One of the voices belonged to Amory. I recognized the other voice, too, but recalling its owner required a deep dig into the dusty corners of my brain. I squinted against the bright light fanning around the edges of my eyelids. My head hurt. I didn't want to open my eyes just yet. I didn't want to face where I was or what had happened.

Lying there, I could feel the hum of motion beneath me and the muffled rush of wind. I was in a car, and I could sense there were other people around me: Amory and the other boy who had spoken. Not opening my eyes, I allowed myself to be lulled into a dreamlike state by the gentle movement of the car.

The Last Uprising

Two cool fingers touched the side of my neck, ghosting over my skin like a raindrop and feeling my pulse. The person next to me sighed loudly.

"I don't know why she hasn't woken up yet." It was Amory.

"That's fine. We'd probably have to knock her out again when we get there. If she's as messed up as you say —"

I grimaced. I didn't like the sound of that.

"I don't want to sedate her."

"We have to."

"You don't know that," he said angrily. *"She might wake up and be fine."*

"I was there when she woke up from getting her tonsils out. Trust me. She's not going to be fine."

Tonsils. *When had I had my tonsils out?*

A memory resurfaced, slowly at first, and then faster and more vivid. I was twelve when I got my tonsils removed, and Greyson had been there when I woke up.

Greyson. That was the other speaker. *Why was he here?* I didn't understand.

After a while, the car stopped, and I felt Amory's arms lift me bodily from the car. The cold air stung my face, but my bare arms in the thin white scrubs had been covered by something warm and heavy — his jacket. *Why did I have his jacket?*

As soon as the cold stopped, I knew we were inside. I heard the floor groan under the combined weight of Amory and me as he carried me to a room and laid me on a soft bed that smelled ancient.

"She doesn't need that."

"It's for her own good," said a much deeper, unsympathetic

voice.

"You know I don't agree with this," said Amory.

"That's fine."

The third person took another step toward me, and a moment later, I felt the hard stab of a needle in my arm.

Something was missing.

There were no voices, but I could feel the presence of several other people in the room — their eyes watching me.

Unsteady light flickered behind my eyelids, and I forced myself to open them.

What looked like a rundown old motel room came slowly into focus: the fake wood paneling, the ugly brown bedspread that smelled like pine-scented cleaner, cheap perfume, and stale cigarette smoke. The concerned faces of Greyson, Amory, and Logan hovered above me.

Logan. I was surprised I recognized her at once, but here she was. She didn't look right, though. She was too pale, rail thin, and wrapped up in a blanket on the chair next to the bed, though the room wasn't cold.

They were all watching me expectantly.

"Haven," Amory breathed. He looked relieved but did not reach out to touch me. Up close, I could see the dark shadows under his eyes and the way his mouth strained to pull up around the edges into a smile.

Realizing what had happened, I sat up with a start, jerking my head around like a caged animal. I pulled myself awkwardly into a seated position. One of my hands was tied above my head, bound to the headboard with a piece of cloth.

"Hey, hey. It's all right." Amory's hand jerked on the bedspread, as though he wanted to reach out to squeeze my arm but thought better of it.

"Where am I?"

"Somewhere safe," said Greyson.

Something about seeing Greyson put me at ease. His caramel-colored skin and warm brown eyes were as familiar as my own, but I didn't understand why. I knew him, but I didn't.

"We removed your CID," Greyson continued.

Amory shot him a deadly look.

Shoulder aching, I reached up with my free hand and lifted my hair to feel the tender skin on the back of my neck. There was a new bandage and, underneath, the bumps of a fresh incision sutured together. It hurt a little. Something inside me seemed to break, and my eyes filled with tears.

"That wasn't your decision to make," I said. My voice shook.

I felt broken and violated. Most of all, I felt confused.

"Haven, we got you out of that PMC brainwashing facility." Logan's voice was strained with worry. "You're safe now. Amory risked his life . . ."

"That wasn't your decision, either!" I yelled.

"What do you —"

"I was fine!"

"They were torturing you," she said.

"They were *teaching* me."

"Teaching you what?"

"Logan," Amory said in a warning voice. "Stop. She's been drugged."

"No, I haven't!"

I *had* been drugged, but I was in control.

Logan was undeterred. "Teaching you *what?*"

"I was finally making progress!"

Why was I screaming?

Now that I was out of there, I knew that these people had been my friends. So why did everything feel so wrong?

Burning hot resentment filled my veins, and the small room suddenly felt too crowded. I hated this room. It made me feel dirty and trapped and estranged.

I took a deep breath, trying to ease the fear that the whole place might crash in on me at any moment.

No. These people were not my friends. They were pretenders. They had taken me away just when things were starting to improve.

"Haven, there's something else," said Amory, reaching out to touch my leg, but I jerked it away, pulling my knees up to my chin and glaring at him.

"Do you really think now is a good time?" Greyson muttered under his breath.

"She deserves to know."

"Know *what?*" I growled.

Amory took a deep breath. "We're at war."

My eyes flitted between Amory and Greyson. "Who?"

"The rebels have crossed the border to fight World Corp and the PMC. We're trying to draw attention to what's going on so the people here will turn against them. If we can get the documented people involved, it will be an easy win. If we can't —"

"You're not going to win," I said automatically.

Amory stopped talking. He was looking at me as though

The Last Uprising

he'd misheard.

The three of them exchanged an anxious look.

"What?" asked Greyson.

"If you try to fight World Corp International, you will die." I took a deep breath. "You're on the wrong side."

Chapter Three

It doesn't matter what side you're on. Being a prisoner anywhere is pretty much the same.

With the rebels, the treatment was slightly better, but it didn't feel humane. I stayed tied to the bed in that dark room, shaking and sweating. Amory told me I was going through withdrawal, and I believed him. Nothing would stay down, and I felt dizzy, nauseated, and disoriented for three days.

Greyson and Amory took turns guarding me, and I glared at them through the haze.

After the effects of the little clear pill had worn off, they explained that I had been held at the facility against my will. I didn't know if I believed them. I couldn't shake the horrible feeling that the three people who told me they were my friends were just as bad as the man whose face rippled above the water as I was drowning in my nightmares.

The food they brought me wasn't anemic and tasteless like the food at the facility, but I told myself they were feeding me well in an effort to lower my defenses and coax me over to their side.

There were days it felt as though it was working. I ate as though I was starving, and the way they looked at me, maybe I had been. After a few days, I felt stronger and more alert.

One day, I overheard Amory and Logan arguing in the hallway, and I thought for a while that they were debating whether or not to kill me.

In the end, Amory seemed to win, but he still wasn't happy. He left for a while, and when he returned, Greyson blindfolded me and tied my hands.

He packed up our scant possessions from the room, and they put me in a van. We drove for a few hours, maybe longer. I lost track of time.

When the van finally stopped and Amory slid the door open to let me out, I could smell pine trees. The cold, fresh air filled my lungs and revitalized me, and I allowed myself to enjoy the warmth of Amory's gentle hand on my back as he guided me through the woods. I counted my steps from the van so I would know how far I was from the road, but I was disoriented, and I had no idea what direction I was walking.

I could hear someone splitting wood and the sounds of dozens of people moving around, so I knew they had brought me to a rebel camp. Since it would have been nearly impossible to cross the border with a hostage in the backseat, I surmised that we were still in the New Northern Territory.

Amory's hands touched my shoulders to steady me and reached behind my head to untie the blindfold. When he pulled the fabric away, the camp came into view: a rough circle of about forty tents clustered in pockets of trees. There was an enormous bonfire burning in the middle of the clearing, and rebels in black milled around fetching water, preparing food, and carrying firewood. No one paid us any attention.

He led me to a tent tucked farther back in the woods than the others, with a crude sign staked in front of it that read "Auxiliary Supplies."

Amory cleared his throat uncomfortably. "Roman thinks it might be best to keep you away from the others until . . . until you recover."

A sharp pang of irritation hit me, souring my words.

"Recover from *what?*"

"I didn't mean . . ." He scratched his head, looking lost for words. "Just until . . . you're back on our side."

I scoffed. "Then you may be holding me hostage for a long time."

"Is that what you think?" Amory sounded genuinely hurt. I wasn't tempted to feel any remorse until he drew back the tent flap and I saw he had pushed all the supplies to one side of the tent and made me a pallet on the other.

I glared at him.

Anger flashed in his gray eyes, and he pushed me inside. "Sit down."

I sank cautiously down onto the tarp with my hands bound in front of me, resting against an enormous bag of flour.

Amory's hands gripped my ankles and yanked them toward him. I felt a flash of alarm and tried to pull away, but he just grabbed a length of rope from the floor and bound my feet together.

By the time he was finished, my humiliation was burning a hole through the tent flap.

Amory looked red around the ears, too, though I couldn't think why he would be embarrassed. *What had he expected? Wasn't this how you treated a prisoner?*

He backed away from me crouched on his heels, his eyes dancing with a challenge. He expected me to break — to say I was on their side and could be trusted. I knew it would be smarter to act as though I had succumbed to Stockholm syndrome or something and was back on their side, but I couldn't do it. I had been confused and powerless for too long. Now that I finally had a clear head, I wouldn't let people control me anymore.

The Last Uprising

I raised an eyebrow at Amory. He could tie me up all he wanted — starve me if he liked. I didn't care. I didn't trust them, and I wouldn't feign trust. I would escape on my own, though I had no idea how or where I would go.

With a grunt of irritation, Amory got up. He grabbed the sleeping bag from the pallet on the floor. With a loud unzipping sound, it came apart as a blanket, and he threw it over me unceremoniously. When I pulled my chin up over the sharp zippered edge, I was alone in the supply tent.

Within three days, I had memorized the rhythm of the camp. Chores started before sunrise, and the crack of splitting firewood echoed through the trees. I could hear people huffing toward the mess tent with buckets of water and the groggy murmurs of people milling around in their tents.

When the sun came up, a bell tolled across camp, and the woods went quiet as they all gathered for a meeting. Then the camp was bustling again as everyone went off to do their daily chores. Some hunted, and others stayed behind to wash clothes, cure meat, and clean weapons. The bell tolled again at noon and a third time for supper.

At sundown, I heard the murmur of Amory and the other guards outside preparing to fan out around the perimeter to watch for approaching PMC. Sometimes I just listened to the guards pacing in the snow.

It wasn't much, but the routine kept me from going insane.

I barely had any visitors, apart from Roman, who brought me my meals in silence and took me out to the woods to use the bathroom. I wasn't sure why he was tasked with taking care of me, but perhaps the others thought him less likely to let his guard down around me. They didn't want me to escape.

I hadn't seen Greyson or Logan since we'd left the motel.

The Last Uprising

Amory was the only one who visited me, not out of necessity, but because he wanted to.

Every day at noon without fail, he would appear with two plates of food and sit with me while we both ate our lunch. It was only half an hour, sometimes less if there was a lot of work to be done, but at least it was human contact.

Part of me was inclined to feel grateful since I knew it was the only time Amory really had that was his own. From the dark purplish shadows under his eyes and his raw, wind-stung cheeks, I knew he was kept busy on lookout duty from sundown to sunrise.

The other part of me felt distrustful. If he was really my friend, why wouldn't he untie me? I did think of trying to escape, but as I turned the idea over in my mind, I realized it would mean certain death. I had nowhere else to go.

During those first few days, Amory tried to maintain a strained, one-sided conversation. He told me stories from the farm, and I knew he was hoping to jog my memory. But the things he brought up were mostly foreign to me. I could only see snapshots of memories, and even those might have been figments of my imagination.

I couldn't remember much about Amory and Logan and Roman. Other than their names and a vague familiarity, I didn't know them at all.

The memories of my life before the Collapse were there — accessible if someone referenced an event or a person from my past — but they were oddly dulled and fuzzy if I just tried to think back.

Amory asked me questions about my childhood — about Greyson — but I was silent, obstinately refusing his attempts to connect. When he talked, I just sat there, trying to mask my fear and confusion.

At first, he acted as though it didn't bother him, though I

knew it did. For a while, he could keep his voice bright and optimistic.

But as the days went by, I could tell my silence was beginning to wear on him. Amory was slipping away.

He talked less, ate quickly, and left. He seemed to grow older and deflate a little each day I ignored him.

Whether I was breaking him or he was breaking me, I couldn't tell, and it didn't matter. It was equally horrible for both of us.

After ten days, I had grown restless and impatient. Amory, Roman, and the others showed no signs of letting me go, and it was clear they didn't plan to kill me. They would probably keep me there forever if I let them.

I realized the only way they would untie me and let me roam around free was if they truly believed I had begun to remember them. That meant I had to earn their trust.

Amory seemed the most likely candidate to believe I'd changed. He was desperate for me to come over to their side — an easy mark. And, as much as I hated to admit it, I was curious about Amory and why he was the only one who seemed so invested in me returning to my former self. There was something odd about the way his eyes settled on me when he thought I wasn't looking — a certain tenderness in his gaze and a deep pain I did not understand.

By the time the noon bell rang out across the camp, my decision was made. I would be amicable and receptive when he tried to talk to me. I would open up a little, act as though I cared, maybe even smile. It was sick, but my escape depended on it.

I sat waiting against the sack of flour that had become my backrest, running through all the things I could possibly say to make him trust me. I had to be careful not to come on too strong too soon, because no matter how much Amory wanted me to remember, he was too smart and too distrustful to be fooled that easily.

Plus, after my long silent treatment, I wasn't even sure I remembered how to maintain a normal conversation.

As I ran through all the possible details I could conjure up from my broken memories, something strange happened. I found myself smiling — actually smiling.

It wasn't the crazy smile of satisfaction that my plan could work; I was smiling at the snapshots of memories I could recall with Logan and a dark-haired boy with devilish blue eyes cooking over a stove.

I swallowed, confused about why these snippets of memories made me feel . . . happy. These people weren't my friends. I knew I shouldn't trust them, yet these memories were *good* ones.

I waited.

Amory didn't come.

Thinking he may have gotten held up hunting with the others, I slumped back and listened to the sounds of guards pacing out in the woods.

I waited for nearly an hour, but he never showed.

Despite my best efforts at indifference, the hurt and anger that spilled into my stomach took me by surprise. I had started to look forward to Amory's visits, even if they were a little painful. He was the only person who seemed to care about me, and now that he had abandoned me, too, I was truly alone.

Chapter Four

After the rest of the rebels had eaten and scattered to go about their afternoon routine, a surly Roman appeared with a hot bowl of soup, two rolls, and a jug of water.

I wanted to ask him where Amory was, but I would not give him the satisfaction. I purposely avoided his gaze so my expression wouldn't betray my hopelessness, and he left without a word.

I watched the steam rising off the bowl of soup and knew I should start sucking it down before it got cold. The rolls looked inviting, too, but I did not reach for them.

If they insisted on treating me like the enemy — depriving me of my freedom and nearly all human contact — I would force them to make a choice: Either I was their friend, or I was their prisoner. I could not and *would* not let them imagine I could be both.

I allowed myself a drink of water from the jug to bolster my willpower. Then I watched the soup grow cold and averted my gaze from the perfect, golden rolls.

Roman didn't show up in the afternoon to take me outside, which was strange. I began to wonder if something had happened that had kept Amory from visiting me at lunch. Surely he had bigger things to worry about than drawing me out of my shell. Maybe the rebels were launching an attack against the PMC. Maybe he'd left on a supply run.

Maybe he'd been injured or captured. The thought gave me pause, and it infuriated me that I was *worried* about him.

I would not let myself care. So what if Amory was kind to me?

It shouldn't have mattered to me, but it did.

When the bell tolled again for dinner, Roman reappeared with another plate of food. His eyebrows lifted in surprise when he saw my untouched lunch, but he set down my supper and whisked away the cold soup without a word.

I waited as the last beams of sunlight disappeared from the crack between my tent and the frozen ground, and I heard Amory's voice in the distance. He was laughing at something another rebel had said — a low, musical sound that rumbled up his chest.

My heart contracted.

It was business as usual in camp. There was nothing that had kept him from visiting me at lunch. He had not left camp. He was not hurt.

He was probably happy to be away from me.

I sat stiffly in the darkness until Roman's silhouette reappeared against my tent flap.

He shuffled inside and untied my ankles roughly. I didn't say a word when he pushed me out of the tent and into the snowy woods. My legs felt like jelly, and my head was fuzzy from a lack of food. Since the warmth of the sun had evaporated in the night, it was also miserably cold.

I didn't even drag out the time to stretch my legs as I usually did. I just let him steer me back to my tent without a single complaint or even a dirty look. I didn't feel like fighting. I was beaten.

The next two days passed at a sluggish pace. Both days when the bell struck noon, I waited for Amory to come, but he never did.

It seemed as though the last of my "friends" had given up on me.

After dinner on the third day of no one but Roman, I heard voices coming toward the woods from camp. The first belonged to Roman.

"Relax. I'm sure she'll eat today. She has to be starving."

"How could you not *tell* me she was starving herself?" snapped Amory. His voice was low and deadly.

"Didn't seem that significant. She was a pain even before she'd been brainwashed by Aryus."

Amory made an angry noise. "You'd better fucking watch it."

"Whatever. I've been on babysitting duty, not you. Remember? Honestly, I didn't think you'd care if she wasn't eating."

"Of course I care," said Amory bitterly. "I never *stopped* caring."

My heart fluttered a little, but I pushed down the warmth that was creeping up my chest.

There was a long pause.

"What about you?"

"I don't blame her. She thinks we're holding her hostage. She wants to die . . . or she's trying to send a message."

I recognized the third speaker as Greyson.

"Does she remember you at all?" asked Amory. "I thought maybe since you two were friends before —"

Greyson let out a long breath. "Did you see the way she looked at me? She doesn't trust me. It's like she doesn't even know me." His voice sounded strained and tired.

"How did they *do* that to her? It doesn't make sense."

"You think she's still in there?" asked Greyson. "Because I'm not so sure."

"Of course she is!" snapped Amory. "She'll come back. It's just going to take a wh—"

"How do you know?" cut in Greyson.

"What?"

"How — do — you — know?" he repeated, stretching out each word. "As far as I can tell, she's not the same. They did something to her. It's like they made her forget who she is."

"She'll come back."

"Did you ever, though? I mean . . . *really*?"

There was a long, strained silence between them.

When Amory spoke next, his words came slower than before. "I'm not saying she'll be the same as before. I hope she will, but I can't be sure. But you *can* fight it. I've done it. You just have to convince yourself that they don't own you."

Their footsteps came to a halt several paces away from my tent, shuffling uncomfortably before they started again and faded away.

For a moment, I thought they'd all gone. But then I heard the distinct crunch of brittle leaves under the snow outside my tent. A silhouette flickered against the canvas, and the flap opened. The newcomer was concealed by shadows, and then he swung in with a lantern.

It was Amory.

He sighed audibly when he saw me slumped against the sack of flour with a plate of untouched bread and potatoes on the tarp next to me.

For the briefest second, his eyes bored into mine, as if trying to register whether I was in the same state of anger and distrust. I looked away first, silently cursing myself for merely confirming his suspicions. I didn't know why I couldn't ignore my feelings and play Amory as I'd planned, but something inside me had broken.

He sighed again and flopped down on the tarp, setting the lantern down between us and rubbing his hands together to restore feeling.

I allowed myself to watch him for a few seconds, noticing the way those sharp gray eyes searched my face.

There was something strange about the way he was looking at me. It was as if he was making a concerted effort to be nonintrusive, even though he knew my face well and could read every part of it.

"Roman says you're not eating," he said finally.

I didn't answer.

"Are you sick?" he prompted.

"No." My voice sounded hoarse, and I realized it was because I had not spoken to anyone in days.

"Then why aren't you eating?"

I sighed, feeling stupid and angry before the words even left my mouth. "I thought if you were going to treat me like a prisoner, I should at least protest being held here indefinitely against my will." I sounded like a child, and that filled me with shame.

Amory's eyes crinkled in surprise. "Oh."

I looked away from his face and focused my gaze on his jacket instead. His eyes were boring into me, and I wanted to turn my head so he couldn't see me anymore. It was awful not being able to avoid someone.

The Last Uprising

"I'm sorry," he said, surprising me. "You're *not* a prisoner. I didn't want you to feel that way. Only . . . Roman and some of the others think you've crossed over to the other side. They think you're working for World Corp now. And honestly, after what they put you through, I don't know what you would do if we just let you go."

"You think I can't be trusted."

"I trust you," he said, his gaze heavy. "But I think you need to remember who you are."

"Did we tie *you* up after you were conditioned by World Corp?" I didn't remember much about Amory being imprisoned — only that, for some unknown reason, I'd helped him escape — but Greyson's words had given me an idea.

Amory's face fell, and I knew I'd hit the mark. "No. But maybe you should have."

We were quiet for a long moment. When he spoke again, it was all in a rush — as though he had to force himself to ask. "Do you really not remember anything that happened after the Collapse?"

I looked at him.

"Do you really not remember *me*?"

In that moment, his face was so naked and unguarded that it made my chest physically hurt. I sucked in a huge breath of air.

"I remember you," I said, so quietly I almost hoped he would not hear. "I remember a few basic details . . . I just don't remember anything to make me trust you. The one memory I have . . . it isn't good."

Amory seemed to deflate visibly. "Well, I don't know what memory that would be."

His answer struck me as odd, but I continued. "What was

it like . . . when we were friends?"

Amory sighed and ran a hand through his hair in frustration. Then, strangely, he broke into a sad smile. "I don't know, Haven. I just really liked you. I liked you instantly . . . even though everybody told me you were dangerous. You and I were the same. We trusted each other."

His words disappeared into the cold, dry air as soon as he said them, and we were left in the quiet on the edge of the woods with nothing between us.

Then, without warning, a sharp pain burst across my skull. It was hot and punishing and bad enough to make my eyes water.

I winced, bringing a hand to my head, and Amory's brow furrowed. He opened his mouth as though he were going to say something, but I shoved the pain down and forced myself to meet his gaze.

"What does Greyson think of me now?" I asked, my voice wavering slightly.

"He doesn't know what to think."

"I thought he was my oldest friend."

"I think that's why he's having a hard time with the fact that you don't remember why you were friends."

"And Logan?"

Amory looked taken aback for a moment and then broke into a slight smile. "Logan . . . she's uh . . . she hasn't been up and about too much yet. Aryus's cure did a number on her. It's not really perfected yet. She's still weak, but she's doing better."

"What does she say about all this?"

"Oh, you know Logan. She's super pissed about our

decisions, as usual."

Amory gave a strained grin, and I had to look away. His features were gaunt, making him look older and tired. He'd said "our decisions," and he seemed to notice his slip right away.

We were both silent for a few seconds, and then Amory stood up to leave. Halfway out the tent, he stopped and turned over his shoulder. "Is there anything you need? Even if you don't remember us, I don't want you to feel like a prisoner."

I shook my head, too miserable to speak, and Amory left without another word. The pain in my head had subsided to a dull ache, but the things Amory had said left me unnerved.

Was I imagining the strange way he'd said "us"? It hadn't sounded as though he was referring to himself, Roman, and Greyson. It was a different "us" altogether.

Rolling over to the pallet and curling up on my side, I tried — not for the first time — to remember something, *anything* about Amory. Apart from his name, his age, and the basic knowledge that he had been in med school training to become a PMC doctor before defecting and running off to the farm, I could remember little else about him. I knew I had somehow helped him escape a World Corp test facility, but I didn't remember the circumstances.

He was the person who confused me the most. If I tried to remember the others, I could now recall snippets of conversations and bits and pieces of my time on the farm. I vaguely remembered learning how to shoot a gun with Logan and eating dinner across from Roman. It was generic and void of emotion, like watching a reel of film, but the memories were there.

With Amory, I was drawing a blank. I knew it was strange that I could recall more details about his life than any of the others', but when I tried to think of us together, I couldn't

The Last Uprising

picture it. The one memory I had was so faint it could have been a dream.

I was lying on the ground, sore, lightheaded, and in pain. Amory had me pinned to the ground, crushing me with his weight. He was wearing a murderous expression that froze me to the core.

I swung at him with a knife, but he knocked it out of my hand like it was nothing. I punched him in the jaw, but he just pinned me down with his knees until my eyes watered.

He was going to kill me.

Then the memory was gone.

Chapter Five

Amory recommenced his daily lunch visits, and I started eating again.

Hating my captors was exhausting. My willpower was dwindling, and I could feel myself starting to let go of the intense fear and distrust. But every time I let my guard down, new emotions crept in to take its place. I almost didn't recognize the feelings of camaraderie and compassion because it had been so long since I'd had prolonged contact with another person.

These emotions gnawed at my gut, and every time they appeared, that sharp pain splintered in my head — a feeling that reminded me of when I'd been running around the house as a child and had fallen into the sharp corner of the oak coffee table. I'd hit my head hard enough to need stitches.

The pains turned into persistent headaches. They started when Amory came to eat his lunch, burst into sharp stabs when he spoke about my past, and throbbed dully like a lingering hangover long after he'd left.

I tried to hide what was bothering me, but somehow, he knew. On the fourth day after he started visiting me again, he surprised me by asking, "When did the headaches start?"

How had he known?

"A few days ago," I said. I tried to shrug, but the pain was intense.

Amory nodded as though he had read my mind. "I used to get headaches like that. For me, they came on whenever I got scared. That was usually when I . . . well, you remember."

There was a pregnant pause, neither of us willing to concede that perhaps I didn't.

"Anyway . . . I would lose myself . . . rip apart anyone who was threatening me. It didn't feel like me, though. It was what *they* wanted me to do."

That I could relate to. I hadn't felt like myself much since they'd taken me from the facility. I didn't have any memories to tell me who I was, and I didn't even know whom I should trust.

Amory swallowed, and his eyes searched my face. "Are you scared? Right now?"

"No," I answered, though I wasn't sure if he was asking if I was scared of him or scared of what I'd become.

"It's okay if you are. You can tell me."

"I'm not afraid. I just . . ." I trailed off, not wanting to tell him that the headaches started whenever I let my guard down around him or whenever I thought about Greyson too long.

Since Greyson was the only one of them I'd known before the Collapse, most of my memories of him were intact — even if the emotions attached to them were strangely distorted. I had begun to study them in the quiet moments before drifting off to sleep: Greyson and me riding our bikes as kids, laughing at school together as teenagers, getting drunk together for the first time at college, me sitting with Greyson after his dad had died.

As much as I tried, I could not find fault with him or understand the reason for my distrust, and that made me doubt the basis of all my fears. The worst part was that whenever I lingered too long in a passing memory, the pain would flare up and send me into a torrent of nausea and dizziness.

"What's wrong with me?" I whispered, not caring that Amory was my captor. Right then, it felt as though he was the closest thing I had to a friend.

A look of pain crossed his face, and he rolled onto his knees. "Hey, hey. It's okay."

I hadn't realized I'd been crying. He moved to close the space between us and put his hands behind my elbows to pull me toward him. But as soon as he touched me, a surge of pain ripped across the back of my skull. I squeezed my eyes shut in a grimace and jerked away from him. I couldn't get out of his reach. His eyes were bright, sad, and sympathetic, and I hated him for the pain he brought on every time he came here.

"Stop!" I yelled.

Amory fell back onto his heels, looking as though I'd physically struck him.

I wanted to care. I wanted to tell him I was sorry, but the pain had only intensified, even though he had let go. Blinding and white hot, it had spread from the back of my head into my eye sockets. There was a vague ringing in my ears, and I curled over my knees and buried my face in my legs.

Rocking there for a moment, I tried to focus on something — anything — besides Amory and Greyson. I focused on my physical space: the tent, the tarp, the crack of sunshine leaking in from outside.

Slowly, the pain ebbed away. Within a few moments, it was only the shadow of hurt, a ghostly prickle of needles at my hairline. I didn't trust it. It could return at any moment. I didn't dare to move or speak.

The Last Uprising

When I finally looked up, Amory was gone.

The next day, I heard the crunch of footsteps through the snow long before Roman was due with my breakfast. It was still dark. I sat upright, drew my arms across my chest, and prepared an expression of appropriate surliness. Then the tent flap was drawn back, and I was surprised to see who it was.

Amory looked younger — refreshed — as though he had actually slept instead of spending the night on lookout duty. His face bore no trace of the hurt I had seen there the day before. In fact, he looked positively cheerful.

"What are you doing here?" I asked, trying to keep my tone neutral.

"I think good behavior has earned you a little time out of here."

The distrust was back in the pit of my stomach, mixed with another odd feeling. I became aware that I was still lying on the pallet, my hair mussed from sleep and stiff from days without bathing. I shrunk away from him as he bent to untie the rope binding my ankles.

"Relax," he said, sensing my unease. "I just think you could use some fresh air. Plus there's someone you need to see."

I knew I should withdraw more, but I just shook my head a little to clear the feeling of needles pressing down at the base of my neck. It was just an outing — even the most despicable prisoners were allotted time out in the open air.

I tried not to focus on Amory's fingers brushing against my ankles as he untied me. But instead of grabbing the rope between my wrists to pull me into an upright position, he grasped my cold hands.

His hands were bigger than mine — warm and callused. I pushed down the briefest feeling of pleasure that was quickly engulfed by a throbbing sensation in the back of my skull.

Once I was on my feet, he held on just a second longer than he should have, squeezing my hands once for good measure. I jerked away, squinting in pain and avoiding his gaze, but I thought he smirked briefly.

He pushed open the tent flap and let me pass in front of him. Instead of grabbing the ropes and dragging me along like an animal as Roman usually did, he let me walk ahead of him.

I kept glancing over my shoulder for him to lead, but he just nodded with a reassuring smile and guided me with a careful hand on the small of my back.

The camp was quiet, but the sky was lightening along the horizon. Soon the rest of them would awaken, and I would once again be on display as a circus sideshow — the freak prisoner everyone shunned.

Amory seemed to sense this and led me quickly around the perimeter of camp, past the still-smoldering fire to a large tent marked with a red cross. Next to it was a smaller one-man tent, and Amory lifted the flap so I could pass under his arm inside.

There was a small shape balled up on a thin pallet in the corner, and I caught a glimpse of golden hair unfurling from the mouth of a sleeping bag. My nostrils prickled at the strange smell filling the tent: the subtle scent of sleep and sickness.

I knelt down on the edge of the pallet and watched Amory lean over the shape. He nudged the sleeping girl and whispered something I could not hear. She stirred slightly for a moment and then seemed to wake fully. She shimmied anxiously up out of her sleeping bag and propped herself on her elbows.

Even with the dark shadows under her eyes, the pale

The Last Uprising

pallor of her skin, and the strange lackluster quality of her once vibrant hair, Logan was unmistakable.

"Haven!" she said in a hoarse whisper. "Where have you been?"

Before I could prepare myself, Logan lurched across the mattress and strangled me in her arms. I stiffened in her embrace, but there was something familiar about her smell. Under the staleness of sleep and the stagnant tent air, I could just make out lavender. *Soap*, I thought. *Homemade soap.* I wasn't sure how I knew that.

Logan released me and pulled back to study my face. Then her eyes fell to my hands, which lay awkwardly between us, bound together by rope.

"Amory," she said. Her tone had shifted instantly from friendly to accusatory. "If this is some kinky new thing you two are —" She stopped, studying my face.

I looked away, feeling embarrassed at her realization.

"Oh my god." She whipped her head around to look at Amory. "She hasn't recovered yet." She looked back at me. "That's why you haven't been visiting me. I've been asking for you, and they told me you were away from camp with Godfrey."

She released my arms, and I sank back onto my heels with caution. From what I remembered about Logan, I knew she had a volatile temper. Something told me she wouldn't hurt me, but that distrust rumbled in my gut like a hunger pang.

"Have you been keeping her tied up like a hostage?" she hissed at Amory, not bothering to mask her disgust. "What the *hell* is wrong with you?"

"You don't understand," he said in a quiet voice.

"I thought *you* would, of all people. She stood by you," Logan said, nodding at me, "when you were ripping apart carriers and beating people up. Haven was the only person who thought you were still you."

"I know," he said.

"Is *this* the deal you made with Roman to bring her here?"

Amory sighed, looking annoyed. "It's not just him. There's a lot of people who were against the idea of me bringing her here."

"Ida wouldn't stand for this. When she gets back . . ."

"She doesn't remember what side she's on," said Amory in a strangled voice, avoiding my gaze. "She doesn't remember us."

My stomach twisted, and a sharp pain stabbed the back of my head.

Logan turned to me. "Is that true?"

I took a deep breath. "I know *who* you are. It's just . . . most of my memories are gone. I don't trust you."

Logan seemed to deflate in front of me.

"She's been *conditioned* not to trust us," said Amory. "They wiped away her memories. But she's coming back." The hopefulness in his voice was enough to break my heart. He couldn't be faking that.

"Amory —" began Logan, casting me a glance.

"She is! She gets headaches *just* like I used to, which means she's fighting it."

Logan was watching me with that same defeated look Amory had the night before. She was tired. Amory seemed to sense this, too, because he motioned to me that it was time to leave.

As I started to stand up, Logan reached out and gripped my arm tightly, pulling me in awkwardly for another embrace. This time, I tried to give in to it despite my bound wrists, and a surge of pain shot from my brain stem down the back of my spine. I backed away from Logan and the ghost of lavender that clung to her hair and out into the early morning sunshine.

"It happened again, didn't it?" asked Amory, coming out behind me. "The headaches."

I ignored his question. I would not encourage his smugness or the fragile hope he held that I would suddenly remember everything about him and want to join the revolution.

"What happened to her?" I asked.

"Don't you remember?"

I shook my head.

Amory sighed. "She was infected. We broke into World Corp headquarters for the cure. It made her really sick. Aryus said it himself . . . it's not ready yet."

The thought seemed to distress Amory more than Logan's adverse reaction, which I thought was strange.

"We're going to need a lot more where that came from," he said, sensing my confusion. "The virus has mutated. The vaccine doesn't protect us against stage-five carriers anymore."

"That doesn't seem right," I muttered. "The New Republic would never . . ."

"What?"

"They wouldn't let people believe they were safe if the virus had mutated."

Amory gave me a strange look. "Was that part of your conditioning?"

My stomach twisted uncomfortably. I didn't like when he

called it that.

"I suppose they covered it in training," I mumbled. Truthfully, I could not remember where I'd picked up that information.

Amory didn't say anything more about it, but I followed him away from Logan's tent across the camp. People were already stirring in their tents, and a few early risers had emerged to relieve themselves in the woods, throwing us curious looks.

I thought Amory was leading me back to my tent, but he cut around it, and I followed him into the woods.

It was like being in a blizzard. White paper birch trees towered all around, shorn of their leaves, rising up through the untouched snow. I instantly felt a quiet calm settle over me, unknotting the cords of stress that had tightened around my chest. Amory continued into the trees, and I had the fleeting thought that he was leading me out to kill me.

I followed anyway. If they *had* just been holding me for information, my fate was inevitable. There was no point prolonging the mental anguish or the horrible uncertainty.

But when Amory turned to face me, it was to sink down on a felled tree. He wasn't looking at me, but he wore a conflicted expression, as if deciding whether or not he dared to speak.

"Come here," he said without looking up.

I stood frozen. Something about the resolve in his face scared me more than anything.

"Please." He patted the spot next to him on the log.

Watching his face carefully, I shuffled over and sank down next to him. For a moment, I just breathed in the crisp, cold open air and reveled in the whiteness of it all. It was untouched and empty, but here the emptiness was not a prison.

"Can I ask you something?"

I swallowed, not sure if I should agree, but nodded.

"What's the memory?"

"What?"

"The one memory you have of me . . . it must be bad if it makes you hate me. It's just . . . it's driving me crazy because I can't think what I've ever done to you to make you think . . ." He shrugged, dragging in a heavy breath and looking away.

"Oh," I said, taken aback. "It's . . . it's just a flash of a memory, really. I'm on the ground, and you're on top of me. You look really angry . . . like you're going to kill me. I swing at you with a knife and hit you, but then . . . I don't know what happens after that."

To my surprise, Amory's eyes crinkled into a grin, and a short, heavy laugh burst from his lips. "I can't believe after everything, *that's* what you remember." He chuckled again. "You really don't remember the circumstances?"

I shook my head.

"That was the first day I met you. I was at the farm, on carrier watch, and I saw you sprinting toward the house. If you could have seen yourself . . . you looked like you could be infected. You were too skinny — half-starved to death — and you were covered in blood and dirt."

Amory looked at his hands, a soft smile playing on his lips. "I thought you might be a threat . . . until you tried to stab me with that dull knife. Then I knew you were just a survivor, like me. I had to know you."

He finished the story, and I couldn't help but stare at him. It made sense, and I was more curious than ever.

"And we . . . we became friends after that?"

He nodded, that cute smile still playing on his lips. I mentally slapped myself for staring. "Oh yeah. Fast friends."

I folded my hands together, not sure what to say. I didn't remember any of that.

When Amory spoke again, his voice was gentle. "Haven . . . I don't know how long it will be before it all comes back to you . . . or if it ever will. But I'm not going to stop trying to find you."

Then he did something I wasn't prepared for. He reached over and clasped my cold hand. He was wearing thick fingerless gloves, but I could feel the warmth emanating from his fingertips. I breathed in sharply, and a hard blow of pain crashed against the back of my head. I breathed again, willing it to stop.

"It's all right," whispered Amory. "Don't fight the pain. You have to let it in."

I closed my eyes tight to stop the tears that were threatening to spill over.

"Trust me," he said. "It's the only way."

When I opened my eyes, he had released my hand, but his bright gray eyes were focused on my face. The look there was so intense and earnest I had to break his gaze.

"Haven, I know it must go against everything they . . . taught you. But you have to tell us what you know. The resistance is not doing very well. We've lost a lot of people.

"The attack on the last World Corp base went badly wrong, and now we have all these refugees who have defected from the northern commune and no real center of leadership.

"We're recruiting faster than we can mobilize everyone. These newest defectors aren't mercenaries like the rebels at Rulon's camp. They're older. Some of them aren't even

The Last Uprising

strong enough to fight. But we can't just abandon them."

"Where are we?" I asked.

"We're still north of the border, which means we're in enemy territory. We don't have the hordes of carriers to deal with, but supply runs are getting too dangerous. The PMC here is much better fortified than they were in Sector X."

I let this information wash over me. Somehow, I knew I should be suspicious and angry with Amory, but I found I was merely curious. The needles prickled at my hairline, but the pain did not cripple me the way it had when Amory touched my hand.

He seemed to be the source of all the pain, which only intensified my fascination with that memory. I'd reflected on it so many times it only felt half-real, and it didn't make sense.

By now I knew my memory had been damaged in training, though whether that was intentional or merely a side effect, I couldn't be sure. But if World Corp *had* withheld some memories on purpose, what was the harm of the Amory memories if he had been hostile? Surely they wouldn't think those events would shake my loyalty.

"What else did they tell you about the New Republic?" Amory asked suddenly, pulling me back from my reverie. "In your training?"

"You know everything I know," I muttered. "You just choose to ignore it."

Amory waited, hanging on my every word, so I continued. "The New Republic formed after the acquisition of the New Northern Territory . . . after the Collapse of the federal government and after the Great Migration. Citizens were protected against the virus and protected against themselves."

"How do you mean?"

"Mandatory Identification. When people knew someone was watching, there was less crime . . . more security. Through order comes progress. We're building a better world. The only true threat left are the rebels who look to destroy everything we have done."

"A better world? What do you mean by that?"

I wanted to stop. I knew I *should* stop, and looking at Amory was making the pain creep up the base of my neck. I shook my head to clear it and continued. "Energy efficiency . . . a republic that is completely self-sufficient. World Corp International has made great strides on the crops we can grow, technology, medicine . . ."

The pain had turned from a dull throb into a sharp stab that seemed to press through my skull, but I rolled on. "We've already conquered North America. We're well on our way to taking the entire western hemisphere."

"How? How does the republic plan to take over? Aryus is losing control in his own stolen territory."

I stopped, turning away from Amory to hide my shame and ignoring the persistent pain in my brow.

Why had I told him all that? Any information I gave would be used against the republic.

"Haven —" Amory reached out to squeeze my arm, but I jerked out of his reach.

"Stop. Just stop. I know what you're doing."

How could I have been so stupid? I thought. Everything Amory had done — every look, every word — had been designed to manipulate me, wear me down, and make me trust him so I would give them information about World Corp's plans.

He sighed, running a hand through his hair in frustration. After a few minutes of silence, he stood up and reached for

The Last Uprising

me. I ignored this gesture, and he seemed to brush it off as I followed him back toward my tent.

I fought the gawking stares of the others at camp as I ducked around to the front of my tent and went inside. Amory looked angry about all the unwanted attention, but he turned back toward me with a slight smile playing on his lips.

Slumping down in the corner, I looked up at Amory with a challenging stare. He hesitated for a moment and then left without binding my ankles.

I knew it was meant to be a gesture of goodwill, but I could not help feeling that he was taunting me. Amory seemed to know I would not attempt an escape because I had nowhere else to go. Or maybe he sensed my curiosity and knew it would weaken my resolve to leave.

I did not see Roman for the rest of the day. Amory took it upon himself to bring me my meals, as though he suddenly felt invested in my well-being.

Around nightfall, Amory left me my supper on his way to lookout duty. I listened to him walk away as I chewed the hard bread crust. Several paces away from my tent, his footsteps suddenly stopped, and I heard the low rumble of Roman's voice.

"Still playing guardian angel?"

"Go away."

There was a brief shuffle of footsteps, as though Roman had blocked his path.

"Taking responsibility for the problem you brought here, I guess," he taunted.

"You're cheerful," growled Amory. "No wonder she's been making so much progress."

"*Progress?*" Roman scoffed. "She's completely brainwashed."

"So was I."

"Yeah, you weren't there that long, though."

"You really think a few weeks make that big of a difference?"

"Of course it does! Especially after they had you to practice on."

An angry growl escaped from Amory's throat. "She's coming back. It's only a matter of time before she —"

There was a rough sound of muscle on muscle, as though Roman had shoved Amory's chest.

"Before she *what*? Escapes and betrays our position? She's not on our side."

"She *is* on our side."

"No, she's not!" Roman yelled.

Amory's voice was so low I could barely hear his next words. "She's one of us. We do not throw away our own."

"Not all of us are as invested as you," said Roman. "I know you two had a thing."

My mouth fell open as the realization hit me.

"That has *nothing* to do with it," snarled Amory.

"I think that has *everything* to do with it," said Roman. "She warps your judgment. Everyone thought it was a bad idea for you to go in there. Greyson and Logan only went along with it because she was their friend and you were tearing around like a fucking maniac."

Amory interrupted in an exasperated tone. "Well, she's here. She's safe. And she's already given us valuable information."

"Information World Corp is happy to disclose to its enemies, I'm sure."

The Last Uprising

"They're planning something . . . taking over the entire western hemisphere. This isn't just a vision — Aryus is evangelizing. He's psychotic."

"See? She's in your head. They're just trying to distract us."

"She's not part of their plan . . . at least she wasn't yet. They still had her there because she wasn't ready. She was still defying them. Have you seen all those HALLO burns on her arm?"

Roman sighed.

"I'm telling you. She was fighting back then, and she's fighting back now. And when she's herself again, she's going to be able to tell us things we need to know."

Amory's words hit me hard. Shame and betrayal seared my insides, burning my throat and choking me. They had made me weak — Amory had made me weak. He'd tried to make me trust him and wear down my defenses.

Maybe he *had* cared about me — maybe he still did — but Amory had tricked me.

I bit down on my lip to stop the tears that were threatening to come, feeling too angry with myself to care about the burning in my head.

Why did I care? What did it matter?

I knew all along I could not trust Amory and the others, yet I had let my guard down. The enemy had poisoned my mind.

I waited until the sounds of Amory's and Roman's footsteps had faded completely.

After a few minutes, the camp fell silent. It wasn't very late, but I supposed the rebels didn't dare gather around the fire at night to talk and relax. They were in PMC country after all, and their survival depended on concealing their camp.

Moving slowly and carefully, I felt my way around the tent. Awkwardly propping myself up with my tied hands for balance, I crawled through the supplies searching for scissors, a knife, *anything* sharp enough to cut my ropes.

My knee hit something hard, and it skittered across the tarp under a sack of beans. It was a box cutter.

Triumph swelled in my chest as my fingers connected with it in the darkness. I settled back onto the tarp and listened intently for anyone approaching. Nothing.

Holding it steady between the soles of my boots sharp side up, I began to saw at the heavy ropes around my wrists. It was slow work. The blade was very dull, but it was enough. Thread by thread, I ripped into the rope until it came apart between my hands and my bonds fell away. Stroking the skin where it had begun to chafe, I marveled at the delicateness of my freed arms.

I longed to run — to leave this camp and never look back — but I knew I had to be smart. An empty paper bag rustled at my feet, and I rummaged around in the supplies looking for food to fill it. I tore into the sack of dried beans and grabbed a box of oatmeal from a crate underneath.

I lamented the pallets overflowing with canned vegetables at the back I would have to leave. My paper bag could not handle their weight.

As a consolation prize, I salvaged a dented tin camp pot from a box of kitchenware and threw that in, too. I had no matches or flint starter to make a fire, but I would worry about that later.

I paused for a moment at the flap of my tent to listen for footsteps, my breath coming hard enough to disturb the heavy canvas. Hearing nothing, I pushed it aside and made my way carefully around the back of the tent.

The Last Uprising

Walking on the edge of the woods wasn't as quiet. Every snapping twig made my heart leap into my throat, but the shadows offered more concealment than ducking between the tents. Plus, if I was spotted, I would have a better chance of disappearing into the trees.

I edged my way around the camp, trying to get my bearings. I had no idea *where* north of the border we were, but if I headed due south, I was sure to find the PMC. I remembered the direction the sun rose and set off at a ninety-degree angle from the side of my tent where the light peeked through every morning.

As I cut through the trees, my foot found a deep divot — tire tracks leading away from camp. I followed the tracks, able to walk more quietly where the undergrowth had been tamped down by wide tires.

When I was thirty paces from camp, the snap of a branch to my right nearly gave me a heart attack.

"Leaving, are you?" called a voice behind me.

Chapter Six

I jumped, looking around wildly for the watcher.

I heard a match strike, and a tiny ball of light briefly illuminated a face. My stomach dropped.

There was a click, and Greyson fiddled with a lantern, throwing light and shadows between the trees. He was slumped on the ground, shivering in what looked like three bulky coats. I hadn't seen him in the darkness, but he was so close it was a miracle I hadn't stepped on him.

"Stealth guard," he said. "It's more effective if someone's trying to sneak into camp . . . or out," he added with a humorless grin.

I did not look at him. My eyes were focused instead on the rifle cocked under his right arm. He followed my gaze and lowered the gun to the ground.

"Seriously?" His face fell into a dark frown. "I'm not going to shoot you, Haven."

There was a note of defeat in his voice, though he had the upper hand.

I glanced quickly down the path, my eyes following the tire tracks until I couldn't see them anymore.

What were the chances they had another guard posted farther down? I knew Amory was on lookout duty, too. Perhaps he would see me and try to stop me leaving.

Greyson let out a cold laugh. "Wow. You really do hate us."

I looked at him, unsure why that cut me so deep. I remembered that Greyson and I had been friends, but there was something artificial about my oversaturated childhood memories — something I didn't trust.

"Go on, then. Leave."

Although he was looking down the path, I detected his poorly concealed resentment and hurt.

"You'll let me leave?"

When he met my gaze, he looked surprised. "Yeah. Haven, when have I ever made you do something you didn't want to do?"

I dodged this strange question by staring at my boots. I really should have grabbed some extra clothes from the supply tent. I would freeze out here exposed to the elements.

"It's probably for the best anyway," Greyson continued. "I don't know if your memory will come back, and honestly, you being here hasn't been easy. We might all be better off . . ." He glanced away, fiddling absently with the lantern.

I didn't say anything. For some reason, his words did not bother me the way Amory's had. Something in the back of my mind recalled that Greyson was prone to these frank, bitter statements. While they were hurtful to some people who didn't know him well, I knew they were just Greyson's way of protecting himself.

"I didn't know you cared," I said.

"Of course I care." He still wouldn't look at me. "You know, I accepted that you were dead. I knew you were. After Amory escaped, I didn't think Aryus would keep you alive. But Amory wouldn't stop digging. He wouldn't believe you were dead."

I felt a swell of emotion that someone had cared enough not to give up, which was strange, considering they had ripped me away from World Corp and tried to get me to divulge the information I knew.

"Finally, we got some intel that you were being held in one of their . . . *treatment* facilities. I didn't think we'd ever get you out — not after last time. But Amory was obsessed."

He stopped speaking for a moment. "Do you remember how long it was before Amory snapped out of it last time?" he demanded suddenly. "I mean, *really*. How long did it take before he was himself?"

I thought back, and my brain seemed to lurch and stall like an old car. Of course I knew that Amory had been held in a facility as I had, but I had no internal timeline to put the memory in context.

"I don't know," I whispered.

Greyson stared at me for a long moment, breathing in deeply. The look on his face told me he had reached a decision. It was as if this answer was enough to confirm his worst fear. I was not myself.

"I guess I expected that." His voice was cold. "Well . . . you should clear off before Amory hears us. It's not fair to put him through this."

I took a deep breath, watching him and wondering what I was supposed to do. I did not belong here. I belonged with World Corp. That was what I had been trained for. These people were not my friends. Certainly Amory wasn't — not after what I'd heard him saying to Roman. It didn't matter what Greyson thought.

As I turned to go, Greyson's voice startled me in the stillness.

"Do you remember sixth grade? Mrs. Sanders's class?" I turned to look at him, startled, and suddenly had a picture of eleven-year-old Greyson. His hair had been longer then — wild, dark brown, and curly around the ears. He was small for his age.

"Yeah," I said, but Greyson wasn't listening to me anymore, and his voice sounded strangely choked.

"I feel a lot like I did then. Like I didn't know what I was supposed to do — ever."

The year we turned twelve was burned into my brain. It had been a horrible year for Greyson. His dad had died, and his mom had sunk into a bad depression.

I hadn't understood that then, but I noticed the way Greyson came to school — as though no one had looked at him before he left the house. He wore the same T-shirt for several days in a row.

A boy in our class, Brock Epstein, took to tormenting Greyson every day in gym class — rallying a soccer-team worth of cronies to make each day a living hell. They stole his lunch money while he was changing into his gym clothes and, an hour later, told everyone that Greyson's mom was too poor to afford food or wash his clothes. To this day, I could still hear the boys' chants of "trailer trash" that seemed to follow Greyson down the hall.

I solved the problem as any sixth grader would: I shared my lunch with him and quietly told Brock and his friends to go away.

"Remember Brock Epstein?" said Greyson suddenly.

I nodded, my nails reflexively digging into my palms as I remembered. The pain had returned, throbbing in the back of my skull as the memory of Greyson's tiny, sad face stared at me.

"I heard he's PMC now."

I didn't say anything.

"Do you remember how you finally got him to lay off me?" He laughed a little. "It still amazes me to this day."

"I snuck three cans of tuna to school in my backpack and poured the juice into his locker while we were in gym," I said automatically, amazing myself with the clarity of the memory. My heart had been pounding the whole time, so sure I would get caught or Brock would turn his taunts on me in retaliation. "They made fun of him for the smell for weeks, and I got Cole Dillinger to tell him he was cursed."

I glanced at Greyson, and we both tried to stifle our laughter. For some reason, this made me feel better than I had in weeks.

Something stirred inside me, which made the pain intensify. I ignored it and focused on the other feeling coursing through me: warmth all over and a great expansion in my chest that lifted the enormous weight I had felt for days. It was so strange to be laughing with Greyson, but tonight, he didn't feel like the enemy.

As our laughter died away in the dark, I could tell the moment was over. Greyson's smile was starting to fade, and we were snapped back to reality.

I had planned on leaving just then, but now it seemed foolish and impulsive. Instead, I turned around and followed the tire tracks back toward camp. It just wasn't the time.

I sneaked back into my tent, which felt much colder than it had when I left.

Now, on top of feeling helpless and betrayed, I was wildly confused. I was starting to think Greyson, Amory, and Logan were telling the truth. We *had* been friends. So what had gone wrong? And why did I feel so sure that World Corp was right?

I had vague shadowed memories of a life, but that seemed so far away. It didn't really feel as though it belonged to me.

Thoroughly drained by the encounter with Greyson and

The Last Uprising

the memories he had dredged up, I didn't have the energy to fiddle with my ropes to make it look as though I'd never left. I curled up on my cold pallet and pulled the sleeping bag over me.

Shivering and still aware of whatever had stirred inside me, I ignored the prickle of needles at the base of my neck and fell into an uneasy sleep.

Chapter Seven

The sound of sirens shattered the stillness of the night. I was up and out of my tent before even opening my eyes, clamping my hands over my ears to block out the incessant, piercing note.

Panic choked me instantly. They were much too close.

Within seconds, beams of blue light flashed between the trees from two different directions, and the rebels started rushing out of their tents, groping for loved ones and sprinting into the woods.

I backed away into the trees. My heart was pounding. I couldn't think clearly. Still in the fog of sleep, I tried to piece together an explanation. The PMC was rounding up the rebels. Already I could hear the screams and shouts and the scuffle of feet in the snow.

I focused on breathing and tried to tell myself that they were not the enemy. The PMC officers were on my side. They would not hurt me. Some foolish part of me half expected one of the officers to demand to know what they had done with Haven Allis.

But this was not a rescue mission. This was a raid.

I saw movement in the darkness: a lone figure sprinting around the edge of the woods toward me — or, rather, toward my tent. It wasn't a PMC officer. He wasn't wearing the reflective white uniform.

Gunshots erupted in the darkness, and I crouched down,

covering my ears and trying to get ahold of myself.

What was wrong with me? After everything I had been through, why *now*? I couldn't freeze up. I had to make a decision — had to move. The PMC raiding the camp wouldn't know my face. They would think I was a rebel.

That thought was almost a relief. Some tiny, demanding part of me was tearing around in my chest, ordering me to run away from the PMC toward the fleeing rebels. It didn't make any sense.

"Haven!"

I heard the sound of my name like a whisper. It was urgent, but I could not identify the source of the speaker. I had lost my view of the dark figure.

"Haven!" It was Amory, and his voice was coming from just outside my tent.

The canvas rustled. Amory swore quietly and tore out into the woods — right toward my hiding place.

Without thinking, without stopping to consider the consequences, I heard his name escape from my own lips.

He stopped, looking around wildly.

"Here," I hissed.

Not bothering to tread quietly, Amory crashed through the frozen leaves and drifts of snow, stumbling slightly on a hidden tree root. I didn't see his face until it was inches from mine, his hands gripping my arms, traveling down my forearms to untie my ropes and feeling only skin.

"Oh, thank god. How did you —" In the dark, I could see his mind working out an answer. "Never mind. We have to get out of here."

Gripping my hand hard, Amory pulled me deeper into the woods. The shouts of the PMC were growing louder.

Gunshots reverberated in the frigid air, making my teeth rattle.

Amory had broken into a run, yanking me through the trees behind him. Stray branches whipped me in the face. I swatted my left hand blindly in front of me, my right still clutched in Amory's hard grip.

I couldn't tell how far we ran or for how long. After a while, my legs went numb, working on their own. I couldn't breathe, but it was from the wild fear choking my airways rather than fatigue.

Amory never released my hand.

As the fear pumped adrenaline through my veins, I noticed a strange clarity I had not felt since my rescue. There was no pain in my head. If anything, my senses seemed to sharpen. My brain had been wired to thrive on this fear — this choking drive for self-preservation at all costs.

Amory would not hurt me. I didn't know why I trusted him, but I did, and I kept running.

I had failed World Corp — that I knew. I had made a decision, leaving with Amory, and now I was a fugitive like the rest of them. The PMC did not forgive traitors.

I could not blame Stockholm syndrome for turning my back on the officers. Hating the rebels in my tent for days didn't count. During a revolution, it was one choice — one split-second, life-or-death decision — that cemented your loyalties and showed the world where you stood. I couldn't even bring myself to regret fleeing with Amory.

Up ahead, a bulky shape emerged from the blackness. The bluish light filtering through the trees gave it a strange gleam, and I slowed my pace. It was an old, rusted-out Volkswagen van. The garish orange paint was washed out in the dark, and huddled near the tires were Logan and Greyson.

"All right?" Amory panted, hands on his knees as he tried to catch his breath.

Greyson nodded. He was hunched protectively over Logan, who looked ghostly pale in the fractured moonlight.

"You guys weren't followed?"

"No," said Greyson. His voice was bitter, and I remembered he had been on watch. "They came out of nowhere. Must have been driving with their lights off ten miles an hour. Then they turned the sirens on and floored it. I grabbed Logan and came straight here."

"They had to have been tipped off," said Amory. "They knew exactly what they were looking for. We're lucky they didn't hem us in on all sides."

"Who do you think it was?" asked Logan.

"Could've been Roman," said Amory in a cautious tone, as though testing the waters for the others' opinions.

"Don't be stupid, Amory," Logan snapped. "He's out. He risked his life to save me and Haven."

"Yeah, but he left us once before, didn't he? I wouldn't say he's beyond betrayal."

"Glad to hear you have such high opinions of me," said a voice from behind us.

We all jumped and looked around, startled. Roman was a huge guy with massive shoulders and a beefy neck that seemed to swallow his ears, yet he moved through the woods with the stealth of a ninety-pound ninja.

He emerged from the shadows with a rucksack slung over his shoulder. "Don't suppose any of you were smart enough to take some supplics?"

Greyson, Logan, and Amory stared at their feet.

"Yeah, didn't think so."

Everyone stood silent. Then, finally, Greyson voiced the question no one else would. "How many of us are gone?"

"You mean killed or captured?" The question was sharp and accusing.

Greyson shrugged, and sympathy tugged at my chest. He felt responsible.

"Couldn't tell. Seems like most of the old crowd disappeared into the woods, but a lot of the commune defectors were being rounded up. They aren't built for this life."

His voice was laced with disgust, but I couldn't tell if it was distain for the commune defectors or general anger at the state of the world.

"Who was on lookout at the point?" asked Greyson.

"Supposed to be Rogers, I think."

Amory ran a hand through his hair in frustration. "How did he not see anything?"

"Maybe he was the one who tipped them off," offered Greyson.

"He couldn't know he would be on watch," said Roman. "We make it random to keep things like that from happening. No, it had to be some fucking commune coward."

Amory sighed. "Whoever it was, he'll be long gone by now."

"It doesn't matter," Logan broke in. "We should keep moving. The PMC is probably searching the area."

Amory nodded, eyeing Roman with suspicion.

"You got something else to say?" Roman snapped.

"No. Nothing." But Amory still had that look in his eye.

"How many times do I have to put my neck on the line for you people before you realize I'm on your side?"

"Enough!" snapped Logan. "Your fighting is what's going to get us all killed." She turned on her heel and plowed off deeper into the woods.

Greyson trailed behind her wordlessly, and Amory motioned for me to follow.

We walked in silence with Roman bringing up the rear. I sensed his presence like an itch on the back of my neck, but I never turned around. I couldn't shake the feeling that he wanted me gone. It shouldn't have bothered me, but it did.

Now I had nowhere else to go. I couldn't return to World Corp after I'd fled. Even when I'd had the perfect chance to escape and bring back intel, I hadn't left. I was a traitor.

After two hours of walking, my legs had begun to burn from crunching through the heavy snow.

"Where are we going?" I asked Amory.

"We're just scouting the area for a good place to camp out for a day. After that, we'll regroup with the other survivors."

"Is that a good idea?"

"The PMC never returns to the same place once they've cleared it. They haven't got the resources for that . . . not with all the rebel activity that's moved north of the border."

"Why do people come north if they aren't documented? Isn't that more dangerous?"

Amory smiled grimly. "That depends what you're more afraid of: the PMC or the carriers. No carriers north of the border, and a lot of people prefer to loot from the PMC than try to make it on their own in the states."

"Let's stop," said Greyson. "We've walked far enough."

He was eying Logan, who still looked slightly pale and queasy. Clearly, she still hadn't recovered from the nasty side effects of the cure.

She shook her head, blond hair rippling like a flag. "We should keep moving. We aren't safe yet."

"Nowhere is *safe*," growled Amory.

"Shhh," Logan hissed. "Listen."

Everyone froze, ears piqued for the sound of an approaching intruder or the gurgle of a creek. For one long minute, all I could hear was the rattle of bare tree branches in the wind, and then . . . *whoosh!*

"That!" said Logan, looking around to verify we'd all heard it. "It was a car."

She turned away from us, crashing through the deep drifts of snow in the direction of the sound. We followed, and I felt my muscles contract, ready to run or fight in the event we ran right into a convoy of PMC vehicles.

The farther we ran, the stronger the wind became. The trees thinned up ahead, and the sky opened up where they disappeared over a steep embankment. We slowed to a stop.

The woods did end, and at the foot of the embankment was a highway, four lanes across. In the silvery mist of early morning, the road was completely empty. But situated on a bare piece of land across the highway was a boxy white building. It looked like a hospital.

"What do you suppose that is?" asked Roman.

Logan's eyes were huge. "A goldmine."

"You can't be serious," said Amory. "We have no idea what kind of facility that is."

"No, but I bet they have some things we need at camp."

Amory threw her a look of caution.

The Last Uprising

"We haven't been on a run in weeks," Logan pressed. "Our supplies —"

"It's not worth the risk."

"You'd think it was worth the risk if Haven was hurt . . . or me or Max or —" Logan stopped abruptly, her face screwed up as though she had swallowed a fly.

Max's name stung the air, and Amory's face clouded over. It didn't make sense how his name meant so much, but an image flitted through my mind. I pictured Max, ghostly and faded at first, but growing stronger quickly. He was wearing his ridiculous apron, making dinner back at the farm.

Then another memory returned.

The PMC opened fire, a dozen bullets hitting Max in the chest. He was falling. I was yelling his name. It all happened so slowly. Then I was running, and Logan was sobbing, her shoulders caving in as she stumbled toward the bridge.

We were fleeing Sector X.

Logan sniffed loudly, bringing me back to reality. It didn't make sense that I had been on the wrong side of the battle lines, but my heart ached for him still.

The others seemed subdued by the mention of Max, too.

Then Logan turned and began feeling her way down the steep slope toward the road. We followed close behind, trying to stick to the shadows of the smaller saplings and brush creeping up the embankment. Light was coming quickly, and there were no cars on the road.

We waited at the bottom in a cloud of tall, prickly grass sticking up out of the snow.

"Now!" whispered Logan.

She sprang from her hiding place, and the rest of us tore after her across the empty highway in the direction of the boxy white fortress.

My breathing was ragged as we sprinted across the road. Months in the facility with little exercise meant I was out of shape. The road was empty as far as we could see, but for a few brief moments, we were exposed. If anyone was watching from the building, they would know we were coming. And, judging by our appearance, they would know we were rebels.

Panting and pink in the face, Logan threw herself into the snowbank behind a cluster of tall weeds. A second later, I heard it: the unmistakable sound of an approaching car. We waited. I held my breath and closed my eyes as the car drew closer, bracing myself for PMC gunfire.

Then the car whooshed past us, and we breathed a collective sigh. After the sound of its tires had faded away, we climbed up the embankment and inched along the low stone retaining wall behind the building.

Even though we were only a hundred yards away, we still couldn't see an entrance. In fact, the exterior looked completely seamless: an enormous white block as large as ten warehouses.

The only defining characteristic was a scroll of messages from a concealed projector: "Sin is lawlessness . . . With goodwill doing service, as to the Lord and not to men . . . World Corp International: doing God's work."

I shivered. We had found one of World Corp's communes, and at any moment, the doors could open for the workday. I tugged on Logan's sleeve and pointed at the messages.

She frowned. "Now they're using God to justify themselves? I thought it was 'perfect science for an ideal world.'"

Amory sighed. "They'll say whatever they need to say."

The Last Uprising

We crept along the rear of the building, hiding behind a row of huge steel recycling bins. There was a parking lot with two dozen white electric vans neatly charging in a row. Snow-covered fields stretched behind the building, but they were not like any barren winter field I had seen.

Frosted leaves and small rosy buds were poking up through the snow. I squinted. No, they weren't buds at all, but perfect, nearly ripe strawberries.

"They've done it," Greyson breathed. "They've been hinting for years, but I never —"

"I don't believe it."

"They can grow food all year round now," said Amory. "Now they really do control the food supply."

Suddenly, the building began to hum, and large panels of white plastic siding began to rise of their own accord, revealing dozens of separate apartments in the upper levels and larger rooms in the lower levels.

"We need to get inside," said Logan, not bothering to conceal the excitement in her voice.

Roman snorted. "You're joking, right?"

"We need supplies, and it could give us valuable information about World Corp."

"No. We *need* to get the hell out of here before they all come out."

Logan whipped her hair around to glare at him. "This could be our only chance to see one of these places in person. I am *not* going to pass this up."

"How do you plan on getting inside?" Roman jerked his thumb at the glass door closest to us, above which was mounted a beady black identification rover.

Logan laughed. "One rover? Seriously? If a dozen people

come out at once, there's no way it can read them all."

"They don't care about the people coming out — only the people going in."

"There's got to be a service door," said Greyson. "That's our best bet."

Logan's eyes grew wide, looking at me and Roman with satisfaction.

I gave a noncommittal shrug, and Roman sighed in resignation. Even though I knew I was on the wrong side, I couldn't deny that I was curious. I wanted to get inside that commune and see how World Corp had taken a country in crisis and made the people live cooperatively.

Ducking behind the vans, we moved carefully along the back of the building. We'd only gone a few yards when the strong stench of decay filled my nostrils.

"Compost heap," muttered Greyson. "We must be near the kitchen."

Looking across, we could see a slope in the concrete, leading to an entrance that was not flanked by glass windows. And, just as Greyson had predicted, the steel service door did not have a rover mounted above it.

But Logan's eyes weren't fixated on the entrance to the kitchen.

There was a loud bang, and a door farther down the building burst open. Before any of us could call to her, Logan was sprinting out from behind one of the vans, throwing herself behind an enormous generator.

I squinted down to the other door and saw a lanky teenager emerge from the building with his rumpled shirtsleeves rolled up to his elbows. A large vent mounted on the side of the building was hissing wildly, creating a cloud of steam as the hot air was released into the cold. The boy was pushing a cart of what looked like garbage.

"Laundry," Logan mouthed at us. "This is it."

Waiting with bated breath, we watched the boy upend the contents of the cart into a dumpster. He turned back around, and Logan jumped out from her hiding place. She had her gun out, and it was pointed at the back of the boy's head.

I wanted to scream, but my throat had gone completely dry. He couldn't be older than seventeen, and she was going to shoot him.

I watched, paralyzed, as Logan stalked him in complete silence, my muscles braced for a gunshot. But she did not shoot.

The boy seemed to be humming to himself, and my eyes settled on the slight bulge of his back pocket and trailed up to the headphones in his ears. Between the clatter of the cart and his music, he was blissfully unaware of the gun trained on the back of his skull.

My breath became more shallow as he approached the door. If he turned around, he was finished. And if Logan shot him, our advantage of stealth would be gone.

But he did not turn around. He waved his arm in front of a scanner on the lock so it could register his CID, and he pushed the cart through the open door.

As agile as a cougar, Logan jumped at the closing door and stopped it with an index finger.

"Hey!" Greyson hissed.

While I'd been watching Logan, he had been climbing over the side of the dumpster, rummaging in the trash the boy had thrown away. I peered over the edge and saw pieces of discarded clothing mixed in with empty detergent cartons and balls of dryer lint.

Greyson tossed me a piece of white fabric, and I heard

two shoes slap the pavement beside me. More clouds of white polyester rained from the dumpster, and I ducked behind it to change.

The piece of clothing Greyson had given me looked like a nurse's dress. It was ripped under the arm and too big in the hips, but otherwise it was fine. The shoes were a fake, plasticky leather — the ugly nonslip kind I had been issued at the facility. Uniform cracks were beginning to appear in the leather just above the toes, but they weren't noticeable from a distance.

Feeling self-conscious, I pulled off my coat and began to undress, hyperaware of Amory and Roman, who were changing on the other side of the dumpster.

Goose bumps erupted all over my skin as the cold air hit my bare flesh. Although the dress was an unflattering, matronly cut that buttoned up to my collarbone, I instantly wished the thin, short-sleeved garment could be more substantial.

Reluctantly, I kicked off my black combat boots, stuffed my feet into the too-small shoes, and pulled my greasy, unwashed hair into a ponytail. I had no idea what I looked like, but I was sure anyone examining me too closely would be able to tell I did not belong among the sterile, freshly bathed commune people.

When I emerged from behind the dumpster, Greyson, Roman, and Amory were already dressed. Greyson and Amory wore thin cotton scrubs, while Roman was looking irritable in a white collared shirt and blue overalls. We sprinted over to Logan, who wore an expression torn between impatience and amusement.

Greyson took over holding the door ajar while Logan stripped indiscriminately and donned a dress that matched mine. I could tell instantly that Greyson should have switched our dresses. Logan's was much too small. The stiff material strained at her hips, and the buttons gaped along her chest.

Logan glared at Greyson as though he'd done it on purpose, but he, Roman, and Amory were carefully looking anywhere but at her.

Once she had pulled her hair into a twisted bun, she blended in much better than I did. She pushed aside a profusely blushing Greyson and wedged open the door to go inside.

Chapter Eight

A rush of hot air hit my face as we stepped into the narrow room. The sounds of a dozen dryers stacked three high bounced off the opposite wall and made it impossible to hear anyone approaching.

As we rounded the corner, we saw the boy standing at a long table with his back to the door. He was nodding his head in time with his music as he folded identical sets of white pants.

Praying he didn't see us in his peripheral vision, we ducked around the corner one at a time, heading toward the door. Amory reached it first. He pushed it open a crack and checked the hallway before nodding at us to follow.

We emerged into a long, empty corridor. White lacquer doors were spaced every few yards along the right, with tiny silver inscriptions neatly embossed to read "Boiler Room," "Linens," and "Sanitation Supplies."

As we walked along, the hum of voices began to grow louder. I hesitated slightly, not sure if we should be going *toward* the crowd, but Amory and the others continued around the corner. I hurried to catch up and was startled to reach a huge throng of people in white streaming from the cafeteria.

"Where are they going?" Amory whispered to Logan.

"No idea."

I threw a panicked glance at Greyson. The herd of people

The Last Uprising

was growing as the corridor widened, and I was worried we would be separated.

The crowd sorted itself into distinct groups. The men in the blue overalls seemed to stick together. They were burlier and scruffier, and they cleared a path easily with their sheer mass and exuberance as a group. The women dressed like Logan and me were huddled together in tight knots, arms linked, giggling conspiratorially.

Suddenly, the ceiling began to slope upward until it disappeared, and the walls gave way as though we were entering a football stadium. My eyes struggled to adjust to the sudden brightness, and when they did, I realized the entire ceiling was one giant skylight. Ornamental white rafters stretched up to give the illusion of a sloped roof, and the entirety of one wall was dominated by a fifteen-foot cross rising up over an altar.

The horde of people began to disperse into rows of pews, and Amory placed his hand on the small of my back to steer me into one of the back rows. I tried not to gawk at the enormity of the worship hall, but its size and grandeur made it nearly impossible.

What I first thought were upper decks of seating was actually a hallway, probably one that led to individual apartments. The last stragglers were hurrying down two spiral staircases in the back corners of the sanctuary.

We took our seats, and my heart nearly jumped out of my chest when I felt a tiny tap as soft as a bird's wing on my shoulder. I froze, dread and fear pumping through my veins.

I tried to arrange my face into an expression of calm friendliness as I turned, but it probably looked more like a grimace.

Behind me was a woman in her midtwenties. She had thin, white-blond hair folded into a neat plait. A cloud of angelic curls framed her pale, heart-shaped face, and her mouth was lifted into a sweet smile.

"Excuse me, sister. You might want to move before Sister Elise sees."

I must have looked puzzled, because her eyes darted to Amory, who was sitting close enough for our arms to touch.

"Sorry to intrude. It's just . . . well . . ." She blushed a little. "You know the rules."

About men, I filled in for her in my mind.

"You're welcome to sit with us." She extended a porcelain hand. "I'm Mary Beth, by the way."

Looking around, I noticed entire pews filled with women in white dresses, chatting in whispers or bowing their heads in prayer. Behind them, unable to hide their stares, were rows of men. Some sat back in the pews looking bored while others kneeled to flirt with the women sitting in front of them, pretending to whisper a prayer behind their folded hands.

"Oh, of course," I spluttered, feigning embarrassment and pumping her limp hand quickly. "I don't know *what* I was thinking."

I got up and excused myself, ignoring Greyson's confusion and Amory's look of panic. I hoped he would not make a scene and reveal that we knew absolutely nothing about the congregation's rules.

Mary Beth motioned for me to sit next to her friend at the end of the pew, who offered me a forced smile. I settled in beside them and looked around frantically for Logan. She was nowhere to be found.

Copying the guys I had seen in the back, I shifted down to the padded kneeler to whisper to Greyson.

"Where's Logan?"

The Last Uprising

"Dunno," he said. He was looking straight ahead and barely moving his lips, but I could feel the nerves coming off him in waves. "I lost track of her when we came in here."

The congregation was beginning to settle into their seats. A hush spread toward the back of the hall like a cold draft. I got back up onto the bench, ignoring the scowl from Mary Beth's friend, who had been watching my whispered conversation with scorn. She must have thought me very Hester Prynne, brushing up against one man and whispering into the ear of another.

A man in white robes was ascending the steps of the altar, and everyone fell silent when he stepped behind the lectern. When he spoke, his voice boomed out in surround sound.

"Good morning, my brothers and sisters."

"Good morning, Brother Jedediah."

"Today, like every day, we celebrate the birth of the New Republic. We give thanks for peace. We give thanks for order. We give thanks for abundance. And, of course, we give thanks for World Corp International, whose fine people are doing the Lord's work so that *we* may benefit from the great gifts He has to offer.

"So if you will all refer to your hymnal and join me in the first prayer of the day for the New Republic..."

There was a rustle in the crowd, and I copied everyone around me as they reached for the white leather books tucked into the back of the pew, *Prayers and Hymns for the Church of the New Republic*.

I fumbled for the right page, but I didn't have to look far: the prayer was inscribed inside the front cover in silver ink.

Dear Lord, we give thanks for the gifts we have been given.

We give thanks for order; we give thanks for peace; we give thanks to our benefactors for the abundance they provide.

I promise to serve the republic as I serve you, so my benefactors may continue with your great work.

I forsake sin; I forsake lawlessness; I forsake the evildoers who seek to destroy the republic, for they are the minions of Satan.

Please give me the strength to do my part, for I remain your loyal servant and a soldier of salvation for the New Republic.

Amen.

A chill ran down my spine as the last words of the congregation resonated in the great hall, and the hairs on the back of my neck prickled. The prayer for World Corp and the New Republic shouldn't have unnerved me, but it did. Something about it felt wrong — artificial.

"Thank you, brothers and sisters, for those lovely words," said Brother Jedediah, as though he had not asked for the prayer himself. "And now, I'll yield the floor to my friend, Officer Ramsey, so that he may share with you a message of caution from World Corp International."

While Brother Jedediah was speaking, I had not noticed the PMC officer standing in the wings. He wore a grave expression that could not conceal the lines of cold hatred in his brow.

"Thank you for that introduction, Brother Jedediah. And thank you all for your continued support of the New Republic, the Private Military Company, and World Corp International. You all have built a wonderful community based on shared values and mutual respect. But I'm here today to warn you all about the dangers we still face."

He pointed an accusing finger. "Outside those doors, evil still walks. There are those who seek to tempt you . . . to *pull* you off the path of righteousness."

Hushed whispers of indignation rippled through the crowd. Officer Ramsey waited for silence, seemingly satisfied with the congregation's reaction.

The Last Uprising

"But this deal with the devil is not without its consequences. For when you walk with demons, they consume your body and soul."

As if on cue, there was the rattle of wheels on the shiny tile floor, and Brother Jedediah reappeared, pushing a human-sized cage.

The crowd recoiled, and the smell confirmed my worst suspicions before I even saw it.

Inside the cage, slobbering from the lesions at his mouth, was a carrier. My stomach clenched automatically, and the panic started to thrum in my veins.

But I wasn't scared of the carrier, I realized. I was scared of Officer Ramsey.

"Now I . . . hate to bring this abomination into a house of God," said the officer. "But I felt it only prudent to warn you all and show you the fate that awaits sinners and enemies of the republic."

The crowd erupted in a frenzy of terror. Women in the front row screamed as Brother Jedediah wheeled the carrier toward the center of the sanctuary.

Officer Ramsey walked smugly around the cage and struck the metal with his nightstick. The carrier howled, rattling the bars, and his yellow eyes darted around the room.

"This is what happens out there to wayward men and women. This *monster* used to be a rebel. See what became of him?"

Brother Jedediah turned to a woman in the front pew, who was crying and shaking uncontrollably.

"Don't be afraid, my child. You are a righteous woman. Evil has no hold on you . . . but be vigilant of sheep that wander from our flock."

The woman sobbed audibly, and the sound echoed

through the huge chamber — magnified in surround sound.

"Let's show the good sister she has nothing to fear from this demon."

Officer Ramsey strode obediently out of the sanctuary and reappeared with a can of gasoline and a blow torch.

I shook my head, silently hoping he did not intend to do what I imagined.

As I watched, he doused the carrier in his cage. Whatever human senses the carrier had left resurfaced, inciting an angry howl. He knew something terrible was about to happen. I imagined his eyes were burning from the gasoline fumes, but the officer kept shaking the can until only a few drips of gas escaped the nozzle.

No. No, no, no. Every muscle in my body had tightened and recoiled. This was wrong.

Officer Ramsey set the can on the ground with the dull echo of empty plastic and picked up the blow torch. I wanted to look away, but I couldn't.

I wasn't watching the carrier — not anymore. I was watching the firelight gleam in Officer Ramsey's eyes as the carrier's flesh ignited. His screams of pain caught in his deteriorated throat and were drowned out by the roar of the crowd, some gasping in shock, others goading Officer Ramsey on.

Dense smoke furled up through a vent in the ceiling, and I covered my ears to block out the shrieks ripping through the carrier's infected lungs.

My heart was pounding against my ribcage. The carrier's screams tore at my insides, and I thought instantly of my mother. *She* had been a carrier. Those could just as well have been *her* screams.

I knew the virus was wrong. It shouldn't have existed at

all. But the monster wasn't the sick, deteriorated human in the cage. The monster was Officer Ramsey — World Corp.

The smell of burning flesh reached my nostrils, and I bent over my knees, willing myself not to be sick. The pain was ripping through the back of my skull.

Between the debilitating headache, the screams, and the horrible stench, I nearly passed out.

People all around me had risen to their feet for a better view. Some looked horrified, but most wore expressions of excitement. Someone bumped my shoulder, grabbing my upper arm and yanking me to my feet. I raised my head slowly, thinking I was *definitely* going to vomit, and Roman pulled me out of the pew and down the aisle toward the back of the hall.

I twisted around, searching for Greyson and Amory, but the crowd was thickening. I had lost sight of them. The congregation pushed forward to get closer to the scene at the altar, and Roman's grip on my arm was the only thing pulling me out.

There was no back exit, and the side doors were blocked by the crowd. The only way out was the spiral staircase that led to the private apartments.

I barely noticed where my feet were carrying me as Roman dragged me up the stairs.

The carrier's screams were echoing inside my head. I saw Officer Ramsey's wicked eyes and then Aryus Edric's — the man who'd hovered over me as I drowned and burned in the facility.

Going up and around in circles was making me dizzy. I stumbled more than once, but Roman was holding on so tightly I never fell.

All the doors upstairs were wide open, probably as a symbol that the commune's residents had nothing to hide.

The rooms were all furnished the same: freshly made beds with crisp white linens, armchairs upholstered with some scratchy blue material, and closets with no doors as one might find in a hotel. If the commune hadn't been so creepy — and if I couldn't still taste the burning flesh on my tongue — the rooms would have looked inviting.

Keeping away from the edge of the railing, Roman pulled me along down the hallway. The walkway wrapping around the sanctuary gave way to a smaller passage with more apartments. A large clear staircase at the end of the hall led down to the cafeteria on the lower level. I could still hear the carrier's shrieks and the roar of the crowd as we descended.

Rounding the corner, we collided with a woman in white.

My heart skipped a beat, and my brain struggled to form an excuse for why I had left the service with a man.

Then I realized it was Logan. She was wearing a white backpack that clashed horribly with her too-small dress and nurse's shoes.

"Oh! It's you," she breathed. "I thought you were someone else."

"Where are the others?" I stammered.

"No idea. I thought they were with you."

"We have to get out of here," broke in Roman. "Now's the time. Greyson and Amory were leaving, too."

I didn't know if that was true, but I followed them down the hall back toward the laundry room. The racket from all the dryers drowned out the sounds from the sanctuary, but the heat was stifling. Logan threw open the door, bathing us in cold air and sunshine, and we stumbled back out into the world.

The first thing I noticed was that Greyson and Amory were not there. Logan reached down to retrieve her

The Last Uprising

discarded rebel garments without breaking stride, and she and Roman continued across the parking lot toward the dumpster.

"Where are they?" I demanded, my lungs heaving as they dragged in the fresh, cold air.

"I'm sure they're coming," growled Roman, sounding as though he couldn't care less.

"Super creepy service, don't you think?" mused Logan as she began to strip.

Roman made a noise of assent in his throat, turning away to change as well. I stood at the back corner of the dumpster, watching the door to the laundry room and trying not to be sick.

The wind ripped through the thin dress, biting at my exposed arms and legs, but I did not notice the cold. All I could think about were the carrier's shrieks and the way that crowd had egged Officer Ramsey on. I realized that this was probably not the first gruesome display. The commune leaders must have given these demonstrations on a regular basis to keep the fear alive in their congregation.

The whole setting disturbed me: the amphitheater-like sanctuary, the morality guise of the commune, the message that linked the New Republic with the divine and the rebellion with sin.

Slowly, I changed out of my torn dress and donned my real clothes. The bulky coat and worn jeans were a welcome relief. I sank down against the back of the dumpster, watching Logan show off the goods she'd stolen.

She had raided the infirmary, probably depleting their supply of antiseptic and medication. She had also managed to swipe some odds and ends that were forever in demand at the rebel camp: matches, batteries, and even a portable radio.

The laundry room door burst open, and Greyson and

Amory came sprinting out. Relief as I'd never known flooded through me — enough to dull the throbbing pain in the back of my head. They were each toting a white bag like Logan's, running toward us as if they were being chased.

"We have to go," panted Amory. "Now."

Greyson was already stripping off his scrubs.

"Were you caught?"

Amory shook his head, pulling on his jacket over the scrubs. "Morning assembly is over. They're all heading out to their jobs in the fields and the factories. This place is going to be swarming in about five minutes."

Logan tossed Amory his cargo pants as he shoved his feet into his boots. "Let's go."

Not bothering to be covert, we sprinted through the parking lot and across the highway, looking over our shoulders every few paces to see if we were being followed.

We reached the other side of the highway and took shelter in a stand of trees to watch the morning commute. Men in overalls were flooding out the back exits toward the fields, while others were piling into white vans and pulling onto the highway.

"What took you so long?" asked Logan, turning in irritation to Amory and Greyson.

"We were getting some food and supplies. And we broke into Brother Jedediah's office and stole this." He retrieved a large packet of information that looked like official documents.

"You *didn't*."

Amory nodded, clearly pleased with himself.

"Now they'll know we've been there."

"I doubt it. They're so confident in their security that

The Last Uprising

they've gotten complacent — don't even lock their doors. It's supposed to 'build trust within the community.' It's all in there." He withdrew a small book and tossed it to me.

I turned the book over in my hand. It bore the World Corp International logo and was titled *Community Standards*.

"This is going to be useful," said Greyson. "If we know how they operate, it will be easier to dismantle everything they have built."

He was right. Even the defectors from the commune up north wouldn't be privy to the strategy the World Corp leaders had devised.

Logan nodded grudgingly. "Good work."

As we plowed through the woods back in the direction we had come, I couldn't shake the nagging feeling that I was missing something crucial. *How had I ended up on the same side as World Corp? How could I fight for an entity that burned carriers alive and was bent on so much evil?*

It didn't make any sense, but here I was, trudging along beside Amory, Greyson, Logan, and Roman. I had been their prisoner, but I wasn't anymore. That much was certain.

After seeing the commune dwellers through the eyes of an outsider, something had shifted in our relationship. We weren't on different sides anymore.

Even though the returning pain in the back of my head told me I shouldn't trust them, I *did* trust them — as much as I *dis*trusted Brother Jedediah, Officer Ramsey, and Mary Beth.

We settled in a protective copse of pine trees near a tiny stream and built a fire. Amory withdrew some tea bags from the stolen backpack, and the comforting warmth of the drink reminded me of my mom and made me feel just a little less hopeless.

I could feel his eyes on me, but I pretended not to notice.

"It's sick, you know?" Roman muttered, finally breaking the silence that had descended upon the group. "Twisting those people's beliefs . . . making them so scared they won't ever leave."

"They believe it," I said, remembering Mary Beth. "They believe all of it, or it wouldn't be so easy for World Corp."

Logan whipped her head around to look at me, and I wondered for a moment if they all thought I was justifying World Corp's actions. I wasn't. I was appalled by everything we'd witnessed at the commune.

"Listen to this," said Greyson. He was skimming the small white book he and Amory had stolen. "Each Community should be built upon the shared values of its intended inhabitants as long as these values are congruent with World Corp International's philosophy of Order, Compliance, and Progress."

"That's the PMC's 'philosophy,'" I said quickly.

Amory nodded. "They're not even bothering to hide that World Corp owns the PMC now."

Greyson continued. "For any Community to thrive, there must be a morality code, both to protect the Populace and to ensure the longevity of the Community. That code must serve the values of World Corp International and protect shared resources."

"What the hell does that mean?" muttered Roman.

"Population control," said Logan quickly.

I thought back to what Mary Beth had said about men and women sitting apart.

"They leave all their doors open to discourage hoarding and stealing."

The Last Uprising

"This is unbelievable," said Greyson. "They have all these rules: curfew . . . required daily worship . . . chaperoned courtship . . ."

"It's just that commune, though," said Amory absently. He was scanning a long list in the packet of papers he had found. "There are hundreds, by the looks of it. All founded on different values. Look!"

"Science, progress, responsibility . . . altruism, order, peace . . . sacrifice, family, security. And here." Amory pointed to a list of codes running down another column. "Some of these are the same. I think they sort them by state, religion, political ideology . . . then they feed them these supposed 'values' that already align with what they believe. They just make sure they're values that don't interfere with World Corp's mission."

"So the commune we saw near the Infinity Building justifies their actions with science."

Greyson nodded. "It makes sense. It's the only way you could get all those people to live together under one roof."

We all sat back for a moment and let Amory's discovery sink in. If World Corp was controlling people with their own beliefs, it would be much harder to break its chokehold on the New Northern Territory.

"We need to show this to Ida," said Logan.

Amory shook his head. "She's not due back at camp for another day at least. We should be gone by then."

"We can't move on yet," said Logan. "Not until she gets back."

"It's too dangerous."

"Why? They've already raided the camp. They think we've scattered. The old camp would be the safest place."

"I don't like it," said Roman. "We're way too close to that

commune. What if they come looking?"

"They're not the PMC," said Logan. "Those people don't leave, much less go out looking for rebels. Don't you see? World Corp wants to draw their focus into the community so they don't see what's going on outside."

Amory sighed. "We'll see what the others say. But I don't like it. I say two days max. If Ida isn't back by then, we leave."

We waited for hours, eventually cooking the frozen meals Amory had stolen from the commune. They were preassembled packets with pieces of real chicken and vegetables harvested from the commune's fields.

I savored all the flavors, wishing the rebels could assemble meals just like it. I hadn't eaten a fresh vegetable all winter. Everything at the rebel camp came from cans salvaged from abandoned grocery stores and warehouses. Even at the World Corp facility, everything had been heavily processed and tasteless.

"No wonder they don't want to leave," said Greyson through a mouthful of chicken. "The food is fantastic."

Logan scowled at him, but none of us stopped eating to form a reply.

Finally darkness fell, and we decided it was time to begin making our way back.

I didn't like being in the dark woods caught between the commune and the raided camp. Every snapping branch and rustle of an animal in the snow made me jump. I was sure the PMC was lurking in the shadows, waiting to capture us and brand me a traitor to the cause.

It was slowgoing. No one was talking, and Amory seemed to be deep in thought.

After two hours of walking, the trees suddenly thinned,

and the hulking outline of a tent emerged in the darkness. We all slowed down considerably, barely breathing as we listened for signs of life.

Amory motioned for us to lay back, and he and Roman fanned out in opposite directions to scan the perimeter of the camp.

For several moments, no one spoke. All I could hear was the thudding of my own heart against my ribcage.

Chapter Nine

The destruction was unimaginable. Deep muddy tracks cut across the snow like fingernail scratches, and dead bodies lay strewn across camp like forgotten dolls.

Near the smoldering embers of the campfire, I could just make out a woman hunched over one of the bodies, her shoulders shaking with grief. It was Ida.

My heart ached for her as I watched her weep, sending a burst of pain across my temple. Though the memories weren't there, I recalled that Ida had always treated me with unfailing kindness.

The man lying next to her in the snow had a bushy gray beard. His weathered brown face was completely slack, so it looked almost as though he were sleeping.

Logan let out a soft gasp, cupping a hand to her mouth. "Murphy."

That name stirred a memory inside me, but it was a foggy recollection. I remembered he'd run a camp for defectors in upstate New York, and I wondered absently how he and Ida had gotten here.

"Oh, thank god!" cried Ida when she saw us. "I didn't think there was anyone . . . I c-can't believe he's gone."

"Where are the others?" Amory asked.

Ida shook her head, lost for words. "We came back early. I thought . . . I thought they'd taken *everyone*." The way she said "everyone" made me realize that the rebels were Ida's family. Fighting in the revolution was all she had left.

Logan sank down into the snow next to her, draping an arm over her shoulders. Kneeling there, crumpled over Murphy's dead body, Ida looked much smaller and frailer than I remembered. Her white-blond hair hung in a raggedy braid over her tattered coat, and her hands were wrinkled, shaking, and covered in liver spots.

"We should see who survived," Roman muttered.

Logan shot him an icy look, but I understood. He wanted to know who else *hadn't* survived.

My legs seemed to move of their own accord as I followed Roman around the perimeter of camp, helping him turn over the fallen rebels one by one to identify them. He didn't speak to me, which made it easier somehow. He didn't even appear angry or disgusted when I flinched away from one man who'd been shot through the eye.

A few people began trickling back to camp, looking tired and defeated. Some clapped hands to their mouths and started to cry; others took in the devastation with blank stares.

One woman staggered over to Roman weeping hysterically and asked if he had found her husband. His mouth tightened into a hard line, and he shook his head. The woman dissolved into tears, though I couldn't tell if she was terrified or joyful. The three of us were all thinking the same thing: Anyone who wasn't accounted for may have survived, or they could have been arrested by the PMC.

After a while, Amory appeared at my shoulder. "We need to bury them and regroup," he said to Roman.

"We can't dig graves for all these people."

Amory's eyes narrowed in anger. "A proper burial is the least they deserve."

"The dead outnumber the living three to one. We need to get out of here before we're next."

"We have to wait for the rest of the survivors."

"Look around you!" snapped Roman. "These *are* the survivors. This is it. Everyone else is either dead or in the PMC's custody."

Amory held his gaze. "We need to wait. People are in shock."

"You think this is smart? We're sitting ducks right now. If the PMC comes back —"

"They won't be back tonight."

Roman sneered. "Oh, right. I forgot you're the all-knowing PMC brat."

Amory's eyes narrowed. "They think they've scared us off. We'll be all right for a while. The PMC has bigger problems to deal with."

Roman made an exasperated noise in his throat. "I'll give you until morning to get your shit together. If you don't have a plan by then, we're doing it my way. I'm not going to get myself killed just because you want to throw these people a funeral."

As he stormed off, I couldn't help thinking Roman's words were much harsher than his actions. He'd told Amory I was a lost cause, yet he'd dragged me out of that sanctuary. He was doing it again now: pretending he didn't care about the dead after he'd painstakingly identified each person.

Amory and I were alone now. He looked at me for a moment, and then his expression changed abruptly, as though he'd suddenly remembered that things were different between us. I wasn't sure why this hurt, but it did.

He left me on my own in the middle of camp, very much apart from the shared grief. I didn't belong here. As far as the rebels were concerned, I belonged with the enemy.

Tree branches snapped behind me, making me jump.

A boy stumbled out of the woods. He was tall and lanky with sandy brown hair and freckles scattered haphazardly across the bridge of his nose. It was Kinsley. The entire left side of his face was covered in blood. He staggered forward wearing a huge grin and nearly collapsed against me.

"I made it," he said with a laugh.

My back bowed as I tried to hold him upright. He was only sixteen, and yet he towered over me by a good six inches. Back screaming in protest, I wondered why he didn't treat me with the wariness the others did. Surely he knew what had happened to me.

"Oh my god. Kinsley!" Logan was running toward us through the snow and grabbed his other side just as my knees gave out. Together, we lowered him to the ground and propped him against a tree.

"What happened to you?" Logan demanded.

"The PMC." He laughed, sounding a little insane. "They weren't going to take me alive. I brought two of those bastards down and ran as fast as I could."

"Did you see how many were captured?" I asked, feeling a sudden responsibility for the people at camp.

He shook his head. "They only took a few. I don't think they cared too much about arrests. I think they wanted to make a statement."

"What do you mean?"

"Raiding the camps . . . making arrests . . . killing anyone who runs away . . . It's just a scare tactic."

I felt a surge of anger that the PMC would go after Kinsley. He was just a kid — completely harmless. It was wrong.

"What about Godfrey?" asked Logan.

He shook his head slowly, as if trying to string the facts together. "I didn't see them take him. Didn't see Godfrey at all, actually. But everything happened so fast. I just ran."

Maybe I was imagining it, but I thought I detected a subtle note of shame and defeat on his last word.

Once Kinsley had recovered, I helped Logan steer Ida back to her tent. I ran to make them a pot of tea, my hands and legs busying themselves without consulting my brain. The pain in my temple had become a dull ache, but I ignored it.

These people were clearly trouble, but I was one of them now. I couldn't fight for World Corp. I was mixed up and confused, but all my instincts told me Amory and the others were good.

Night blanched into a cloudy gray morning, and Amory, Greyson, and Roman helped drag the dead out into the woods. The ground was frozen, so they buried them in the snow. More was falling in huge wet flakes, and I hoped it would be enough to cover the bloody patches, the muddy tire tracks, and the evidence of death that hung over the camp.

Amory and Greyson went into Ida's tent to share what we'd learned about World Corp's control of the communes, and I felt sorry that Ida couldn't even spend one evening grieving for her friends without worrying about the fate of all the people who were depending on her.

By the afternoon, the sky was still a sickly gray, and I heard a shout from outside Ida's tent. I ran out in a panic — not knowing what to expect — and saw a hooded figure approaching from the woods. The limp, pronounced by the uneven ground, and the bushy black beard were unmistakable.

"Godfrey!" Amory shouted.

Godfrey didn't break stride as Amory and the others surrounded him, demanding to know what had happened and where he had been. He was headed straight for me — straight for Ida's tent — and I instinctively stepped out of the way.

As he ducked into the tent, a memory danced through my head: Godfrey in a rumpled white PMC uniform. It clashed wildly with his unruly beard and weathered face, but it was real. He was a mole, and he had helped me break Amory out of Isador. As poignant as the memory felt, it was like watching a movie about someone else's life. I felt so disconnected from that person I had been.

Logan's hand on my arm snapped me back to reality as she pulled me away from the tent.

"He kicked me out," she hissed indignantly. "As if Ida's not going to turn around and tell me everything he says."

As Logan pulled away, I noticed the strained look on her face and the way her hand clasping my arm shook a little.

Everything she said was pushed aside by the question that had been burning in my mind. "Logan, what happened? What did the cure *do* to you?"

She released me abruptly and took a step back. From the way she was looking at me, I couldn't tell if she was angry, surprised, or both.

"It's just . . . you weren't like this before."

Logan's startling green eyes went cold. "Oh, *really*? Tell me, Haven. What *was* I like before? I guess you know everything about me, but you don't remember that we're supposed to be *friends*."

I staggered backward, the smack of anger stinging my

insides. "It's not my fault I don't remember. I don't know why I don't, but —"

"You don't know *why*? World Corp brainwashed you into thinking we're the enemy. They turned you against all your friends and left you with *nothing*! And today when they raided camp, they *left* you here." She said the last few words with relish. "Did you ever think that maybe they're not your friends and we are? Maybe if you tried to remember us, you'd see the truth."

I *had* thought about that — more than I was willing to admit. I understood why Logan was angry with me, but it was all too much to take in.

"Look around, Haven!" She gestured wildly at the destruction. "We're at war! This is why the rebellion is happening. They kill people. They poisoned them with the virus, and now they're hunting down innocent families who escaped those horrible communes. Is that the world you want to live in?"

I stared at her, utterly lost for words. My head was throbbing.

None of it fit with what I had been taught. It made sense, but if what Logan was saying about the virus was true, I couldn't justify anything World Corp had done. They had killed too many people — civilians. They had killed my mother.

"Amory may be in denial, but I'm not," said Logan. Her words sounded confrontational, but her tone was steeped in hopelessness. "We're done holding you prisoner. If you want to leave, leave. If you want to stay, you're with us. But you can't stay here and be loyal to World Corp." Logan shot a glance at two grown men weeping together in the snow. "Not now."

Even though I knew it was a test, her words fortified me. It didn't sound as though she was pushing me away at all;

she was asking me to make a choice.

As tough as she was, Logan could never hide how much she *cared*. She cared so much about Amory and Ida and Greyson that it physically hurt to watch, and her tone told me she cared *deeply* whether I stayed or left.

Right then, that meant everything to me. And for the first time since I'd arrived at camp, I felt that maybe I had friends after all.

It was nearly dark by the time Ida and Godfrey emerged from the tent.

I was sitting next to Kinsley because he was the only person who didn't make me feel wildly out of place.

The camp fell silent as she stepped into the center of the circle near the fire. The frailness and grief were gone. She was Ida again.

"Friends," she began. "We lost a lot of good people today." Ida dragged in a breath, and I knew she was thinking of Murphy.

"We feel beaten because the PMC took them from us, but they have not won. As long as we are still fighting, we are still a threat to them."

The crowd was silent, soaking in the sorrow.

"Our friends and loved ones wouldn't want us to surrender. Many of those we lost were good friends of mine, and I know they'd want us to pick ourselves up and keep going. This fight is bigger than us. It's bigger than today."

There was a murmur of assent in the crowd, and this seemed to strengthen Ida for what came next.

"But our situation has changed. We cannot stay here now that the PMC knows our location. Godfrey has been gathering intelligence, and it is his assessment that we should be safe for a few days at least. What we really need are new strongholds south of the border to demonstrate the power of the resistance and force them to divide their resources."

The crowd bristled, and the fearful muttering spread like a horde of wasps.

"I have not forgotten those living in terror in the World Corp communes. We still intend to infiltrate those facilities and free those who wish to join the cause. Some of them could be great allies in the fight against World Corp, and thanks to some new information we've uncovered, we have a greater understanding of how Aryus Edric has been manipulating those under his control.

"Right now, my intention is to send a small party across the border to establish a new base, rally the rebels in the states, and show World Corp we are still strong. The rest of us will remain in the area to start with the communes closest to the border. Anybody who wishes to have his or her voice heard is welcome to speak now and be a part of the discussions. Just know that by this time tomorrow, we will have a plan, and our decision will be final."

Ida drew a breath, and I waited for everyone to start chiming in.

Finally, a mousy woman who had escaped from one of the communes spoke. "You want people to go across the border?"

"It *is* dangerous, but many of us have done it before successfully."

The woman looked stricken, as though Ida had suggested death by firing squad.

"Why would we want to go back to the states?" snapped an older man. "The place is crawling with carriers. I'm not going back!"

"Me neither," said a shrill woman.

There was a general murmur of agreement, and Amory and Roman threw them all looks of disgust. Everyone who was speaking had come from the communes, so it made sense that they were the most frightened. It was fear that had driven them to the communes in the first place.

"As I said," repeated Ida. "This is up for discussion, and no one will be *forced* to cross the border. If you have anything else to say — or if you wish to stay behind — please join me in my tent."

As people dispersed, I found myself alone with Logan, Greyson, Amory, Roman, and Kinsley.

Roman looked sick. "They're cowards. All of them."

"Think of what they've heard about the border," said Logan. "They've spent months listening to the World Corp propaganda about how terrible it is down south."

"Well, I'm not going to crawl back into that creepy place to liberate a bunch of people who don't want to be freed."

"They've been taught to fear the states," she snapped. "They don't know any different."

"They need to learn to think for themselves."

Although I knew Roman was talking about the commune dwellers, his words felt highly personal. Amory was watching me closely, but I didn't turn to look at him.

"Well, if Ida wants people to cross the border, I'll do it," said Kinsley.

Logan turned to look at him, a mixture of pride and concern in her eyes.

"So will I," said Greyson.

Amory nodded.

"We're all going," growled Roman. "It's obvious nobody here has the balls —"

"What about you?" asked Logan, turning to me.

My face burned, and I was grateful for the low light. I didn't know what to say. All of them were staring at me.

Logan's face fell. "Yeah, that's what I thought."

"I'll go," I said. My voice sounded small, almost a squeak.

Amory's eyebrows lifted in surprise, the ghost of a smile playing on his lips.

Roman was staring at me with a challenging expression, but I was too weary to fight. I didn't have to prove myself to him. Somehow, I knew Roman and I had always been reluctant allies.

Logan left, looking satisfied, and Roman strode off in the direction of Ida's tent — probably to put our bid in to be the party that went south.

"So you're in?" said Amory. The hope in his gaze twisted my heart.

"I'm in."

Greyson shook his head slowly in disbelief. "What changed?"

I took a deep breath, not knowing how what I was about to say would be received. "I don't know what I was like before this . . ." I said slowly. "I just know what I was taught in the facility. My memories don't make sense."

I shook my head, trying to organize my thoughts.

"But what happened today . . . it wasn't right. None of it. Good people don't do this. I don't know what to believe, so I'm going with my gut. Right now, my gut is telling me that I should trust you."

Amory's face fell a little at this explanation, but Greyson looked satisfied.

It struck me that Greyson cared most about the facts. He

valued logic and always wanted to know how people arrived at their decisions, whereas Amory had other reasons for asking me. I knew whatever I said wouldn't make him happy.

"You want to go for a run?" Greyson asked suddenly.

Amory looked surprised and then shot him a warning look. He still didn't trust me not to run away.

"A run?"

He shrugged. "Yeah, you know . . . like old times. I feel all cagey." He feigned a shiver and shifted his weight on the balls of his feet like a boxer. Despite everything that had happened, this made me want to laugh.

"Yeah. All right."

We weren't dressed for a run. We were wearing layers of rebel black — sweatshirts and cargo pants and combat boots — but a run sounded nice. I shed my heavy coat, and Amory looked amused.

I was surprising him tonight, I thought with satisfaction.

Greyson set off at a brisk pace and I followed, my heavy boots clomping through the snow. I was happy this snow was crunchy and tacky. I was able to gain traction and push off without slipping.

Soon we fell into an easy cadence with Greyson leading the way — just as in the old days. I knew he was setting a slower pace than he would have a year ago, since neither of us was in as good of shape as we had been before the Collapse. He had a lot more muscle, and he was strong from fighting, but I had grown skinny and weak in the facility. And after today's brush with the PMC, I had a feeling that Greyson's runs in my absence had been adrenaline-fueled sprints, not long pieces.

I felt a slight stitch in my side, but I liked it. It was a different kind of pain than I'd experienced since leaving World Corp. The headaches made me dizzy and nauseous, whereas the pain from the run energized me.

As we ran, I listened to the soft, rhythmic tread of our feet and our staggered breaths. It was music to my ears.

For a long time, I'd been alone, but now I had someone beside me. We moved as a unit, and there was an unspoken bond between us now.

Greyson set our pace. When he moved, I moved.

I didn't have to worry about my foggy memories or that horrible voice in the back of my head that told me he was the enemy. All I had to do was move my feet and breathe.

I let my mind wander. If I squinted, the white snow looked almost like the sun-soaked limestone trail we'd run on back in Columbia.

It was summer, and I had the freedom of breezy running shorts and light sneakers. It was hot enough that Greyson was running shirtless, sweat glistening between his lean shoulder blades. His mocha skin was already dark with a tan. He wouldn't burn all summer, whereas I already had pink lines around my sweat-soaked cotton tank top.

I was itching with thirst, but I knew we were headed for the trailhead with the good water fountain.

Greyson veered off to the concrete sidewalk marked by a trail map. He slowed to a walk and turned back to me.

He was drinking in heavy, rhythmic breaths, but his eyebrows were raised in satisfaction. I nodded, trying to catch my breath. He checked his watch. We'd made good time.

We both drank our fill of lukewarm water and flopped down in the grass to rest. As I sat there, grass prickling my legs, I felt completely at ease.

We got up to double back, and the cadence of my feet blended with my heavy footfalls in the snow.

The memory was gone, but I felt that happiness still. It expanded in my chest, a warmth that spread through my whole body.

Something clicked into place, and I knew I had been right to place my trust in Greyson and the others. He always ran ahead, but he was constantly listening for my footfalls behind him. He never led me astray.

Suddenly, Greyson stopped. It was so dark that I almost bumped right into him, and he held up his hand for me to be quiet. I choked down my labored breaths, ears piqued for a sound.

Then I heard it: the snapping of branches and the wet, raspy intake of breath from the trees. I heard the mucus rattling in his lungs and his stumbling footfalls.

It wasn't possible. They couldn't be *here*.

But then a shadow appeared to my right — not the source of the noise — and I knew there was more than one. There was a scuffle in the trees and then more snapping. A third shadow appeared, stumbling into a fourth.

Carriers.

I was frozen, and the sounds of snapping branches and the low rumble of dying breaths reached my ears.

"Run," Greyson breathed.

I staggered backward, nearly tripping over an exposed tree root, and took off through the trees at a sprint. I could hear Greyson behind me, and this time I was leading.

I pushed my legs harder, and they burned in protest. My boots and clothes felt too heavy, and I wished I was in better shape. My breathing was fast but controlled. I knew we could outrun them, but I needed to put as much distance between us as possible to buy us more time.

We had to warn the others.

Chapter Ten

I tore into camp breathing heavily. "Carriers! In the woods!" I panted.

There was a moment of silence as everyone stared at me, trying to work out what I was saying. Then there was chaos.

The rebels jumped to their feet and ran. Ida, Godfrey, and Roman emerged from the leaders' tent, and Amory was already at my side. The blazing fire burned my corneas as I tried to focus. After the relative stillness of the woods, there was too much to take in.

A curtain of blond hair whipped around, and Logan materialized in front of me. "That's impossible. There *are* no carriers north of the border."

Greyson appeared on my left, trying to catch his breath to explain. "I saw them, too."

Amory turned to me with a grave expression. "They're *here*? You're sure?"

I nodded, still breathless.

"How many of them?"

"I don't know. I saw at least five, but I heard more moving in the trees."

"There have to be more," added Greyson. "The hordes are growing. We haven't seen a pack of less than thirty since the riots."

"Not here, though," snapped Roman. "There are no carriers in the north."

Greyson rounded on him, clearly exasperated. "Well you can tell them that when they're ripping your throat out."

Roman bared his teeth but didn't say anything else.

Logan snapped into fighting mode at once. The steely veil dropped over her face, and suddenly she was a soldier again. The rifle was already in her hands, and her hair was in a ponytail.

But out of the corner of my eye, I saw her fingers shaking as she loaded her gun. Something was off.

Roman stepped around Logan and handed me a rifle. The way he placed it in my hands made me think he was acting against his better judgment. Roman clearly didn't trust me, but I could shoot, and they needed all the help they could get. He held out a box of ammunition, and I took a fistful of rounds.

I marveled at the familiar coolness of the metal in my fingers. It was strange how something that had once made me so uneasy now gave me comfort. This was something I could do.

The five of us, Kinsley, Ida, Godfrey, and a few defectors I vaguely recognized fanned out near the perimeter of the trees — close enough that we could almost touch each other and prevent the carriers from breaching our first line of defense. I positioned myself between Greyson and Logan, feeling the comforting weight of the ammunition in my pocket.

Some of the other rebels and defectors stood behind us wielding sticks and tools as weapons, but I could tell they were terrified. Most of them had come straight from the states to the communes. Many had never even *seen* a carrier, let alone killed one. They were inexperienced as fighters, and

I for one was glad they weren't holding rifles at my back.

"Take 'em down clean," shouted Godfrey. "Shots to the head. Don't let them break through. If any do, we'll fall out from the edges to kill them. Stagger your reloads."

My heart was pounding with adrenaline. I didn't even feel scared. I felt alive.

Silence fell over the crowd as we waited, poised to fight.

Uneven footfalls crashed through the underbrush. There was a low growl and the sound of damaged lungs panting. Then the first carrier emerged — bald, emaciated, and with oozing flaps of angry red skin around his mouth.

He barely had a chance to gnash his rotten teeth before Amory aimed and landed a bullet right in the carrier's skull. He let out a howl like a dying animal and collapsed in the snow.

There were more footsteps. Branches cracked sharply in the stillness, and the hulking outline of half a dozen others appeared in the trees.

I held my gun on one, waiting until she showed herself in the dancing light from the campfire, and shot her right between the eyes. A shot fired from my left, but it missed the next carrier completely. I took aim and fired at the same carrier, catching him in the chest. The carrier went down.

Sneaking a glance to my left, I saw Logan jut out her lower lip, looking livid.

Something was definitely wrong. Her hands shook as she took aim once more, missing another carrier.

I shot that one, too, before he could fully disentangle himself from a snarl of thorns, and Logan let out a desperate little breath as she reloaded.

I tried to focus on the shadows moving in the trees, but I was distracted by Logan's clumsy movements beside me.

Logan, the deadly PMC-trained soldier — I'd never seen her miss a shot.

As she fumbled with her rifle, I felt a surge of pity in my chest. She looked close to tears. My heart ached, and pain shot up the back of my head again.

I blinked furiously, tearing my eyes away from Logan to refocus on the kill. Three more carriers had emerged, and I aimed for the middle one. I missed and had to reload, cursing myself silently for allowing myself to be distracted. I finished reloading before Logan did and fired again.

As my carrier fell to the ground, another three stumbled out from the trees to take his place.

In the time it had taken me to bring down one, the other two had advanced. I shot desperately, but the horde was coming more quickly now, as if the carriers had been waiting just out of range to hear how many of us were shooting.

Most of them were stage five, but they were faster than they should have been. Dread pooled in my gut. They were mutant carriers, and none of us was immune to this strain of the virus. Letting carriers through our line wasn't an option; one bite was enough to end someone's life.

My shoulder was aching from the kickback of my rifle, and my fingers were nearly frozen in the cold. I wasn't wearing gloves.

But while the others' shots seemed to be coming more slowly, I took the discomfort in stride. If my time as a runner had taught me anything, it was how to convert pain into power. Two carriers were coming my way at once, but I zeroed in on one and then took down the other.

The others weren't faring as well. Two carriers had breached our line, and Amory had broken off from the end to dispatch them with his knife. Worry prickled on the back of my neck, but I forced myself to keep my head straight forward and concentrate on those emerging from the woods.

I fumbled in my pocket to reload and came up empty.

"I'm out," I shouted to Logan.

Her eyes flickered with panic, but she didn't put down her gun. I didn't know if she'd managed to take down a single carrier, but she wasn't going to give up.

"Hey! I need to get more ammo," I yelled to Greyson. He nodded once without looking at me as he aimed at a particularly nasty carrier ambling toward him.

I ran around to the crate of ammunition Roman had left in the snow and shoved a handful of rounds into each pocket. I heard a shot coming from near my post, and I looked over my shoulder in time to see an enormous carrier tearing through our line of defense. Greyson and Logan continued to shoot, and another broke in near Kinsley. They were overwhelming us from the left side.

I rushed to reload, but the huge carrier was stumbling too quickly — a drunken sprint in my direction.

Amory was busy struggling with another that had broken through a while ago. Blood was gushing down the front of the carrier's ragged shirt, but he didn't seem to want to go down without a fight. Amory stabbed again, and the carrier howled in pain. The sound pierced my eardrums like nails on a chalkboard — the sound of vocal chords ripping and the carrier's dying breath.

I felt for my knife at my side and found nothing. I wasn't wearing my holster. I had no other weapons.

But then the big carrier adjusted course. He was headed for Amory, who had just finished the carrier he was fighting and was already fending off another.

For a moment, everything slowed down. I watched Amory's deft swipes through the air — a graceful, deadly dance. His brows were knitted together in fierce concentration, but I didn't see that cold, empty look from my memories. His eyes were bright and clear, and they were full of terror.

The carrier he was fighting lunged, knocking him off-balance. He stumbled, and the carrier fell on top of him. Amory yelled, stabbing him in the back with his right hand while holding him by the throat with his left. Meanwhile, the other carrier was still charging toward him.

Something shifted inside me, like the right puzzle piece snapping into the last empty space. I couldn't recall moving my legs, but a second later, I was there.

I jumped between Amory and the carrier, wielding my rifle with both hands like a staff. With as much force as I could muster, I thrust it upward into the carrier's jugular. He howled, but he was too large. He pushed against me, and my feet slipped in the wet snow. They flew out from under me, and suddenly the carrier was on top of me.

I jerked the butt of my gun upward, catching him hard in the jaw, but my limited range of motion weakened the blow.

His putrid breath burned my nostrils, and warm saliva flecked my face. I could see his rotten teeth snapping and the crusty, oozing sores festering around his mouth. I couldn't let him bite me. I wouldn't.

"Haven!" Amory cried.

He was still buried under his carrier, which was fighting like a hyena as he bled everywhere. Amory's arm was pinned under the carrier, shaking as he held him off. I caught the look of fear in Amory's eyes. We were going to die.

In a final, desperate move, I reached over to Amory's thigh and clasped the knife he couldn't reach. The leather handle was warm and deadly in my hand.

I brought the knife down as hard as I could, aiming for

my carrier's heart through the back. My blade sank in easily, as though I were cutting into a watermelon, and he let out a terrible shriek, neck stretching in pain. I took the opportunity to jerk the knife out of his flesh and plunge it into his eye socket. Blood spewed all over my face, and I closed my eyes and mouth instinctively.

The carrier made a noise I knew would haunt me for the rest of my life, but he tumbled off my chest, and my lungs expanded instantly.

In one motion, I flipped over onto my knees and drove the now-sticky knife into Amory's carrier. He howled, and I shoved him off Amory with all the strength I could muster.

Amory climbed out from under the carrier, getting shakily to his feet and holding out a hand for me. I took it, trembling with adrenaline and relief, and he pulled me up.

For a second, my vision narrowed. I had no idea what was going on around us. There was a loud ringing in my ears, and I was shaking with nerves. Amory's intense gray eyes met mine. Both of our faces were spattered with blood.

I didn't know what I expected — rejection and disgust, perhaps — but Amory reached for me and yanked me into his arms. The side of my face collided with his strong chest, and he held me tightly against him, his shoulders heaving with exertion.

He was making a labored noise, but whether he was panting, crying, or both, I couldn't tell. I felt my body relax and a magnificent warmth spreading through me. The pain in the back of my head was dull — overwhelmed by the heady feeling I got as I breathed him in.

This was right. *He* was right. My need to be this close to Amory was almost overwhelming, and I reveled in the feeling of his arms around me. It was brief.

Within seconds, Amory released me, and we staggered

back to the line of people fighting near the woods. In the time we'd been down, several more carriers had broken through. Godfrey and Kinsley were dispatching them with their knives one by one, and several of the commune dwellers lay bleeding or dead in the snow.

Kinsley was slashing at two carriers at once. They were faster and stronger than the others, but he was lightning fast with his blades. If I hadn't been terrified for him, I would have been amused. His lanky, overgrown frame should have been awkward and messy as he swooped his arms through the air, but his movements were skilled and precise.

I jumped in on his left and stabbed the second carrier through the heart. She howled and fell to her scraped knees. This one still had her cropped auburn hair. She was in her midthirties — stage three, as far as I could tell — and she looked unnervingly human.

As I stabbed the carrier, Kinsley's let out a horrible wail and charged him with renewed fury. Kinsley stumbled. The carrier grabbed him by the shoulders, sinking his teeth into the boy's neck and ripping into the flesh.

Kinsley yelled, and I stabbed my knife into the carrier's back, shoving him to the ground. Kinsley gasped, clutching his throat as it spewed blood, and I lurched forward to clasp him under the arms.

I barely slowed his fall to the ground. Kinsley was numb with shock. Reaching down to slit the hem of my shirt with Amory's knife, I tore off a length of fabric and wrapped it around his neck, trying to stem the flow of blood.

"Help!" I cried. "Somebody help me!"

I wheeled around, ears ringing from the gunshots, searching desperately for someone who could help him.

Kinsley shook his head once, and I was alarmed to see a fresh deluge of blood seeping through the cloth. "S'all right," he croaked. "Go."

"No. No! I'm staying with you."

"Haven . . . you c-can't."

My hands were shaking as I tightened the rudimentary bandage around his neck. I had no real first aid training. I didn't know how to help him. Godfrey and Amory were wrestling a pair of stronger carriers that had broken through the ranks, but the others' shots were growing farther apart. They had nearly exterminated the horde.

I staggered to my feet, unsure what to do. I wouldn't leave Kinsley. All I could see was the helpless boy who'd trailed after Rulon and done all the rebels' dirty work. He was only sixteen, and he had no one.

There was too much blood. It was all over me. I fell to my knees, hands shaking, trying to put Kinsley back together. I looked around, but everyone else was still focused on fending off the last group of carriers emerging from the woods. Bodies fell, and no one noticed the boy bleeding on the ground.

Finally, the last carrier lurching from the woods went down, and Greyson lowered his rifle.

Godfrey stopped pummeling his carrier, and his hand came away gleaming. He was wearing brass knuckles. Then he shuffled to his feet on the crimson snow and aimed his handgun at the carrier's head. The shot rang out, and everything went quiet.

Chapter Eleven

After the last carrier huffed his final breath, the woods were still. Everyone looked lost, shell-shocked, and broken, but the silence roused my urgency.

Kinsley's face was deathly pale, and his eyelids were half-closed.

I pushed myself to my feet and gripped him under the arms, but he was too heavy.

"Help!" I croaked. "Help me move him!"

A few defectors cowering near the campfire looked at me but did not move.

"Please!" I yelled. "Help me!"

Amory was the first one at my side. His hands went around my waist, pulling me away from Kinsley. His expression was grave, but he hunkered down and hoisted Kinsley off the ground and over his shoulder as if he weighed nothing.

I followed him to the medical tent, where a woman with spiky black hair was rushing toward us. She was dressed in a navy medic jumpsuit and covered in blood, though whether it was human or carrier blood, I could not tell.

A memory stirred in the back of my mind, and I remembered her giving Logan a blood transfusion and patching up my wounds after an attack on Rulon's camp.

"Shriver!" I yelped in recognition.

Amory's eyebrows shot up, and his face went slack with shock.

"Shriver! You have to help him!"

She exchanged a look with Amory but did not speak. Amory shook his head once, and I shoved him in anger.

"Do something! He's losing a lot of blood!"

Shriver stared at me wordlessly but ducked into the tent and helped Amory lower Kinsley onto one of the low cots crowded into the small space.

The dim light from the lantern hanging on the bar across the top of the tent threw gaunt shadows on Kinsley's pinched white face. His eyes were closed, and the rudimentary bandage I had made was caked with blood. It seeped down his neck and had left a large stain on Amory's shoulder.

"No," I murmured.

Desperate, I sank down beside him and shook his shoulder gently. Kinsley's eyes fluttered, and I snapped my head to Shriver to make sure she had seen. Then Kinsley coughed, and I heard the miserable gurgle of blood. It bubbled from his lips, and his eyes wrinkled in pain.

Shriver reached for a syringe on the shiny metal table and plunged its contents into his arm. "That should take the pain away," she said in a gentle voice I'd never heard her use.

"What are you doing?" I asked, panicked. "Can't you stop the bleeding?"

But Shriver's eyes were fixated on the ugly ripped flesh sticking out from the crusty piece of fabric.

"I'm afraid there's not much I can do for him," she said.

"W-What do you mean? The carrier wasn't stage five."

"His carotid artery has been severed. He's not going to

make it."

"No!" I cried, gripping Kinsley's arm. But I could already feel him slipping away. His body was still.

Despair washed over me as I stared at his motionless face dotted with light freckles. I wanted to shake him awake — to do something — but I couldn't move or breathe. It felt as though someone were sitting on my chest, choking the life out of me.

There was a commotion outside, and then Roman and Godfrey burst in carrying a man who was bleeding profusely from his abdomen.

Shriver turned to the man, and I reached out to grab her. "No! You have to do something."

But I knew it was futile. She turned, and that detachment I remembered was back. Her eyes had gone cold behind her huge glasses, and she jerked her shoulder away. I wanted to scream at her for failing to save him, but it felt as though *I* had failed. I couldn't reach him in time. I couldn't save him.

Amory touched my arm. "Haven. He's gone."

I looked down at Kinsley, lying there bloody and broken. He looked *so* young. It wasn't right.

Tears clouded my vision, and I was gripping the edge of his cot so tightly my fingers ached.

"Come on," Amory muttered, putting an arm under me and hoisting me to my feet. I dug in my heels, but he pulled me away easily.

I knew he wanted to get me out of there so Roman and Godfrey could cover Kinsley's face and haul him out of the tent to make room for more wounded rebels. I didn't want them to take him. *What if he was still alive?* I didn't want him to think I'd left him alone when he needed me most.

Logan and Greyson nearly collided with us as we stepped

into the darkness.

Logan's eyes were tight as she spoke. "Is he . . .?"

"He's dead," I said. My voice sounded flat.

Logan's face went rigid with shock, and tears flooded her eyes.

"We need to haul off the carriers," said Greyson. "The smell of the dead ones will attract more."

Amory threw him a warning look, but I appreciated Greyson's pragmatism most when things were the worst — even when he seemed insensitive. Taking care of practical matters left less time to mourn, less time to feel sorry for yourself.

We followed him out to the center of camp where the rebels were gathered. Ida was speaking to a small group of older defectors I recognized, and she looked grim. A hush fell over the crowd, and Ida stepped onto a log to speak.

"We faced a great loss today. This was nothing I ever prepared you for, and for that, I am sorry."

"How did it happen?" yelled a woman hysterically. She was cradling one arm across her chest, and her hair stuck up everywhere, making her look crazy.

"Yeah!" said a man. "How did carriers get through the border?"

Ida pushed her hands down toward the ground, and the crowd hushed on her command. "I have been away containing a situation at the border. A rebel leader by the name of Rulon Jacobson has been threatening to release carriers across the border. He represents a radical group of insurgents who started the riots in Sector X, and his violence has escalated in recent months.

"Rulon was killed — by his own pack of carriers at the border crossing — and we were able to contain the situation

The Last Uprising

. . . or so I thought. This must not have been his first attempt to compromise the border. I suspect he is responsible for releasing this horde and others into the New Northern Territory."

A murmur of terror ripped through the crowd, and I was reminded that the majority of the defectors from the communes had fled the states to escape the virus.

"Now that we face threats from every side, we cannot stay here," Ida continued. "It's too dangerous. We'll tend to the wounded and then be on our way."

"Where will we go?" asked a small man in the front.

"I said before that a small group would cross the border to establish a base in the states while the rest of us attempted to infiltrate the communes. I have reached a decision. Godfrey will lead the party south. Amory, Roman, Logan, Haven, and Greyson have experience with the dangers of the states."

Ida turned to us. "The PMC took my farm, but if you can reclaim it, I think it would be an ideal place to gather our forces. Find yourself a small contingency of soldiers in the states, and take it back if you can. Take whatever weapons you need."

Logan nodded, but Roman and Amory both crossed their arms over their chests. I didn't say anything.

"The rest of you, please prepare to be on the move within the hour."

A rush of chatter spread through the crowd, and Logan straightened up, looking excited. "We're going back," she said. "I can't believe we're going back."

"If we can take the farm," added Amory. He looked angry, but I didn't know why.

Greyson shrugged and trailed off after Logan to go gather

supplies.

I turned to Amory, unsure what to say. I was in this, and I was confused by what I had felt after saving Amory from the carrier. I was still missing so much of my past, and I didn't know where I fit in anymore.

"You could have told me," said Amory, staring at me with a stormy expression.

"Told you what?"

He looked disgusted. "Don't lie, Haven. I'm not an idiot."

"What are you talking about?"

He lifted a dark eyebrow, his gray eyes flashing. "You remember."

"Just some things," I said, thinking of my memories of Greyson, Max, and the urge to protect Amory when that carrier almost killed him.

Amory shook his head bitterly. "Like what?"

"I remember going on runs with Greyson. I feel like I felt back then." I shrugged. "He's my best friend."

Amory nodded again. "So that's how it is now."

"How *what* is now?" I snapped. I already didn't like whatever conclusions he had formed.

"You can't have it both ways."

"What?"

"I *know* you remember, Haven. You remember everyone else, so you have to remember me, too."

"Who else?"

"Greyson, Logan, Shriver, *Kinsley*," he spat. His emphasis on Kinsley's name felt like a low blow. "I know you remember Roman, too, because you lock horns with him as much as you did before."

"I *remember* everyone, but I don't remember . . . the important things," I finished, knowing it didn't make any sense.

But Amory was still shaking his head. He didn't believe me. "And you don't remember me?"

I opened my mouth, but no words came out.

"If you didn't want to be with me, you could have just said so."

For a moment, I just stared at him, and I could see the deep hurt behind his anger. Then he tore his eyes away and stormed off.

I trailed behind him, desperately curious and terrified at what I was missing. From his conversation with Roman, I surmised we had been *together*, but it bothered me that I couldn't remember it.

Amory was walking so fast I almost had to jog to keep up. When I finally caught him on the edge of the woods, I grabbed his arm and yanked him around to face me.

"*Tell* me then! If I can't remember, you should at least tell me what I'm missing. What was I to you before?"

Amory's face was conflicted. Rage and confusion and hurt were fighting for dominance. "You really don't remember?"

I shook my head.

And then he did something I hadn't expected. Amory grabbed me by the arms and pulled me into him. He pressed his lips against my mouth, hot and angry.

My mouth went slack in shock, and his lips worked around mine. The kiss wasn't warm or romantic, but he was pouring so much of himself into every breath that it made my chest ache.

Part of me didn't want him to stop, but this wasn't right. I didn't like him kissing me when I felt I was missing something crucial.

After a second, I came to my senses and shoved him away with both hands. His arm was locked around my waist, crushing me to him, but his lips disconnected with a wet smack. He pulled back, looking smug.

"What was that?" I spluttered.

"You remember?"

"No," I said, wiping my mouth with the back of my hand. "I think I would remember such a violent kisser."

For a second, I saw the shadow of laughter playing in his eyes, but then they narrowed into steely slits. "Why is it just me?"

"It's *not!*" I shouted. "I barely remember anything good about my life! Do you know how that feels? To have no idea who you are or the type of person you were? For all I know, I was working against you all the whole time. Maybe I was a terrible person. All I know is what I was taught and what I feel now."

Amory looked momentarily shocked. "And what do you feel now?"

I shook my head, lost for words. I didn't care that I couldn't give him the answer he wanted. This wasn't *about* him, yet he was angry at me for things I couldn't control.

He looked hurt but swallowed it down and walked away, leaving me standing in the snow.

Chapter Twelve

Twenty minutes later, we'd left the chaos of camp behind and were piling into a rusted old Jeep concealed in the woods.

Roman sat in the passenger seat and spread his legs luxuriously, while the rest of us squeezed into the back together. Logan was sitting in Greyson's lap blushing furiously, and Amory was jammed against the door on my other side wearing a stony expression. It wasn't as though we could avoid touching, and the entire right side of my body was ablaze with heat where it was pressed against his.

Godfrey climbed into the driver's seat, grumbling something indiscernible about PMC roadblocks, and coaxed the engine to life. He kept his eyes in the rearview mirror as he pulled away, and I knew he was thinking of Ida and the commune dwellers we were leaving to their own devices.

"Don't know *what* she was thinking," Roman said aloud to the quiet car.

I stared at him, startled.

"If she takes them to one of the communes, how long do you think it will be before they crawl back into their hole?"

"They're scared," said Logan. "They don't know any different, and now they're in danger. It's a lot to take in."

Roman shifted in his seat, thrusting his thighs out even wider. "They're cowards."

"You're one to talk," snapped Logan.

He let out an irritated huff. "Not this again."

"Well maybe if you don't want it brought up again, you should lay off people who made the best decision they thought was right at the time. Maybe they had families."

"Yeah, I had a family, too . . . once."

Logan leaned back with a huff. "So did I. They'd be considered among those 'cowards' you were talking about."

"Ladies, please," said Godfrey in a lazy drawl. "I can't listen to your bickering all the way to Missouri." He met Logan's gaze in the rearview mirror. "He wasn't trying to insult your family." Godfrey threw a sidelong look at Roman. "You. Stop antagonizing her."

"Why are we going back to the farm if we know it's occupied?" asked Amory suddenly.

"We're going there because Ida believes it will be the strongest position for the movement."

"I think she just wants us to take her home back from the PMC."

Godfrey's expression went dark. "Do you make the decisions around here?"

Amory's eyes flickered away, plainly irritated but unwilling to argue with Godfrey.

"Did it ever occur to you that Ida knows what she's doing?" asked Godfrey. "Did you ever consider that the commune people could be the best to coax others into leaving the communes, even if they're scared shitless? Do you think maybe Ida has connections in Missouri . . . that she knows the area . . . that the farm is defensible?"

Amory was staring out the window, sulking for being told off, but I was listening intently. I was fascinated by the rebels' strategy and eager to know what they would do next. World Corp seemed unshakable, but Ida was undeterred. She

The Last Uprising

had a plan.

"So how are we crossing the border?" asked Greyson. "Don't you think they'll recognize us after last time?"

Godfrey guffawed. "Honestly, I doubt it. But Ida seems to think they're smarter than they let on. And after the carrier breach, they're going to be tightening security — mostly on inbound traffic. In any case, we're taking the stealth approach."

We pulled onto a small back road that hadn't been plowed, the Jeep making slow progress on the snow-covered gravel. We drove in silence for nearly an hour, winding through the trees and passing long stretches of farmland, before pulling onto another county road. This road seemed to take us deeper into the woods, but it was slightly smoother.

Finally, Godfrey slowed to a stop and jumped out of the Jeep. He opened the tailgate, grabbed a pair of bolt cutters from the cargo area, and slammed the door shut.

I watched him warily in the side mirror as he stepped into the tree line. There was a narrow path obstructed by snow with a chain link barrier draped across.

Godfrey cut it easily, got back in the Jeep, and pulled onto the path. The engine groaned as we plowed through the snow, and we shifted around on the uneven terrain.

"Where are we going?" asked Logan. She looked nervous.

"To the border fence."

I glanced at Amory, but his face was unreadable. The off-road path seemed to narrow the farther we drove.

"They built these service roads so people could access the controllers for the electric fence that seals the border. But no one's been to this one for a while."

"You want us to climb an electric fence?" asked Greyson,

looking alarmed.

Godfrey snorted. "No. Hell, I thought you were smarter than that."

Godfrey stopped the Jeep and killed the engine. Logan and Greyson stared into the trees with apprehension, but Amory pushed the door open and half fell out of the Jeep. I ignored the sting at his haste to get away from me and followed, looking around for the fence.

I heard it before I saw it. In the relative stillness of the snow-covered trees, I could discern a faint humming of electricity. Then, as I squinted, the metal grid came into view. It rose up out of the snow, eight feet tall with barbed wire curling at the top.

"Are there cameras?" whispered Logan.

Godfrey shook his head. "Not here. But there are sensors that will be triggered as soon as this part of the grid goes down. That's why we'll need to hurry."

He walked off to the left, and we followed at a distance. My ears were piqued for any sound other than our footsteps, but my heart was pounding so loudly I could barely hear anything else. I was sure the PMC had eyes and ears this close to the border, and I was just waiting for them to swoop down on us.

Suddenly Godfrey stopped, and I knew he had found what he was looking for: a huge metal box mounted on a fence post. It was locked. He rummaged in his pocket and drew out a small square of black plastic. He slapped it on the door, and a tiny light blinked red.

"Clock starts now," said Godfrey.

I ducked away from the box instinctively, and the others did the same. There was a faint beep — then nothing.

Then a loud *bang* cracked the door off its hinges, making

the metal hum like a tuning fork. Godfrey approached the box tentatively and reached inside.

"As soon as a section of the fence goes down, the PMC will be on high alert," he grunted, his voice echoing in the metal box. He withdrew a screwdriver from his pocket and began prying something away from the back panel.

My heart pounded harder as he worked, and I waited with bated breath. After a few moments, Godfrey stepped away, shooting a look at Roman.

"This section is down, but we don't have a lot of time. They have a fail-safe. When a section loses power for more than three minutes, the system restarts itself automatically."

"So —" Logan started.

"So we have three minutes before either the PMC shows up or we get electrocuted."

Logan threw me a panicked look, and Roman hunched down near the bottom of the fence and began cutting away the wire. He cut about a foot and a half up the fence and pulled it aside.

"We're leaving the Jeep?" asked Greyson in alarm.

"Unless you think you can fit it through that hole in less than three minutes," Godfrey grumbled.

Needing no further instruction, Greyson pushed Logan forward, and she crawled on her hands and knees through the hole Roman had made. It was a fairly tight fit. Greyson shoved her bag through and went in next.

"Hold this for me, will ya?" said Godfrey to Roman. Roman held the wire fencing up, and Godfrey got down on his elbows like a soldier in the trenches and shimmied through the opening. Roman followed, pulling his rucksack behind him.

"Get the guns," snapped Godfrey.

Amory grabbed the crate and shoved it toward the hole, but it was too big. I hunkered down next to him with the bolt cutters, struggling to cut through the thick wire. My hands hurt, but I cut away two more squares, and Amory shoved the crate through ahead of him. I tossed his rucksack through the hole and got down to follow. The others had disappeared into the trees.

The snow seeped through my pant leg as I got down on the ground, and I ducked my head low to avoid catching my hair in the wire. My upper body was through, and I dug my elbows into the mud as Godfrey had done. But as I pushed my legs off the ground for leverage, I felt myself get yanked backward.

I twisted to free myself, but something was caught in the wire — my jacket. I tried to reach back to extricate whatever was caught, but I couldn't fit my arm between my body and the fence.

I yanked myself forward, which only caused the piece of wire to dig into my skin.

I pulled again, wincing as the wire cut deeper. I tried to shimmy out of my coat, but the fence was flush with my shoulder blades, restricting my range of motion. I couldn't move.

My chest heaved as I panicked, but my lungs couldn't expand fully.

I could no longer see the others.

"Help!" I yelled. *How long had it been?* I knew I couldn't have more than a minute before the system restarted.

"Help!" I shouted, louder this time.

No one was coming.

Then I heard a rustle in the trees, and Amory appeared, looking terrified.

"Come on!" he yelled, eyes darting around me.

"I can't! I'm caught!"

I knew he was thinking the same thing I was: I had only seconds before I would be electrocuted.

His eyes went dark with fear, and he lunged forward, putting his hand on my back to feel where my coat was caught.

"Hurry!" I yelled. The tears were burning in my throat. I didn't want Amory to get electrocuted, too.

He let out a breath of frustration as he tried to free me.

"Just go," I said, my voice breaking. "I don't want you to—"

"I'm not leaving you," he growled in his throat. His sharp gray eyes were darting furiously from my coat to the fence to the woods behind me. I knew he was watching for approaching PMC.

"Go!" I yelled. "Now!"

I could hear the sirens in the distance. They were coming.

Amory made a noise of anger in his throat and put his arms around me, gripping my upper body. In one fast motion, he pulled, freeing me from the fence in a rip of fabric. I fell on top of him, and he fumbled to pull us both to our feet.

"Run!"

As we flew through the trees, my heart was beating so hard in my throat that I couldn't breathe. The shriek of PMC sirens was growing louder, the flashing blue lights inching toward us through the bare branches. I didn't stop.

Then I caught my ankle in a snarl of underbrush and pitched forward. My elbows screamed as they scraped the dirt, but the rest of my body was still pulling me forward.

Before I could right myself, Amory yanked me to my feet, and we were running.

When Godfrey and the others saw us careening toward them, they took off, too. As we ran, I barely noticed the cold wind on my face or the way Amory's hand was clutching mine.

Something jogged my memory as my legs found their cadence, and I had a flash of us running away from an exploding building.

I could practically smell the burnt plastic on the air and feel the warm ash raining down. Amory's hand was in mine. The look in his gray eyes was the same as it had been pulling me out of the fence: raw fear mixed with pain.

Hours later, I'd seen that look again.

We were on a bridge. It was snowing lightly. Tanks were barreling toward us, and I could see the flash of PMC lights. I was in Amory's arms.

I felt the warmth of his lips graze my temple, and then he threw me over the bridge into the icy water below.

He'd been protecting me.

Even though Amory had told me we were together, I hadn't really believed him until now. A tidal wave of emotions hit me, but I pushed them down. It was too much. These weren't homey and comforting like my memories of Greyson; they were laced with painful longing, grief, and fear.

"Over here!" someone yelled, pulling me out of the memory.

I looked up to see the others headed toward a shiny black 4Runner. Godfrey tossed the crate of weapons inside, and we all piled in. Roman sat in the front, and Greyson dove into the very back with Logan, but I stayed glued to Amory's side in the middle row. Godfrey hopped in the driver's seat, turning the keys in the ignition.

For a horrible moment, I thought the car wasn't going to start. But then the engine roared, and the headlights flooded the line of trees in front of us. Godfrey put the vehicle in gear and pulled around in the opposite direction. We were all panting heavily, and Roman's face was beet red, beads of sweat clinging to the short hairs at the base of his neck.

None of us spoke as we bounced along over the uneven forest floor. I glanced at Amory, who was staring at me out of the corner of his eye.

I realized I was still holding his hand. Embarrassment flared in my chest, but I didn't let go. It was as if my hand had a mind of its own. He didn't pull away either, but continued to watch me long after I had looked away.

"Find us a route," Godfrey grumbled to Roman, tossing a battered map from the console into his lap.

Roman unfolded it gingerly. It was an ordinary road map that had been heavily scribbled and highlighted with different colors. There were little notes running over the lines and Xs denoting which routes were no longer safe.

We drove through the trees, none of us daring to speak. Branches snapped beneath us, and our tires groaned through the snow and frozen dirt. The sound of the sirens was fading, but my heart was still thundering against my ribcage.

"We should hit the road soon if we keep heading due south," said Roman. "But they're bound to have a roadblock set up now that they know someone's breached the fence."

Godfrey let out a low noise like a growl.

Roman continued. "But if we head west, we can pick up a smaller road. It's not as direct, but I don't think we'll run into the PMC's patrol units."

Godfrey turned the wheel to change our course, nearly colliding with an enormous tree.

We drove for an hour before the woods started to thin. Then, without warning, the vehicle pitched forward sharply as we drove over a ditch. I threw out a hand to steady myself against the driver's seat, and the tires connected with smooth pavement.

We were on a county road flanked by tall trees. Even though we were more exposed on the open road, I no longer had the uncomfortable feeling that the PMC was going to materialize out of the darkness or step out from behind a tree.

There was a quiet *tick* as Godfrey switched off the headlights, and everything was thrust into darkness.

It was strange to feel the movement beneath us when I couldn't see the road. I gripped the seat, my stomach clenched for our imminent collision with another vehicle, but then I remembered no one drove on this road anymore. We were south of the border now, so the only people we could encounter were the PMC or other illegals.

After several minutes, my eyes adjusted to the darkness. The night took on a velvety blue hue, and I drank in the gorgeous scenery. Something about being back in the states and away from World Corp International made me feel less confined. The trees looked fresh and welcoming covered in pure white snow. I knew if I stuck my head out the window, the air would be cold and crisp and wonderful.

We had escaped. I was a name without an identity. I could start over.

I could feel Amory's eyes on me and knew he was thinking the same thing I was. Something had changed. We were no longer mired in despair. I was no longer their prisoner.

I kept replaying the memories of Amory over and over in my mind. Now I knew I could trust him — that I *should have* trusted him all along. We had been united once. I'd never been a mole for World Corp.

I realized it didn't matter what I had been taught in the facility. Most of what Aryus had told me was probably a lie.

I was a rebel now in every way that mattered. When the PMC came to camp, I had fled. I had chosen Amory, Greyson, Logan, and Godfrey. Now I was a fugitive once again, yet I felt hopeful.

In the back row, Logan was slumped against Greyson's side, fast asleep. He looked exhausted, too, but the happiness in his eyes was unmistakable.

"Is she okay?" I wondered aloud.

Greyson shrugged. "She's been really tired ever since . . ."

"The cure?"

Roman scoffed. "That poison Aryus gave her nearly killed her. She wouldn't eat . . . couldn't keep anything down. She slept for weeks trying to burn off her fever."

"But she's better now."

Greyson cocked his head. "She's not infected anymore, if that's what you mean." His voice was soft, and I could tell he didn't want to rouse Logan. "But Shriver thinks it gave her permanent nerve damage."

I remembered Logan's shaky hands during the carrier attack and felt a pang of sadness. Fighting and shooting was what Logan was good at. It was all she'd known for the last several years.

A memory flickered in the back of my mind: Amory, pulling me behind a stolen cruiser in the parking garage, begging me not to go into the Infinity Building.

"None of us could have known the cure would do that," said Amory. There was a note of defensiveness in his voice that warmed my heart.

Breaking into World Corp hadn't been his idea; it had been mine, and Amory had fought me on it.

"Yeah," said Greyson in a tired voice. "At least she's alive."

"So we're supposed to be *grateful* World Corp just maimed her after they infected her?" snarled Roman.

We all fell silent. Somehow I knew Roman's anger had nothing to do with me. If he blamed me for taking Logan to get the cure, it was only because he was trying to find a target for his pent-up hostility against World Corp. In a way, the angrier he became, the sorrier I felt for him. I knew how heavy that resentment was to carry.

No one spoke for several hours. The scenery changed to fields, and the exposure gave me an uncomfortable prickle on the back of my neck. We were the only car on the road — no signs of life anywhere.

We passed several farms, but the land had a fallow, neglected look to it. There were no animals out in the pastures, and the houses we passed were derelict, the windows boarded.

The snow thinned to patches the farther south we drove. When we pulled off at an exit to salvage some gas from an abandoned filling station, the air felt almost warm. Spring was on its way.

As the hot afternoon sun filtered in through the window, I drifted off to sleep with the door handle cutting into my side. I dreamt of Amory and icy waters.

Despite my slumped position, I slept soundly for the first time in weeks, knowing that when I awoke, we would be closer to home.

The Last Uprising

As we drove past an exit for Columbia, I felt a shiver of recognition. Part of me wanted to go back to see if more memories would resurface, but part of me did not want to drag out old ghosts. This was where Greyson had been captured — where he had lived in fear like a rat for months while the PMC prowled the city.

Finally Godfrey turned off the highway onto a smaller road. We slowed considerably, and I studied the shabby, abandoned houses tucked back in the wasteland of untended cornfields.

Most of the snow had melted here. With the setting sun illuminating the fields, it should have been beautiful, but I only saw people whose lives had been taken from them by the PMC. They had been forced from their farms and relocated to a sterile, crowded commune or taken prisoner.

As we drew closer to the farm, I couldn't sit still. My nerves were tingling, and I could only release some of my pent-up energy by jiggling my leg against the car door.

"You better prepare yourselves," murmured Godfrey. "We don't know what we'll find here."

Logan reached into the crate and began passing out rifles.

Roman took his and began loading it with relish. "Let's go hunting."

"Now, hang on," said Godfrey. "We've got to be smart about this. If it *is* PMC occupied, there's bound to be more of them than there are of us."

"We should park down the road and ambush them," said Amory.

Godfrey nodded grimly. "That's exactly what we're going to do."

"Ida said they wanted her farm for food production," Logan said. "So won't they be gone until spring?"

Godfrey shook his head almost imperceptibly, his eyes scanning the road. "They didn't want it for that."

"What then?" said Amory. "Why did they take her farm in the first place?"

"I don't know."

As we drove, the cornfields turned into pastures, and the pastures turned into woods. We turned off onto a narrow gravel road, and the trees became even denser.

Godfrey pulled off the side of the road and killed the engine. We all spilled out of the 4Runner, and I checked my pockets for extra ammunition. My heart was thudding hard in my chest. It was one thing to take out a bunch of carriers; it was another thing to fight a troop of PMC officers. They were properly trained — lethal. I would die trying to escape rather than be taken prisoner again.

Nobody spoke as we picked our way through the trees along the gravel drive that led to the farmhouse. It seemed years since I had first stumbled bleeding and starving through the woods to the cornfield on the other side of Ida's property. The relief and hope I had felt that day grew stronger with every step. It no longer felt like watching a film of someone else's life. The farm was rescuing me all over again.

Suddenly, I heard the dull *thunk* of metal, and Roman let out a fluent stream of profanity. "What the fucking hell?"

I squinted through the dim light and could just make out something hanging from the tree in front of him at eye level. Dangling from a piece of string was an empty Spam can. I watched it sway there for a moment like some bleak Christmas ornament, mocking us and making me a little hungry.

"That's weird," he said, tugging down the can and tossing it into the underbrush.

The Last Uprising

It was. Nobody threw away food like that . . . unless they were trying to attract a bigger animal.

We started walking again, and Logan swallowed down a shriek. She'd smacked into another strange tree ornament, but this wasn't a can of Spam — it was a dead opossum strung up by the neck.

I backed away from the accusing stare of its beady crossed eyes and swallowed down the bile burning in my throat.

Who had hung these things here? Ida was certainly eccentric, but I didn't remember her ever doing anything like this. It would have drawn —

The realization came too late.

That was when I heard it: the low rattle of dying breaths, the rip of metal, and the drunken cadence of uneven footsteps.

Chapter Thirteen

I whipped the beam of my flashlight toward the source of the noise and saw the shadowed figure of an emaciated carrier pawing at a suspended tuna can. Her skin took on a sickly grayish hue in the artificial light as her sunken eyes drifted lazily toward me.

Amory was the closest. He raised his rifle and shot the carrier cleanly in the head. She looked surprised. Then she teetered for a second before collapsing into a tangle of bushes.

I heard another one shuffling around somewhere behind me. I raised my rifle, but I couldn't see it. Darkness was descending quickly, and I was just as likely to shoot Logan or Roman as I was to hit the carrier that was ripping into the rotting flesh of the nearest dead animal.

Godfrey dispatched him before he got too close. The carrier pitched forward and fell at my feet, and I realized he had been eating the opossum. I was simultaneously disgusted and a little sad. This carrier had been a person once, and now he was so desperate he would eat the rancid carcass of a dead animal.

"Let's keep moving," Godfrey growled in his scratchy voice.

My pulse was still throbbing too fast, but I picked my way around the hanging bait. *Who would do such a thing?*

We didn't encounter any more carriers, but my ears were ringing in their desperation to pick up the slightest rustle of dead leaves or the clang of the perverse wind chimes.

Finally, the gap between the trees widened, and the farm came into view. I wasn't prepared for what I saw.

This was not the farm from my memories. The once meticulous vegetable patches had been trampled by PMC boots. There were no animals grazing on the hill. The old red barn was gone. Wood debris and trash lay everywhere, as though it had been demolished with dynamite. The cheery green farmhouse was still standing, but it had warped two-by-fours nailed over its doors and windows. It looked condemned.

The tall trees that had stood between the house and the field were gone, and the fields looked as though the dirt had been churned by heavy machinery. It was drenched in the last slivers of light from the blood-red sun, which threw shadows from the lone, angry backhoe parked in the middle of the field. Orange construction tape draped over an area in the middle, where a concrete foundation had been poured, taking up nearly half of one field.

Logan clapped a hand over her mouth, her eyes swimming with tears.

Ida's farm had been destroyed.

Godfrey, Roman, and Amory fanned out to my sides, and I stepped out of the trees with my rifle raised.

I didn't see a single living soul. It looked as though the PMC construction crew had stopped in the middle of what they were doing. Perhaps a winter storm had taken them by surprise, or maybe they had simply abandoned the project. *Had they set the bait for the carriers, or had the carriers run them off?*

It only took us a few moments to prowl the perimeter of the field and boarded-up house for World Corp personnel. Greyson took out a third carrier that had dragged a dead squirrel out of the tree line to feast in the backyard, but other than that, we were alone.

Logan was already standing on the edge of the field, squinting at a sign I had missed. It was an illustrated mockup that showed a nuclear power plant in the middle of the field. The picture showed a building where the barn had once stood and a smaller outbuilding where the farmhouse was now.

"They destroyed her farm for this," whispered Logan.

I nodded.

"What a waste."

"It makes sense. World Corp needs power."

I regretted my words as soon as I'd spoken. Logan turned to me, anger burning in her teary eyes.

"How can you be so cold about this? Do you really not remember anything about this place? Don't you care about Ida?"

"I remember," I said. "I remember how much I loved it here."

Logan's eyes widened. "You do?"

I nodded. I wasn't sure how or why, but running with Greyson and Amory had opened the floodgates to my memories: Greyson being hauled away by the PMC, Amory kissing me outside Sector X, Greyson by my side at Rulon's camp, Amory writhing in pain, our bodies tangled together in a darkened room . . .

"What else do you remember?"

"Things are coming back," I said, feeling a smile playing on my lips. "And it's not just the memories . . . I'm beginning to feel like myself."

Logan broke into a huge, watery smile, and before I could say or do anything, she threw her arms around me and crushed me against her.

"That's wonderful, Haven. I'm so happy!" She pulled back. Her eyes were swimming again. "I couldn't lose you, too. I'm not strong enough to lose anyone else."

I thought of Max and felt a pang of sorrow. "I'm here."

"What about Amory? Does he know?"

I shook my head. "It wouldn't be fair to him. It only just started coming back in pieces."

"Do you love him?"

I swallowed, unsure what to say. On the one hand, the feelings that had come rushing back last night had been overwhelming. I knew I *had* loved him, but those old feelings still felt so new.

"I don't know," I said. "I think I *did* love him. And if everything comes back . . ."

Logan squeezed my arm, unable to contain her excitement.

"Please don't say anything to him," I said quietly. "I don't want to get his hopes up."

Logan rolled her eyes. "You don't give yourself enough credit. You *will* remember."

As though that settled everything between us, Logan looped her arm through mine and steered us back toward the house. Roman was already fighting the two-by-fours, trying to pry them away from the front door with a crowbar. Godfrey walked back down the road to pull the 4Runner around while the rest of us watched.

Finally, after a lot of swearing and sweating, there was a crack of wood, and Roman fiddled with the front door. It swung open with a groan, and we walked inside, rifles raised.

A musty stench hit my nostrils. The house was freezing,

and the air was thick with dust. Roman walked into the living room, a flashlight balanced between his teeth, and began yanking the sheets off the couches. It made my stomach ache to think of Ida covering her furniture, so certain she would return.

I walked into the kitchen, and more memories ghosted through my mind. My heart contracted when I remembered Max hovered over the stove in his ridiculous apron, Frank Sinatra blaring as he fried eggplant.

The worn kitchen table was still there. So was the ugly wallpaper in the dining room. Everything was exactly the same — as though time had stood still. A cold draft of air hit me from the sliding glass door, which was cracked open beneath the boards.

Then I heard a loud *thud*. There was a high-pitched cry that didn't sound human, and Roman swore again.

I tore up the stairs after him, rifle poised.

As my eyes adjusted to the darkness, I saw him standing halfway up the stairs near the landing, breathing hard. I followed his gaze of horror, holding my breath in preparation for a carrier's putrid stench.

But it wasn't a carrier.

Just a few stairs above Roman, glowering down at us with huge yellow eyes, was Ida's cat.

"Magnus," I said without thinking, surprising myself when I recalled his name.

"That fucking furball is a menace! I could have broken my neck tripping over him."

I bit my lip to suppress a laugh.

"How is he still . . . alive?"

I grinned. "Why didn't Ida take him with her?"

The Last Uprising

"He's a stray. He was just here all the time because Ida fed him."

"I think she left the back door open so he could get out of the snow."

"Stray cats . . . carriers . . . that woman doesn't know where to draw the line."

I stomped up the stairs past him, giving Magnus a wide berth. I reached the first landing with the bedrooms that had belonged to Logan, Roman, Max, and Ida. Max's door was wide open, and I closed it discreetly as I passed. I didn't want Logan to have to see it until she was ready.

Anxious to reach the comfort of my old room, I bounded up the narrower staircase leading to the attic, as though drawn by a magnetic force.

I was remembering everything.

On my left, I saw sudden movement coming from inside Amory's room. I jumped, but it was just Amory sitting in the dark on his bed, staring out the window in a daze. He looked around when he saw me.

"Hey," he said in a hoarse voice.

"Hey." I shifted uncomfortably from one foot to the other, unsure what to say. "Happy to have your old room back?"

He nodded, eyes raking over his shelf of books, the cozy sloped ceiling, and the starlight filtering in from the tiny window. "Yeah. This was the only place where I ever felt . . . at home."

I nodded. "I hope we'll be able to save it."

"Yeah. Ida couldn't stand World Corp controlling it."

"Do you think they'll be back?" I asked.

"I don't know. It's possible the carriers made them

abandon the project."

I shivered. "You think that bait was from someone else? One of us, I mean?"

He nodded slowly. "I'm not sure. But if that's the case, it means there are others out there. We need to scout the area to see if whoever it is will help us defend the farm if they do come back."

"We should rebuild the barn," I said. "I hate seeing the place like this."

Amory gave me a funny look that was a mixture of amusement and wariness. "I'm curious . . . when did it become 'we' again for you?"

The heat rushed to my face, and I immediately wanted to run away. He probably thought I was crazy.

Amory must have sensed my discomfort, because his face softened, and his eyes flickered over my face.

"I'm sorry . . . about earlier. I shouldn't have kissed you like that. I didn't mean to put you on the spot."

Amory shrugged, his shoulders relaxing, and I had the strange urge to tackle him to the bed and wrap my arms around him.

I expected that impulse to earn me a sharp stab of pain to the back of my head, but all I felt was the dull shadow of pain.

"I won't interrogate you again," he said. "I just . . . I wanted to know when you came back on our side."

I smiled in relief. "I think I was always on your side. It just took the raid, the commune, and everything else for me to realize it."

I looked away, focusing on his bookshelf so I wouldn't have to meet his gaze.

"You probably think I'm so weak. They had such a hold on me when I first got out . . ."

Amory's face crinkled in distress. "No," he said, shaking his head. "I never thought that."

Before I could say or do anything, he stood up, filling the room at his full height and crossing to where I stood. "Haven, I never thought you were weak or somehow less because you'd been brainwashed. I of all people understand what they're like, and you were there for almost two months. I only had three weeks of it, and I felt like I was losing my mind."

He enveloped my hands with his bigger ones, staring down at the way they swallowed mine. My breath caught in my chest.

"I'm so sorry I didn't get you out sooner." He looked up, his eyes pleading. "I swear I tried. After you broke me out, they tightened security significantly — facial recognition that cross-referenced the database of wanted illegals, guards, multiple pass codes to enter the building. Godfrey didn't have any more of those CIDs, so we had to wait until we could buy some.

"Then he had to find a way to bring down all their extra security. Even then, it wasn't a sure thing. That's why I didn't want anyone else going in with me. I figured at least if I got caught, Greyson or Logan could try."

I looked at him and felt the familiar warmth spreading from my chest. This wasn't a memory of what I had felt for Amory; it was a new surge of affection that didn't rely on my scattered memories.

"Not a day went by that I wasn't thinking about you and how I would get you back," he continued, his voice cracking.

"I know," I said. "I remember what it was like being on the outside when they had you. It was awful."

Amory shook his head. "It was so much worse knowing how I felt when I first got out and wondering how far gone you were going to be. I thought they would just try to turn you into a killer, like they did with me." His voice hitched. "I didn't know they would make you forget me."

"They tried."

Amory's eyes widened hopefully, but his expression cleared in an instant.

"I'm sorry I pushed you. It wasn't right, and I won't do it again. But just know that it doesn't matter if you never remember." A smile flickered across his face. "I've decided I'm going to start over."

I stared at him, so sure my mouth was hanging open like a cartoon. This couldn't be happening. I'd only just begun to remember him, and now he was giving up. It was foolish and irrational, but I wondered instantly what other sorts of girls he could possibly meet on the run from World Corp and the PMC.

He must have caught my expression, because he added, "I'm starting over with you, Haven. I got you to like me once. I think I can do it again."

A dam broke inside me, and pure joy flooded in. I let out a strangled laugh. "I think you can, too."

I pulled away, still smiling, and backed down the stairs. I needed to leave, because I knew if I stayed there one more minute, I was going to tell him that I'd started to remember. I didn't want to give him false hope in case my full memory never returned, but I also wasn't ready for his reaction.

If he thought I remembered him, he would want to pick up where we left off, and I wasn't ready. Just picking through the scattered memories left me blushing.

As I descended the stairs, I heard someone rummaging in the kitchen cabinets. Logan was kneeling on the countertop, opening all the empty cupboards.

She groaned when she saw she had an audience. "Ida didn't leave us a single scrap to eat."

"We have the provisions that Godfrey packed."

Logan wrinkled her nose. "Beans, beans, and more beans? I think I'll pass. We'll have to raid some stores tomorrow."

"What about the cellar? Do you think Ida cleared out all the stuff from the garden we used to can?"

She wheeled around. "Haven, you're a genius! I can't believe you remembered that and I didn't!"

I grinned at the casual way she'd referred to my muddled memory. At least I could always count on Logan not to mince words.

She hopped off the counter and started rummaging in one of the open drawers. A second later, she withdrew a tiny key.

I followed her out the back door and around the side of the house in the dark, where two rusted doors were sticking up out of the ground. Trying to ignore the prickle on the back of my neck, I occupied myself with scanning the yard for encroaching carriers. We were alone.

Logan turned the key in the lock and jiggled the handle. It didn't budge. She turned the key again, and this time the lock clicked back.

Her brow furrowed. "That's weird. Ida's so stingy with her strawberries . . . I've never seen her leave this unlocked."

I shrugged, and Logan pulled up on the handle. The door creaked open, and the stench of damp earth filled my nostrils. Logan descended the rough stone steps, waving her arm in front of her to find the hanging cord for the light. She caught it and yanked it down, and a single bulb illuminated the dusty cellar.

Dozens and dozens of canning jars winked at us from shelves around the room, but they were not Ida's jars filled with pickles, strawberries, rhubarb jam, and tomato sauce. They were filled with a clear liquid.

I jumped down the stairs after her to investigate.

"What the —" She snatched a jar off the shelf and twisted the lid. She smelled the liquid, and her nose wrinkled instantly. "It's alcohol."

She handed the jar to me, and the strong stench hit my nostrils before I even sniffed.

"Not even good alcohol," I amended.

"Awww, shit," crowed a voice from behind me.

I jumped, and the jar slipped from between my fingers. It shattered, bathing the brick-and-dirt floor in the foul liquid. I jerked my head up toward the entrance to the cellar, squinting to make out the figure in the shadows.

"Now that hurts my feelings, sweetheart."

My heart was pounding in my throat. Boots scuffed on the rough brick, and dirty denim-clad legs began descending the steps. This man could have been a friend of Ida's, but we were alone in the dark, and something about his shifty voice made my skin crawl.

I saw his shotgun before I saw his face. He was wearing a heavy brown jacket over wrinkled flannel, and his face was covered in a scratchy-looking gray scruff. He had a halo of wispy hair around a huge bald patch, and he was missing several teeth.

"Now this is a shame. Usually I only have to kill ugly guys — not a couple-a pretty girls."

His black eyes flickered toward Logan, and I threw him a

warning look.

"But since you don't like my moonshine, I really don't see a way for this to work out . . . unless you decide to be *real* friendly."

He took a step toward Logan, reaching out with a dirty hand, and Logan lunged at him so fast, I didn't have a chance to react. She twisted his hand, and he bucked forward, howling like a coyote. Her knee shot up, connecting with his groin, and he doubled over in pain, sending the shotgun skidding across the floor.

"You filthy piece of trash," she growled. "This place doesn't belong to you."

"No?" said another voice.

I flew to the ground, grabbing the man's shotgun and pointing it at the entrance of the cellar. Even the man's gun felt dirty.

Another pair of boots appeared at the top of the stairs, and then another, but the two seemed to be engaged in a struggle.

"You first," the man above growled. The second pair of feet descended slowly in front of him. As his face came into view, my heart sank.

The man had Greyson around the neck, a handgun pressed against his temple. Greyson's face was contorted in anger. There were more footsteps from outside — several more pairs of feet.

Greyson's captor was younger than the man Logan had pinned, shorter than Amory but taller than Greyson. He was wearing a dirty camo baseball cap and an orange cutoff shirt despite the cold. One of his flabby biceps was pressed against Greyson's windpipe. The man had all his teeth, but he sucked his saliva in a sickening way and spit out a dark stream of liquid.

When the man saw me pointing the shotgun at him, he broke into a condescending smile. "If I was you, I'd put that down real nice and slow. Otherwise, I'll blow your boy's brains out."

"You hurt him, I'll kill you," I growled.

The man smirked. "I see he's not your fella." He pushed the gun harder into Greyson's head and turned to Logan. "He belong to you?"

Logan glowered.

"We got the old man, too," called another voice from above.

Godfrey.

"Now," said the man holding Greyson. "What's all the trouble? I heard you mouthin' off to Denny."

"You and your other lowlife friends better get the hell off Ida's land," said Logan. Her voice was steady, but I could see her hands shaking.

"Aww, Hank," said Denny. "These pretty girls don' like our alcohol."

Hank let out a guffaw. "I don't give a flying fuck in space what they like or don' like. But now they've found our stash, not much we can do with 'em."

I wasn't listening anymore. I was thinking about Amory and Roman. They were still out there. I just hoped they would be able to get the jump on the others outside.

I decided the best thing to do would be to keep the men talking long enough for Roman and Amory to wonder where we'd all gone.

"Listen," I said, trying to keep my voice calm. "We don't care if you use this place to store your moonshine. That's your business. We only want the house. Our friend Ida used to live here, and we are just reclaiming it from the PMC. You can still use the cellar. I promise no one will interfere with your operation."

Hank laughed. "Well, lookie there, Denny. The little bitch says she'll *let us* use the cellar. Isn't that nice?"

Denny chuckled stupidly. "That's real fuckin' hospitable."

"But see, this place belongs to us now. *We* drove off the PMC. They won't be back 'til spring, and we can move a lot of shine before then at the Exchange."

"It was *you*," I breathed, thinking of the crude carrier bait.

Hank ignored me. "See, I know your friend Ida. I know she's joined up with the rebels now. She wants you to turn this place into one of them rebel camps. What do you think'll happen when the PMC gets wind that y'all are postin' up here? Now, I ain't no fortune-teller, but I'd bet my ass the PMC won't like that. We can't have you all making trouble for us. It's bad for business."

"She was just being polite," said Logan, twisting Denny's arm harder and eliciting a howl. "We aren't going to let you fucking hillbillies squat on our land."

In the second Hank had been distracted by Denny's yell of pain, Logan had reached down to her boot to retrieve her knife. Now it was pressing into Denny's throat, and I saw that gleam of fierce satisfaction in her eyes. "Unless you think you won't miss him — and I wouldn't blame you — I suggest you let our friend go."

Hank laughed. "See, I thought you might feel that way." He turned his head toward the entrance of the cellar. "Hey, Roy! Why don't you see how our handsome new friend feels about that?"

There were sounds of a scuffle outside and a muffled yell of pain. I would have recognized that yell anywhere.

It was Amory.

Chapter Fourteen

As we climbed the cellar stairs, all I could think was that I would rather be mauled by a horde of carriers than die at the hands of these men.

We cleared the top of the cellar, where two men were holding Amory by the arms. He had a bloody nose and a split lip, but the two moonshiners looked even worse for the wear.

Two other men had their guns pointed at Godfrey's temples, and three men were holding Roman down. He lay as still as a corpse. He had to be unconscious.

I still had Denny's shotgun trained on Hank, and Logan had her knife at Denny's throat, but there was no question we were at a serious disadvantage.

"Now, I'm in a real fix here," said Hank, dragging Greyson along. "I really don't want to dig six holes today. But on the other hand, I know if I tell y'all to skedaddle, you'll just turn around and rob me."

"Why would we want your shitty alcohol?" Logan growled, digging her knife into Denny's skin so a line of blood appeared.

Hank cocked his head, his mouth breaking into a dangerous grin. "*Woo*! I was hoping you'd give me a reason, darlin'."

He shoved Greyson to the ground and kicked him hard in the ribs. Greyson grimaced in pain but strangled his yell

The Last Uprising

before it left his throat. I felt the anger burning in my chest and thought about gouging Hank's eyes out with Logan's knife.

Greyson stayed on the ground, and another man shifted to cover him with his gun.

Hank strode toward Logan, his steps slow and pronounced, until his gun was pressed against her forehead. She didn't even flinch.

"Now, you let Denny go nice and easy, or I'll blow your brains out . . . and then Roy'll blow your *boy's* brains out."

Logan's eyes flickered once to Greyson. He shook his head almost imperceptibly, but Logan's face crinkled in fury as she let Denny drop to the ground. He scooted away on all fours like a mangy dog and righted himself beside his companions.

"And you!" Hank yelled in my direction. "Put that fucking gun down, or we'll all shoot our way out of here. Now, maybe you can shoot — maybe you c'aint — but I guarantee *I* won't miss."

I scowled but lowered the shotgun. Even if I could shoot Hank before he shot Logan, the other men would open fire.

"That's it. Now put it on the ground *real* slow."

I bent to lay the gun in the grass.

"Now kick it over here," called the man holding up Greyson.

I glared and kicked the gun — softly — until it was just out of my reach. Another rifle shifted to point in my direction.

Hank's eyes were gleaming in wicked satisfaction. "Good girl." He turned to Logan. "Now, sweetheart, you drop that knife, and I promise I'll be gentle."

Logan was wearing an expression I'd never seen — such intense hatred that it sent a shiver through my entire body. "Go to hell."

Hank reached to grab her wrist, but Logan was too fast. She slashed the knife up and across his face, and Hank howled in pain. "You *bitch*." Blood was streaming down his face.

He lunged at her, but she struck him so fast, her arm was a blur. He howled again, and I knew she'd broken his nose.

"Are y'all just gonna stand there and watch?" Hank grunted.

One of the men standing over Roman's unconscious form handed his gun to Denny and came up to Logan's other side.

Her elbow flew up and connected with his jaw, but I saw none of Logan's usual joy in her movements. Her face was blank — focused — but I knew she was scared. She had to win, or this fight would not end well for her.

Greyson's expression was pained, and Amory was watching in fury. Godfrey looked strangely serene for someone with two guns pointed at his head.

I didn't want to watch the men fighting Logan, but I couldn't look away. Even two against one, they were no match for her. Logan was incredible.

Their movements were clumsy and predictable, while she was precise, economical, and deadly fast. She knocked Hank's feet out from under him and sent his companion crawling with a hard kick to the groin.

Then a shot rang out.

Logan yelped in pain and fell to the ground.

My heart stopped. She was clutching the outside of her leg, where her black pants were shining with blood.

The Last Uprising

Hank's eyes gleamed from where he lay, and he stood up and sauntered over to her. "Not so tough now, are ya?" He grabbed her by the throat, and Logan looked at him with disgust. "That's the thing about pretty little bitches . . . they *always* try to fuck you, one way or another. You don't belong in a fight, baby. You belong on your back."

Logan spit in his face.

Hank closed his eyes once, and when he opened them again, he shoved her head against the ground. He had both his hands on her windpipe, choking her. Logan was flailing, trying to get back in a fighting position, but he had all his weight on her.

Before I could react, Greyson lunged at him, and another shot rang out.

I gasped, but Greyson wasn't hit. He had tackled Hank. When they rolled over, I saw an arrow sticking out of Hank's back.

I still couldn't discern the source of the gunshot, but one of the men who'd been holding Godfrey was lying dead in the grass.

Were we being ambushed again?

Without thinking, I dove for Denny's shotgun and aimed for the other man pointing his gun at Godfrey. I shot him in the foot. He doubled over, losing his aim, and I put a second bullet in his chest.

Amory had gotten the jump on his two captors, but he was still struggling. Hank was still alive. He and Greyson were rolling around on the ground. Godfrey was fighting with Denny, and Roman was stirring.

I glanced over my shoulder again, looking for the shooters, but I didn't see anyone.

I threw myself into the fray with Amory, striking one of

the men in the nose with the butt of the shotgun. Amory brought the other man down and delivered a hard kick to his gut.

The man I'd hit swung a fist in my direction. He was uncoordinated, and I used the opportunity to put him in a chokehold and knee him in the stomach. He doubled over, but before I could finish the job, he threw all his weight into me. I lost my balance and hit the ground — hard.

I smelled his disgusting, unwashed body all over me. The stench of alcohol and decay on his breath made my stomach turn inside out. I struggled to right myself, but he was too heavy. The man sneered, and I caught a glimpse of rotten teeth.

Then an arm wrapped around his neck, yanking him off me. My lungs expanded instantly, and I gasped for air.

Amory was on top of the man, pummeling him with a rage that terrified me. The man cried out, but Amory kept going. His knuckles were bleeding, and the muscles in his back rippled with every move, so I knew he was throwing his full force behind each blow.

Finally, he stopped. The man was whimpering.

Amory got up, grabbed one of the fallen moonshiners' guns, and shot each of his two attackers in the head.

I looked around. Everyone was still and quiet except for Hank. He was curled up in a ball on the ground, and Logan was pummeling him with all the force she could muster. She was breathing heavily, her hair mussed and her green eyes feral.

I watched Greyson lay a careful hand on her shoulder. She jerked around, and he raised an eyebrow.

Logan stopped, looking a little ashamed, and took the handgun he was holding. She hovered over Hank, who was still smirking through bloody teeth. It seemed Greyson had done a number on him before Logan had her way.

Logan's nose wrinkled once, and then she shot him in the head.

She lowered the gun, and Greyson took it from her gently, emptying the chamber and pocketing the bullets.

"Your leg," he murmured, dropping to his knees to examine Logan's bloody thigh.

"He missed," she said. Her voice was hollow. "Barely grazed me."

Greyson dragged in a deep breath. "Still, Amory should—"

"What a *mess*," called a voice from behind me.

I whipped around, searching for the source of the voice, and heard Logan and Amory point their guns toward the trees along the side of the house.

The shooter.

I squinted into the trees. There was a dark shadow moving toward us, sending my heart into overdrive.

"Who is it?" called Amory.

"Considering I just saved your asses, I'd say a friend."

A chill shot down the back of my neck.

Roman had just pulled himself into a standing position, but he was already alert.

"What's your name?" he called.

"Marcus. Marcus Hooper."

"Well, I'll be damned," murmured Godfrey.

I turned. "You know him?"

Godfrey nodded once, a shifty smile breaking over his face.

The Last Uprising

"Show yourself!" yelled Amory.

The shadow moved again, and I glimpsed a pair of broad shoulders and a buzz cut.

Marcus was a large man in his early thirties. He had a thick, beefy neck that stretched out his camo jacket and small, suspicious eyes. He was clutching a crossbow in his thick hands, looking from Roman to Amory with a wary scowl.

"Marcus Hooper, as I live and breathe," murmured Godfrey. "Last time I saw you, you had your daddy's pickup truck wrapped around a tree."

Marcus's face lifted in a crooked grin that looked out of place and held out his hand to Godfrey.

Godfrey pumped his hand once, and I noticed how fierce he looked despite his smaller stature.

"How you been, Mr. Godfrey?"

Roman snorted, and Godfrey shot him a warning look.

"Been better, now you mention it."

"I'll say." Marcus glanced around at the dead moonshiners lying at our feet.

"Thank you . . . for your help," said Amory, stepping over and offering a hand to Marcus.

Their hands collided with a hard, manly smack, and I noticed the dark look smoldering in Amory's eyes.

His greeting wasn't a welcome; it was a warning. A muscle twitched in Marcus's jaw, making him look like a wolf with his hackles raised.

"It wasn't a second too soon," said Greyson. His voice was burning with uncharacteristic anger.

Marcus looked over, as if just noticing Greyson. The

The Last Uprising

marked difference in the way he sized up the two guys irritated me instantly.

"Sorry about that," he said casually. "I was waiting to see what other information they might spill."

He strode over to Hank, nudging the man's head with his boot. "This is Hank Burns. Those two are his brothers, but there are more of them."

"What do you mean?" I asked.

"They live around here — the whole nasty family. Real trash."

"So there's more of them?"

Marcus nodded. "Bound to be a *lot* more of them if all their relatives have regrouped since the Collapse."

I glanced at Denny, who was lying with his eyes wide open.

Then I did a double take, and something else clicked into place. I hadn't noticed it before when he was threatening us, but with the moonlight reflecting off his glassy eyes, there was no mistaking it.

His eyes were yellow around the edges, and his skin had a sickly grayish tinge.

"This one's infected," I said.

"What?" snapped Marcus.

"He's an early-stage carrier. They both are," I said, gesturing to the man who'd attacked me with the noxious, rotten breath.

"How do *you* know?"

I threw him a challenging look. "I've seen it."

Marcus still looked doubtful.

"Check the others," Amory prompted. "Haven can spot

an early-stage carrier like no one I've ever met."

Marcus bent down next to the two who'd held Godfrey. Their eyes were half-closed, but the signs of infection were there.

"How did this happen?" asked Greyson. "You think a horde attacked their family?"

Roman snorted. "I doubt it." He flipped one of the other men over. "They're meth heads. Every last one." He yanked up the man's sleeve. "See the track marks? Rotten teeth? My guess is one of them ran afoul of the carriers they were baiting, and then they were all sharing needles."

"So if there are more of them left somewhere . . ."

Roman nodded. "We're going to have a much bigger problem."

Marcus ran a hand over the top of his short hair. "Well, I'll be damned."

My gaze fell to the heavy crossbow in his grip, and something clicked into place.

"Hang on . . ." I said. "Where's your friend?"

Marcus glanced up at me in irritation, as though I were a fly he wanted to swat. "What?"

"There were two shooters," I said. "Your arrow hit Hank, but someone else took out one of the men holding Godfrey."

Marcus shrugged, but I could detect a flash of nervousness in his eyes. "Wasn't me."

"I know it wasn't," I pressed, urgency and distrust humming in my limbs. "The shots came too close together. You wouldn't have had time to switch weapons."

Amory stepped up beside me. He was glaring at Marcus. "If it wasn't one of us and it wasn't you . . . who the hell was it?"

Chapter Fifteen

Suddenly I was on high alert again. *Was there no one we could trust?*

All around me, the others had picked up weapons and were scanning the trees for whomever Marcus wasn't telling us about.

"Stop," said Marcus. "It's all right. They mean you no harm."

"Who's 'they'?" snapped Roman, striding over to Marcus and training the rifle on his chest. "What are you hiding?"

Marcus sighed loudly, and I heard the crunch of leaves coming from the shadows. My spine went rigid, and Amory spun to point his gun toward the source of the noise.

"Krystal, I said stay out of sight," growled Marcus, seemingly oblivious to the rifle pointed at his heart.

"Oh, I think I can take 'em," called a female voice.

A severe-looking woman stepped out of the tree line, a challenging smile playing on her lips.

She had deep olive skin, and her straight black hair whipped out behind her, taking on an almost bluish hue in the light from the moon.

Marcus sighed. "This is my kid sister, Krystal."

"And you didn't trust us enough to tell us you weren't alone?" asked Greyson sharply.

Marcus ignored him.

With a gleam in her dark eyes and a shotgun in hand, Krystal cleared a path between Godfrey and Roman like a tornado. Her baggy jeans and flannel shirt didn't fully conceal her figure, and Roman's eyes trailed after her every step.

"Your 'kid sister' is a better shot than you," she snapped. "You couldn't even finish the bastard you took out."

"He was moving too much," growled Marcus. "And I didn't want to hit the girl."

Logan's eyebrow quirked in irritation.

"Krystal's right," said a third voice, swallowing down a burst of musical laughter. "She is a better shot."

There was the sound of someone crashing through the trees behind the woman, and another man appeared. He was much younger than the other two — about our age, by the looks of it — and he was beautiful. He was six feet of pure muscle with short brown hair and golden skin.

Marcus rolled his eyes. "Meet Jason. He's our younger brother."

Jason shrugged. "Younger brother . . . best brother . . . whatever."

He flashed a mischievous grin, and Logan shot me a look that I took to mean something like, *damn.*

"Why are you all here?" asked Roman. He didn't bother hiding the edge to his tone.

"We'd been hunting about a quarter mile out when we heard the yellin'," said Jason. "We knew no one was supposed to be living here, so we thought we'd check it out."

"Just to make sure no one was trespassing besides you?" Roman muttered.

Marcus shot him a look. "Ida was a friend. She's always

let us hunt on her property."

"Said we kept the deer from eating all her corn," Jason chortled.

"Well, thank you for your help," said Godfrey. "You saved our lives."

Krystal's eyes landed on him for the first time, and her expression softened slightly. "Godfrey! What are you doing here?"

"We're on assignment from Ida."

Krystal's eyebrows shot up. "She isn't here with you?"

"She's up north right now, rallying the documented people to stand with the rebels. She asked us to come back here to establish a stronghold in the Midwest."

Krystal looked suspicious. "That doesn't sound like her."

"You don't know what it's been like."

Krystal shook her head. "I know Ida wouldn't be running with the rebels."

"She didn't have much of a choice," growled Godfrey. "The revolution has started."

Krystal and Marcus exchanged a look.

"There's not gonna be a revolution," said Marcus flatly. "The PMC is taking over. S'only a matter of time before they bulldoze our house and everything else along with it."

Godfrey shook his head. "The PMC is acting under the orders of Aryus Edric, who owns World Corp International."

"World Corp is behind all this?" Jason laughed. "No way."

Godfrey continued. "Aryus's focus is up north. If we can raise hell on all sides, they won't be able to hold it together."

"Oh yeah?" said Marcus. "You and what army?"

I felt a stab of fury, and Amory, Logan, and Roman shifted angrily on either side of me.

"We're trying to rally whoever is left in the area," said Godfrey, clearly used to Marcus's brusque manner.

"No offense, but we're doing just fine on our own," said Krystal. I could feel the distrust wafting off her, though I didn't understand why. Clearly, she knew Godfrey and Ida from before the Collapse.

"I'm sure you are," said Godfrey. "But this is about more than that. We need to make this farm defensible so we can put up a real fight against the PMC."

"You're on your own," said Krystal.

"Hey!" snapped Jason. "I want to fight."

She shot her brother a deadly look. "No, you don't." She turned back to Godfrey. "You won't have our help raising the PMC's ire."

"Krystal. Stop," said Marcus.

Godfrey raised an eyebrow.

Krystal folded her arms across her chest. "The answer is no."

"It's not up to you!" yelled Marcus.

"I'm not interested in being the PMC's prisoner," she shot back. "Or *worse*."

Amory took a step forward, glaring at her. "If you think there's anything worse than being the PMC's prisoner, you've been hiding in the woods too long."

A look of rage flashed across Krystal's face, and for a moment, I thought she was going to hit Amory.

Marcus had been watching him out of the corner of his

The Last Uprising

eye.

At Amory's words, he seemed to make up his mind about something, and he leveled Godfrey with a fierce look. "What would you need from us?"

Godfrey shrugged. "You join us, help us rally others . . . then we reclaim this territory from the PMC. It gives us a foothold in mid-Missouri, and this base serves as a nice diversion. The goal is to hem them in on all sides . . . divide their focus."

Marcus nodded slowly. "Makes sense."

Krystal had fallen silent, but the sullen look on her face told me this was not the last the brothers would be hearing from her tonight.

"So you'll join us?" I asked.

Marcus didn't answer right away. He seemed to be mulling it over, while Jason was bouncing on the balls of his feet waiting for a verdict. Krystal was the voice of the group, but it seemed Marcus had the final word.

Finally, he nodded. "Count us in. We'll pool our resources . . . food, ammunition, anything we got."

Krystal scoffed but didn't say a word.

"Look for us the day after tomorrow. And when you talk to Ida, you can tell her . . . we're with you."

The Hoopers disappeared into the woods, and I had the immediate feeling that we must have imagined the whole thing. In one fell swoop, the Hoopers had saved our lives and increased our numbers by fifty percent. Plus, they were bringing supplies.

"What was *that* about?" Roman asked. Clearly he also found our turn of luck a little disconcerting.

"The Hoopers are good people," said Godfrey. "They've

just been through a lot, is all."

"What do you mean?" I asked.

Godfrey sighed. "Their mother died years ago, God rest her soul, but their father and brother . . . Back in the early days of mandatory migration, the Hoopers took in an infected family . . ."

I felt my jaw drop.

"The family was so early stage the Hoopers couldn't have known," he said quickly. "They were on the run from the PMC — a family with three young kids and a sick father. They were living in the Hoopers' barn, and the father was stage three. Violent. Unpredictable. He broke into the house in the middle of the night and killed Mr. Hooper and his youngest son."

"There was a fourth Hooper kid?" Amory asked.

Godfrey nodded grimly. "Thirteen years old. The infected man ambushed Mr. Hooper, and the boy got caught in the middle of it all. Krystal heard the struggle and shot the man, but it was too late."

"What happened to the others? The family?"

Godfrey's face fell. "Marcus went out to the barn. The mom and the three kids had heard the shots, so of course they were terrified. The mom was clearly infected, too, but the kids . . . well, I guess we'll never really know one way or the other.

"Marcus will always insist those kids looked infected, too. I think he was just scared. Back then, see, no one knew *how* the virus spread."

"He killed the whole family?" I asked, horrified.

"Yep."

"And that's why Krystal didn't want anything to do with

The Last Uprising

us."

Godfrey nodded. "After that, the Hoopers really went underground. Ida would come around every now and then to bring them supplies and check to make sure they hadn't turned. I'm surprised they've survived this long, to be honest. It's hard to make it these days if you're not out west or with the rebels."

As Godfrey's chilling story sank in, I realized there probably wasn't a family out there that hadn't been touched by the devastation World Corp had wrought on the world. My family's end had been tragic, but I couldn't imagine having to witness it.

Greyson wouldn't rest until Logan let Amory examine her leg wound. While she argued with them and insisted the bullet had only grazed her, I helped Roman and Godfrey drag the dead moonshiners out to the field and returned to the cellar to lock up. It was late, but I didn't feel tired with all the adrenaline still coursing through my veins.

As I came around the side of the house, I heard yells echoing in the still night air. I flattened myself against the porch rails, listening intently.

One voice belonged to Greyson, and he was furious.

"You could have gotten us all killed!"

"But I *didn't*!" snapped Logan. "If anything, I kept him from blowing your brains out."

"Right," Greyson said in a clipped tone. "Because that went *so* well."

"In case you haven't noticed, we're all fine."

"Yeah . . . thanks to Krystal and Marcus."

I remembered Greyson tackling Hank, and I realized he had tried to save Logan, knowing he would be shot.

"I was just trying to keep them talking," Logan persisted. "We needed *time*. Roman was unconscious . . ."

"You were *antagonizing* them!"

"Would you rather I surrendered?" snapped Logan. "Huh? Let him . . . do whatever he wanted to me?" Her voice was shrill but deadly serious.

"No. No! Of course not."

"Then what was I supposed to do?"

"You shouldn't have provoked them."

My insides contracted, and I knew Greyson had said the wrong thing.

"*Provoked* them?" Logan snarled. "They came at us, remember? What would you have done?"

"We were outnumbered."

"So I was just supposed to let them kill us?"

"We might have been able to walk away."

"*Walk away*? Are you serious?" Logan's voice was just getting higher. "Do you have *any* idea what he was thinking of doing to me?"

"Of course I do!" yelled Greyson. "Do you really think any of us would have let that happen?"

"You had a gun pointed at your head."

"So did you."

"I don't care. I wasn't going down without a fight."

"Neither was —" Greyson sighed in exasperation. "I would have *died* before I let him hurt you."

"It wouldn't have made a difference."

There was a long, heavy pause, and I cringed with dread. I'd forgotten a lot about my past, but I remembered that driving Greyson to speechlessness never meant victory in a fight.

"So that's it, then?" His voice was ragged. "You think I couldn't protect you?"

"I don't need your protection," she said quietly.

"Just because I'm not as good in a fight as you, you think I'm *useless*," he spat bitterly.

Logan's voice was softer when she next spoke. "I never said that."

"You didn't have to."

"I just don't think you *get it* sometimes."

"Get what?"

"How bad the world is now." Logan's voiced hitched. "I've been out here a lot longer than you have."

Greyson paused, and I could almost feel the anger emanating from him. "What's *that* supposed to mean? You think I don't know what the real world is like because I was in *prison* for three weeks? While you were here, on the farm?"

"No. Because I was like them once. I was a bad person, Greyson. I did *horrible* things to plenty of innocent people when I was in the PMC, and I didn't even care. Whereas you . . . you've been good your whole life."

"That doesn't make a difference."

Logan sighed. "Yes, it does."

There was a long, painful silence. Then someone sighed and walked away.

I hesitated, unsure who had left. As a friend, I should have been there to comfort either of them, but I knew instinctively that one would want me to be there and the other wouldn't.

When I rounded the corner and saw Greyson standing there, my heart sank. I'd known him long enough to know he would rather have time to pull himself together than let me witness his pain and humiliation.

He had his back to me as he watched Logan walk away with long strides, and his shoulders were hunched forward in defeat.

She had wounded him and insulted him as a man, yet all Logan saw was the boy I did — the boy I'd grown up with who *was* good.

His head jerked around when he heard me coming, and I tried to arrange my mouth so there was no trace of pity in my expression. It was hard once I saw his face.

"You heard, didn't you?"

"Not everything."

"She's impossible!"

"She's Logan."

"She thinks I'm weak because I wasn't trained by the fucking PMC."

"No, she doesn't. Logan just has a hard time letting people in."

"She makes me *crazy*."

I grinned at the intensity of his tone.

"It's not funny. She could have gotten us all killed mouthing off like that."

"But she didn't."

"I thought I was going to have to stand there and watch him do something horrible to her."

"You wouldn't have let it get that far. None of us would have."

"But she doesn't think that," he yelled, throwing his hand in the direction she'd gone.

My heart ached for Greyson. I wanted him to be happy so badly, but I had the horrible feeling that he would never get anything but grief from Logan.

It wasn't that Greyson wasn't her type; it was that they were too similar. Both were stubborn beyond belief and emotionally idiotic. Each would die refusing to yield rather than give in.

"Do you want my help?" I asked, trying to suppress a grin.

He threw me a furious look that burned out in an instant. "Yeah."

I tried not to look taken aback by his willingness. "Stop trying to prove that you're strong enough to take care of her. Logan doesn't need to be taken care of — she doesn't want to be."

"I get that."

"No, you don't. Fighting is what she's good at, and if you try to take that away from her, she'll hate you for it."

For a moment, he looked surprised — not by what I had said about Logan, but by me. "I'm not trying to take anything from her," he whispered.

"That's not how she sees it. Give her something she actually needs."

"What?"

"A challenge . . . a distraction . . . a good laugh. Take your pick." I took a step toward him and squeezed his arm once. "She'd be lucky to have you."

Greyson broke into a smile that made me feel as though I could finally breathe.

"Thanks."

I turned to go, but he reached out and tugged at my arm. "Haven? You give really good advice for someone who doesn't remember her friends."

My head twinged slightly, but it was nothing like the debilitating pain I'd felt a few days ago. I dragged in a huge stream of air, trying to find the right words. I didn't want to get his hopes up, but I owed him an explanation.

"I'm starting to remember the important things," I said.

I left him standing there heartsick over Logan, and I wondered what it was going to be like having them living under the same roof.

Mulling over the scattered memories I had of them, I realized they were both my best friends for a lot of the same reasons. Both were intense and loyal — hell-bent on doing whatever they thought was right. Either they would kill each other, or they would be the most annoyingly in-love people in the world.

Chapter Sixteen

The next day, I awoke to the sound of Roman swearing loudly from the backyard.

I lay there for several minutes, willing him to stop, but if anything, his shouts just seemed to be growing louder.

I pulled on some clothes and padded out into the hallway, where Logan was slumped half-asleep, still in her pajamas.

"Too early," she yawned. "I need my beauty sleep."

"We need to get the place ready for the Hoopers."

Logan groaned. "This is the first time in days when I haven't been in imminent danger. I just want to sleep in."

I nodded and waited for her to change, and then we both went down to the kitchen and out the back door.

By the time we came outside, Amory had joined in the shouting match. He and Roman had lugged Ida's old emergency generator up from the shed, and by the sound of it, they were having trouble getting it to work.

Greyson was leaning against a tree, watching the argument with amusement.

"If you can't play nice, you can't play at all," Logan crooned from the step.

"Oh!" said Roman, turning his sweaty face to her. "So nice of you to join us, princess."

"What's got your panties in a twist this morning?"

Roman opened his mouth to let loose what I was sure would not be a nice explanation, but Amory broke in first.

"He doesn't like the idea of the Hoopers coming to live here."

"Why not?" I asked.

Roman's eyes darted to me. "They're trouble."

"You just don't like the oldest one . . . Marcus."

Roman rolled his eyes and went back to the generator. "*Him* I can deal with."

That took me by surprise. "Who else didn't you like?"

"The sister — Krystal. I don't trust her."

"He finally met the woman who could make an honest man out of him," Logan teased.

I bit back a laugh. So I hadn't been the only one who'd noticed how Roman looked at Krystal.

"What?" snapped Roman. He didn't turn around, but I could see his brain working furiously to get ahead of whatever Logan was about to say.

"You *like* her," said Logan. "Well . . . you like the way she looks."

A dark cloud rolled over Roman's face. He was such an angry person that it was hard for me to imagine him having a love life. But with Krystal, he had definitely met his match.

"She's a lunatic," he muttered. "We'll be lucky if she doesn't kill us all in our sleep."

"You'll keep an eye on her," Logan mused. "I don't imagine you two would be sleeping much."

A laugh burst out of Greyson's mouth, and he tried to cover it with a cough.

"Whatever," growled Roman. "Since you slept in, you get

to clean out the guest house." He tossed the extension cord in the grass and stalked off in a huff.

Amory grinned at me, and I felt something flutter in my chest.

"You shouldn't provoke him," Greyson told Logan.

She shrugged. "He's really more of a teddy bear than a grizzly bear."

"If you say so."

I smiled. If anyone could get away with teasing Roman, it was Logan.

He'd treated her like a porcelain doll ever since he'd found her weak and dying at the Infinity Building. Logan, of course, *hated* being treated differently, so she'd been goading Roman more than usual, as though she were trying to lure him into a fight just to prove she could still hold her own.

We each grabbed a power bar for breakfast and went off to the guest house to get it ready for the Hoopers. In the last few years, it had only been used occasionally to house illegals staying at the farm when the main house overflowed, and it had fallen into disrepair.

There were ten dusty rooms that needed cleaning and a broken-down kitchen with cupboards full of cobwebs. The bed linen was moth-eaten, and the whole place was overrun with mice.

It took the whole day to get the house in a condition that would be livable. It was nasty work sweeping the cobwebs, dust, and rodent excrement out of the rooms, but it felt good to sweat and do something productive.

While we cleaned, Roman and Godfrey scouted the rest of the nearby farms for food and supplies. Amory and Greyson busied themselves with dismantling the PMC's work out in the fields. They began filling in the foundation of the plant and cleared away the mess the builders had left during construction.

When we all gathered around the kitchen table for a late supper of noodles in thin broth, we were sweaty, exhausted, and irritable.

Amory still hadn't managed to get the generator running, and Roman and Godfrey's supply runs had not been very fruitful. At this point, we faced the strong possibility that we would run out of gasoline and be unable to make more trips into the city to gather food.

"We need to rebuild the barn by spring," said Roman. "We need more room for people."

"How can we house people if we can't feed them?" Amory muttered.

"Well we can't defend this place with just us and the Hoopers. We may be able to drive off the workers, but the PMC will send in reinforcements."

"Once they know we're here, all they'll have to do is set up a roadblock. They'll be able to starve us out."

"We can still hunt," said Logan.

Amory shook his head. "All the carriers drove off most of the game in the area. That deer the Hoopers shot was probably the last of its kind."

"We have enough gas for one more run," said Godfrey. "We'll have to go far and wide this time. With any luck, we'll find enough fuel left to make it worth our while. That's what we need to worry about. As long as we have gas, we can do runs to get more food."

We finished our unsatisfying meal in irritable silence, and I went upstairs to be the first at the bathroom. I didn't care if the water was cold. I just wanted to wash away the filth and grime from the day.

When I emerged, Logan was sitting outside the door, waiting her turn. Amory, Roman, and Godfrey were talking downstairs, but Greyson's door was cracked.

I knocked half-heartedly and pushed the door open before he could respond. He might have wanted to be alone, but I didn't.

He had his back to the door, and he sighed when he heard me come in.

"Can you shut the door?" he asked.

I pushed it closed and walked around to the bed.

Greyson was leaning against the wall, the side of his jaw twitching as though he wanted to cry. He had something in his hands I couldn't quite see.

Cautiously, I sank down next to him.

"Why are we here, Haven?"

I was startled by the lump in his throat. "W-What do you mean?"

"I mean . . . why am *I* here?"

He sighed, and I could sense the energy this confession took from him. "I feel like I'm just an extra person . . . like I don't belong with you guys."

"Of course you belong with us!" I said, taken aback by this statement. I'd never considered that my friendship with Logan and Amory had made him feel left out, or what it must have been like for him when I wasn't myself.

He shook his head. "I should have gone west. That's what we planned on doing, and that's where I should have gone."

"We *will* go west," I said, my voice wavering despite my resolve. "I promise."

"When?" he demanded. "When will we go? It seems like everything we do just takes us farther and farther away from my family . . . farther from what we wanted in the first place."

I was taken aback by his words. I vaguely remembered Greyson *wanting* to fight with the rebels after Sector X fell. *I* had been the one who wanted to flee, but I'd joined up to save Amory.

"I thought . . . I thought you wanted this," I said quietly. "I thought you wanted to be a rebel."

"That was after I got out of prison," he said, his face contorting in pain as he remembered. "I was angry. I wanted to get back at the PMC for what they took from me. But now . . . I just want to live my *life*."

His voice was tired, defeated, and that sobered me more than anything.

"I don't want to be on the run anymore . . . to go to bed every night thinking I might be killed in my sleep or hauled back to prison."

"What brought all this on?" I asked. "This isn't you talking."

"I don't belong here!" he snapped. "I'm just in the way!"

It seemed odd that Greyson was telling *me* he didn't belong — after I'd spent two weeks tied up in a tent while the others debated whether or not I was going to turn on them.

But then Greyson shoved what he was holding into my hands, and I understood.

A stack of glossy Polaroid pictures slipped between my fingers. They were all pictures of Logan: Logan laughing, Logan lying in the grass with the sun in her eyes, Logan perched in the old tree with a rifle slung across her lap.

"Where did you get these?" I asked. I knew he couldn't have taken them.

"They were under the bed. They must have belonged to —"

"Max," I finished, closing my eyes. That stung me deep down — not just because I missed Max, but because of what he had lost, and because of the pain it caused Greyson to bear witness to what had slipped away from Logan.

I gripped his arm and felt him flinch a little. Greyson wasn't emotional. He didn't wear his pain on his face the way Roman and Logan did. I knew it killed him to break down like this in front of me, but I gripped him harder, devotion blazing in my chest.

"Listen. You're not an outsider here. *You* helped me save Amory from Isador. *You* helped him get me out. And *you* are the reason I'm remembering everything."

He looked at me, and I could see the effect my words had on him.

"*I* am?"

"Yes," I said. "That night the carriers attacked the camp . . . that run triggered my memory."

The dark haze that had settled over him seemed to be lifting, so I kept going. "You belong here as much as any of us — probably more than me. I went into Sector X for you, and I would do it all over again. You're the closest thing I have to family, and I promise we'll find your mom and Dani."

"You can't promise that."

"I can promise we'll *try*. If we're still alive after all this, we'll go up north and find them. But we have to fight the PMC. How long do you think they'll let illegals live free out west? They postponed migration, but they didn't escape it

The Last Uprising

entirely. You'd be living in fear out there, too. Things aren't how they were before. You can't just choose to be free. We have to fight for it."

There was a long pause. My heart was pounding against my ribs. I didn't want him to be angry, but he needed to hear the truth.

"Thanks," he said finally, sniffing loudly and forcing a laugh. "I think I actually feel better now. That was just the ass-kicking I needed."

I grinned. "I know." I shuffled the pictures into a neat stack and pressed them into his hand. "Now stop whining. Stop tiptoeing around the Max issue. If you don't face this head-on, he's going to be the giant elephant in the room every time you're with her.

"Give these pictures to Logan. Tell her you'll give her time. But tell her that when she's ready, you'll be waiting."

The Hoopers arrived the next day, hauling a rickety open trailer behind their black pickup truck. The three of them were crammed into the cab, and the trailer was overflowing with their belongings and supplies.

Marcus killed the engine, and Krystal and Jason hopped out.

Logan emerged from the guest house. She'd been cleaning furiously again, fighting a losing battle with the spiders and mice. When she saw the Hoopers, she pulled her hair out of her bandana, and it tumbled down around her shoulders in golden waves. Dressed in baggy overalls with no rifle in her hand, she looked oddly domestic.

Jason ogled her. "We brought all the supplies we have," he stammered, pulling the first crate out of the open trailer. "Where should it go?"

Logan smiled. "We can cook and eat in the main house, so just bring it inside. Any extra can go in the guest house and the cellars."

The boys wandered out of the house to help unload the food, and we each carried a load inside while Godfrey took inventory of the ammunition. Logan directed the organizational process in the kitchen, making Roman and Amory move each box around two or three times until she was satisfied.

Outside, there seemed to be some sort of commotion going on. I heard someone yell but thought little of it. I'd only just met Jason, but already I knew he was the family loudmouth.

Then, without warning, a gunshot shattered the cheerful sunlight streaming through the kitchen window.

Amory and I exchanged a look, and we both ran for the back door. He snatched up two rifles that were resting against the wall, and I followed him around the house.

We hadn't even made it to the front yard when two more shots rang out. I pushed my legs harder and then slammed to a halt.

In the front yard, a dozen carriers were rushing the trailer. Their withered skin was drooping around those unnerving yellow eyes, and their pale bald heads gleamed in the sun.

Godfrey stood frozen inside the trailer, hovered over a crate of canned goods with his rifle trained on the nearest carrier.

As I watched, more shuffled out of the woods, drawn by the scent of food. A few were rocking the trailer or trying to crawl up the sides. Godfrey was taking them out with methodical, precise shots to the head, but there were too many.

Amory and I started shooting, and Godfrey jumped into the bed of the pickup truck. One carrier tried to scrabble up the side, but I raised my rifle and shot him in the back.

Out of the corner of my eye, I saw a knot of them gathered near the far corner of the trailer. Someone whipped past me, and before I could stop him, Marcus had thrown himself into the fray.

"No! Don't!" I screamed.

But it was too late. He'd disappeared into the horde, slicing their jugulars from behind with a butterfly knife.

Suddenly, I knew why the carriers were gathered like that. Looking down, I saw a familiar pair of boots thrashing on the ground. There was a guttural yell, and I realized the boots belonged to Jason.

I aimed at the carriers around him, but I couldn't kill them quickly enough.

Roman and Greyson were already shooting by my side, and Logan ran into the horde with knives flashing in her hands. I knew she didn't trust herself to shoot with Jason entangled in the mess, but I wanted to throttle her. There were too many carriers. I wouldn't be able to stop them rushing her.

"Jason!" Krystal yelled, her voice high-pitched and hysterical. She took aim and was surprisingly accurate, despite the panic in her voice.

Logan had nearly cleared the knot of carriers around Jason. Even after the long-term effects of the cure, she hadn't lost her touch in hand-to-hand combat. She moved her knives artfully, slicing and stabbing as though she were dancing, and they fell off one by one.

Jason lifted his head. He'd shoved his body between the trailer and the ground for cover, but one of the carriers had gotten hold of his arm. Now he had it cradled against his chest, trying to stifle his cries of anguish.

Logan moved into position to fend off three carriers who were still trying to claw at him, and Jason stumbled out behind her.

Then everything slowed down.

A fourth carrier nobody had noticed was crouched on the trailer, rummaging through a box of supplies. He lifted his head at the sound of Logan's heavy breathing and pounced.

I cried out, but the carrier had already tackled Logan to the ground, and the other three were joining in the frenzy.

I couldn't shoot at them. I was paralyzed. All I could see was a flash of golden hair as the four carriers overpowered her.

I yelled again, but my voice only gurgled in my throat.

Before I knew what I was doing, my instincts had hijacked my common sense, and I was running into the horde.

"Haven!" Amory yelled, but I ignored him.

I didn't have my knives, but I grabbed the carrier on top of Logan around the neck with all the force I could muster, pulling him off her and striking him in the face. There was a vicious crunch that told me I'd broken his nose.

As he staggered out of the way, there was a sharp crack. Amory had shot him.

I fought the carriers as though they were humans: quick punches to the gut and well-placed kicks that brought them to their knees. They were slower than humans — softer — but they were still bigger than me.

I used every ounce of strength I had as I gouged out their eyes and elbowed them out of the way. As soon as I pushed them off Logan, Amory would shoot them.

Logan staggered to her feet, bleeding and disheveled, and relief rushed through my limbs. Then I saw the bite along her neck and the bites on her arms.

I took a quick survey of the carriers on the ground. None of them had sores around their mouths yet, so they weren't contagious.

More gunshots rang out like thunder claps. I tried to keep sucking in oxygen, but the rush of adrenaline in my veins was beginning to subside. I could feel the ache of the bones in my hands and the sting of air on my bleeding knuckles.

The growls of carriers were growing further apart. Half of the horde had scattered, and the other half lay dead and dying at my feet.

I looked around wild-eyed and watched Logan skewer the last one with both of her knives. The carrier fell to the ground, bloody and defeated.

Logan was too pale, but she was alive.

Suddenly I didn't know what to do. There were so many dead carriers.

I focused on breathing in and out, my arms hanging useless at my sides.

Everyone on the porch was watching us. I wanted to run or crumple into a heap of bones on the ground, but I did neither.

As I surveyed the death all around me, I felt a warm hand on the small of my back that made my skin tingle. Amory was already standing beside me, looking concerned, and I let his touch steady me.

"Are you hurt?" he asked.

I shook my head, not trusting myself to speak. The stench on the air was a mix of rotten lettuce and stale sickness. My stomach was a flimsy bag of nausea.

"Haven . . .?"

"I'll be all right," I said. But in truth, I didn't think I

would. I didn't know how much more killing I could physically tolerate.

Amory pulled me over to the porch and made me sit down. He didn't say anything as I pulled myself together, but I could feel the subtle contact of his knee against mine, rooting me in place.

Greyson found Logan and pulled her inside to disinfect the bites, and I knew Amory needed to go examine Jason's wounds. Somehow I'd come out unscathed, though it didn't feel like it. It never did.

Every death, carrier or human, cut me inside and burned like a thousand paper cuts. They never healed over, and every death was a thousand fresh slices, crisscrossing over the old ones and shredding me to pieces.

Chapter Seventeen

Over the next few days, we fell into a rhythm at the farm. With the Hoopers' supplies, we finally had enough to eat, and surviving the horde's attack gave us a new urgency to fortify our defenses.

Roman and Marcus found some lumber on an abandoned farm, and Greyson and Amory took it upon themselves to design the new barn we would build where the old one had stood.

Neither of them knew anything about construction, but we didn't have much of a choice. The plans Greyson had sketched showed a building with a larger loft to double the available space for people and a smaller annex to shelter livestock.

A week after the carrier attack, we were already attempting to frame the barn, sweating in the unseasonably intense heat.

I tensed when I heard the crunch of gravel that signaled an approaching vehicle, and Amory stiffened automatically. I found my rifle, and the others fanned out around me, weapons in hand.

The seconds slowed as we waited for the dust to clear, and the 4Runner appeared, followed by a beat-up Ford pickup truck.

At the sight of Godfrey and Marcus leading the caravan, I lowered my rifle slightly but continued to inch toward the newcomers in the truck.

The Last Uprising

"Easy now," Godfrey grumbled as he got out of the vehicle. "They come in peace."

So Godfrey had been recruiting. He'd brought Marcus along because he knew all the families in the area that were in hiding.

Piled in the truck were three stocky-looking men in dirty jeans and worn-out T-shirts. They got out, and I watched their scuffed boots shuffle over to where we all stood. Something about their rugged look and beefy frames reminded me of the moonshiners, but at the sight of our shaky construction, they let out a collective rumble of warm laughter that put me immediately at ease.

"Gang, meet the Holts."

The man closest to me removed his sun-faded baseball cap and held out a calloused hand. "Name's Ray Holt, and this is my brother Bobby." He pointed to the shortest man. "That's Matt, our cousin. We're here to help."

"Haven Allis," I said, taking the man's hand. It was rough and warm — a hard grip built from honest work.

"What brings you here?" asked Amory, materializing at my elbow.

"We heard ol' Ida's fighting back. We want to be of service." Ray turned back to me. "Plus Marcus here told us how y'all fought off a whole mess of carriers the other day."

"We didn't have much of a choice," I said grimly, remembering Logan's screams.

"Where'd you learn to fight like that?"

"Out east," I said. "The hordes near Sector X were much bigger."

"*That's* where y'all come from?"

I nodded, not wanting to share our whole life stories with

these people. It didn't matter if we were all *really* from Missouri.

"Damn," said another of the men. "You on the run or something?"

"Something like that," said Amory, an edge to his voice.

Maybe I imagined the arch of his brow or the challenge in his gaze, but he looked as though he were trying to shield me from this man, which I thought was cute.

It wasn't jealousy. No matter how many times Amory and I had fought side by side — watched *each other's* backs — he always felt the need to protect me in situations where there was no real danger.

"We live a few miles south of here," continued Ray. "We've been laying low since the PMC started to overtake this area. But then Godfrey and Marcus came by and said you were establishing a base. We'd like to fight those bastards."

"Good man," said Amory, finally offering his hand. "I'm Amory."

Ray shook it enthusiastically. "Good to meet you." His eyes flickered over to our shaky construction. "Tell you what. You teach us how to fight, and we'll help you build a barn that won't collapse in one good strong wind."

Amory broke into a grin, and all signs of tension disappeared.

The Holts helped us frame the barn, and we were halfway done by sundown.

I couldn't help but think that these men would be a huge asset. Ray had worked in construction before the Collapse, and Matt and Bobby had run their family's farm. Our inexperience was evident next to men who had been farming and building things their whole lives.

The Last Uprising

After dinner, Ray cornered Amory and Roman to ask for a fighting demonstration, and Logan rolled her eyes in my direction.

She tolerated men's stares and took their doting smiles in stride, but I imagined it grated on her nerves that these men assumed Amory and Roman were the best fighters among us — especially since Roman and Amory hadn't even fought the carriers hand to hand that day.

The boys weren't *asking* for attention. I could tell by the droop in their shoulders that they were tired, but Logan and I knew that neither would object to a fight with the other standing right there.

The other two Holts were enthusiastic, and even Krystal and Marcus looked up with interest.

We all went out into the yard, and Roman lit some of the Tiki torches Logan and I had found in Ida's cellar off the guest house. The torches formed a ring in front of the house, and I felt the excitement radiating from Logan.

I was excited, too, but not about the fight. Since the aftereffects of the cure had hampered her shooting abilities, I just wanted to see Logan in her element again. Never was she so much herself than when she was fighting.

I was surprised when Roman jerked his head at Amory to step into the ring. Amory approached him warily, his mouth set in a grim line. I wasn't sure why Logan wasn't fighting, and by the look on Marcus's face, he was confused, too.

I suspected Roman and Amory didn't want Logan to overexert herself. The way she'd fought the moonshiners and the carriers, it was easy to forget she was still recovering from the side effects of the cure.

Logan and I exchanged a glance. If they were fighting each other, it meant we would have days of pouty silence from whoever lost.

Amory was normally humble, but it shook his confidence whenever he lost a sparring match to Roman. Since Roman was already moody and joyless, I secretly hoped he would lose instead.

Amory pulled off his jacket and tossed it to Greyson, who was playing referee. Greyson gave him a slight nod, which I took to mean he hoped Amory won, too.

It gave me a little leap of joy that he and Amory had become such good friends, although I wasn't sure why I cared so much.

Roman and Amory squared off, and I watched the cords of Amory's back muscles tense through his navy T-shirt. With his tree-trunk arms and thick torso, Roman had the advantage of size, but Amory was strong, fast, and more agile.

"Three hits is a win," said Greyson. "Go!"

As expected, Roman swung first.

Amory dodged his hit expertly and came back around with a swing. Roman avoided his punch, too, and I marveled at how quickly he dodged despite his size.

His hits weren't as fast. He swung at Amory, lumbering like a giant, and Amory parried each of his blows with a jerk of his forearms or a swift duck.

It went like this for a while, neither making contact, and both appraising each other silently in the dancing torchlight.

It wasn't hatred I sensed between them. It was pure rivalry, wariness, and respect for each other's skills.

After a few minutes, the small crowd was beginning to grow restless. Marcus looked unimpressed, and the Holt brothers were growing bored. They didn't know Roman or Amory, so they probably thought the Hoopers had exaggerated our group's skills.

Finally, Amory pulled one of his lightning-quick one-two fakes, connecting with the side of Roman's jaw.

"One to Amory!" shouted Greyson.

Roman shot Amory a crooked grin as a challenge, and his fists flew at him.

Amory managed to block two hits, but the third was too powerful. I heard it rather than saw it, and Amory grimaced and ducked out of the way of another blow.

"One to Roman!"

Moving more quickly now, Amory swung out his foot and brought Roman crashing to the ground. Amory jumped on top of him with his fist raised, but before he could deliver a punch, Roman flipped him over, and in a second, the roles were reversed.

My muscles tensed as I watched Roman wind up and smash his knuckles into Amory's jaw.

I winced. I didn't like this part.

Then Amory elbowed Roman's inner thigh with a painful-sounding *thwap!* Roman let out a strangled grunt, which was the closest he ever got to admitting real agony.

"Two-two!"

Come on, Amory, I urged silently.

With a great heave of his hips, Amory bucked him forward. Roman caught himself with his hands, and Amory used the opportunity to collapse his left arm and throw him off balance. Roman's shoulder smashed into the ground, and Amory staggered to his feet.

The two squared off once again, and Amory advanced with a combination I hadn't seen before. It capitalized on his agility and speed and allowed him to push Roman back as he dodged. But one of Roman's moves was too slow. Amory took his chance, jabbing Roman in the stomach — hard.

"That's it!" yelled Greyson.

Roman lurched backward, glaring at Amory, but Amory held out a hand. Roman shook it begrudgingly.

The group clapped and whistled, but Amory seemed utterly unimpressed by his own victory. He tucked his chin, embarrassed by all the fanfare.

One of the Holt brothers leaned in to clap him on the back, and I heard Amory deflecting his praise.

"That wasn't anything great," he said between gasps. "Roman and I spar all the time."

He took in another two dragging breaths and turned to the rest of the crowd, hands at his sides, clutching his abdomen. "I want to fight Haven next."

My heart stopped, and everyone's heads turned in my direction. A murmur rippled through the group, but the corners of Marcus's mouth curled into a grin.

This was what he'd wanted to see, I realized.

Amory was staring at me with those burning gray eyes. His gaze was a challenge.

Why was he doing this? Was he hoping to beat me to show you couldn't have mercy on your opponent? Did he want me to fight back to prove I'd been hiding some sort of hidden skill I'd learned during my time with World Corp?

A thousand possibilities had erupted in my mind, but I pushed them aside and walked into the ring.

It didn't matter *why* Amory wanted to fight me. I would do it anyway. I wasn't afraid.

No, that wasn't true. Even though I trusted Amory, I knew a fight against him would be brutal.

The Last Uprising

I stepped into the ring, eyeing Amory warily. When I was close enough, he touched my shoulder and pulled me in.

He leaned over to block me from the crowd, so close I could see the heat beneath his skin. He looked anxious.

"Hey, is this okay?"

I met his gaze through narrowed eyes. "It's a little late now. You want to fight, let's fight."

My reply seemed to concern him, because his eyebrows knitted together. "I just want you to show them what you can do. Plus, *you're* the one who impressed the Hoopers the other day, not me and Roman. You're the one they want to see."

"You want to fight, so do it," I said, a hard edge in my voice. I wasn't sure why it sounded like that.

I could tell he was nervous, though I didn't know why.

"I'll only use fifty percent power. I'm not going to hurt you."

I shook my head. "Don't hold back, Amory. I've got it."

He raised an eyebrow, and it looked as though I had finally solidified something he had been struggling with. "Fine."

"Come on, Haven. Kick his ass!" shouted Logan from the sidelines. She was bouncing on the balls of her feet, unable to conceal her excitement.

Logan had trained me on the farm and in Rulon's camp. She was responsible for the basic skills I had, and she was such a proud teacher.

I squared off against Amory, shaking out my arms to loosen up. He raised an eyebrow, which I took to mean he wanted me to remember what we had agreed upon.

Greyson caught my eye for a long second, and then he

shot Amory what I could only guess was a look of warning.

"Ready . . . Go!"

Amory advanced first, his body moving like a panther's. I tore my eyes away from him and concentrated on my footwork, careful not to let him drive me back. I heard Logan's voice in my head: *If they're pushing you around the ring, you've already lost.*

I changed directions. Amory smirked, following my movement effortlessly.

When I got too close, he swung his fist out hard — and slowly. I dodged his hit easily and pushed him back with punches of my own. He deflected each one but didn't seem to be pushing offense.

What was he doing?

I aimed a kick at his knee, but he moved out of the way. I lost my balance slightly. He swung at my head, and I ducked.

He expected me to retreat, but I grabbed him and jabbed my knee into his gut. I didn't use full force, but I knew he still felt it.

"That's one!" Greyson bellowed.

I blocked two hits and stumbled back, throwing a cross and a hook. Then Amory swung out his other hand, broad and fast, connecting with the side of my head as Logan had done in training whenever I'd dropped my left hand.

"One to Amory!"

I dragged in a breath, shaking my head to clear the jarring pain. But before I could recover, Amory jumped behind me and wrapped an arm around my neck, choking off my airways. He was stronger than I was prepared for.

I yanked down his arm to keep him from crushing my windpipe and elbowed him in the gut.

"That's two," yelled Greyson. I could hear the smirk inching around his mouth through the commentary.

Amory was doubled over in pain, and I used the opportunity to twist into him and wriggle out from under his shoulder, pulling his elbow close to my body and locking his arm behind him.

Amory's eyes widened. He was impressed but surprised. I was, too.

My victory was short-lived. Suddenly, my feet flew out from under me, and I landed on my back.

I gasped. I'd had the wind knocked out of me. Suddenly Amory was on top, pinning me down. He was breathing heavily, and his eyes were burning as he met my gaze. I became very aware of his thighs pressed against my sides and the look of his chest as he towered over me.

Then his fist swung out and hit my jaw, the pain reverberating up the side of my face.

"Two to Amory!" said Greyson. He sounded as shocked as I felt.

The Holt brothers were booing, which gave me a smug sense of satisfaction.

Amory hadn't hit me hard at all. I could tell he was only using maybe ten percent of his strength, but it was the shock that he'd actually *done* it that had me flying into a rage.

Without thinking, I reached up and boxed his ears with my palms — a dirty move Logan had taught me.

He growled, and I used the second he'd been distracted by pain to buck my hips and roll him off me.

I should have ended it right then, but suddenly my face was too hot. I was straddling Amory with everyone's eyes on me. I stumbled to my feet, but he caught my ankle, pulling me back to the ground. Before he took me down, I closed my fingers, twisted my wrist, and brought my hammer fist around behind me, colliding with his nose.

"That's three!" shouted Greyson, not bothering to hide the relief in his voice.

I yanked my ankle out of Amory's hold, but he struggled to a standing position and gripped my arm tightly. I was about to punch him again when he did something that surprised me.

He pulled my arm up and held it in the air as though I were a world champion.

The group erupted into applause — the Holts cheering and wolf-whistling. Logan was screaming at the top of her lungs, and Greyson was grinning like an idiot.

I shot a half-hearted glare at Amory and was startled to see his nose bleeding from where I had hit him.

He grinned sheepishly. "What do you *want* from me, Haven?" he asked, his voice so quiet that only I could hear.

"What?"

He smiled again, but his expression was caught between adoration and sadness. "What do you *want* . . . from me?"

I shook my head wordlessly, painfully aware that I had no idea how to answer him. There were too many people around.

He lowered my arm and brushed his thumb over my jaw where he'd struck it. It didn't hurt at all anymore, so I knew he must have hit me *very* lightly — barely a graze.

"I'm sorry," he said. "This fight was a bad idea. I didn't want to hit you, but I thought if it was just the two of us again, doing what we did before —"

I jerked my head, confused but not regretting the fight. "They loved it."

Then Amory dove in so fast I didn't have time to react.

Instead of what I was hoping for — what I really needed right at that moment — he brushed his lips against my cheek, barely an inch from my mouth.

As he pulled away, he growled low in my ear, "You have to tell me what you want."

I looked at him, a little shocked, but nodded numbly.

"That's my girl!" squealed Logan from behind me, dragging me away from Amory and shattering the bubble of our private exchange.

Logan thrust my arm into the air again, throwing her hair back like a party girl and letting out a high-pitched "Whooo!" I'd never heard her make.

The Holts were slapping my back and grinning. They wanted to learn how to fight like us. It felt good.

Of course I couldn't know how much Amory had held back to let me win, but it still felt like a victory in more ways than one.

Soon the Hoopers and the Holts wandered off to the guest house, and I followed Roman, Greyson, and Logan into the main house.

Godfrey hung back, and I could tell all the torches and sparring had been too much excitement for him. Perhaps when you'd seen as much fighting and death as Godfrey had, even a playful match lost its appeal.

Chapter Eighteen

Over the next two weeks, the farm changed so dramatically it was hardly recognizable. With the Holts' help, the barn construction went quickly, and it was beginning to look even nicer than it had before.

Godfrey was almost always away from the farm, recruiting rebels and searching for supplies. Some of the things he returned with didn't make sense to me, like when he'd raided a chemical manufacturing plant and carted the unlabeled jugs out to the shed. I didn't question it. Godfrey had always been eccentric and paranoid.

The guest house overflowed with illegals from Columbia, Kansas City, and St. Louis, and we hauled sleeping bags and blankets out to the barn. None of the newcomers seemed to mind. Most of them had been on their own for months, scrounging for food and water. From the stories they brought with them, I knew that the deserted cities were much worse.

So many new recruits meant there were more people to take turns on carrier watch, but Roman never seemed to stop prowling the edges of the woods. None of us had seen a single carrier since the attack, but hordes of that scale rarely kept quiet for long.

To ease my troubled thoughts, I threw myself into farm operations and supplementing our food supply. I planted early crops of beets, broccoli, cabbage, and onions in the trampled vegetable patches and asked Matt and Bobby to look for livestock. One afternoon, they returned with two cows, three goats, and chickens in the Hoopers' trailer.

Logan and Amory were busy training everyone twice a day in hand-to-hand combat. Although Marcus was deadly with a crossbow and Krystal, Jason, and all the Holts could shoot, none of them had any experience fighting carriers.

One night in the barn when I was feeding the cows, I caught myself staring at Amory. He was just doing a demonstration for the Holts, but I couldn't help thinking of our fight — the way his body had moved, the way it had felt against mine.

I kept glancing over at him, marveling at the way he looked in his faded jeans, barefoot in the hay, with his snug gray T-shirt clinging to his tan arms.

They were laughing about something, and I glanced over the wooden partition to steal another look.

Amory laughed with his whole body, throwing his head back and arching his shoulders. Then his eyes crinkled closed in a way that sent a thrill through me.

Before I could look away, Amory caught my gaze.

"Haven! Come here!" he called.

There was a slight sparkle in his eyes, and I felt the flush spreading up my neck.

What an idiot. He'd caught me watching him.

"It'll just take a second," he coaxed. "I need to show them something, and you've done this before."

The nerves tingled down my back all the way to my fingertips at his words "done this before," but I forced myself to cross the barn to where the four of them stood.

The Holts grinned. They were hoping to see Amory and me fight again. Somehow, word had spread that Amory and I had both been subjects of World Corp's brainwashing experiments and had fought our conditioning, so we had become objects of morbid fascination for the rebels. Most of them seemed to think we were killing machines.

Amory adjusted his posture, and I knew he would be playing the role of the attacker. My heart skipped a beat.

"I'm trying to show them how to ward off a carrier that gets ahold of them and pins their arms," he said. "Especially if there's more than one. You're smaller, so this will show that it works no matter how big the carrier is."

I nodded. My throat was dry.

"Ready?" he asked, arching an eyebrow as if he sensed my nervousness.

"Ready." At least my voice didn't give away how on-edge I felt.

Amory smiled briefly, and then he lunged at me. My whole body went rigid as I braced for impact, but I heard Logan's voice in my head: *Stay relaxed.*

Amory hit me like a linebacker, and his strong arms wrapped around my torso, pinning my arms to my side and squeezing me like a boa constrictor.

I gasped for air, and my senses were assaulted by his fresh, woodsy smell, the warmth of his body, and the adrenaline from the attack. His breathing was ragged in my ear.

Without giving myself time to think, I smacked him in the thigh and brought my knee up, careful just to feign striking his groin.

Amory faked doubling over, and I used his new posture to wiggle out and yank his arm away from his body, pushing the blade of my forearm into the side of his neck. I held his head down and faked an elbow strike before aiming a kick just above his knee.

The Last Uprising

The kick *wasn't* fake, and he stumbled.

It was amusing to see him so graceless for once. I laughed, and he threw me a sideways look with those bright gray eyes that made my stomach squirm with pleasure.

"That's how it's done," he panted, breaking into a grin.

The Holts wolf-whistled, and my face burned when I realized my eyes were lingering on Amory's chest and shoulders. I couldn't help it.

What was wrong with me?

I forced my feet to start moving, but Amory's hand found my wrist and pulled me back into his orbit. I didn't fight it, and he didn't let go.

"Can you stay a little longer? Help me with some more demonstrations?"

I smiled before I could stop myself and nodded. My brain felt fuzzy. I couldn't think about anything except the warmth of his fingers pressed into the tender skin inside my wrist. Amory cocked an eyebrow, and he looked me up and down, eyes lingering longer than they should have.

Did he know?

"A little longer" turned out to be another hour — another hour of being put into headlocks, bear hugged, and knocked down so I could show the Holts how to ward off an attack.

For an hour, I breathed in Amory and deflected his advances, trying to ignore the feel of his abdominals through his shirt or the way his strong arms softened around me.

When I finally left the barn, sore and light-headed, I realized I would have sparred with Amory for another three hours just to be near him, and he knew it. My feelings were strong and unreasonable — intensified somehow by the months he and I had spent apart.

The Last Uprising

I felt the uncontrollable, girly smile tugging at the corners of my mouth all the way across the yard, and I realized I was in deep trouble.

Now that we had a sizable army at our disposal and spring was upon us, we needed a real plan. Greyson, who had studied military strategy briefly in school, had been pouring over maps of the area for days.

He called a meeting, and Amory, Logan, Roman, Greyson, and I crowded around the kitchen table to strategize. Godfrey had been gone for several days, and I was starting to get nervous.

We all looked at Greyson and the county map spread out in front of him. He cleared his throat nervously and circled his finger around a plot of land.

"This is us," he said. "These are the two roads the workers could come from when they return for construction. I think we should have someone stationed here . . . and here . . . with walkie-talkies to give us a warning when they're on their way."

"When do you think they'll show?" asked Amory.

Greyson shrugged. "The moonshiners said spring. I say we play it safe and operate under the assumption that they'll be here sooner rather than later."

"So what do we do when they arrive?" asked Amory.

"I think we should ambush them before they even get to the farm. There's a blind curve here." He pointed on the map. "We'll have plenty of time to head them off. We should be able to take them out with ten or twelve people."

"These are the workers," Amory reminded him. "Civilians. You want to kill them?"

"Who cares if they're civilians!" growled Roman. "They're working for World Corp."

I glared at Roman. His callousness was so hypocritical, considering he'd elected to join up with the PMC after the riots in Sector X.

"We don't need to kill them," said Greyson. "In fact, it's better if we don't. They're not the target — just the messenger. Keep the troop small . . . just enough people to drive them off, but not enough to show our hand to the PMC. With any luck, they'll underestimate our numbers when they send out reinforcements. If we can kill the troops they send, then the PMC will know we mean business."

"Then what?" broke in Logan.

Greyson shrugged. "Then we'll have to pull out everything we've got to defend the farm. I wouldn't count on them coming by the road a second time. They could try to ambush us from the woods."

"If we want to defend the place against the PMC twice, we'll need a lot more people than we have now," said Logan.

"How many of us are there?"

"Only forty."

"We can fit another ten in the barn, maybe," said Amory. "But after that, we'll need to start moving people into the main house. It's going to get really crowded."

"We're going to need more than that," said Logan. "At least a hundred if we want any real chance."

"A hundred people?" said Greyson incredulously. "How do you expect to keep a hundred people on this farm? We'll be lucky if we can feed the people who are here now! We don't even know if we'll be able to keep running water once the PMC gets wind of us."

"We managed it in Rulon's camp. And we didn't have running water there."

Greyson waved a dismissive hand. "That was when we

were five miles from Sector X and could steal PMC supplies. We need to be able to sustain these people for at least two years."

"*Two years?*"

"How long do you think it's going to take to rally people up north?"

"You want all these people to hang out here for two years?"

"Probably longer," said Greyson, his voice almost a growl. "Jesus, Logan. These things take time!"

"Well it's going to take a lot longer if we're trying to fight the PMC with forty people. All it takes is one bad carrier attack or one fight against the PMC, and it'll be down to us and five other people."

"How can you say that?" asked Greyson. He had raised his voice, fighting a tremor that told me he was getting angry — truly angry. "We've been training them, and they're learning."

"I'm telling you, half of these people aren't going to make it, so it's best not to get too attached."

"Is that *really* how you think?"

Logan whipped her hair over her shoulder, leaning over the table to yell at him. "It's how you *have* to think if you're in charge of our defense strategy, Greyson. You have to be realistic. People are going to die. We need more bodies to throw at the problem because we're unprepared to face a PMC attack right now."

"They'll do fine," Greyson snarled. "Not all of us are PMC trained, but we manage." His voice was rough.

"What's *that* supposed to mean?"

"It means maybe you should think a little less like them

and a little more like us." I could feel the anger rolling off him in waves. "People. Aren't. Disposable."

Logan looked as though he'd reached across the table and smacked her. Before I could prepare myself for her torrent of fury, she lurched forward and upended the table. Greyson's maps fluttered to the floor, and Amory and Roman leaned back in their seats.

Logan's fists were clenched at her sides, and I waited for her to yell or hit him. She took a step forward, and Greyson looked scared.

"This is a fucking joke," she said in a low voice, punctuating each word. "You don't know what you're doing, and you're going to get us all killed."

She stormed out of the room and up the stairs. The rest of us just sat there, staring at Greyson. I didn't know what to say. I knew Logan would expect me to go comfort her, but I wasn't sure who needed me more.

Logan would never be able to outrun her PMC past, and as soon as those words left Greyson's mouth, I knew this argument would resurrect itself whenever they fought. It wasn't as though Greyson held Logan's time with the PMC against her, but she thought he did, and that was enough. To Logan, Greyson's hatred of the PMC somehow extended to her.

"What the hell happened in here?" Godfrey growled from the back door. "*Christ.* I leave you all for four days, and everything goes to shit."

Amory cleared his throat and quietly righted the table. Greyson was still standing frozen, his face contorted in anger.

I wished for a moment that the others weren't there. I just wanted to give him a hug and tell him he wasn't incompetent or stupid. If he hadn't hit Logan in the only place that could truly hurt her, she never would have said those things.

Then again, I suspected they were both doubly hurt by what had been said simply because of who had said it. Logan's opinion *mattered* to Greyson — probably more than anyone else's.

"Where's the kid?" asked Godfrey absently, shrugging off his wet coat.

"She's . . . in her room," I said.

Godfrey didn't comment.

"Where've you been?" asked Amory.

"Up north. Didn't think I was going to make it back, to be honest."

"Why?"

"It's an absolute circus up there, that's why. Two of the communes near the border have fallen, and Rulon's old gang shut down three of the PMC's major supply lines."

I was glad to hear that Ida's efforts at the communes had been successful, but if Rulon's crew was still interfering, it wasn't good news for either side.

"Supply lines?" repeated Amory. "How?"

Godfrey raised a grim eyebrow and flopped down in Logan's abandoned chair. "IEDs."

"Shit," said Roman.

"Yeah," said Godfrey, rubbing his head. "Those fuckers mean business, but they're getting reckless. Rulon's forces took a hit in the carrier breach, but he created a bunch of monsters in that camp of his. Now that he's dead, there's nothing to stop his thugs from running amuck. They've split off from the revolution — vigilantes, I guess you could say — made a fucking mess for Ida and the rest of us."

Godfrey removed his knit cap and ran a hand through his wiry hair. "It's costing a lot of lives on both sides."

"That's just the price you pay, though, isn't it?" said Roman.

"It's a war," murmured Amory.

I looked at him, sure he didn't mean to sound so uncaring.

"Where will the people from the communes go?" I asked.

Godfrey shrugged. "I supposed they'll stay up north, and Ida will set up a camp. They probably won't see any combat. After the last raid we had, well . . . they aren't cut out for battle."

"So what will happen to them?"

"Best case scenario, we win. They head south and go home. Worst case, we lose, and they'll get the same as you or me. I don't imagine the PMC would have a hard time rounding up a bunch of scared city people roughing it in the woods. But they'll sit tight for now."

It didn't feel right that the people from the communes should be caught in the middle of the revolution when they'd taken no part in the upheaval. But then again, I hadn't wanted to be part of the revolution, either. I'd just been swept up along with it.

As I watched Godfrey limp up the stairs, I couldn't help thinking he looked years older than he had a few days ago.

All of us looked older now — tougher. We had been hardened by all the fighting, all the death, and I doubted any of us would ever be the same.

I'd watched people die. I'd *killed*. World Corp had stolen my identity.

Everything about who I was before had been peeled

away, broken, and reset like a bone. I was functional, but I'd always be able to feel the cracks and scar tissue. There was no going back.

Two days later, I awoke to the sound of frantic knocking on my bedroom door. I peeled my eyes open lethargically, still in a haze of sleep and reeling from my latest nightmare.

In my dream, I was drowning at the bottom of a shallow pool of freezing water. Aryus was hovered over me, barely visible through the ripples. Water was rushing into my lungs, and I was quickly losing consciousness. I was going to die.

Aryus's lips moved, and I heard his voice echoing inside my head.

You are my greatest achievement, Haven. You can't fight it. You will be the end of this revolution.

Trying to shake the eerie feeling that this was some sort of premonition, I shuffled across the room and opened my door.

I barely had time to register Amory's panicked look and smoky gray eyes before he pushed his way into my room and pressed me against the wall. His fingers were thrumming with nerves, and his face was as white as a sheet.

"The workers," he breathed. "They're back . . . with PMC."

Chapter Nineteen

I stared at Amory for a long moment. Our days of peace had reached an end, and there was still so much left unresolved. Something heavy passed between us as his gray eyes bored into mine — a silent acknowledgement of everything that had gone unsaid between us.

Not bothering to change out of my borrowed sweatpants and oversized T-shirt, I bolted down the stairs to the kitchen. Greyson and Logan were already waiting, looking grim. I stuck my head out the back door, and I could see a white PMC cruiser coming up the road through the trees.

"Drop your weapons and surrender," boomed a voice from the cruiser's intercom. "Resisting Private Military Company forces is an act of treason. You are all trespassing on World Corp International land and interfering with official operations. Please put down your weapons . . . and put your hands in the air."

I stood frozen in the doorway, watching the cruiser approaching as though this wasn't happening to me. Blood rushed through my ears, drowning out the panicked voices of Greyson and Amory behind me.

I stepped outside, barely thinking clearly enough to grab my rifle. The Hoopers, the Holts, and all the other rebels were already crouched in the yard behind cars, trash cans, and other makeshift barriers, their weapons poised. I ducked behind the 4Runner, pulling Greyson down with me.

The cruiser stopped where the trees met the driveway.

Nobody moved.

Behind the cruiser leading the convoy were three heavy-duty construction trucks. Several vehicles back, I heard car doors slam and the sound of heavy footfalls. I suspected there were two more PMC cruisers bringing up the rear.

"This is your last chance to surrender peacefully," said the officer. I could see him speaking through the windshield, but the booming voice did not match the pale, mustachioed man sitting behind the wheel. "Drop your weapons and place your hands over your head. If you do not surrender, we will open fire."

The rebels were all staring at the officers with the same challenging expression. The officer was talking into his radio again, but no voice came over the intercom.

Then four officers from the front of the convoy got out toting riot shields, rifles pointed at the rebels nearest them. They looked vaguely surprised. Clearly, the PMC had only been expecting to defend the workers against a horde of carriers.

As the officers advanced, the rebels opened fire. The shots cracked through the trees and sent a violent surge of adrenaline through my veins. Two of the officers went down at once, but not before they'd hit one of our men.

More PMC were spilling out from behind the trucks. There had *not* been two cruisers in the back as I'd thought. Over a dozen men were marching toward us, and they kept coming.

I looked at Greyson, whose face had gone white. We had not prepared for PMC defense of this scale.

I raised my rifle and aimed at the officer nearest me, but it hit him in his vest. He went down, clutching his chest in agony, but he wasn't dead. I aimed at his head, but my second shot ricocheted off his vehicle.

A bullet whizzed past my head, and someone behind me cried out in agony. I ducked and aimed again at the officer I'd shot. This time I hit him squarely in the forehead, and I watched him slide down the closed door of the cruiser, his eyes staring straight ahead.

Behind the line of officers, there was a strange commotion going on in the construction vehicles. Men in blue overalls were jumping out and fleeing toward the back of the caravan, but a few had picked up the fallen officers' weapons and were using the dead bodies as shields as they shot at us.

It struck me as very odd that these men — the scared people who had been cowering in the communes since the Collapse — were rallying behind the officers who had enforced mandatory migration in the first place. These were the people Ida was trying to convert, but the look in their eyes told me they had taken World Corp's message to heart. They truly believed we were the evil ones.

I saw one man leaning across the seat of the cruiser, speaking into the radio. I aimed and shot. The window shattered, and the man slumped back. He was still alive. I had hit him in the shoulder. He was speaking frantically into the radio — calling in backup — and I shot again. This time, he fell down across the console, a pained expression frozen on his face.

As I watched him die, a cold vise gripped my chest, squeezing the life out of me. My limbs were all pins and needles. I was just a floating pair of lungs and a cold, dead heart.

He had been one of the men in blue overalls — just an ordinary person, probably with a family back at the commune. He hadn't truly been part of this — he had just been caught in the crosshairs.

And I had killed him.

I lowered my rifle. Suddenly I was looking at the others in a different light. We were the ones dressed in black. We were the ones shooting innocent people.

Not for the first time, I had the horrible feeling that I was doing something very wrong.

It didn't matter. The battle continued to rage around me, and after a while, the shots quieted. Most of the officers and workers lay dead and dying in the gravel. Half a dozen workers had fled.

I looked around to our forces. A few of our men were wounded, and a small group was clustered around another man.

My heart sank. The PMC had come here expecting only a horde of mindless carriers, yet we'd lost one of our own already.

Looking grim, Godfrey shuffled over to the officers lying by the cruisers. I tore my eyes away, not wanting to watch him put any of the men out of their misery.

I set my rifle down in the gravel. My hands were shaking too badly to hold it.

"Haven! Haven!"

I turned around. One of our men — a man whose name I did not recall — was limping over to me with one hand over the wound in his leg.

"What should we do with Jimmy?"

"I —"

"He's bad. They shot him in the stomach. He needs help."

My mind was racing. *This man was dying, and the others were looking to me to save him?*

I opened my mouth, unsure what I was going to say,

The Last Uprising

when Roman stepped between us and put a hand on the man's shoulder.

"Joe, take him straight into the kitchen. Amory will see what he can do."

Amory heard his name and wheeled around.

I was relieved to see he was still in one piece, but I regretted the position he was in. I knew he didn't feel ready to treat serious wounds like this — and maybe he wasn't — but he was the closest we had to a doctor on the farm.

He nodded at Roman and squeezed my arm as he passed.

Roman ducked down to eye level with me, looking anxious. "Haven, what's the plan?"

"What do you mean?"

"That worker you shot . . . he was in the middle of radioing for backup, wasn't he?"

"It looked like it."

"Well, we need to be ready in case they send another wave. We won't have the advantage of surprise this time."

I nodded. "You're right. Tell the men —"

"I'm not telling the men anything. They take orders from you and Amory."

"Why me?"

Roman shrugged. "They see you as a leader. You escaped Aryus and came back to our side when no one thought you would. You need me, I'm here to help. But I'm not a general."

I stared at him. He was looking at me with those tough grizzly eyes, but for the first time since I'd known him, it wasn't a predatory stare. Roman was addressing me with respect.

I cleared my throat, wishing my voice sounded deeper, steadier. "All right, guys. We don't know for sure, but it looked like one of them might have had a chance to call for backup."

The rebels let out a collective groan, and my stomach twisted uncomfortably like a wet rag. They were angry and tired, and I somehow had to get them ready to fight again.

"Listen . . ." I said, gathering my resolve and letting it build in my chest until it was a low buzz of adrenaline. "That was *nothing*. There were only a handful of officers, and they weren't prepared to find us here. We won't be facing a few officers and unarmed workers next time. The PMC means business. It's up to us to defend this place and send them crawling back north."

There was a murmur of approval from the crowd.

"If you're wounded, get into the kitchen and form a line. Amory will treat the most serious wounds first."

A few of the rebels limped off, clutching bleeding shoulders, arms, and legs. Some leaned on their comrades, while others toughed it out on their own, eyes watering.

As Godfrey brushed past me on his way back inside, I grabbed his sleeve.

"What should we do?" I asked. "We need a defense plan for when they send reinforcements."

Godfrey wiped the sweat off his face and sighed irritably, as though I'd asked him to take out the trash, not save a few dozen rebels' lives.

"I say we try Greyson's plan," Roman offered. "Head them off on the road if we can."

"Sure, that sounds good," Godfrey grunted, shifting his gaze away.

I stepped in front of him to block him from going inside.

The Last Uprising

"Wait. If you have a better plan . . ."

"Go with whatever plan you want. It doesn't really matter."

I stared at him, so sure I'd misheard. "What?"

Godfrey glanced around to make sure no one else was around and opened his mouth reluctantly. "It doesn't really matter what we do. Ida sent us here to be a distraction, not to single-handedly end this war."

Somewhere inside me, the frayed thread of my nerves snapped. "*What?*"

"You heard me."

"A distraction?"

"Uh-huh. What? Did you think she would send a bunch of kids to win a revolution?"

"So we're just supposed to die?" I spluttered. "Just . . . accept that we're . . . what? A sacrifice?"

"You can accept or not accept whatever you want," said Godfrey in a low voice. "It doesn't change the facts."

"Ida wouldn't do that," said Roman. "We can fight this."

"All I'm saying is that it was never her intention for us to win."

"Well, screw that," Roman snapped. "I'm not just going to lay down and —" He looked at me, his eyebrows scrunched together in determination. "I'm taking the others to set up a blockade down the road. That will give us cover and keep them from driving in."

I nodded numbly. I was still in complete shock. Then I turned to Godfrey, looking up into his rough, terrifying face with as much resolve as I could muster. "Listen. I'm *in* this. You have to be in this, too. These are people's lives we're talking about. Yes, we might die, but I would much rather live. Is that understood?"

Maybe I imagined it, but I thought I saw a ghost of a smile flit across Godfrey's weathered mouth.

That just stoked my anger. "Do something!" I snapped, pushing him hard in the chest.

Godfrey gave me a long hard look before limping off across the yard.

I felt a little sick as I watched the others move the trucks, revealing big pools of blood in the gravel. The bodies were still there, and I didn't know what we were going to do with them.

Roman rounded up a group of the beefier-looking rebels and disappeared down the road with a few of the vehicles for a blockade. That left us with fifteen able-bodied men and women to defend the farm if they should fail.

Had Ida sent us here on a suicide mission? I wouldn't accept that.

While the rest of our forces reloaded, I ran inside the house to help Amory patch up some of the less serious wounds.

Greyson was already working on one of the men, and Logan had busied herself at the stove boiling water, sanitizing instruments, and collecting fresh supplies. She hated blood, and it was beyond her ability to patch up a bleeding man without throwing up.

I fell in with Greyson and applied pressure to one man's wound. He had taken a bullet to the shoulder. His face was roughly the shade of cooked oatmeal, but I knew it was mostly due to shock rather than blood loss.

Amory was bent over the man on the table — the one called Jimmy with a bullet in his stomach. I watched him reach up with a bloody gloved hand to dab the perspiration gathering on his forehead, and I felt very sorry for him — sorry he had this responsibility.

Godfrey's words were still ringing in my ears, but I pushed the sick feeling down.

We were *not* a sacrifice.

Amory's strong back muscles were working furiously, but then he stopped again, and his back buckled. Suddenly, he swore loudly and slammed his fist on the table, making his instruments rattle.

He stood there for a moment, breathing heavily, before turning to face us. "I need help moving him." Amory's voice was thick. "He's gone."

Greyson got up, and the two of them carried the dead man outside.

I wanted to reach out for Amory — comfort him — but there was no time. I was scrubbing the kitchen table with soap and water, and Amory was already helping me heave the next man onto the table.

For a moment, I just watched him speak to the injured man. His voice was as even and controlled as ever, but his jaw was stiff, and those beautiful, intense gray eyes were tight with grief.

He turned to grab a fresh pair of gloves, practically colliding with me. Before I could stop myself — before I could think — I reached out and threaded my fingers through his.

For the briefest moment, his eyes met mine, and the corners of his mouth lifted into a tired smile. His trembling hand stilled.

Then the back door banged open, and Godfrey strode in. "They're back."

The rebels had used the cruisers and trucks to form a

barricade to shield us from the immediate line of fire. They'd parked the trucks bumper to bumper and piled cinder blocks, lumber, and debris from the PMC's construction site on top of and underneath the vehicles. It wasn't an impenetrable wall, but it was better than nothing.

I was relieved to see that the bodies had been moved away, though the blood-soaked gravel was a stark reminder of what had transpired. There were little bumps of gravel here and there, as though someone had tried to cover up the blood but had given up.

The sound of gunshots coming from up the road cracked through the air and bounced off the trees, giving them an almost organic tenor. My heart was pounding, and I nervously checked my pockets for extra ammunition.

There was just Roman and fifteen of our men between the PMC and the rest of us. If they couldn't hold them off, it would just be us.

We had no backup — no one to pick up our guns and rally. I didn't even have anyone who would miss me if we all died today, I realized. We would be permanently erased — a welcome void on the PMC's radar.

Suddenly, the gunshots drew closer. Two rebels standing next to me hit the deck, and I ducked behind the wall of cinder blocks, too. I scrambled to find a good vantage point to shoot, but I still didn't know where the shots were coming from.

Then I saw officers through the cracks in the cinder blocks. Some were emerging from the woods, and some were running toward us from the driveway.

Their bullets ricocheted off the trucks, but the vibrations still shook my chest. I aimed at one officer standing out in the open and fired. He yelled and collapsed on the ground. I'd just hit his leg.

The Last Uprising

I shot again, and he went still.

A bullet flew over my head and shattered the window of the truck I was hiding behind. Glass rained down on my back, and I scooted away carefully. Logan had made herself a hole in the cinder blocks and was in full sniper position.

With the stability from the ground, she was able to take out three men in a row, but the rest of our forces weren't doing as well. A couple had caught stray bullets, and the rest weren't great shots. We had wounded and killed a few officers, but more were encroaching, spilling out like dozens of white spiders.

As more officers appeared, any hope I had felt was absorbed by a black hole of cold resolve. Roman would never have let so many through — not unless the PMC had overwhelmed our forces. It was just us now.

Amory reappeared from the house covered in blood and threw himself behind the barricade to help us take down the officers.

Part of me felt glad he was here by my side, but the other part wanted to die hoping he might have survived.

Death. That was what I was preparing for now. I refused to be taken — refused to have my mind hijacked again.

Officers were approaching slowly and cautiously, taking their time. They had us outnumbered, and they knew it.

I pointed my gun at one who was crouching in the trees. He was inching along, trying to get a good shot around the side of our barricade. I had him in my scope, but then he stepped forward, his toe nudging one of the tiny bumps in the gravel.

An explosion erupted, throwing the officer backward in a burst of flames. I threw myself onto the ground closer to the house, and the wave of heat washed over my back.

Stars erupted behind my eyelids, and three more booms echoed through the trees in quick succession. They shook the ground and rattled my ribcage. My body was a tuning fork, quaking from the blast.

I heard yells and screams and saw fire licking at the ground as I forced my eyes open. The smoke burned, and tears streamed down my face. Everything was blurred and shaking.

I didn't know who was hit. There were bodies everywhere.

Amory.

I crawled on my hands and knees through the smoke until my hands found his arm. *Please don't be dead.*

"Haven!"

"Are you hit?"

"I'm . . . I'm all right," he coughed. "You?"

"I'm — yeah," I choked, gagging on the acrid air.

I opened my eyes cautiously, squinting through the smoke. Amory was lying back against the truck, but he was still in one piece. I threw an arm around him and looked around.

The PMC officers were gone, languishing in the flames. The smell of burning hair, flesh, and polyester stung my nostrils, and Logan bent over and retched on the ground.

The explosions hadn't touched our people, who were poking their heads out over the trucks hopefully. No one seemed nearly as shocked as I was.

Then Godfrey strode out from behind the house wearing an expression of grim satisfaction.

"Why didn't *we* think of that?" Logan coughed.

Explosives were his specialty. I wasn't sure how I'd forgotten, though now I realized he'd been building homemade bombs in the shed.

I glanced up toward the road, searching for more officers, but I didn't see anyone. The relief I felt mixed with horror and dread. I didn't want to be here when the fire died down, but we needed to know if any officers had survived.

Worst of all, we needed to know if any of *our* men had survived.

Roman.

I didn't know if he was dead or alive, and the thought gave me a surprisingly strong ache in my gut.

Roman and I had never been friends exactly, but he was part of the family I'd known on the farm since the very beginning. He and I had formed a grudging acceptance of one another, and if he was gone, I knew I would feel the loss.

We all waited, holding our breath. We didn't dare approach the road in case the remaining PMC had planned an ambush.

But then I heard footsteps. Everyone's heads snapped toward the drive, listening to the scuff of boots on gravel.

Just as the smoke began to clear, I could see half a dozen figures rounding the bend. Several rebels raised their weapons, preparing to shoot down the officers who had survived.

But I didn't see the flash of PMC whites. The figures were too close to be shadows. They were clad in rebel black.

Walking in the middle, toting an AK-47 from a dead officer in each hand, was Roman.

Chapter Twenty

It took the rest of the day to clear up the devastation from the attack. Several men in Roman's squad had been killed, and many more were wounded. I served as Amory's assistant, removing bullets, cleaning and bandaging wounds, and getting the injured rebels settled in bed.

When the bodies had been cleared away and all the wounded had been treated, I gathered around the kitchen table with the others.

With five wounded men sprawled out on cots in the living room, we couldn't conduct our meeting in secret, but we needed to plan our next move.

"Any thoughts?" grumbled Roman.

Logan rolled her eyes. The joy of finding Roman alive had worn off slightly since the attack.

Sitting there nursing a black eye from the butt of an officer's gun and scrapes from asphalt all down his arms, Roman looked even more smug than usual. I could tell he was incredibly pleased with himself — even if he had let half the PMC's forces slip past the blockade.

"We can't take another attack like that," said Greyson. "Not with twenty men."

Godfrey let out a breath of frustration. "Not with *fifty* men. The PMC won't underestimate us again, and we can't recruit fast enough. But maybe we can distract the PMC by taking out some of their supply lines in the Midwest."

"Like Rulon did, you mean?" Amory asked sharply.

"No . . ." Godfrey cracked a shifty grin. "Not entirely. I've got more style."

"Oh, we know," muttered Greyson.

"I say we do it," said Logan. "If it buys us more time."

"If we could just hold them off until summer . . ."

"What's that going to do?" snapped Roman. "A few months —"

Godfrey shut him down with a single look. "It'll give us time to recruit and train a proper army. This group of misfits may have gotten us through on sheer piss and luck, but we won't survive a second wave of attacks. Mark my words."

"He's right," said Logan. "We need to double down on our forces. I don't care if we have to bring twenty more people into this house."

"The men we have need more training," said Amory. "We're hemorrhaging ammunition, and we won't be able to afford missing shots at the PMC next time."

I nodded, feeling slightly numb at the prospect of rallying for another fight. I was starting to think I wasn't cut out for this — the constant fear and having so many people's lives in our hands.

I knew we needed to gather the survivors for a debriefing. Even though we'd managed to overpower the PMC, it didn't feel like a victory. We'd lost too many people.

Logan and Greyson gathered our forces in the front yard, and I scanned the waiting crowd nervously. They looked tired but satisfied. Perhaps they were more resilient than I gave them credit for. They certainly looked stronger than I felt. I was overwhelmed.

I nudged Amory, hoping he would understand. I couldn't

The Last Uprising

address these men. I could barely stand.

He looked surprised but gave me a tender look and stepped up beside me. He cleared his throat, and the crowd fell silent.

"You all fought well today," he said. "Truly. You pulled together to operate as a unit and performed much better than we could have ever expected. We managed to subdue the enemy . . . but the PMC will return."

He paused. His hands were hanging loosely at his sides, and he kept clenching and unclenching his fists, which were shaking slightly.

"We lost six men and women today, and more are wounded."

Amory swallowed, and I took a long, deep breath, hoping it could somehow steady him, too.

"We feel their loss, but we cannot dwell on the people we failed to save."

Amory's voice caught, and for a moment, I wondered if he would continue. There was a line in his brow, and I ached to take his face in my hands and smooth it out.

"We have to think about what we have left to lose — everything we have that's still worth fighting for." His eyes flickered to me, and my breath hitched. "Personally, I still have a lot I'm fighting for. And even if your loved ones are gone, we all still have our freedom. That alone is worth saving."

He took a deep breath, and for a moment, everyone just stared.

There was a long pause as Amory's words sank in, and I wondered briefly if the others would give up and abandon us — if they were too scared to continue.

But then a man in the back clapped his hands together,

and the sound spread to the front until it was a solid wave of noise. People cheered and nodded as though Amory had spoken to them personally, and I had the strong urge to wrap my arms around him.

He stood there, looking slightly awkward from the attention but stronger than ever. His eyes were blazing with a bravery I loved, and his shoulders were strong despite the weight he carried.

He glanced over at me, unsmiling, holding me frozen in place with the intensity of those eyes. There was a question and a challenge dancing behind his stormy gaze, but I couldn't move or even speak.

Right then, our thoughts were connected, and I knew that Amory was what *I* was fighting for.

After Greyson and I helped the wounded men to bed, we walked back to the house together in the dark. The farm was strangely peaceful after all the shooting and the bombs, but it felt as though we were waiting for something much worse.

We didn't know what was coming next — only that something *would* come. The PMC would not allow us much peace now that we had killed nearly thirty of their soldiers.

"What was with you and Amory today?" asked Greyson out of nowhere.

I stopped walking, taken aback. "What?"

Had we been that obvious?

"After his speech. I thought you two were going to start making out right in front of everyone." He grinned. "I mean, don't get me wrong. It was a good speech, but —"

I shoved him lightly. "Shut up."

My face was burning up, and I was glad it was dark.

Greyson grinned. "I'm just saying . . . it's about time. We

need you guys to make up, actually. Amory's been a little off his game since . . ."

"Since?"

Greyson stopped, letting out an exasperated sigh. "Since you were taken. You should have seen him those two months you were gone. He was . . . he was tough to be around."

I stared at Greyson. The way he said "you were gone" made it sound as if I'd been on vacation or something.

He seemed to sense my unease, because he started walking again, raking an agitated hand through his curly hair. I was glad to see it was fanning out around his face again now that his prison crew cut had grown out.

"Then you came back, but nothing was the same. It was like you were a stranger to him."

When Greyson turned to look at me, his dark eyes were serious. "He's not been able to trust many people in his life, and you . . . you were important to him." He smiled. "You're *still* important to him."

I bit back a grin.

Greyson was lecturing me about Amory. My best friend was defending my . . .

Well, Amory wasn't "my" anything. The thought gave me a twinge of sadness.

"I know," I said. "I'm not the same . . . but I *am* myself again. As much as that's possible."

"Are you?" It wasn't an accusatory question. Greyson seemed happy to hear me say it.

"I think so. I remember most things."

"And Amory? Do you still like him?"

I swallowed twice, trying to keep the words down, but they burst from my lips as though they'd been trying to get out. "I think I might love him."

Greyson's eyebrows shot up to his hairline. "You *love* him?"

I nodded. "I think I have for a while."

We paused, me giving Greyson time to process. I wasn't sure why I'd told him instead of Logan — maybe because Greyson tended to be reflective rather than reactive when he got news like this.

"You have to put things right with Amory," he said. "Soon."

"Put things right?"

Greyson raised an eyebrow. "We all saw you two fight, Haven. There's so much . . . tension between you two. Amory's still licking his wounds. He feels rejected."

"Rejected? I didn't *remember* him."

He laughed. "That's almost worse. Trust me, when you go from being something to nothing to a girl, it makes you . . ." He trailed off, searching for words. "Just know that Amory's handled it really well considering everything."

"I know he has," I said, a little defensively. "And he could never be *nothing* . . . not to me."

"Put yourself in his position — having to keep you at arm's length when he used to be able to . . . do whatever he wanted with you."

I felt my face growing hot. I wanted to extricate myself from this conversation as quickly as possible. Greyson was my best friend, but we didn't talk about this stuff.

In the past, Greyson might have been the better choice for Amory-related advice since he had a more objective

The Last Uprising

opinion than Logan. But now that he knew Amory, he was invested, too. Amory was his friend as much as I was.

We had reached the house, and a lone figure overlooking the field came into view. It was hard to tell in the light of the small fire he'd made, but it had to be Amory.

"Go," said Greyson. I could tell he was smirking. "Not doing anything is much harder than telling him."

"I just . . . I feel like I've waited too long," I said.

Greyson laughed. "You wouldn't say that if you'd heard the things he tells me. He loves you, Haven. He'd wait forever. But you shouldn't make him." His expression became grave. "I don't think we *have* forever."

Before he could stop me — before he could feel awkward or diffuse his own kindness — I threw my arms around his neck and squeezed. "Thanks," I muttered into his jacket.

"Don't mention it."

I pulled away, and he backed toward the house. Even as his features disappeared into the darkness, I knew he was wearing a mischievous grin.

It felt like a long walk out to where Amory was sitting. It struck me as odd that he was out here, considering it was Roman's night on duty. Maybe Roman was out there somewhere, stalking through the trees looking for carriers, and Amory had just come out because he couldn't sleep. His rifle was lying in the grass next to him, as though he didn't think he'd be needing it.

"Hey," I whispered, not wanting to startle him by sneaking up behind him.

He jumped, spinning around, and his face fell into a relieved expression when he saw it was me.

"Sorry. I didn't mean to scare you."

But he was already smiling, truly happy to see me. Maybe I was imagining it, but there seemed to be a slight droop of sadness to his eyes. He looked tired and beaten down — as though he were muddling through everything himself, despite his encouraging speech.

"No. I'm glad you're here," he said, spreading out his blanket so I could sit down.

It was freezing, but he was only wearing cargo pants and the same black rebel jacket he'd worn in camp. His gloveless hands were shoved into his pockets, yet I was shivering in the huge down coat I'd found in Ida's closet.

I certainly wasn't dressed for any romantic declarations. I'd at least changed out of my bloody clothes, but I hadn't even combed my hair that day. It was lying all over my shoulders in unruly waves.

Meanwhile, he was sitting there, eyes smoldering, looking annoyingly sexy despite everything that had happened.

"I'm sorry about today," I said. "I know how hard it must be to watch someone die like that and . . . and not be able to do anything."

Amory took a long, labored breath. "The thing is . . . I knew he was going to die. But I still feel like I failed."

"No!" I said, taken aback. "You didn't fail. You were *amazing* today."

Amory looked at me, and I was a little embarrassed by the naked passion in my voice.

I cleared my throat. "You did so much better than me. I couldn't have rallied the men like you did. Earlier I . . . I just choked. I'm not cut out for this."

"What?" Amory leaned in closer. "Yes, you are." He sighed. "You're a leader, Haven. That's one of the reasons I pulled you into the ring to fight that night. I wanted them to see how *good* you are. These guys . . . they're guys' guys. They needed to see that you could hold your own before they'd let you send them into battle."

"That's not *really* why you fought me," I reminded him.

His mouth lifted into a crooked smile, and I could have sworn I saw him blush. He dug the heel of his boot into the grass, looking anywhere but at me. "It's one of the reasons."

I knew then I couldn't fight all the feelings that were rushing through me. It wasn't just that Amory believed in me and trusted me when no one else did; Amory and I understood each other better than anyone.

Only he knew what I had gone through when I was Aryus's prisoner, and he loved me despite how messed up I had been. He was steady and kind and courageous.

"You know . . . most of the time, I only feel like I can do this because of you," I whispered.

His eyebrows lifted in surprise, and I could see his jaw muscle twitching. His features looked all the more pronounced in the dancing firelight, and I could tell he was holding something back — as though he didn't want to hope for anything.

My face was growing hot, but I kept talking. "You're the only one who believes in me most of the time."

He shook his head. "You keep us going. Everybody knows that."

"But you're the one who keeps *me* going. You're what I'm fighting for in all this."

Before I could stop myself, I had reached out and touched his leg.

He took in a big breath of air, his whole body stiffening, and I pulled it away.

The Last Uprising

I cursed myself silently. I was throwing this all at him too quickly. I couldn't expect to push him away for weeks and then ask him to come back to me.

"Amory, I . . . I'm sorry. I'm so sorry for everything I put you through when you got me out. I'm sorry you thought I remembered everyone but you. I know you think I was pretending, but those memories of us were buried so deep. I think World Corp must have done something to make sure I forgot you."

He sighed, shoulders sagging. I realized he thought I was breaking things off for good. He thought I would never remember.

"These past couple weeks, though . . . my memories have been coming back."

Amory looked up, and that hope was back in his eyes.

"You remember me?" he croaked. "Us?"

I nodded. "Yes. But I didn't even have to remember. I started to like you all over again — not because of the memories of what we used to be like, but because of how we are now."

He looked away. He opened his mouth, but no words came out. I knew he was processing that thought, but I couldn't stop or I would lose my nerve.

"I know I pushed you away. I know it might be too late to pick up where we left off, but . . ."

"Too late?" he gasped. "Are you kidding?" He shook his head, shoving down his own hope. "Please don't say this for my benefit, Haven. I don't want to be without you, but I don't want you to feel obligated to be with me — even if you have remembered."

"You told me to tell you what I want. I *want* to be with you," I whispered, feeling my face grow hot as I said it. "If you want me."

His eyes met mine, and he looked as though I'd gone crazy. "Haven . . . I've *always* wanted you."

Those words sent my heart into overdrive. That was all I needed to hear. It was all I'd ever needed.

Amory reached for me, and I met him halfway.

His hand wound around the back of my head, and he threaded his fingers through my hair. In one rough motion, he pulled me into him and crushed me against his chest. I could feel his heart beating hard beneath his shirt.

His hands fumbled up my sides, ghosting all over me until they reached my face. When his lips met mine, the heat spread from my mouth all the way through my body.

I shuddered with pleasure. Every emotion — every delight — came flooding back in a wave of feeling.

Kissing Amory felt familiar in the most wonderful way, but also new.

His mouth was hot and inviting, and I drank him in as though I'd been thirsting for weeks.

He kissed me with such desperation and longing it scared me. It was as though he couldn't get enough, and the way he gripped me made me think he was worried I would disappear. I returned his kiss with fervor, tasting and touching every bit of him I could reach. I was drunk — absolutely ridiculous in how much I wanted him.

His arm wrapped around my waist, and he rocked me back onto the soft blanket. My hair fanned out behind me, and I shivered a little as his chest grazed mine.

"Oh, god I've missed you," he groaned into my mouth.

"You have no idea."

That seemed to send him into a frenzy, and I felt his

hands shake a little as they trailed up my sides, burrowing under my shirt. I let him feel his way up my ribs and around my back, and he pulled me closer to him.

I grabbed his belt loops, pulling him down and dragging him against me. I wanted to crawl inside him and never leave.

Amory's kiss had fire behind it, and I thought we might both combust if I didn't rip off his clothes right there in the yard. He seemed to sense this, and after a moment, his kisses burned out a little and became playful and full of joy.

We were back, and after today's victory, it felt as though we had all the time in the world. We had earned this happiness a hundred times over, and now that we were together again, I felt invincible.

I didn't know how long we kissed, but it wasn't long enough. We finally pulled apart, but Amory's hands were still wrapped around me, one behind my knee and one tangled in my hair. I lay back into his arms, and he held me tightly.

"I've wanted to do that for so long," he breathed.

"Me, too."

"Why didn't you tell me you'd started to remember?"

"I didn't want to get your hopes up . . . in case I never remembered how I felt about you. But it didn't even matter." I smiled. "I would have done that anyway. I couldn't hold it in anymore."

"I've been holding in a lot of things," he said with a laugh.

My face prickled with heat, but my stomach squirmed with pleasure.

He must have sensed my awkwardness, because he whispered, "We'll take it slow." A laugh rumbled through his chest. "Even if we couldn't quite manage it just now. I know it must be a lot to get used to."

It's not, I thought.

"When did the headaches go away for you?" I mused. I could hardly remember the last time I'd felt that shooting pain in the back of my head.

Amory shrugged. "The last bad one I remember happened when you were about to go into the Infinity Building."

I strained my memory to recall the time he was talking about, but that was still a little fuzzy. I remembered Greyson warning me about Mariah, Amory's goodbye, Mariah handing us over to Aryus, and Jared falling onto the marble floor. He had tried to save me, and they had shot him.

"I still get a twinge now and then," Amory continued. "Like this morning . . . any time I'm really afraid."

"That's not when I get them," I said slowly. "For me, they came on whenever the feelings started coming back . . . like when Greyson talked me out of leaving and when you —" I broke off. I did not like remembering myself that way.

The time I had not known whose side I was really on had been dark and lonely. And even though I knew it was the result of World Corp's brainwashing, I hated myself for it.

"So . . . when you're feeling *love?*" Amory asked. The way he said the last word sounded very shy, as though he were testing the waters.

I smiled. "Love . . . sometimes. Or compassion, I guess."

"That fits."

I shifted in his arms so I could look at him. "Why do you say that?"

"I remember when Sector X fell. The way you felt about killing a carrier . . . I thought that guilt would end you. Even though you thought their humanity was gone, you still hated ending a life."

I thought hard for a moment, trying to remember any of my World Corp training, but that time in my life was a completely blank canvas. I had no idea what simulations they had put me through or how they had tried to tamper with my brain.

"The pain is the result of conditioning, right?" I asked.

"I suppose. That's why they made adjustments to your CID. As your pain tolerance grew —"

"But why would we have a ghost response to two very different things? Unless they were trying to prevent us from feeling those emotions while we were there. Fear and compassion . . . those are completely unrelated."

"Not necessarily. Maybe that's what they saw as our greatest weakness. That's what they needed to stamp out of us before we would make good soldiers."

I jerked my head around to look at him.

Amory was staring straight ahead, his face pale. He had figured it out, and it sent a horrible chill throughout my whole body. World Corp's manipulation had been more sophisticated than I had thought if they could condition us to reject compassion, reject fear, reject love — whatever threatened their mission.

Just then, I heard an inhuman wail, followed by a strangled, familiar scream. It had come from the edge of the woods around the field.

Roman.

Chapter Twenty-One

Amory and I jumped to our feet. Another howl drifted across the field, but Roman was silent.

My mind conjured up horrible images of carriers tackling him to the ground and tearing into his flesh. No carrier had ever gotten the jump on Roman. He had to be outnumbered.

The horde we had feared had been laying low, just waiting for the right opportunity to attack.

"Go back to the house!" Amory yelled, taking off toward the woods. "Get help!"

I shook my head, not wanting him to go out there on his own. But I hadn't brought a weapon with me. How stupid.

I turned and ran to the barn, pounding on the huge sliding door. "Get up!" I yelled. "Carriers!"

I kept banging on the door until a woman with frizzy hair answered my frantic knocks. I ducked inside and felt desperately along the walls for the old rifles Logan always stowed there. Nothing.

A few rebels had awoken and were grumbling. Others had gotten out of bed in alarm to see what the commotion was about. When somebody lit a lantern, I saw a dull knife lying on the shop table.

"Get the others at the main house!" I yelled at them. "Roman's been attacked!"

I shrugged off Ida's coat, stuck the knife in my boot, and

The Last Uprising

tore out of the barn in the direction Amory had run.

It was an inky starless night — impossible to see anything around me. I worried I would collide with someone — or something — in the dark, but there was nothing but open field between me and the woods.

I was sure everyone within a mile could hear my feet crashing through the flattened skeletons of corn stalks, but I didn't care. I was ready to fight.

As I drew closer to the tree line, I heard low growls and scuffling. Then there was a wounded cry like the sound a dog might make. *Carriers.*

My blood pounded in my veins, and all thoughts and emotions seemed disconnected from my body. I wasn't afraid of anything anymore. For a moment, all I could see was the cloud of my own breath, but then I caught movement in the trees.

As I entered the woods, the growls of the carriers grew more pronounced. More than a dozen were lumbering toward me in the shadows, but when I squinted, I could see them everywhere: carriers clawing out of the ravine, carriers lurking under trees, carriers staggering around looking for food.

Roman *had* stumbled upon the horde, though I knew it hadn't been there yesterday. Panic gripped my entire body. Amory was nowhere to be seen.

I staggered backward, away from the swarming carriers, and my boots connected with a body. I tripped, and the body groaned.

"Roman?"

No answer.

He was slumped beneath a tree, limp and motionless. I squinted at the ground, where three dead carriers were sprawled in the dirt.

"Amory," I hissed, not daring to shout.

Something moved on the other side of the tree, and then Amory was at my shoulder. "Haven!" he whispered, brushing his hand up my arm. "Why did you come alone?"

"The others are on their way. Where did all these carriers come from?"

He shook his head. "The Burns family must have turned and joined up with what was left of that horde."

My stomach clenched remembering Hank and Denny, their foul breath and rotten teeth.

"Haven, get Roman out of here. Now!"

I bent down and felt my way up to Roman's face, but my hands were covered in blood before they reached it.

"Oh my god. Amory . . ."

"I know," he growled. "They must have jumped him. That's as far as he got before he collapsed. Get him out of here."

I didn't want to leave Amory, but Roman was in bad shape. If I didn't get him back to the house and stop the bleeding, he would die.

Ignoring the warm blood seeping through his sweatshirt, I reached under his arms and pulled. I waited for him to struggle into a standing position, but he was practically unconscious — dead weight. My back screamed in protest, but I couldn't shift him.

"He's weak," I whispered. My voice was shaking. "I can't carry him. You'll have to take him."

"I won't leave you."

"Can you shoot them?"

The Last Uprising

Amory shook his head. "Once I start, they're going to swarm. I can't take them down fast enough."

I tried to breathe, but my lungs wouldn't expand fully. We didn't have a choice. We had to fight them.

I bent down to retrieve the dull knife from my boot and straightened up, standing shoulder to shoulder with Amory.

"Let's go."

We flew at the mob of carriers, and I sank my knife into the deteriorating flesh of the nearest one's shoulder, just missing her heart. She cried out in agony, and I yanked the knife out for another go.

The carrier threw out an arm, catching me across the face with such force that I staggered backward. I squinted to find my aim, but the moon was behind the clouds, and there was no light.

This time I aimed lower, and I felt the satisfying gush of hot blood as my blade sank into the carrier's stomach. I yanked it out and elbowed her in the side of the head, and she collapsed onto the ground.

It wasn't a clean death, but I would take it.

Another was lumbering toward me, and Amory was struggling with two others just feet away. He was fast, and his knife was sharp, but these carriers were early stage four. Their humanity was gone, and they still had their strength.

The second carrier I stabbed put up a fight, lashing out at me with his fists. I avoided one hit purely on instinct, but the other connected with the side of my jaw. I staggered backward, feeling my face starting to swell, and bumped into another carrier that was wandering over to Roman.

I turned around and shoved my blade into her back, hoping I had somehow pierced her heart. The carrier cried like a banshee, and I pulled the knife out.

It was much more difficult to work with a dull blade, and my shoulder was already aching from the extra force required for each stab.

Footsteps were approaching from the field, and relief washed over me. There seemed to be a never-ending supply of carriers emerging from the woods, and we would need all the help we could get.

Logan and Greyson stood at the front of the crowd. Logan looked ready for a fight with an enormous knife in each hand, but her face paled when she saw the great swarm of carriers lurching through the woods. We had to contain them before they reached the farm.

I swiped at one carrier that was encroaching on my space, and he stumbled backward, bumping into a tree.

"Greyson!" I yelled. "Help Amory take Roman back to the house. He's losing too much blood."

Greyson gave a shaky nod, but Amory looked over his shoulder with reluctance.

"I won't leave you," he growled, slicing his knife viciously across the throat of a carrier he was holding in a headlock.

"You have to. You're the only one who can help him."

The look on his face said he knew I was right, and I jumped between him and the next carrier so he could get to Roman.

Roman groaned loudly as Amory and Greyson pulled him up, and they staggered back up toward the house with his huge form hanging between them.

In the few minutes I hadn't been paying attention, the carriers seemed to have multiplied. I took up the knife Greyson had left and plunged it into the heart of the nearest one. The strangled scream echoed through the trees, and a heavy shudder rumbled through my gut and out my throat.

The other rebels were fighting like cavemen with whatever they had found up at the farm. They were taking out carriers with the sharp edges of shovels, rakes — even a hammer. It didn't look effective, but their blows had so much force and fury that they were mowing them down faster than I could with a proper weapon. It was a grisly scene, and more than once, I felt the overwhelming urge to vomit as blood spattered my face.

After a few moments, tunnel vision set in. My shoulder was burning, I was out of breath, and my hair was plastered to my forehead with a sticky mixture of sweat and blood.

Suddenly I felt a shooting pain in the back of my neck, and cold fear clamped down on my chest as something heavy overtook me.

Teeth — human teeth — were digging into my skin.

I lashed out, trying to buck the carrier off me, but his teeth were embedded in the flesh between my neck and shoulder. His nose was buried in my hair, sniffing the dinner I had cooked. He was starving.

I jabbed my elbow back as hard as I could, and the carrier jerked away. But in the moment I'd been incapacitated, another carrier had stumbled up to me. I swiped my knife at him, but the carrier behind me wrapped his arms around my neck, pulling me backward and latching on to my shoulder. I felt the flesh being ripped from the bone, and I screamed.

I stomped down on the carrier's instep and jabbed my elbow back again with as much force as I could muster, skewering the second carrier in the abdomen. He fell away, but the carrier behind me stumbled, pulling me down with him.

Pain shot up my side as I hit the ground, and the carrier who'd bitten me clambered onto my chest. His putrid breath filled my mouth, and I gagged. I squinted desperately at his mouth. It was covered in blood — my blood — but I

The Last Uprising

couldn't see any sores.

The bites in my neck and shoulder burned as the carrier pushed me into the ground, grinding dirt and dead leaves into the wound. I swung out my fist, knocking him back for a moment, and I felt along the ground for my knife.

Nothing.

The other carrier was elbowing in, trying to fight off the one that had me pinned. I swung at him as hard as I could, but my hit was weak. I was exhausted and defeated, with no fight left in me.

The first carrier was hunkering down, the saliva coating his bloodied mouth in dripping ropes. His yellow eyes flashed across my face. He knew I was weak, and he could smell the food.

I was going to die, and he would still go hungry.

Then, in a daze, I watched the flash of a blade glide across the carrier's throat. A disembodied boot swung out of nowhere and connected with his skull. The same knife dispatched the second carrier, and he collapsed beside me in a pile of rags and rotten flesh.

I looked up for my savior and saw a rugged-looking man wielding a switchblade. He was pale with a shaved head and a dark, dirty scruff obscuring his expression. He held out an arm, and I took it, eyeing the sleeve of tattoos snaking up under his leather jacket.

"Thank you," I gasped, trying to catch my breath.

"Thought I would give you a hand," he muttered. "You were doing pretty good on your own, but once they had you on the ground, I knew you was a goner. You're too small."

"You're right." I tried to stand up straight, but the pain from my wounds was spreading down my back.

"Did that one have the sores yet?"

I shook my head, knowing my savior was referring to the carrier that had bitten me. "I don't think so. It could have been a lot worse."

He gave me an approving look and turned back to the knot of carriers shuffling toward us.

As he turned his head, I saw the patch of scarred, destroyed flesh twisting up the back of his neck like a braid. This man was no stranger to carriers.

I grabbed my knife and turned to the two lumbering toward me. My near-death experience seemed to have given me a second wind, because I went at the carriers with renewed ferocity.

But the other rebels' energy was flagging. We needed to end this fight soon or retreat to the farmhouse to shoot them long range.

I stabbed another carrier and felt the warm blood soak my sleeve. I shoved her aside and watched her twitching on the ground. I shuddered, wishing it wasn't real, but this was my life now — fighting hand and tooth just to stay alive.

I was so engrossed in the fight that I hardly noticed the eerie silence spreading through the trees. The horde was nearly exterminated, and a few stray carriers had retreated into the woods. I didn't like to let them go, but we were all exhausted.

I dropped the bloody knife on the ground and realized my hands were shaking. I couldn't fight anymore.

Chapter Twenty-Two

As I watched the man who had saved me dispatch the last carrier, I had the sudden urge to cry. The moon had emerged from behind the clouds, bathing the forest in a sickly silver light.

Dead carriers were piled on the forest floor, blood soaking into the soil. One had taken a few bites of me with him to the grave, and another might have killed Roman. The cost of World Corp's manipulation was high.

"Oh my god, Haven," gasped Logan. "We have to get Amory to look at you."

I shrugged, feeling strangely detached from the wound seeping blood into my shirt.

"How did it happen?"

I shook my head, unnerved that the carrier had snuck up on me. "I don't know . . . but he saved me."

I nodded at the man with the tattoos and scars who was cleaning his blade on a dead carrier's tattered rags.

"Switch?"

"Is that his name?"

She eyed him warily. "No. But that's what they all call him. He fought off a horde all on his own during the riots with nothing but a switchblade. He's a scary guy."

"He saved me."

Logan let it drop but dragged me through the trees back

toward the house. The lights were on in the main house but not in the kitchen. I quickened my pace, wondering why Amory wasn't treating Roman.

My neck was throbbing, but I ignored it. I couldn't think about that now.

I didn't think the carrier that bit me had been stage five, but truthfully, I couldn't be sure. I tried not to imagine the virus ripping through my veins, turning me into one of them. I'd watched Logan grow weaker and lose herself a little more each day, and I didn't think I could handle what she'd gone through. It was too horrible to consider.

We came through the back door. I looked around, but there was no sign of Amory, Greyson, or Roman anywhere.

We took the stairs two at a time. Roman's door was cracked, and light flickered from inside. I knocked softly and pushed the door open.

Roman was lying in bed with his eyes closed, looking deathly pale. If he hadn't been so badly injured, the sight of his huge overgrown body in the tiny twin bed might have been comical, but he had bandages wrapped around his neck and chest, and he was breathing slowly and painstakingly. Three long parallel scratches ran down the left side of his face, the blood caking like muddy tire tracks.

Amory was hovered over him, injecting a clear liquid into his beefy arm.

Greyson was standing in the corner, looking at Roman with a grim expression.

"How is he?" I asked. I was startled by the scratchy croak that came out of my mouth.

"He's —" Greyson glanced in our direction and then did a double take. "Holy shit. What happened to you?"

I shook my head. "I'm fine. How is he?"

Greyson's eyes were huge. "Not good."

Amory looked up. The relief that flashed across his face was quickly replaced by panic when he saw me from the side.

"Oh my god! Haven!"

He crossed the room in two strides and put his hands on my arms. He turned me gently to examine the bites, and I heard Greyson and Logan's collective intake of breath.

"What stage was it?" Amory asked. His normally strong voice was shaking, and that sent a wave of fear through me.

"I-I don't know. He didn't have the sores yet."

Amory squeezed my arms and stared into my eyes. "Are you sure?"

"Yes," I lied.

"Go up to my room," he said. "I'll be up in a minute to clean those."

I nodded and took one last glance at Roman lying in bed. Despite his size, he looked so weak and fragile, strangely exposed with us watching him sleep. If he were conscious, he would scowl and tell us all to go to hell.

I left the room, and the full pain of my injuries washed over me. The blood had started to dry around the wound, leaving it crusty and stiff.

Instead of heading for Amory's room, I went into the bathroom and started to fill the tub. I undressed, peeling my ruined shirt away from the destroyed flesh and nearly screaming as a piece of skin ripped away.

I put a shaky leg in the tub and sank into the lukewarm water. I dunked my head in first, washing away the spattered blood and sweat. I cleaned away the grime until my wounds stung in protest and the bathwater had turned an ugly shade of gray.

Once I was clean, I wrapped myself in one of Ida's fluffy towels and climbed the small flight of steps to Amory's room.

Someone had already lit a lamp, and there was a small pile of clothing on the bed. I smiled at Logan's thoughtfulness and quickly pulled on the clean sweatpants. I finger-combed my hair and sank down onto Amory's bed, covering myself with a towel so Amory could clean my wound.

There was a soft knock at the door, and Amory opened it slowly. He looked nervous, though I didn't know why.

"Do you think Roman's going to make it?" I asked in a scratchy voice.

Amory sighed. "It's hard to say. His wounds are serious, but he's one tough son of a bitch."

I tried to smile, but it was hard to ignore the exhaustion and hopelessness in his voice.

"The truth is," he continued, "I just don't think there's anything more I can do for him."

Amory sank down next to me on the bed and ripped open a package of bandages.

"I think you've done more than was fair to ask of you," I said.

"I just feel like I'm letting everybody down. If this had happened a few years later, I'd know a lot more, and I'd be able to *do* more."

He looked up to examine the wound and sucked in a stream of air through his teeth.

"Is it bad?"

"I really hate those things," he said, avoiding the question. I was startled by the note of anger in his voice. Usually when Amory was treating a wound, he was calm and collected.

"I have to disinfect this," he murmured. His warm breath tickled the exposed skin of my back. "It'll sting."

I smiled at Amory in doctor mode, but it quickly disappeared as the alcohol burned. Amory worked quickly to clean the torn flesh from the top of my spine across my shoulder blade and up the back of my neck.

"I'm going to look like Switch," I said. "He has a horrible scar all along the back of his neck."

"The scar won't be that bad," Amory murmured, a smile playing on his lips again. "Not after a while."

He was quiet for a beat. "I'll still find you beautiful."

My stomach did a funny little backflip. Turning to look at him over my shoulder, I saw he looked a little flustered. He was staring at the spot where my shoulders met my spine, and I watched his eyes trail down to the small of my back.

"Are you checking me out?"

Amory's eyes snapped up to mine, heat rushing to his temples. "Uh . . . yeah, I guess I was."

I turned slightly, ignoring the painful tug of my wound, and found his lips with mine. He returned the kiss with fervor and then pulled away with a smile.

"Sorry. That was really unprofessional," he whispered.

"Good."

He grinned, and I saw a little shiver pass through him as he tried to return to the task at hand, spreading ointment over my wound and pressing a bandage into place.

"Haven?" He pulled a piece of hair back over my shoulder and sighed. "I'm sorry I wasn't there. I'm sorry I didn't stop this."

"It wasn't your fault," I whispered, pulling the towel a little tighter against the chill of the room. "I wasn't paying attention."

His eyes were burning with regret. "It won't happen again. I'll be there next time."

"You don't have to be," I said gently. "I can handle myself."

He grinned. "I know you can. But I still want to be there to watch your back."

Now that I was looking straight at him, I felt extremely exposed under the towel. Amory seemed to be thinking along the same lines, because he was looking at me as though he was about to jump off a cliff into rough, icy water.

Then there was a knock on the door, and I heard Greyson's muffled voice. "Hey! We've got company. You'll want to see this!"

Amory was on his feet before I could draw a breath, and he shuffled uncomfortably with his back to me until I was dressed and ready to go.

When we came down into the kitchen, a handful of wounded rebels were already seated around the table waiting their turn. A chill whipped down the hallway, carrying the smell of a storm. The front door was ajar.

It was raining outside, and a dark silhouette was superimposed against the bright headlights of three trucks idling in the driveway. I squinted. There was something oddly familiar about the figure.

She was short and slumped, draped in a heavy coat. Then she threw back her hood, revealing a mane of short, spiky black hair.

"Well don't just stand there," she growled to Amory, who looked just as shocked as I felt.

I would have recognized that gruff voice anywhere. "Shriver!" I yelped, utterly bewildered.

She pushed her way past Amory, a reluctant smile playing on her lips. "Go put some food on. We're starving."

"You have *no* idea how happy I am to see you," Amory murmured.

"Well, I can see why."

She'd just laid eyes on the motley crew of rebels slumped around the kitchen table.

Outside, I could see more figures moving around in the darkness, and Godfrey strode in after Shriver, looking more excited than I'd ever seen him.

"Godfrey," said Amory. "Who else is here?"

Godfrey broke into a crooked grin that was oddly disconcerting. "The rebels who are going to save our asses."

"What the hell happened?" asked Shriver, tilting one man's head back to examine the bite on his neck.

"There's been a carrier attack."

Shriver rolled her eyes. "And here I was hoping the PMC had suddenly started biting people instead of shooting them. I *mean*, how did it get so out of hand?"

Amory looked at her blankly. "There were too many of them."

"The hordes are growing in strength," growled Godfrey. "I don't know how, food being as scarce as it is. But they must be running together so they can overwhelm human settlements. It's the only way they haven't starved."

Logan materialized at the foot of the stairs. "Shriver?"

Shriver wheeled around, tossing her head like an angry grizzly bear.

"It's so good to see you," Logan gushed, running up to take her coat.

"Why do people only say that when somebody's bleeding?" Shriver muttered irritably. "None of you look too torn up," she said to the men. "Now beat it. People gotta eat. Can't have you bleeding all over the place."

"I'll . . . clean them up in the living room," said Amory.

Shriver nodded as though this were obvious and began scooting the kitchen table toward the dining room. Clearly she had been here before.

Did all the rebels know Ida? I wondered.

We'd barely pushed the tables together when the front door opened again. Greyson and Amory were busy, so Logan stayed in the kitchen to help me throw together something for the travelers to eat.

Logan didn't really know what she was doing, so she just hovered beside the stove, talking in a fast, excited whisper and sliding between me and the counter whenever she thought I wasn't listening. Once I had some canned green beans and a huge vat of chili warming on the stove, she seemed to grow bored with my inattention and breezed off to the dining room to talk to Shriver.

I peered out into the hallway and watched the travelers coming in. Most of them were in their thirties, but many had bushy beards like Godfrey's and darkly tanned faces, as though they'd spent a lot of time battling the elements. They were dressed in snow boots and heavy coats.

I grabbed Greyson's arm as he passed and pulled him into the kitchen.

"Who are these people?" I hissed.

"Rebels . . . from out west," he said in a hushed voice. "Ida must have sent them."

"Really?" My heart pounded harder in my chest. "So it's true? There really are settlements out there?"

"Seems so," he whispered. He was trying to sound offhand, but I could detect the hope and yearning in his voice.

"What sector are they from?"

Greyson shook his head. "There are no sectors. It's all off the grid out there for a few hundred miles."

"No," I said, feeling skeptical. "They can't have held off the PMC for a year and a half."

"They have."

I shot him a disbelieving look.

The rebels were already gathered around the elongated table, squeezing in extra chairs around the corners. They were talking in loud voices and laughing, looking more carefree than any of the rebels I'd seen before.

When they saw me carrying in the food, their voices seemed to rise with excitement. One of the youngest rebels with unruly honey-colored hair saw me struggling and ran over to help maneuver the heavy pot of chili.

"Need some help?" he yelled over the din.

I smiled gratefully. "You have no idea."

He grinned back, showing all his teeth, which stood out against his windburned lips and ruddy face. "Yeah. Godfrey said you had back-to-back PMC attacks and just got hit by a major horde of carriers."

I nodded, thinking of Roman lying unconscious upstairs. He had no idea what was going on or who was here, and I felt a little leap of affection in the pit of my stomach when I thought about how he would disapprove of the westerners' cheeriness.

The Last Uprising

"How many of you were killed?"

"Too many," I sighed.

"I'm sorry." He nodded at the bandage around the back of my neck. "The carriers give you that?"

I nodded. "The one that bit me was early stage, though. I should be fine."

"You're a lot tougher than you look." He sounded genuinely impressed.

I shrugged. "It's not the first time a carrier took a bite out of me."

He smiled, but it did not quite meet his eyes this time. I was getting the awkward feeling that maybe he really did think I was insane.

"Do you have carriers out in sector . . .?" I trailed off, testing to see if he would supply the name of the sector or confirm what Greyson had said.

"Oh, we're still independent of the New Republic," he corrected. "Our settlement spans all across the Rocky Mountains."

"Seriously?"

He nodded. "It's the worst kind of guerrilla warfare for the PMC. They aren't good in the mountains. We've managed to secure a pretty sizable territory."

"All the way to the West Coast?"

He shook his head. "Colorado. Most of the Southwest was hit really hard during the outbreak. Utah and Nevada are no man's land. Illegals and carriers are dying off. SoCal is a different story . . . total carrier country."

I smiled at his use of slang I hadn't heard since before the Collapse.

The Last Uprising

"We do a little better where we're at near Estes Park. The carriers have natural predators up there."

"What?" I asked, feeling dense.

"Mountain lions . . . black bears." He made a gnashing motion with his teeth as though he were ripping the skin off a turkey leg.

Soon all the newcomers had been served, and I returned the pot to the kitchen and settled in the empty chair between Shriver and Godfrey.

"Where did you come from?" I asked Shriver.

"Ida asked me to go west after everybody scattered. She knew we would need to rally every rebel from east to west to take down World Corp. She had a lot of contacts in the Rockies, so I headed out there first."

I nodded and noticed that Shriver was searching my face.

"So . . . are you back with us?" Shriver asked, the edge in her voice cutting through her careful wording. "Last time I saw you . . . you were a poster child for World Corp's brainwashing experiments."

I grinned. Shriver didn't sugarcoat anything — a trait I'd always appreciated. "Yeah. Most of my memories are back. I'm all in."

"I'm glad to hear it. Being around Amory at camp was like attending your own fucking funeral: awkward and depressing."

I laughed, wanting to change the subject. I didn't like thinking about the way Amory must have felt after my rescue. "What's it like out west?" I asked.

"Quiet. They're worried about surviving the winter, not fighting off the PMC. They also don't get the big hordes like we do out here."

"And these guys are the only ones who wanted to come?"

"Oh, no. More are on their way. We're supposed to radio that we made it safely." She smirked. "You all must have done a number on the PMC. We had to avoid about ten checkpoints between here and Kansas City alone."

"Really?"

She nodded. "You've made them nervous. But they won't be away long. They're just waiting until they have a good tactical strategy. They want to avoid drawing the fight north at all costs."

"Why?"

"They're losing control of the communes. Between that and trying to contain the carrier breach, well . . . they've got their hands full."

"I still can't believe Rulon did that."

"Believe it. Soon there won't be a corner of North America that's safe. Joke's on World Corp, though. Aryus didn't plan for these massive hordes to form. He thought the carriers would die off too quickly for that, but since the mutation, they're living a lot longer. They're adapting — latching on to one another for survival."

That was a horrific thought. I wasn't sure our forces could handle another horde like the one we'd just faced.

There was a rustle behind me, and Amory appeared at my shoulder. He smelled like antiseptic and latex gloves, which made me worry instantly.

"Hey, Shriver," he said. "Do you think you could give me a hand? It's Roman. He's hurt pretty bad."

"It's been a while since someone's asked me for a second opinion," said Shriver, getting up excitedly and following Amory out of the room.

I turned to Godfrey, a little confused.

"She's talking about Doctor Carson," he muttered. "Real piece of work from CU Denver."

I looked down the table to the man Godfrey was nodding at. His dark hair was turning gray around the temples, receding into his skull, and he wore round glasses that gave him a buggy, know-it-all look.

There was something off about the way he was speaking across the table and eating — never gesturing or moving his mouth more than was necessary, as though he were listening and forming judgments rather than engaging.

"He's known for his carrier research — premigration and postmigration. But he's also the resident doctor in his camp. It's put Shriver's nose a little out of joint."

I grinned in amusement at the thought of Shriver sharing her med tent with anyone, but I was more than a little curious about the doctor.

"Godfrey says you do carrier research, Doctor Carson," I said, drawing his attention from across the table.

He turned, the corners of his mouth rising incrementally. "Indeed I do. I've got less to work with than before, and I'm afraid the facilities aren't what they were before the Collapse."

"Well . . . we've got plenty of dead ones in the woods if you want to take a look." I couldn't quite keep the bite of challenge out of my voice. There was something off about this man.

The doctor looked a little startled at this turn in the conversation, but his expression cleared smoothly.

"It doesn't help me much to study expired subjects," he said, taking a tiny bite of his food. "I've been focusing my research on the amygdala and the temporal lobe of the carriers. We've seen this type of aggressive, antisocial behavior in psychopaths, though not to this extent."

"Really?" I asked, feeling a little sick.

Dr. Carson nodded. "We've also been studying how the virus's progression breaks down the body. We're concerned that the stages don't accurately reflect the . . . *severity* of the virus."

I glanced at Logan, who had stopped talking to Greyson and was listening with interest.

"How do you mean?" I asked. "I don't think anyone would argue the virus isn't severe."

He laughed — a cold, hollow sound that made my insides curdle. "True. But once carriers reach stage four, there really isn't anything we can do. Even if you could stop the virus from eating away at their brain, the nerve damage, decline in organ function, and the deterioration of their spinal cord would be irreparable. We have not seen any survive longer than twenty-four days once they reach this stage."

"And what about the stage-three carriers?"

Doctor Carson grimaced. "That's where we find the stages to be misleading. World Corp believes the virus can be completely cured as long as it is administered before stage three."

"And you disagree?" I said, my eyes darting to Logan.

"Yes. Based on the data we've gathered, a stage-three carrier that receives the cure will live, but the effects of the virus are irreversible. In my opinion, it's misleading to say the virus can be cured. Of course, I haven't had the opportunity to study anyone who's received the cure, but judging by the brain activity I've observed in earlier-stage individuals, a return to healthy brain function would never be possible."

The Last Uprising

"So what then?" snapped Logan from across the table. "What happens to them?"

Doctor Carson regarded her with curiosity but did not seem put off by her poisonous tone.

"Based on what I've seen . . . I would say any individuals who have been infected with the virus for any reasonable period of time would suffer permanently from violent, unpredictable, antisocial behavior. They would be, in essence, a sociopath."

Logan slammed her hand down on the table, causing the silverware to rattle. "A sociopath?"

"Yes," said the doctor. His expression was neutral. Clearly, he had no idea what he had just stepped in. The others sitting around them had lowered their voices to listen.

"That's enough," said Greyson through gritted teeth, who was glaring down the table at Doctor Carson.

"I'm sorry . . . I hope I have not caused offense. I myself have had many friends succumb to the virus —"

"And have any of them *lived*?" snarled Logan. "Have they lived with this psychopathy?"

"Not yet," he said, his expression turning grim.

"Well, I have. I was infected, and I've had the cure."

"I'm sorry to hear that," said the doctor. He didn't look abashed. He was staring at Logan with a mixture of interest and amusement. "It is possible, I suppose, with the appropriate rehabilitation . . ."

Logan's mouth curled in disgust. "Rehabilitation?"

"With your permission, I'd love to study your case to see how you progress in your transition back to functional behavior. With many convicted felons, we've seen great progress being made —"

The Last Uprising

"Shut up," growled Greyson. "She isn't a convict. And you aren't *studying* her. You know nothing about her or people like her who've survived. You said it yourself."

"I do apologize," said the doctor. But his tone and expression did not match his words.

Greyson wasn't having it. "Maybe you should worry a little less about hypotheses and a little more about what's going on in the real world," he said nastily.

Logan wasn't glaring at the doctor anymore. She was looking at Greyson with a mixture of gratitude and adoration.

Doctor Carson was studying Greyson with fresh interest. "You were in the prisons in Sector X, weren't you?"

"Oh, I suppose you've studied actual felons, too, then?"

The doctor threw Greyson his empty smile. "No. I just noticed the way you keep glancing at the doors out of this room. Having this many people in such a small space makes you nervous. You've grown your hair out too long, which leads me to think you're thumbing your nose at the PMC. You're undocumented, but your HALLO burns say you've had a run-in with World Corp. Now, I can only think of one reason why you would have escaped undocumented."

Greyson opened his mouth to retort, but the rest of the rebels were getting up to leave. They would be bunking at the Hoopers' farm and returning in the morning to discuss our strategy against the PMC.

Doctor Carson shot us another cold smile and followed his companions back out into the hall.

"I should go see if the others need help moving the dead carriers," said Greyson, getting up to leave.

I could tell by the tone of his voice that he was trying to rein in his temper and regain his dignity. I knew Greyson was ashamed of the time he'd spent in Chaddock — if for no other reason than the fact that he would be considered a felon for as long as World Corp was in power.

Logan followed him out into the hallway and grabbed his arm — a bold move, considering he was trying to shrug off the fury the doctor had unleashed.

Greyson turned to her, looking wounded and surprised. Logan's face was as light as I'd seen it since I'd been rescued. She leaned in to Greyson, who looked momentarily speechless, and planted a soft kiss on his lips.

"Thank you," she whispered, reaching up on her tiptoes to touch her forehead to his.

Greyson's mouth fell open, and his eyes grew round and warm.

Then, without another word, Logan pulled away and darted toward the stairs, leaving Greyson standing frozen in the hallway.

Chapter Twenty-Three

After a while, the chatter in the dining room died down, and the house was filled with the sleepy yawns of rebels from the west saying goodbye and heading out to the Hoopers' farm.

I trudged up the stairs, feeling the weight of my muscles with every step. My entire body ached, but with the rebels' arrival, all I noticed was the relief I felt.

Roman's door was closed, and all the other rooms were silent. As tired as my body felt, I was too wired to sleep.

Moving lightly so my feet would not disturb the squeaky floorboards, I crept up to the second landing, where I saw the light emanating from the bottom of Amory's door. My heart sped up a little, though I didn't know why I was so anxious.

I ran a shaky hand through my hair, conscious that I hadn't really paid any attention to my appearance in the entire time Amory and I had known each other. Back in Columbia, I would have obsessed over my clothes and hair and makeup every time I saw him. My mind would have raced, always searching for the right thing to say, and I would have kicked myself any time my voice hitched in his presence.

But it wasn't like that with Amory. The words tumbled out of me before I could think, and I talked to him as easily as anyone I'd ever known. I might wish I looked cuter around him most of the time, but the attraction between us was deeper than that.

Things that had felt so important then seemed insignificant now.

I knocked softly, my skin tingling from the memory of our last encounter. The door opened immediately, but he looked surprised to see me. A huge grin spread over his face as he stepped back to let me in.

"How are you feeling?" he asked.

Was I imagining it, or did he look nervous, too?

"Much better," I said, trying to suppress the slight waver in my voice.

"Good. I might have Shriver take a look at you when she's done examining Roman."

"Not tonight," I said, trying to sound casual. "I feel fine. Besides . . . I'm in good hands."

Amory swallowed, a light flush creeping up the back of his cheeks. "I don't know . . ." He flashed a grin. "I think I've got a blind spot when it comes to you."

He sank down on his bed, which seemed so small for someone his size. He watched my every move as I paced around his room. I was finding it difficult to breathe normally.

"Come over here," he murmured. It wasn't a command. It was a request that left him exposed.

I crossed the room and sank onto the soft red blanket, remembering how I had awoken here, in this room, when I had first arrived at the farm and passed out from hunger and blood loss.

Amory's arms came around me, one behind my back and one under my knees. With surprising ease, he pulled me onto his lap and leaned back against the wall. I let my weight fall against his chest, savoring the warmth and strength of his arms.

He was staring at me through half-lidded eyes, his contentment barely masking the intensity simmering beneath the surface.

There was so much going on behind those bright gray eyes it made me nervous: hunger and longing, but also fear. My gut ached remembering how I had rejected him just a few weeks ago when I had not remembered who I was.

"It's hard to believe, isn't it?" he whispered.

"What?"

"Everything that's happened since I first brought you up here."

I nodded. "I remember. You trusted me when no one else did. I wouldn't be here if it weren't for you."

"Neither would I," he reminded me, fingers absently brushing the back of his neck, where he had a scar identical to mine.

I shivered. I didn't want to think about those horrible three weeks he'd been World Corp's prisoner any more than I wanted to remember my own imprisonment.

"I'm so *glad* I met you," he said.

The swell of emotion this simple statement triggered surprised me. Amory wasn't talking about me saving him anymore, at least not in that way.

"Me, too."

"These last few weeks have nearly killed me, Haven." He shook his head. "The way you looked at me like I was the enemy . . . It made me feel like I didn't even know who I was anymore."

His words were painful, but there was no accusation in

his tone. He was just sharing the burden, something we'd done since the beginning.

"I didn't know who I was either."

He shook his head. "You don't understand." He took a deep breath. "Before I met you . . . I *hated* myself sometimes. I hated that I was a coward, and I hated what I had almost become . . . with the PMC."

My chest hurt, and I longed to throw my arms around him and kiss him until he forgot.

Amory smiled absently. "You changed all that. You made me feel strong . . . like I finally had something to fight for."

A muscle was working in his jaw, and he was avoiding my gaze now. "When you were taken, I didn't just feel empty because I love you . . . I felt empty because the one person in the world who thought I was worth something was gone."

The wind was knocked out of me so fast it felt as though I'd fallen flat on my back.

He'd said he *loved* me. He'd said it once before, when we'd been traveling north to steal the cure, but it had been in a rush of anger and passion. This felt different.

Amory seemed to realize the weight of what he'd said, too. He looked up at me, his eyes burning, deadly serious. "I love you, Haven."

Those words — I could listen to them on repeat all day long.

"Amory . . . I've *always* loved you. Even when I didn't remember, it was in there. I never stopped."

That was it. That was all he had to hear. Suddenly he was two Amorys: the Amory I only saw when we were alone together — raw and exposed — and the fighter who attacked everything with ferocity.

His hand came around my neck, lifting my hair off my back and cupping my head gently. His arm tightened around my waist, pulling me against him.

His lips were burning with hunger when they found mine, and I returned the kiss just as fervently.

He groaned softly — almost too low to hear — and brought me closer. Even in his eagerness, his hands were gentle and moved expertly around my injuries as though he'd memorized every cut and bruise.

Amory's long, dexterous fingers tangled in my hair, and I felt the roughness of his calluses graze my ear. Before I knew what I had done, I had swung my legs over to straddle his hips.

He wasn't resting against the wall anymore. He was leaning into me — urgent and alert — his hands gripping my hips. I tried to savor the taste of him on my tongue, but it made me too hungry.

I wanted more of this, and it felt as though he was going to be yanked away. *Who knew how much time we had?*

I pulled in to close the paper-thin breath of air between us, nearly sending us both crashing off the edge of the bed.

Amory steadied me, his hands trailing dangerously high up my waist, feeling every inch of me and sending a shiver down my spine. I bit his lip, wanting more, and his fingers slipped beneath my shirt, caressing the bare skin at the small of my back.

I reached down to the hem of my shirt, pulled it over my head, and looked down. For a second, Amory looked genuinely nervous, but the look faded as quickly as it had come, melting into adoration as he studied me.

I raised an eyebrow. He took the hint and yanked off his own shirt. My mouth fell open a little as I took in his perfectly sculpted torso. His skin held traces of a tan, his smooth chest narrowing at his hips and fading into cut abdominals. Not for the first time, I noticed that the muscles of his shoulders and arms were lean and feral, formed from lifting and building and fighting.

I let my fingers ghost over his bare shoulders, pulling him closer so I could study him. His arms wrapped around me, eyes locked on mine.

He didn't break eye contact, but his fingers drifted to the clasp of my bra. He was breathing a little faster than normal. I felt every rise and fall of his chest through my whole body. The clasp released, and he pulled it away, his eyes blazing.

I touched his jaw, feeling the barely-there stubble beneath my finger.

"You're beautiful."

"So are you."

Then his arms came around me. He rested his forehead against mine, pressing our chests together, and for five whole seconds, I couldn't breathe.

Gently, he lowered me onto his pillow, and I had the opportunity to study the subtle lines where his abs trailed into the hem of his pants — teasing me.

"Is this okay?" he asked, brushing my hair to the side.

I nodded, trying to find my voice. "Yes."

It wasn't okay. It was perfect.

His lips met mine again, and I gave into it fully. He returned my energy with everything he had, and my fingers fumbled at his belt, hands shaking. A small chuckle rumbled through him.

"Never thought you'd be ripping *my* clothes off," he whispered.

I let out a low growl that surprised me and finally

managed to undo the belt and the top button of his pants. Now that I had, my heart was pounding. There was no going back now — and I didn't want to — but I was a little scared. I wondered if things would change between us.

Then Amory's lips teased my collarbone, leaving a light trail of hot kisses down my chest and my stomach. His lips grazed my waistband, and my nerves evaporated.

The rest of our clothes seemed to disappear, though I had no recollection of how it happened, and I could finally run my hands over all of him. The rest of his body was even more wonderful than I could have imagined — all hard lines and soft touches. I caught him staring at me with the same reverence.

"You're incredible," he breathed, his hand trailing up my leg.

I couldn't wait any longer — couldn't breathe.

"Amory. I want you."

That did it. He dove in for another kiss so fierce, I physically ached. Our hands were everywhere.

When we came together, I felt the warmth of him in every part of my body. It trailed up from my abdomen and spread from my arms to my cheeks. My blood ran hot, pounding in my veins.

It was slow and tender at first, and then it shifted into something deeper — a desperate, passionate need.

When it was over, he collapsed against my chest. I matched his breaths until I couldn't tell where he ended and I began, running my fingers through his dark hair.

Chapter Twenty-Four

Three days later, the sound of breaking glass made me topple out of Amory's bed in a panic.

I was foggy and disoriented from sleep, and it took me a moment to remember where I was. Amory was gone.

Then a strangled yell drifted up through the walls — the unmistakable sound of pain. I ran into the hallway and down to the main landing toward the source of the noise.

Roman's door was ajar, and he was sitting bolt upright in bed. His face was drained of color, and Shriver was staring openmouthed, a glass bottle lying in shards at her feet.

"Shriver? What is it?"

She shook her head, completely speechless, and then removed her glasses and looked at the floor. "Come see for yourself."

Carefully avoiding the broken glass, I stepped into the room to look at Roman. He was still bedridden and as pale as cauliflower, but at least he was awake. I didn't know what had startled Shriver until I crossed to the bed and met his wary gaze.

Then I saw it.

The morning light was filtering through the bedroom window, throwing a column of light across one side of his face.

His eyes were bloodshot and puffy, and a faint yellow

The Last Uprising

tinge was spreading around the edges of his irises.

I did a double take, scanning his body for signs that his eyes betrayed him, but there was no denying it. His skin was glistening with cold sweat, and the wounds blotting his neck and chest were oozing yellow with infection.

Shriver had a hand to her mouth, so I said what she couldn't. "You're turning."

Roman stared at me, but he didn't look surprised. If anything, he was leveling a challenge with his gaze. It was as though he were saying, *Come closer. You scared?*

But then something happened that I had not been expecting. His face fell, and for the first time since I'd known him, Roman looked genuinely helpless. "How long do I have?"

I shook my head, turning to Shriver. "I don't know."

"It depends on how quickly the virus progresses," she murmured.

"How long did it take Logan to get like that?" he snapped.

I swallowed, remembering how bad she had looked when he'd seen her at the Infinity Building. When I didn't answer right away, Roman seized another bottle off the bedside table and hurled it across the room.

"How long?" he demanded.

I didn't even flinch. The broken glass was nothing.

"Three days," said Logan.

I whipped around to look at her. She was standing in the doorway wearing rolled boxer shorts and an oversized T-shirt, her hair piled on top of her head in a messy bun. Her expression was controlled, but I could feel the weight of her misery in the air.

The Last Uprising

"Shit," Roman muttered, his voice hitching.

"Everyone's different," I said, looking to Shriver for help. "And Logan was off and on. One moment she would be okay . . . and then the next . . ."

"I'd be delirious," she finished.

Roman's shoulders sagged in defeat. "Well, I hope I can at least take out a few more PMC before I go."

I swallowed, thinking that was an odd thing to say. But we all knew that Logan would have gone full carrier if we hadn't gotten our hands on the cure at World Corp, and it was unlikely we would be able to make the trip for Roman before it was too late.

"You should go," I said suddenly, not wanting him to die. "Take a few men and drive north now. If you go before it gets any worse, you might be able to break in, kill Aryus, and take the cure."

Even as I said it, I knew it was hopeless, but I felt desperate — out of control. I couldn't lose anyone else.

"I'll go with you," said Logan quietly.

"I'm not going anywhere," he growled.

I looked up in surprise.

"The fight is here. I'm going to kill as many PMC as I can before . . . before I change."

I bent my head, willing my eyes to stop stinging. Roman was going to die, and he'd already accepted it.

"I'll go . . . get something to clean this up," said Shriver.

I followed her out into the hallway to give Roman and Logan some time alone. Only she truly understood what he was going through.

"How long does he have?" I whispered as soon as the

door closed. "Really?"

Shriver hesitated. "With Logan, the virus progressed very quickly due to her weakened immune system. But with Roman . . . it could work more slowly."

I let out a long, ragged breath. "How long, Shriver?"

"Two months at most. After that, the brain damage will be too much to bring him back. He might live, but he won't ever be the same. Within a week, he'll be stage two, like Mariah was. He'll be violent, unpredictable, angry . . ."

"So basically himself," I muttered.

"I should warn you," said Shriver. "The longer this goes on, the harder it's going to get. Logan was nothing. When he's stage two, it will be a constant up and down. One day you might think he's getting better, and the next hour he won't know you." She sighed. "They never get better — not on their own."

"I know," I said, thinking of my mother. Shriver didn't have to tell me how hard it was to watch someone go through that.

I could hear the soft murmur of Logan's voice through the door, and I felt a surge of affection for her unflagging strength. If anyone could help Roman come to terms with his fate without fear or self-pity, it was Logan.

I paced back and forth in her room, finally sinking down on her bed to wait for her. I expected her to return soon, but she and Roman had been talking longer than I'd ever heard Roman speak.

I couldn't sit there soaking in despair any longer. I needed to talk to Amory.

I knew he wasn't in his room or downstairs. Since Roman had been injured, Amory had taken over his nighttime carrier patrol in the woods, scanning the perimeter like a ghost in the trees.

I pulled on my boots and a coat and tiptoed down the stairs, careful not to rouse the rebels who were sprawled out on the living room couch and across the floor. These days, every available room was overflowing with people.

Slipping out the front door, I felt the cool morning dew stick to my skin, chilling me instantly. The sun was rising over the field, illuminating the glistening frost on the ground.

As I stepped off the porch, I stopped dead in my tracks.

Amory was standing in the middle of the front yard, looking at me as though he'd been waiting.

Something was wrong. He was standing stiffly, as though he had a rifle jabbed in his back, and he watched me cross the lawn to him with an uncharacteristic amount of dread.

I noticed the way his eyes shifted all around him and back to me, trying to warn me about something.

"Amory?"

He didn't answer. His mouth was a tight line, and the planes of his face stood out like cut granite. There were bruises spreading along his jawline and over his eye, as though he'd been struck repeatedly with the butt of a gun.

When I was ten paces away, everything became clear. There was a bulky black vest strapped to Amory's chest with wires snaking out around the pockets. Explosives.

On his chest, where there should have been an insignia, was a digital display. It was counting down from nine and a half minutes.

"Oh my god!" I whispered. "Amory?"

I stepped toward him, examining the vest. I wanted to reach out to hold him, but I was afraid to touch anything. I took a shaky breath, and Amory's eyes widened. He was holding back his fear.

"What —"

"Go get Godfrey," he murmured. "Quietly."

I nodded and stumbled back inside, nearly falling over my own feet. I tripped up the stairs and staggered onto the landing.

I tried Godfrey's door, but it was locked. I pounded on it, hot tears rushing to my eyes. A heavy lump in my throat was choking me, but I refused to cry.

"Haven?" Logan stuck her head out into the hall. "What is it?"

I didn't answer but continued to pound on Godfrey's door.

Finally I heard footsteps shuffling across the floorboards, and the door creaked open. He appeared, disheveled from sleep, irritation etched across his face.

"It's Amory. You have to come," I gasped.

He didn't need any further explanation. He followed me downstairs and out the door.

When he saw Amory standing in the yard with the explosives strapped to his chest, his face drained of color. He strode toward him, examining the vest with rapid precision.

Amory held out his arm. In his hand was a crumpled piece of white paper. When Godfrey took it, the silvery PMC insignia caught my eye. I read over Godfrey's shoulder.

Your destruction is imminent. A small sacrifice can be your salvation, or all will meet their end.

"So if you let me die, they'll save the rest," croaked Amory.

The Last Uprising

"No," Godfrey muttered. "They don't mean you." He gestured at Amory. "They mean this whole damn place."

Godfrey turned to me. "I don't want to risk moving him. Go in and evacuate the others. Bring them around the back, and keep them in the fields."

I nodded, threw Amory one last look — hoping it conveyed everything I wanted to say to him — and tore off toward the house.

I banged on the front door and saw Logan standing in the makeshift office. By the tears swimming in her eyes, I knew she had seen everything from Roman's window.

"Haven, what do we —" she blubbered.

I clamped a hand over her mouth to stop her blurting it out and pulled her into the corner. "Get everyone out the back. I don't want to start a panic, but keep them in the fields."

"Why Amory?"

I shook my head. "We don't know. Just do it."

Logan nodded, and I released her. I jumped over all the people sprawled around the living room and went out the back door toward the guest house.

I knocked frantically on the front door until someone came. It was Shriver.

"Get everyone out," I breathed.

"What?" She was grumpy and muddled with fatigue.

"Evacuate everyone. Take them out into the field, and don't go through the front yard. Do you understand?"

She nodded, looking stricken, and I left her without another word. I sprinted toward the barn and banged on the sliding door. The animals shifted nervously, as though they could smell the fear in my blood.

The Last Uprising

The door slid open, and I was startled to see Switch staring down at me.

"We need to get everyone out," I breathed. "Evacuate to the fields."

Switch turned his head, the carrier scars stretching along the back of his neck. "You heard her! Out!"

I heard the mumbles of people stirring from sleep.

"Get out!" yelled Switch. "Head to the field. Let's go! Move it!"

People were scrambling up in the loft now, pulling on pants and coats and jumping down to the ground level.

"Stay out of the front yard," I yelled over the noise.

The rebels poured out of the barn, and I was relieved to see the last stragglers leaving the main house and the rest running around the back of the guest house.

I crossed the yard to where Godfrey and Amory still stood. Godfrey's large, dirty hands were moving deftly around the front of the vest, cutting with a tiny pair of sheers that looked as though they belonged to a toiletry kit.

He severed a wire, and I forgot how to breathe.

The display flickered, and the red countdown disappeared.

I let out a sigh of relief, but then the ground shuddered, and the farm erupted in a burst of flames.

Chapter Twenty-Five

A great wave of heat and pressure knocked me to the ground. It hit me with such force that the air left my lungs and I struggled to breathe.

My head hit something solid. There was another explosion. Then another.

I gasped for breath and peeled my eyes open, but everything was a blur of bright light.

I was dizzy and disoriented, and there was a strange ringing in my ears. Only one thought flashed through my head, and it was louder than anything else: *Amory.*

I looked around, my body still glued to the cold, wet grass. My vision began to adjust, and I realized the brightness was not my eyes playing tricks on me. We were surrounded by a ring of fire. The barn was in flames, and the blaze was spreading to the nearby trees. The main house was still standing, but the guest house was fully engulfed. People lay sprawled everywhere, but some were bleeding and screaming.

I struggled to my feet, my head still ringing. Someone next to me was trying to stand.

It was Amory.

A funny sob got caught in my throat when I saw him. He was alive. I wanted to grab him and squeeze him as hard as I could.

Amory tugged off the vest and threw it into the grass

The Last Uprising

several yards away, meeting my gaze with a look of relief and bewilderment.

Godfrey was already standing again, his face to the sky as if he expected the fire to rain down from the clouds.

Then I saw what he saw. There was a white helicopter heading toward us with the PMC's insignia emblazoned on the side. My heart thudded against my ribcage. They had learned from their last ground assault. Now they were coming for us from the air.

"Drop your weapon!" said a voice over the speaker of the helicopter. "Drop your weapon, and place your hands on your head."

I realized Godfrey had a gun in his hand, and he was staring at the helicopter as though the officers were addressing him directly. A red rifle sight appeared on his forehead, and I realized they *were*.

"Drop your weapon!" said the voice again, this time more insistent.

Godfrey was staring up at them with a challenge in his eyes. He seemed unaware that two more red dots had appeared on his body: one on his chest and another on his forehead.

What did they want with Godfrey?

I glanced at Amory, who was frozen, staring at him.

No. We could not let them take Godfrey.

As I watched, a strange calm came over him. Everything slowed down.

Then Godfrey raised the gun and pressed the barrel to his temple.

I wanted to run to him — close the small distance between us and yank the gun away — but my feet were frozen in place. Godfrey would not be taken alive.

There was a long and complete silence, and then a shot shattered the stillness.

Godfrey stood upright for two long seconds, looking as though he'd surprised himself. Then he began to fall.

I felt a tug on my arm, barely aware it was still attached to my body.

Amory was pulling me away from the house — toward the wall of fire. There was a sharp chemical stink in the air, mixed with the tang of blood. Bodies lay everywhere, but we didn't stop. I heard a strangled cry, not realizing it had come from me.

I was tripping after Amory, sobbing and gasping for air. My hair whipped around my face as the helicopter moved in our direction. I stumbled several times over bodies, debris, and who knew what else. I didn't look down.

Hauling me into the trees, Amory slowed his pace slightly to avoid giving away our position. Once the fire and bodies disappeared, I realized what was happening. Amory was taking me away from the farm — away from the other rebels, Greyson, Logan, and Roman.

"No!" I gasped, stopping and yanking my arm out of his grip. "We have to go back for them!"

"It's too dangerous," he panted. "The PMC will shoot us down."

"Amory! Are you insane?" We stood several feet apart now, and I realized I had raised my voice beyond what was safe. "This isn't even an option."

"They will get away," he hissed. "We'll find them . . . but we're no good to anyone dead."

He was right. If Greyson had been here now, he would have said the same thing. Even though every part of my body was screaming in protest, I had to admit I wasn't thinking clearly.

I gave a shaky nod, and Amory grabbed my hand. We moved through the woods, half running, half falling over snarls of vegetation. Amory never released my hand.

From the direction we were moving, I knew we were making our way around the field through the woods. If the others had made it, this was our best chance of running into them.

I heard shots in the distance and people screaming. I focused on running, wishing desperately I could shut my ears off. I didn't know if we had shot at the PMC or if they were shooting down our people. Logan would have been able to tell from the sound of the shots.

Logan. If we never found her and the others, I didn't know what I would do.

Up above, I heard the low hum of a helicopter. Instinctively, Amory and I threw ourselves onto the ground, rolling into the undergrowth and trying to conceal ourselves as the chopper passed over our heads. The trees around us shuddered in the heavy gust of air from the propeller blades, folding in on themselves so much I thought they would snap in half.

Then the chopper disappeared.

The silence that followed was chilling. I could no longer hear people screaming or the sound of the barn's rafters cracking in the fire. The air was still heavy with the stench of burning wood and flesh.

After the chopper left, we picked ourselves up and kept walking. I didn't know if it was fatigue, worry, or fear that had slowed Amory down, but I was glad. The slower we moved, the more likely we were to run into the others.

Suddenly I heard voices up ahead, and my heart sped up.

The Last Uprising

We were too far off to distinguish the speakers, but I could tell they weren't PMC. The voices were pitched lower, quiet and afraid.

Amory raised his hand, signaling a slow, quiet approach. We hunkered down and inched forward.

Up ahead, I could discern half a dozen figures crowded together in the shelter of two large maple trees.

"Can you make it?"

"Of course I can. I'm not an invalid."

I recognized those voices.

Swallowing down a grin, I pulled out of Amory's grip and charged through the trees.

"Haven!" Amory hissed.

"Stop right where you are!" said the female's voice. *Logan.*

I froze, realizing she probably had a rifle trained on me. *Stupid,* I thought — *sneaking up on them in the woods.*

"Logan, it's me," I called, my voice registering my relief.

"Oh, thank god," she cried.

I heard the crunch of dead leaves as Amory came up behind me.

I approached Logan and the others at a run, careening into her and throwing my arms around her neck. The lavender smell of her hair hit me, wrapping me up in a comforting embrace.

"Godfrey's dead," I murmured into her shoulder.

Logan's arms tightened around me, and I felt the shudder of a sob roll through her.

As she squeezed me, I looked around the clearing at the people with her. I saw Roman slumped against a tree, his face pale and sweaty.

The Last Uprising

Once I'd registered the faces of the surviving rebels, my eyes automatically began another circuit, convinced they were mistaken. I saw Switch, Marcus, Ray, Shriver, and Krystal — no one else.

"Where's Greyson?" Logan asked, her voice vibrating my shoulder.

My stomach turned.

"What?" I pulled away, eyes raking the crowd again in desperation. "I thought he was with you."

Now Logan looked panicked. "He's not with you?"

I shook my head, a million thoughts firing at once.

"We have to go back," I said. "We have to find him. He could be there right now . . . and others who are wounded. He needs us."

"Haven," said Amory in a scratchy voice. He was looking at Logan as though he didn't want to break the news alone. "We can't go back."

"We *have* to." My voice was an octave too high. I sounded like a crazy person.

"The PMC will be back. They crippled us, but they'll want to make sure we've been completely wiped out. They won't let us go on at the farm, and we can't fight them now."

"What are you saying?" I asked, even though I knew what he was saying. The farm was gone. Most of our forces were dead. Our supplies were destroyed.

We could not carry on the mission Ida had sent us here for. We had failed.

Godfrey was dead.

"Come on," said Logan. "We can't stay here. Let's see if we can meet up with the others at the Hoopers' farm."

I'd almost forgotten about the rebels from the west. At least they had escaped the attack unscathed . . . or so we hoped.

Logan and Amory helped Roman to his feet. He shrugged them off as soon as he was standing, his exhaustion and irritation fighting for dominance.

If he was experiencing what Logan had, he was running a high fever. He would be weak, but he would muddle through. Then he would seem to recover — right before losing himself in delirium.

We had lost everything. We'd lost the farm. We'd lost Godfrey. I'd lost my best friend, and we were close to losing Roman as well. Suddenly, the full misery of our situation hit me. We had no supplies and no guaranteed shelter from the night. I didn't even have my rifle.

I listened to the sound of the others' shuffling footsteps, and I forced my feet to follow.

Greyson couldn't be dead. I knew I would feel it if he were suddenly gone from this world — as though a part of my own soul had been snuffed out. But then, I hadn't felt anything when my parents were killed. I hadn't known until much later that I was alone.

I didn't know how many miles we had walked. At one point, I thought Marcus was leading us in a circle. All the trees looked alike. Then we crossed a blacktop road, and I found my bearings. We hadn't walked as far as I had thought. I had a vague idea where the Hoopers' farm was, and we were nowhere close.

It was nearly noon by the time we found the road that would lead us there. My stomach knotted into a pit of dread when I saw the roof of the barn jutting out over the trees. If the westerners were gone, too, I didn't know what we would do.

When we reached the fields, I squinted out at the huge farmhouse at the end of the gravel drive. Its windows looked dark, and the door was boarded just as Ida's had been. It didn't look as though anyone had been there in months.

We walked straight across the field toward the house. If the rebels were there, we did not want to sneak up on them.

Then I heard a low whistle coming from the lone tree out in the middle of the field. My chest swelled in relief. It had to be their sentry, signaling the others that friendly visitors were approaching.

As we came closer to the house, I saw one of the boards on the windows lift, and two eyes appeared. I knew how we must look: dirty, tired, and covered in soot from the explosion. Switch was limping, although I wasn't sure if that was a new injury or an old one flaring up.

The front door banged open, and Jason strode outside. His face was blackened by smoke, but his obvious distress turned to relief when he saw Marcus and Krystal.

"Come inside. Quickly," he muttered, ushering us into the house.

Logan explained what had happened in a scratchy voice, and my eyes traveled over the rebels gathered in the dusty living room. They had been here playing cards, talking, and relaxing while we had been running for our lives.

With each face that turned out not to be Greyson's, my heart fell a little lower in my stomach.

"Has anyone else arrived?" Logan asked.

Jason shook his head, and I felt like crying.

A woman was shooing me and Logan into one of the rooms upstairs to wash up and get our wounds treated, but I was in a daze.

I was given clean black rebel clothes, a felt blanket,

bandages for the cuts running up my arms, and a hot bowl of rice and vegetables, but I didn't register any of it.

Amory was huddled with a knot of the rebels from the west, no doubt strategizing, but I wanted no part in it.

When no one was looking, I slipped outside through the side kitchen door and sank down onto the warped wooden steps. Here, I could watch for approaching stragglers from the farm without any of the others looking at me with pity. They knew whom I had lost.

The bowl of food grew cold in my hands as a few rebels stumbled up to the farm. Every time I saw a knot of people approaching from the south field, the breath caught in my lungs. And every time Greyson wasn't among them, I sank a little deeper into the crevices of the old steps.

At one point, Amory shuffled out and put his arm around me. He didn't say anything because he was thinking what I already knew: Greyson was dead. Dead or lost — perhaps wounded. I knew I should go looking for him, but truthfully, I had no idea where to begin. I didn't know the area well, and it was likely I would get lost, too.

As the sun sank over the quiet field, I heard a rustle behind me. I glanced up at the window and caught Logan's gaze. She was watching for Greyson, too.

"Haven, you have to come inside," said Amory once darkness had settled. "He might turn up in the morning, but he won't be on the move now."

I heard him, but I didn't answer. I wanted to shout at him — say he didn't know how I felt — but I knew that wasn't true. Amory had lost his best friend. He'd watched him die. If anyone knew the sinking helplessness I felt, it was him.

He took my silence for refusal and instead brought out an extra blanket to drape over my shoulders. It smelled as though it had been in storage for a long time, but underneath, I could detect a whiff of summer and sunshine — Greyson's smell. Or maybe that was wishful thinking.

Just like that, I was lost in the light pounding of our feet touching over the limestone trail. The cadence was everything: the staggered rhythm of our breathing, the sound of our feet, the pattern of sunlight flashing between the trees. He was leading me, and I was hovered near his left shoulder — always two paces behind, but always there.

I wasn't there now. I had let him down.

But then Greyson was running again. He wasn't running up ahead. He was running right toward me.

No, he was stumbling. He was staggering across the field, only a shadow in the darkness. But I would recognize that stride anywhere.

My breath caught in my throat, and I made a little noise of excitement like a gurgle. Tossing the blankets aside, I sprinted out into the field toward him.

When Greyson saw me, relief flashed across his face. I threw my arms around him, crushing him in a hug. His arms wrapped around me, and he dragged in a shaky breath against the top of my head.

I savored everything about him just then. He was alive. He was here. I wasn't alone.

Pulling back slightly, I took a silent inventory of his wounds. He had a bad cut that had crusted over at his temple and plenty of scrapes and bruises running down his arms. His legs were shaky, but it was the way he was hunched to one side that had me worried.

"What is it?" I asked, pulling his hand away from the small of his back. "Where are you hurt?"

He winced. "The explosion threw me against a fence post. I hurt my back pretty bad."

Behind us, I heard a strangled little cry. I turned to see Logan dashing toward us.

Greyson's big brown eyes lit up, and the corners of his mouth lifted into a grin.

Logan careened into him, unaware of his injuries. I saw a slight cringe flash across Greyson's face as the full force of her hit him, but I could feel the happiness wafting off him. He grabbed her up in his arms, and to my surprise, Logan planted a brief kiss right on his mouth.

It was quick, but it was there. Greyson looked as though he couldn't believe it.

"What the hell happened to you?" Logan breathed, pulling away.

"Got lost."

A small laugh exploded out of Logan, and I tried to hold mine in. It wasn't funny, but I felt giddy.

"I couldn't remember exactly where the farm was," he said. "I knew it was in this general direction, but I stayed in the woods for a few hours in case the PMC came back. I was looking for you, but you were long gone. I knew you probably came here. Then I ran into a pack of carriers."

My stomach twisted with dread. I hadn't even considered the danger he had faced alone in the woods without a weapon.

He continued. "They must have broken off from that horde we took out. Obviously I wasn't going to try to fight them on my own, so I got as far away from them as I could. I got turned around, though. I was walking for hours in the wrong direction before I realized it."

"I was so worried," I said.

"You don't have to worry about me," he said. His voice sounded casual, but I wasn't buying the subtle lift at the corner of his mouth. "I always find my way back, don't I?"

Logan looped her arm through his and walked him back toward the house.

When Amory saw us from across the living room, a huge smile broke across his face. He ran into the kitchen to get Greyson some food, and I brought him over to Shriver so she could tend to his injuries. I was worried about the cut on his temple and whatever had happened to his back.

The rest of the rebels had gathered in the living room, discussing what our next steps should be. I could tell Greyson was itching to give his input, but once Shriver was satisfied that he would live, I sent him straight upstairs to rest and ice his back.

"We should reclaim the farm," said Logan. "We can't just fold now that they've launched a serious attack."

Amory looked at her as if she were crazy. "We lost most of our men," he said. "Another hit like that would kill us all."

Roman shook his head. "The farm's destroyed. Even if we could defend it, barely any of it's still standing."

I was surprised to hear him echo Amory's sentiments, but it was hard to argue with the fact that the guest house and the barn had been completely destroyed in the bombing.

"What I don't get," said Roman, "is why they strapped a bomb to you if they were just going to give Godfrey enough time to disarm it."

"They wanted to lure him out," said Amory. His voice was tight, and there was a strain of grief in his eyes. "They knew he would try to diffuse the bomb, and they wanted to capture him. It was also a distraction. They knew everyone would be so focused on the bomb they could see that no one would notice them arming the bombs they couldn't."

"But they couldn't have done all that in a few minutes,"

Roman said.

Amory shook his head. "They must have done it in the middle of the night. It's my fault. I was watching the road, mainly. And patrolling the woods on the far side of the field. I didn't expect them to come from the north side."

Roman didn't say anything, but the tension hung thick between them. He blamed Amory, and I sensed the others did as well.

"It wasn't your fault," I said, a little louder than I should have. "You couldn't watch everything by yourself. Besides, they would have found another way in."

He nodded. "I guess. They were watching me. When I went into the woods to patrol for carriers, two of them jumped me. One hit me on the head. I blacked out for a second. The next thing I knew, I was lying in the yard in front of the house."

"They wanted to show they could manipulate us," I said. "Drive us out, capture Godfrey, destroy our base, and then shoot down anyone who thought they could escape."

"Well, they don't have Godfrey," Roman muttered.

"That's right," Logan said weakly. "They don't have Godfrey."

A strained silence fell over the group. Even among the rebels from the west, the grief for Godfrey was palpable. The westerners might not have known us, but everyone knew Godfrey.

A staticky outburst from the radio on the cabinet in the corner made us all jump. It was a huge setup I hadn't seen before, and I realized the newcomers must have brought their own communication equipment with them.

"This is the farmer up north, over."

"That's Ida," Amory said.

Shriver crossed the room and picked up the handheld. "Farmer, this is the runaway doctor, over."

I could hear the warmth in Ida's voice as she addressed Shriver. "It's good to hear your voice, Doc."

Shriver's mouth fell into a hard line. "I'm guessing that's not why you called?"

"No," said Ida. Her voice was heavy. "We've had some problems at our other bases in the states. I . . . I was wondering if you'd returned home. What is your position, doctor?"

"The cows have come home, but . . . we've been hit."

There was a long pause, and I felt my heart breaking for Ida.

"That's what I was afraid of." Ida's voice was strained. "What's left of home, doctor?"

"Not much. A few survivors, but most of us from the west made it."

I heard a shaky intake of breath over the static. "Bring them north, then. We've got work to do. I'm calling everyone to the castle."

"Message received, farmer."

My heart sank.

If Ida was calling all the rebels north, that meant she had given up on fighting the war from the states. She was rallying the troops for one last fight.

Chapter Twenty-Six

I didn't sleep at all that night, and I barely slept the entire drive north. I couldn't shake the idea that this was the rebels' last stand, and I knew Amory, Roman, Logan, and Greyson were thinking the same thing.

We hadn't brought anything other than the clothes on our backs. Everything I owned in the world was gone.

As we sped toward the New Northern Territory, I rested my head against Amory's shoulder, savoring what I hoped was not one of my last days at his side.

Roman's fever was worse, and he was sprawled across the back row of seats, shivering and sweating under his blankets. I tried to ignore his groans of pain, but all I could think was that maybe it was better this way. I knew Roman would prefer to die quickly fighting the people who were responsible for the virus rather than wither away slowly on Ida's farm.

We took turns driving and staring out the window, and I began to see signage for the border.

"No CID — No Entry."

I almost wanted to laugh. There had been a time when I'd been afraid to travel by the interstate, and now we were barreling toward the border — all of us illegals — without fear.

We took strange detours to avoid the rovers, but the rebels had such an intimate knowledge of the safe routes

The Last Uprising

along the highway that Shriver never blinked an eye.

It was the middle of the night when we finally pulled off on a smaller back road. I knew we would have to cross the border by taking down a portion of the electric fence, and that made me uneasy.

When we pulled off the road into the impressions another SUV had left in the mud, my heart sped up. Amory squeezed my hand, and I returned the pressure.

Shriver slowed down, her eyes scanning the darkness for the metal grid of the fence. I wasn't sure how she knew we were close. She couldn't have made this journey more than once, and the forest was pitch black.

Then, in the distance, a pair of headlights flashed. They blinked twice, and Shriver flicked our lights in response.

The tires crunched slowly over dead leaves and crackling branches, and the outline of a Jeep came into view on the other side of the fence. The metal grid towered over us, and I could almost hear the hum of electricity on the air.

A tall figure emerged from the Jeep and disappeared into the shadows. There was fumbling and some scraping of metal on metal, and the person on the other side shorted out a portion of the fence.

Then the figure sprinted back into view and grasped the fence, pulling it backward. I gasped a little as the entire section detached from the rest of the fence and swung out. This was certainly more sophisticated than our first crossing. The figure waved Shriver through, and we pulled forward into the New Northern Territory.

I watched in the rearview mirror as the rebel ran to swing the fence back into place, and I knew it was live again. As far as World Corp knew, the border was secure.

The Jeep did not follow us, and I suspected the sentry remained posted at the fence to let the other cars in our caravan pass. We had left the farm in staggered waves so we wouldn't attract the attention of any PMC cruisers lingering on the highway south of the border.

I expected we would be headed to a camp similar to the one we had fled in the winter, but I was surprised when the trees began to thin and we returned to the highway once again. I didn't ask Shriver where we were going. Trees along the road disappeared, giving way to fields and derelict towns. Fear was unfurling in my stomach. I didn't like being without cover in PMC country.

Finally, we reached a cluster of old buildings — a factory. The broken windows along the front looked dark, but as we pulled off and drove around the back, I began to see the flicker of firelight coming through the squares of glass.

Shriver parked, and we got out. As we climbed the crumbled old steps to the back door, I stayed right between Greyson and Amory. A strange wariness had come over me. This was nothing like any rebel camp I'd ever been to.

But then a pair of familiar eyes appeared in the tiny window in the door. The door swung open, and there was Ida, beaming down at us.

"Oh my god!"

She threw an arm around Logan, who was closest, and crushed her against her chest. "I didn't know . . . I didn't know if any of you survived." Ida pulled away, patting her eyes with the back of her lumpy sweater. "When they told me about the attack, I thought for sure . . ."

"We made it," I said.

"All of you?"

"Not quite all of us," said Roman in a low voice. He staggered up behind us, looking ashen. "Godfrey's gone."

The light disappeared from Ida's eyes, and the warm,

The Last Uprising

motherly lines around her mouth sagged.

"No," she breathed.

I prayed she wouldn't ask how it happened. A lump was forming in the back of my throat, and I looked away. Now that I'd seen her face, I knew Godfrey had been wrong about Ida sending us back to the states. She had never meant to sacrifice us.

"Of course . . . that's how he would have wanted to go," said Ida. "In service to the cause."

Those words almost made me lose my tenuous grasp on my emotions. "The cause" sounded so pitiful now, when our numbers were diminished and we were retreating back to the north. World Corp had taken the states, and Aryus wouldn't surrender it.

Ida's watery eyes flitted from one of us to the next, as though she was hoping someone would contradict Roman's words. When her eyes landed on him again, they widened in shock.

"Oh my . . . oh my dear. You're not . . .?"

Roman nodded.

"How long?"

"I was bitten a few days ago."

Ida's eyes quivered again, threatening to spill fresh tears, but she swallowed them down.

"He's doing well so far," said Shriver gruffly, which I took to mean that Roman was hanging in there despite his inevitable death. In her own way, Shriver's brand of kindness was the best.

Ida nodded. "Well, you're here, and we're still fighting. With any luck, we'll be able to get our hands on the cure again."

I smiled weakly because it seemed like the right response, but my heart wasn't really in it. Judging by the note of defeat in her voice, Ida thought it just as unlikely as I did that we would be able to get the cure in time for Roman.

"And . . . and the farm?" she asked. "Is it really gone?"

"We're not sure," admitted Logan. "The barn and the guest house burned. It's possible the house is still standing."

The corners of Ida's mouth twitched, as though she was trying to smile but not quite managing it. "That farm has been in my family for over one hundred years."

"I'm sorry, Ida," said Greyson.

"Don't be silly, dear. I should be the one to apologize. It was wrong of me to send you and Godfrey there without any real strategy. Taking it back from the PMC when World Corp had every intention of using the land was foolish. Godfrey said I let my sentiment get in the way of the cause, and he was right."

With a shaky deep breath and a fortifying nod, Ida ushered us inside. The building was freezing and smelled of smoke and mildew. I preferred the rebel camps with their blazing campfires and the shelter of the trees around a city of tents.

"It isn't ideal," called Ida as she led us up the stairs. Her voice echoed off the filthy cinderblock walls and damp floor, making me feel a bit claustrophobic. "But the woods have become too dangerous."

"PMC?" Amory asked.

She shook her head. "Carriers."

"How bad is it?"

"Bad," said Ida grimly. "We thought at first it was all Rulon's doing, but there are too many for that. The hordes have been tremendous. We listened in on the PMC frequency and discovered that a huge portion of the fence was still down. It took them nearly a week to repair because they were losing so many officers to attacks."

"Why are the carriers swarming the north?"

"We don't know. But when they first came, there was a glut of stage threes."

"The carriers are fighting back while they still can," I whispered.

Ida sighed. "That's what we think, too."

As we reached the top of the stairs, the sound of voices bouncing off the walls grew louder. The flicker of light told me they had lit a few small fires for warmth inside, and in the dim light, I could discern the outline of hundreds of rebels. Some were huddled together shoulder to shoulder, while others were wrapped up in their sleeping bags against the chill in the air.

"We've got room for you down at the far end," said Ida, motioning with her flashlight. "And Shriver, I hate to ask after your long drive, but I could really use your help. We've got a few cases of walking pneumonia, I'm afraid."

"Just lead the way."

We shuffled down the narrow aisle toward the tall, broken windows at the end of the factory floor, Ida's flashlight throwing tall shadows of old machinery and sleeping bodies against the blackened walls. The smoke from the campfires itched my throat, and I heard a few hacking coughs as I passed sleeping rebels. When they shifted away from the light, I caught glimpses of their ragged, unshaven faces.

Ida pointed out the rebels who were sick, and Shriver fell in to check on them.

It hit me that these rebels had probably been holed up in

the factory since we had left camp. Seeing the misery of the cold, cramped conditions, I began to think I would rather rough it outside with the carriers.

"They're not accustomed to fighting carriers," said Ida, as though she had read my mind. "Or the outdoors, really. Most of these people came from the communes, so they're still . . . acclimating."

"Oh," I said, only because I didn't know how to respond to that. If they were commune dwellers, it meant that they were mostly inexperienced and terrified of the PMC.

"After the disaster at camp, I couldn't expose them to that kind of danger again. Even if it meant we had to stay here."

"Then how will they fight?" asked Roman a little harshly.

"We'll fight with what we've got," she said.

We had reached the end of the factory floor, where half a dozen pallets and sleeping bags were stacked neatly in the corner.

"I'll have someone bring you some food. You must be hungry."

I nodded, wanting to throw my arms around her. I was so glad to see Ida. She was like the mother of our little group.

"Get some sleep. Tomorrow we strategize. Everyone must know their role. Then we attack."

"What about the others?" I asked, thinking of all the rebels from the west who had been following us in the caravan.

"I'll put them in the basement," she said carefully. "I'm not sure they will . . . mix well with the others."

I felt a little pang of guilt when I caught her meaning. She thought the westerners would regard the commune dwellers with contempt for fleeing to the north, since the rebels out west had managed to find safety and abundance through sheer determination. I realized I was no better in my own quick judgment of the commune dwellers. But then, none of them had faced what we had.

Ida placed the palm of her hand against Roman's cheek — a gesture I was sure he wouldn't allow from anyone else. Her lips pursed together in concern, and she shot us all one last warm smile before scurrying away.

Amory grabbed two pallets and unrolled them side by side. I smiled and sat down on the one next to his. Logan and Greyson flopped down across from us, and Roman hunkered down a few feet away.

"Bit of a downgrade from Murphy's camp, isn't it?" murmured Greyson.

Roman snorted. "It's a hellhole."

"Is it really this bad?" Logan wrinkled her nose. "The carriers, I mean. So bad they'd have to retreat closer to the city and camp out in here?"

"You were there," I said, feeling as though I should defend Ida. "You remember the carrier attack. It was a bloodbath."

I caught the four of them exchange a glance. I knew they usually avoided mentioning that time. It had been horrible for all of us.

"We remember it," said Roman darkly. "But I'm surprised *you* do."

Logan's face lost its color, but a small laugh burst from my lips.

The feeling was infectious. Amory's shoulders began to shake, and he started laughing, too. Even Roman managed a shifty grin, and he made a weird rumbling sound that hummed in his chest. Pretty soon, Logan was laughing so hard she was crying, and Greyson was sprawled out on his back trying to recover.

The rebels around us took notice, some shooting us irritated looks, but we ignored them. It felt good to laugh, and it had been too long since we had all shared an easy moment.

"So do you think we even stand a chance?" asked Greyson. "Against World Corp . . . with a bunch of commune dwellers?"

"We have the rebels from the west."

Roman snorted.

"That won't be nearly enough," said Logan.

"Ida's smarter than that," said Amory. "If we're here, that probably means she's called in everyone. This is the last uprising."

"What do you think they'll do with all of us if we lose?" asked Logan.

Amory's brows lifted. "Kill us, if we're lucky."

We all fell silent. Killing us would be the merciful choice, but we all knew Aryus better than that.

One of Ida's men came over with a warm pot of thick stew, a loaf of bread, and bottled water. We all ate quickly and fell back onto our pallets to stare at the cold metal ceiling.

Even with warm food in my stomach, the misery of the huddled rebels and the dying revolution hit me. Never in a million years would I have imagined I would be sleeping on the floor of an abandoned factory in the New Northern Territory. I was homeless, with nothing but the clothes on my back, and I was about to fight to the death to overthrow World Corp.

The Last Uprising

Then Amory's warm fingers laced through mine, and slowly, the heavy weight of sadness lifted. I snuggled into him, wishing we weren't surrounded by hundreds of other people. More than anything, I wanted to feel him all around me again, with nothing between us. That was the only thing that would take my mind off what we were about to do.

As if he could sense what I was feeling, Amory tugged me closer. I settled into the crook of his arm and rested my head over his heart, savoring his warmth. The steady beat, accompanied by the rhythmic rise and fall of his chest, was the most soothing sound in the world.

"Whatever happens," he whispered, "at least we have this."

"This is all I want," I said.

His arms tightened around me momentarily, and then the exhaustion overtook me.

Chapter Twenty-Seven

The next morning, I awoke pinned to Amory's side. I heard movement all around us, but I didn't want to get up. I knew we had to face all the commune dwellers and hear what our role in the coup would be.

There was a long line for oatmeal and bread, and I used the time we were waiting to get a feel for the situation we'd walked into.

In the dark, all the rebels had looked scruffy, unwashed, and rugged, but in the light of day, I could see that there was a stark difference between the commune dwellers and the rest of Ida's forces.

In fact, it was easy to tell all the different groups apart. The commune dwellers were pale, dirty, and skinny. If anything, they looked scruffier than Ida's rebels, who had more meat on their bones and a controlled grunge about them. Rebels who had been roughing it in the wilderness for months were accustomed to shaving with their own knife next to a frozen creek, and the rebel women had learned how to conceal their greasy, unwashed hair in tight braids and ponytails.

The commune dwellers' hair hung in matted tangles, and they wore their rebel blacks with a certain self-conscious distain. After eating perfectly portioned meals complete with out-of-season fruit from World Corp's supercrops, I was sure the rebels' offering of runny oatmeal and stale bread paled in comparison.

I could even tell Ida's rebels apart from the rebels who'd come with us. While the westerners looked easygoing and capable, Ida's rebels were watching Roman warily with a tightness to their faces that told me they knew he was infected.

But it didn't matter where we had come from or the hardships we'd experienced. Tomorrow, we would all have our roles to play. If we failed, we would all be killed or imprisoned.

Once we'd eaten, Ida gathered everyone on the first floor of the building. I noticed that the different groups sat together, Ida's rebels peering over at us with distrust. Everyone ignored the commune dwellers.

"With our numbers," said Ida, "we should have over a thousand fighting in rebel black tomorrow."

I looked around. Hundreds certainly, but I doubted very much if there were even near a thousand.

"We do not outnumber the PMC, but we have the element of surprise. We strike first to gain the upper hand. That is our only choice."

Ida pointed to the map she had duct-taped to the wall and explained how she planned to attack the different bases throughout the city. She knew the routes the officers would take when they called in backup, and she planned to ambush them.

Once the moving parts were explained, Ida chose three leaders who would select their teams and lead each strike. I noticed she picked a commune dweller, a rebel from the west, and one of her own men to head up the groups. Ida was a terrific leader with a knack for bringing people together, but she wasn't subtle.

"Once we've crippled most of their forces, we need to take out Aryus Edric in the Infinity Building."

At Ida's words, my chest seized up. A murmur of outrage whipped through the crowd. I'd been to the Infinity Building. It was the last thing I remembered before all my memories were taken.

"We *must* kill Aryus," Ida continued. "Without him, their leadership will crumble. He has the vision. He symbolizes everything World Corp stands for."

"It's a suicide mission," said a burly rebel from the back of the room.

I recognized that voice. It was Switch. Through the jungle of limbs between us, I could see the tense muscles in Switch's neck working. His carrier scars stood out sharply in the bright light streaming in through the factory windows. "No one will ever get in and out of there alive."

Logan and I exchanged an angry look. I couldn't believe Switch was talking back to Ida like this. I knew Ida well enough to know she would ask for anyone with objections to come forward later, but he was just being rude.

"With all due respect, Switch," said Ida, "there are those among us who have been inside the Infinity Building and lived to tell. They infiltrated the building to get their hands on the cure and spoke to Aryus themselves. They will guide the unit through what they know of the building and its security."

Ida's gaze flickered over Logan, Roman, and me, and my cheeks flamed as a few rebels looked curiously in our direction.

"It is my assessment that whoever goes into the Infinity Building will have to take down every officer on the way in before getting to Aryus. That's the only way they can reach him and get out safely."

"And who do you suppose is willing to take that on?" drawled Switch.

I wanted to hit him. Carrier survivor or not, he was being disrespectful. And at the moment, he was being a coward.

"I was going to open the floor to volunteers," said Ida brightly, unruffled by his distain.

There was a hush of silence. Nobody moved.

Then two arms shot up in my peripheral vision. I looked over.

Amory was leaning back on his elbows, his arm in the air. There was a look of determination in his eyes. On his other side, Roman had thrown up his beefy arm.

A flash of anger rolled through me. I understood why Roman wanted to be the one to assassinate Aryus. He was the one who had started the virus. He had created the monsters that had slaughtered his family. He was the reason Roman was dying.

But Amory? I didn't understand why he was undertaking such a dangerous task. He knew there was a strong possibility he would never even reach Aryus and a very slim chance he would come out of that building alive.

As I stared at him dumbfounded, his gaze fell to the side. He would not meet my eyes.

Without thinking, I raised my arm, too.

Now it was Amory's turn to look shocked and angry.

On my other side, Logan put her hand up, and Greyson's followed. A tight coil of dread settled in the pit of my stomach. I didn't like this. The more of my friends who went inside the Infinity Building, the more I would lose. There was no chance we would all make it out unscathed.

I shook my head at Greyson, but he just grinned at me, as though we were going for pizza instead of assassinating a crazed corporate visionary who had overthrown the U.S. government, started an epidemic, and taken over two countries.

Ida looked surprised but pleased by our willingness. None of the other rebels had volunteered, but I couldn't imagine she was thrilled at the prospect of us being responsible for taking out Aryus. This called for a team of Navy SEALs, not a handful of twenty-somethings whose training consisted of shooting at coffee cans and target practice on carriers.

"Right," said Ida. "That's about the gist of it. Of course, once we overtake the city, our work won't be done. Other PMC units will come. Once we have the city stabilized and the civilians to safety, I am happy to simply imprison the rest of the officers."

"What about the PMC leadership?" asked Amory.

The realization hit me in the gut like a sucker punch. Amory's father was a captain. I could only imagine how he felt.

"Those who surrender peacefully will have to await the scrutiny of the U.S. justice system," said Ida. Her voice was firm, but I could detect the gentle undertones there. "If we want a peaceful restoration of the federal government, that's what we have to do. We cannot continue to operate as vigilantes. We will have to fall in line once the government knows which way is up."

"And the carriers?" Logan asked. Her voice was small, but it carried through the crowd.

"They are not our biggest concern right now," said Ida. "We don't know how much of the cure has been produced. Once the Infinity Building has been secured, our number one priority will be recovering the formula. Hopefully, once the dust settles, we'll be able to cure a substantial number of them."

"By then it will be too late," said another voice. It was Doctor Carson.

The Last Uprising

I looked at Roman, whose hands were balled into fists on his knees. The yellow around his irises was starting to spread. He looked feverish and slightly unhinged.

"Ida, be reasonable," said Shriver. "The cure has the potential to save thousands of lives."

"We will do what we can," said Ida. "But neutralizing World Corp and the PMC should be our first priority."

The crowd murmured in agreement. Clearly they didn't believe the carriers were worth saving.

I knew differently. I had watched Logan and my mother succumb to the virus; I didn't want to watch Roman's slow decline.

"I need you all to come with me," said Ida.

I looked up and realized she was addressing me and the other members of our little assassination squad.

She led us over to a table with a more detailed map of the city. Ida put a finger on one of the roads and traced a line to the center.

"This is your best route to get to the Infinity Building from here. If all goes according to plan, these bases will be neutralized. But if they're not, we cannot wait. If we give Aryus enough time to flee, it will be nearly impossible to find him again. He has unlimited resources. Even with all international flights grounded, it would not be out of the question for him to charter a plane to another country."

I nodded. I knew Aryus's first priority would be self-preservation.

"Do not engage in the fighting," said Ida. "Your only task is to get to Aryus."

Her eyes lingered on Roman for a moment before snapping back to me. "Haven, I need you, Logan, and Roman to share everything you know about the building."

I nodded, everything inside me screaming in protest. I didn't want to tell them anything. I didn't want them attempting the impossible.

I looked to Roman and Logan, but Roman was expertly avoiding eye contact. Since he had been working for the PMC at the time, I knew he was ashamed to be singled out, but we were beyond that now. This was about survival. I started talking, and Logan jumped in to relay everything we knew about the layout.

Greyson drew a diagram of the lobby with all the exits we could remember. I explained how the woman at the front desk controlled all the elevators.

We would need two people to stay behind in the lobby to kill any officers who entered the building after us and ensure we could get back to the first floor.

"Aryus had a few doses of the cure in his office," I said. "But our best bet for the main supply is the lab. I don't know where it is, though."

I recalled the wretched nurse who had stood over my bed, but I had no memory of being brought there.

"It's the twenty-fourth floor," said Roman in a scratchy voice.

"How many officers can we expect?" asked Amory.

Ida shook her head. "It's hard to say, but Aryus has grown paranoid. After Mariah and Jared sneaked in as uniformed PMC and Roman betrayed him, he doesn't trust his own officers. He's likely to have only those closest to him guarding his chamber."

Amory nodded, his eyes cold. The full weight of what was about to happen hit me. We were really going to kill Aryus.

When Logan and I had exhausted everything we knew and formed a plan, Amory's hand clamped over my arm, and he pulled me away from the others.

"Where are we . . .?"

He didn't answer but continued to tug me toward the stairwell.

Once we were out of earshot, he whipped around, anger burning in his eyes.

"Haven, what the *hell?*"

I staggered back, unprepared for his fury.

"What?"

A dark cloud passed over Amory's face, and a derisive laugh burst out of him. "What? *What?* Why did you volunteer?"

"Because you volunteered!" I spluttered. "Did you think I was just going to let you go in there with Roman alone?"

"Yes!" he burst out. "And you should have. Do you think this is a game?"

Now it was my turn to feel the anger sour in my blood.

"A game?"

Amory caught my expression, and a tangle of emotions flew across his face: frustration, regret, and embarrassment.

"In case you've forgotten, I was the one who was in there. I talked to Aryus. I watched him cure Logan, not knowing if she would live or die. I watched Jared die trying to come back for me. Trust me — I know it isn't a game."

Now Amory's face was all regret.

Realizing I'd been shouting, I lowered my voice. "Why is it so terrible for me to go but not for you?"

"Because I want you to *live*," he said before he could stop himself.

"And you're preparing to walk in there thinking you won't?"

"N-No. I didn't mean —" He sighed. "The more of us that go in, the lower the chance that we'll all come out alive. I want to be able to walk in there knowing you're safe."

I took a step toward him, wanting to reach out and bridge the short distance between us. "But I won't be. No matter what. You need a team, and I don't want you doing this without me."

Amory let out a burst of air in frustration, spinning away from me with his hands in his hair. "I can't lose you, Haven!"

I stared at him, shocked by the terror and fury etched across his face. "That's how *I* feel."

"You don't understand . . . there's a good chance we *will* die."

"I'm well aware of the facts. But after everything I've lost, I can't lose you, too. At least not without putting up a fight."

He sighed, and I sensed he knew I could not be persuaded to hang back.

"Wait . . . why did *you* volunteer?" I asked, peering up at him with suspicion.

"I have my reasons . . ."

He was sulking now. Perfect.

Rolling my eyes, I took two steps forward and wrapped my arms around his waist, closing the space between us. He stiffened, vaguely surprised, and then he relaxed into me and draped his arms over my shoulders.

"Tell me."

Amory sighed. "I couldn't let Roman go alone. I knew he would volunteer so he could try to get the cure."

I nodded, thinking there was probably more.

"Plus I hate Aryus for everything he stole from me," Amory whispered into my hair.

Of course. Guilt stung the words on my tongue. With everything going on, sometimes it was easy to forget what Amory's own father had put him through. "Your father?"

"No. The PMC didn't make him the way he is," he said bitterly. "Aryus stole you from me."

I pulled back a little so I could look him in the eyes. "No. I'm here now. I'm yours."

Amory's look was so intense it knocked the air right out of me.

Without warning, he tugged me up until his warm lips found mine. I ran a hand through his hair and sighed against him. His hands trailed down my waist, pulling me closer.

He put everything he was feeling behind that kiss. He was angry and loving and scared. He pushed me back against the wall, and our bodies fit together until there wasn't a hair's breadth between us.

We clung to each other, both thinking our time together was limited.

Why did we take such stupid risks? I wondered.

But I knew the answer. We took risks because none of us could stand doing nothing — not after everything we'd been through. We had to fight. I felt that urge deep in my bones, a toxic need that would fester inside me long after the last PMC officer had fallen.

Chapter Twenty-Eight

I didn't sleep at all that night. From the minimal snoring and the constant shifting of blankets across the factory floor, I knew most of the other rebels were lying awake, too.

It was different than any other night I had slept awaiting battle. This was the first time I genuinely felt as though we wouldn't make it back.

When the first rays of sunlight peeked through the broken factory windows, I was already sitting up in the folds of my sleeping bag, watching Roman's fitful tussle with his blankets.

He'd gotten worse. The fever no longer kept him incapacitated, but he now had that unhealthy pallor all the time. He'd lost weight, and he looked suddenly much smaller.

It was strange that I should feel protective of Roman, since he and I had never really been friends. We tolerated each other, but he didn't like me.

Still, if we didn't get the cure, he would be dead soon — one more member of my family gone from the world. I didn't think I could take it, no matter how infuriating Roman could be.

Greyson stirred next. We sat without talking, him watching Logan and me watching Amory, and my heart went out to him. Greyson had followed me all over the country and had brought me back to my old self. Watching him

The Last Uprising

sitting there, rubbing the sleep out of his eyes and tousling his now-messy dark waves, I felt a surge of comfort and strength that reminded me of home.

Ida called a meeting over breakfast, which was just as well. None of us was very hungry. I picked at my oatmeal and chugged a mug of weak instant coffee as she ran through the plan once again.

I already knew our part. It was simple: Don't get killed, get to the Infinity Building, blast our way in, kill Aryus, grab the cure, and get out.

When she finished, I watched the rebels milling around in their black combat gear, prowling at the edges of the room like caged panthers. Some of them owned Teflon vests, which made me jealous. Others were being a bit theatrical, spreading tar paint over their cheeks to read "XX" as they had on the night of the Sector X riots.

It seemed tactless now. Then, the rebels had been attacking a military base to free prisoners who were innocent, including Greyson. But now, we were about to stage a violent overthrow of a region where civilians lived. The weak and cowardly had fled to the communes, but so had families, the elderly, and the sick. If anything went wrong, innocent people could be killed.

I waited in line with the others to be issued weapons, trying to think about anything other than what we were about to do.

Logan was ahead of me in line, and when Switch tried to pass her a dainty little handgun, I thought she was going to take his head off. That made me laugh. I couldn't believe there was a rebel alive who didn't know what a sharpshooter Logan had been.

She didn't stop until she had locked up five of the best rifles for each of us, and I was grateful when she handed me an FN SCAR. This was the weapon I was most comfortable

The Last Uprising

with, and she knew it.

I caught her eye, wishing I could put my gratitude into words, but she understood. It wasn't just the gun; Logan was always looking out for me.

"She shouldn't be doing this," Amory murmured over my shoulder.

He was right. How would Logan take out officers when she could barely shoot straight? She was still a deadly fighter in hand-to-hand combat, but that didn't matter to the PMC. They would shoot her as soon as look at her.

We fell out, piling into the vehicles parked behind the factory. Amory, Roman, Greyson, Logan, and I had an old Xterra all to ourselves. Judging by the silence in the car, they were all as nervous as I was.

We took the route Ida had given us, staying off the main highway. The rebels would be hitting from three strategic points in the city, but we were to go another way. Ida wanted us to station ourselves by the base nearest the Infinity Building and lay low. When the base fell, we would know it was our best opportunity to find Aryus.

As we approached the heart of the city, it struck me how quiet and deserted the streets looked. The commune dwellers should have been on their way to work at the World Corp factories, fields, and labs, but I didn't see the people in white.

Then I remembered Ida had persuaded several of the communes to riot. She must have chosen those communes specifically to get the civilians out of the way. That made me feel slightly better about storming into the city and staging an overthrow.

We passed under a rover, and I panicked as the light turned red. They knew we were here now. I imagined rovers all over the city setting off alarms and the PMC scrambling

The Last Uprising

to discover why there were so many illegals fanning out across the city.

Did they think it was another carrier attack? Or had they been expecting a rebel invasion?

I sensed Logan's and Greyson's nervousness as we watched one rover after another blink red.

There were so many in the city center, and I realized they must record everything the commune dwellers did. I couldn't imagine living under such intense scrutiny.

Amory parked the car in a garage facing the base and killed the engine. We would not be in disguise this time, hiding in PMC whites. That sent a defiant thrill through me, but it also made me nervous. This mission was not about stealth. We were taking a stand.

We got out, and I checked my gun out of habit. The extra ammunition weighed down my pockets, but it didn't seem like enough. Amory got out, and I watched him stick a knife in his boot and clamp on his weapons holster. His gray eyes were cold and focused, his movements precise. He was all business, and I was struck — not for the first inappropriate time — by how incredibly sexy he was.

Not two minutes after we'd parked, sirens were blaring up the street, drawing closer. Amory grabbed me and pulled me behind the SUV, shielding me with his body. If I wasn't so scared, I would have blushed at the way he was pressed against me.

Blue lights flashed in my vision, and several cruisers blazed past the garage. They knew what direction we had gone, but they hadn't expected us to stop.

Nobody dared speak, but I knew everyone's thoughts were the same: *When would the rebels attack?*

My muscles tensed. My ears were piqued for a sound, my body poised to run and fight.

What were we waiting for? An explosion? Gunfire?

Then more sirens sounded, farther away this time, and I knew PMC units were responding to other reports of illegals. Then there were three gunshots in quick succession and a loud crash.

Somewhere in the distance, a car alarm was going off. More gunshots ricocheted off buildings, no more than half a mile away.

Sirens were blaring again, approaching from the opposite direction this time. There was a volley of gunshots, and then glass shattered.

"It's starting," breathed Logan.

It didn't feel right, standing here waiting for the rebels to take down the PMC bases. We should have been out there fighting.

No. We shouldn't have been there at all.

Suddenly I felt very young. I wanted to go back to college and never think about fighting or killing again. I wanted to go to parties, go on runs with Greyson, and spend late mornings lounging in bed with Amory.

But Amory was part of *this* life. Without the fighting, I wouldn't have him or Logan or Roman or Ida. I was completely different now.

I stared out at the street. PMC officers were flooding out of the base, some fanning out to defend it, others breaking off to subdue the nearby violence.

The rebels' plan was working.

Logan was kneeling by the low concrete wall of the parking garage, her rifle propped up on the ledge. At first I thought she was just resting it there, but she was lining up her shot.

The Last Uprising

"Logan! No!" Amory hissed.

"Do you expect me to just sit here when I've got the perfect shot?" she snapped.

"Yes," said Greyson, sliding down the wall beside her and pulling her rifle down. "We have to stay out of sight. We have a job to do."

She looked irritated, but I could tell Greyson's soft brown puppy eyes were more persuasive to her than Amory's bark.

But I was getting antsy, too. From my vantage point, I could make out a battered rebel SUV speeding down the street toward the swarm of officers, an arm swinging out the window. Something flew through the air, landing in the crowd of officers. Before they could do anything, an explosion shook the entire street.

Momentarily blinded, I stumbled back as the wave of heat reached us. Amory's arms fumbled for me as we both hit the hard concrete. Somebody screamed, and the acrid stench of burning plastic and hair reached my nostrils.

"Those crazy fuckers," yelled Roman, his deep, booming voice echoing off the walls.

There were more gunshots, and a few streets over, another explosion rocked the parking deck.

The cacophony of gunfire, sirens, and screaming mixed together in a horrific pulse that shook my ribcage as I lay curled on the concrete under Amory's arm.

Finally, we hoisted ourselves up and crawled over to Logan. She was coughing loudly, and I could tell she had inhaled a lot more smoke than I had.

"You okay?" I croaked.

She gave a shaky nod, and we all turned to look at the base.

The Last Uprising

Windows all along the first few stories were shattered. Bodies clad in PMC whites lay sprawled everywhere, covered in bits of brick and rubble. A few officers were staggering to their feet and dragging themselves from the wreckage, but another rebel truck was approaching from the opposite direction. There was a volley of shots, and the remaining officers fell.

"Do you think that's all of them?" Greyson wondered aloud.

"No," said Amory. "But I think it's as good as we're going to get."

"Let's get this shit over with," said Roman, strapping on his holster impatiently.

Once Logan had recovered from her coughing fit, we vaulted the low wall and sprinted across the deserted street. My legs were moving without consulting my brain, and I didn't even feel the burning in my lungs as we flew full force toward the Infinity Building.

It was only a block away — an imposing titanium formation that consumed the skyline.

We ducked behind a parked cruiser, and Amory checked that no officers were headed toward us.

"Go!" he breathed, and we all took off toward the building at a sprint.

I hefted my rifle in my hands, preparing to shoot, my legs and arms working of their own accord.

Logan was in full sniper mode now. Her hair was pulled back into a slick ponytail, and her beautiful face was set in stone.

The last time we entered the building, we had come up from the parking garage in an elevator. But since the visitors' entrance would be on lockdown, we were planning to storm the front steps. Four heavily armed officers were standing outside the door, which didn't seem like very much security to me.

Roman threw out an arm, and my chest slammed into his rock-hard triceps. With the wind knocked out of me, I didn't fight as Amory pulled me behind another parked car.

He pointed up, and I followed his gaze to a building across the street. From one open window, I could just discern the tiniest flash of white. A sniper was perched there.

"They probably have more. We need to move fast."

"We can't just rush them all at once," said Greyson. "That would be exactly the scenario they've planned for."

"So what, then?"

"We take them from two sides," offered Logan, following Greyson's train of thought with ease.

Amory nodded. "Roman and I will approach them head-on. You three take them from the sides."

"You have to let us go in first," I said. "We'll have the element of surprise. It will be less dangerous if you let us take out as many as we can before you move in."

He nodded, clearly distressed that I had circumvented his efforts to keep us out of danger.

We dashed out from behind the parked car, skirting around a building that was out of the sniper's line of sight.

Please don't let there be any PMC, I thought.

If we had to open fire this close to the building, the guards would hear, and we would lose our advantage. More would come rushing in to fortify the building, and we'd have a much harder time shooting our way in.

The street was eerily quiet as we moved down the rows of buildings. Suddenly I wondered if they were empty or if they

The Last Uprising

were businesses run by displaced Canadians living under World Corp's regime.

Greyson turned up an alley, and I followed, hoping his sense of direction had magically improved overnight.

As we skirted down the narrow street, the corner of the Infinity Building came into view. We were at the perfect vantage point to take out the officers.

We crouched down behind a dumpster, and I checked my gun. Here, we could each get a clear shot at an officer.

"I've got the far right," said Logan, lining up her shot.

A pang of worry hit me as I watched her fingers shake on the trigger.

"I'm fine," she hissed, irritated by my pointed gaze. "I won't miss."

Forcing myself to swallow any doubts, I found my target. "Second from the right."

"I got far left," said Greyson.

That was smart. The final guard left would look to both sides, giving us one extra second to take him out.

"One . . . two . . ."

But then one of the officers raised his rifle, and a shot rang out from farther away. To my horror, I saw Roman sprinting out from his and Amory's hiding place, shooting at the officers. Amory was nowhere in sight.

Roman staggered, and I knew he'd been hit.

"Shit," breathed Greyson, lining up his shot again.

I didn't waste any time. I found my target again, shooting and praying. I hit my officer straight in the chest, and he went down.

Logan shot, missed, and swore loudly, lining up another

The Last Uprising

shot. "He moved," she growled, fending off a remark I had no intention of delivering.

My heart was pounding too loudly. Roman was still staggering, lifting his gun despite his injury. I still couldn't see Amory.

"Is he out of his mind?" Greyson yelled after he'd shot again. There were still two officers standing.

"It's the virus," said Logan. "He's not himself right now."

Why hadn't Amory appeared? Had he been hit? I had heard two gunshots, but I assumed one had been the fatal shot to the officer.

"We need to move in before we lose our window," I said. "Now!"

Greyson and Logan didn't argue. We shot out from behind the dumpster and sprinted toward the building. The officers heard us approaching and aimed their rifles in our direction, and then one shuddered and fell to the ground.

Amory.

I shot at the other officer and hit him too low. He fired at Logan as he went down, missing by inches, and she delivered another shot to his head.

We had reached the marble steps. An alarm was sounding within the building. It must have been triggered by the gunshots' reverberations.

A blistering sting of heat unlike anything I'd ever experienced hit my shoulder.

My eyes watered and I froze, but my feet kept moving without consulting my brain. I stumbled, feeling warmth spreading down my arm — pain. Something was wrong.

I raised my hand to my shoulder, and it came away sticky with blood. The sniper had grazed me. I'd been *shot*.

The Last Uprising

I wanted to throw up, but a delirious laugh bubbled out of my mouth, and I threw myself against the glass doors. They wouldn't budge, and I bounced off like a mosquito hitting a light bulb. Blackness was pushing at the edges of my vision as though I were wearing blinders.

"Get out of the way," growled Roman. He had come up right behind me, clutching his arm.

He was bleeding profusely. He fumbled with his rifle, but he didn't seem to be able to raise his left arm.

"I got it," said Amory, flying to the door. He snapped two black devices I'd seen him use before onto the glass and then pulled me with him until we were in the shadow of a large planter, hidden from the sniper's view.

Everything was moving very slowly, and the numbness was overtaking my body. I couldn't believe all my limbs still worked.

Logan, Roman, and Greyson hit the deck, and I crushed my hands over my ears as the rhythmic beeping began.

There was a wave of heat and a tremor that shook the marble steps. The doors shattered.

Unwilling to give the sniper any more chances, we scrambled to our feet and dashed inside. We were barely inside the building, and two of us were already shot. We were such amateurs.

"You're bleeding," said Amory.

I tried to shrug, but the tiny gesture sent a wave of pain down my arm. Now that the shock had worn off, the burning feeling was intensifying. At least I could raise my rifle. Roman threw his down and reached behind him with his good arm. He produced a handgun, and I wondered if he'd lifted it when Switch wasn't paying attention.

I could hear movement in the lobby. There were more

The Last Uprising

officers inside. Greyson lunged around the corner first, sending an officer in white sprawling across the floor as he fired.

Greyson ducked back around the corner, panting.

"How many?" I breathed.

"Fifteen or so."

Amory swore.

Roman ducked around the corner, and a volley of shots cracked through the air. For a moment, none of us breathed, but then he jumped back around, his arm bleeding worse than before from exertion.

"Make that thirteen. They're guarding the elevators."

That was it. We were done for. We knew this place — only one way in or out, now that the visitors' entrance was sealed. The walls were sheets of titanium. Between the officers and our own ricocheting bullets, there was no way all of us were coming out of here alive.

We looked at each other, knowing we didn't have much time.

"The desk," I said suddenly. "Run for the round desk in the center of the room."

Roman nodded reluctantly.

My pulse was racing, but my head felt clear. I couldn't even feel my shoulder anymore. The tears had dried in my lashes.

I reached up and kissed Amory briefly, and when I pulled away, he wore a fierce expression that mirrored everything I felt.

"Let's go," Roman said.

I nodded, steeling myself for the worst, and we dashed

around the corner.

Taking aim at the officer nearest me, I hit him in the abdomen — not a clean kill. The others were firing behind me, but I focused on pumping my legs and propelling myself toward the round desk in the center of the lobby. I didn't stop.

Across the room, an officer raised his rifle, and I knew he was aiming at me. His partner was aiming at Amory. *What were we thinking?* These officers were trained. Of course they had a strategy.

I only had one option.

I dove onto the floor, their shots echoing off the walls. I hit the ground harder than I'd wanted to, but it worked. The officer who'd been aiming at Amory stopped, training his rifle on me instead.

I struggled to get to my feet. Roman was already at the desk. He vaulted it and poked his head up. His arm came up, training his gun on the officer aiming at me. It all happened so quickly I wasn't sure who fired first. All I knew was there was a gleam of satisfaction in the officer's eye, and Amory was diving down in front of me.

He fell on top of me, unable to cushion his landing, and I felt the warmth of blood that wasn't mine. The officer who had shot at me fell to the ground. Roman's gun was still raised, pointed in his direction.

Greyson and Logan slid over the desk, but I couldn't feel relief. Amory let out a low howl of pain.

There were more gunshots. My ears felt as though they would bleed. Every shot and every echo reverberated deep in my bones.

"Amory?" I whimpered. "Amory?"

He mumbled something I couldn't understand.

The Last Uprising

"Where are you hit? Amory?" My voice was two octaves too high. I couldn't think. I couldn't breathe.

I tried to shift Amory. We had to *move*. We had to take cover.

A bullet whizzed past me, narrowly missing my head. With every ounce of strength I had, I pushed Amory off me. He fell back onto the white marble, his eyes squeezed together. He was clutching his chest, and my heart tripped erratically.

No. No, no, no. This wasn't happening.

Somebody else shot, and I raised to a crouch and whipped my rifle around. Miraculously, I took out an officer, but two more were encroaching.

I didn't know what to do. I had to move Amory, but I couldn't stop shooting.

My hands were starting to shake. I gripped my rifle tighter, trying to maintain control, but I was cornered.

Another shot made me jump.

Greyson had taken down one of the remaining officers, but there was still one crouched behind a bronze bust, his dark eyes flashing behind his helmet. I moved to raise my gun, but his was already trained on me. There was nothing I could do.

Instead of raising my rifle to fight the inevitable, I dropped toward Amory, falling onto my knees and reaching out for him one last time. I braced myself for the inevitable pain — the choking cold that would clamp down on me as the blood poured from my chest.

A final shot cracked through the air, the echo cutting up the high ceiling and piercing my eardrums.

My knees hit the hard marble floor, but I hadn't been shot.

The Last Uprising

I looked around. Logan had her gun pointed where the PMC officer had been. Now he was slumped against the brushed titanium wall. I'd given her a clear shot.

It only took a fraction of a second for reality to sink in. Amory was in front of me, bleeding — dying.

A heavy silence descended.

"Amory?" I gurgled, tears stinging my eyes and throat. I moved his hand, and he winced.

Hot, sticky blood coated his fingers, and more was seeping down his shirt.

Now that I was this close, I could tell the bullet was embedded too high to have hit his heart, but he was bleeding heavily. I pressed my hands over the wound, applying pressure.

"Haven . . ." he murmured.

"Why did you . . .?" I swallowed down the messy tears that were burning in my throat. "Help me," I choked. "Help me. They shot him."

A second later, Greyson, Logan, and Roman were at my side.

"We have to move him," I said. "More PMC will come."

"There's no time," said Roman, his voice surprisingly gentle. "We have to keep going."

I shot him a nasty look, but I knew he was right. We could not fail. We had to kill Aryus.

"You keep going," I said. My voice was shaking. "I'll take care of him."

"You can't move him," said Logan.

She was right. I glanced at Roman, but he was already reloading his gun, wincing as he used his injured arm. Even if he *could* move Amory in his current state, there was no way he would agree to stay behind.

"I'll stay," said Greyson quietly. "You go."

My tears doubled when I looked at him. Greyson really was the best friend I could ask for, but leaving him with Amory would put him in more danger. If another wave of officers came, he would be on his own.

"Go," he repeated. "You know this building."

Feeling like a blubbering idiot, I threw a bloody arm around Greyson's neck. Then I turned to Amory, pushing his hair back. His eyes were fluttering closed.

"Stay with me," I whispered. "I love you."

And we were gone.

Chapter Twenty-Nine

It was easier than I thought it would be to leave all thoughts of Amory and Greyson behind as we entered the small, sterile-looking elevator.

I *couldn't* think about them. If we didn't kill Aryus, I would have failed everyone.

The elevator doors closed, and I knew Greyson had punched in the correct floor from the console at the desk when the robotic female voice spoke.

We shot up through the building, and I tried to block out the steady sound of Roman's blood dripping on the clean white floor. Logan looked as though she might be sick, but my hands were surprisingly steady on my gun as we waited. I felt deadly calm. We had to finish the job. There was no other option.

The elevator doors flew open with a friendly *ding*. We each raised our weapons, expecting officers to swarm the elevator. But the hallway was deserted.

I recognized the sound of trickling water coming from the industrial fountain snaking along the sharply rounded hallway. We inched around in a tight circle, and I caught a glimpse of Roman's face out of the corner of my eye. He looked a little green around the edges, and I knew he was fighting the exhaustion, fever, and blood loss.

Then we rounded the corner, and I saw a flash of white. I aimed, but a familiar voice stopped me.

"I wouldn't do that if I were you."

The officer turned. It was Mariah.

As I took in her smug smile and that greasy blond hair pulled back into a tight bun, a million hateful remarks burned on my tongue. I longed to toss my rifle aside and tear her apart with my bare hands.

"You shoot me, and that robot will shoot you." She gestured over her head to the swiveling weaponized rover.

So Ida had been right. In the end, Aryus guarded himself with the only person he could trust.

"He's in there, you know," she teased, the light glinting off her smartlens. She was stroking the trigger of her rifle as if it were a shiny black bird, reveling in the power she held over us. "He's pacing." She threw us a mock pouty expression. "Poor baby. He does that a lot."

"Jeez, you really *do* fuck your way to the top," Roman blurted.

Mariah's rifle moved toward him with a metallic jerk. Something about the way she turned on him reminded me of a cobra, poised to strike.

I mentally pleaded with Roman not to do anything stupid. Mariah was volatile. Doctor Carson would say her behavior was the result of residual brain damage caused by the virus. But her cockiness made her stupid. If given the chance, Mariah would let her guard down. The briefest second was all we needed.

"I didn't fuck him, you asshole," Mariah spat. "He just knows he can trust me." She seemed to toy with this notion for a moment. "Stupid, really . . . you should never trust anyone. Given half a chance, anyone will turn on you."

"Like Aryus did, you mean?" I asked.

Mariah's gaze snapped to me. "He lied, yes. It doesn't

matter." Her lips formed a poisonous sneer. "I'm used to it. People are liars by nature."

She took a step toward me, and I could see the dark shadows under her eyes behind the smartlens — the way her skin looked pinched around the mouth. She wasn't much older than we were, but she looked it.

"You're a funny one, Haven. We bring you over to our side, and you still end up crawling back to the rebels. Such an idealist.

"I tried to tell Aryus the conditioning would never hold. Once a defector slut . . . always a defector slut."

I smiled — happy I got under Mariah's skin even half as much as she got under mine. I took a deep breath, trying a different tactic.

"His men killed Jared," I said quietly. "They shot him like a dog in this very building. Doesn't that *bother* you?"

By the shadow that crossed Mariah's face, I knew I had struck a nerve.

"*Liar*," she spat.

I hadn't expected that.

"You're lying to try to get a rise out of me. Aryus told me Jared went back with you."

I shook my head, hardly able to believe Mariah had taken Aryus's words to heart. Then I realized that besides her brother, Aryus was probably the person she'd trusted the most since he had cured her.

"You liar!" she screamed.

The more she called me a liar, the more her hardened expression cracked. She believed me.

"I'm sorry," I said. "I thought you knew." As much as I hated Mariah, I really was sorry. The love she had for her brother was the *only* thing that ever made her seem human.

But something was changing inside her. All the hatred and despair and helplessness were welling up behind those catlike eyes. Suddenly she wasn't the PMC officer anymore. But she wasn't Mariah the rebel, either — the dangerous, cunning mind behind Rulon's leadership.

All the power and cruelty was gone, leaving an empty, dull husk of a human being behind.

She lowered her gun. I watched her reach up to her brow and tap the lens. Instantly, the swiveling rover stopped tracking us, and the light went out.

Mariah tugged off her smartlens and threw it on the ground.

"I won't stop you. But you probably only have a couple minutes before this place will be surrounded."

I could hardly believe what had just happened.

As she stormed off, I could see the sag in her shoulders and the uncertainty in her gait. She was a woman with nothing left to lose. Mariah — the person I knew I could never trust — had just become our greatest asset and Aryus's undoing.

"Come on," said Logan, nodding toward the door.

Needing no further instruction, Roman kicked the door in. It flew backward, banging off the titanium wall, and the three of us ran inside, rifles raised.

"Mariah, I —"

Aryus was standing in the center of the room, swiping furiously at a tablet resting on a high glass table. He looked up at the sound of our rough entry, all the color draining from his too-tan face.

He recovered almost instantly, pulling out a smirk to

match the sharp lines of his goatee. He was dressed all in white as he had been the last time, but he was wearing light suede slippers and an impeccably tailored jacket. He was fleeing his fortress.

"Going somewhere?" Roman snarled.

"As a matter of fact, I was," said Aryus, clicking a button on the rounded wall.

Instantly, the enormous, ceiling-wide skylight defrosted, and a helicopter came into view, resting on the glass.

"There's quite a hullabaloo going on in the city, as I understand it," Aryus continued. "My advisors tell me I should relocate for my own safety until this whole mess is sorted out."

He smiled, and I got that horrible sick feeling in my stomach that reminded me of my time as his prisoner.

"A little late for that," said Roman.

"Oh, Roman . . ." Aryus clicked his tongue with regret. "You could have been such an *officer*. You were on the fast track, my boy. What with your size and brains . . ."

He gestured to the sky, and I wanted to roll my eyes at his own sense of self-importance about his military company.

"You're done," I breathed.

"Oh . . . no, I don't think so," Aryus scoffed. "No. For one thing, I can tell Roman here is in stage one of the virus. He wants the cure as much as he wants me dead.

"For another, there's a much bigger problem than you originally anticipated going on down below."

It was silent for a moment, and I listened intently for the sound of gunshots, but I couldn't hear anything except the persistent hum of Aryus's helicopter on the roof.

"Carriers," Aryus breathed. "A huge swarm of them. This

is what happens when you have a security breach of undesirables." His gaze lingered on me for a long moment. "They bring all kinds of trash with them."

I opened my mouth to retort, but then I knew what we had to do. I raised my gun, but before my finger closed on the trigger, a shot pierced my eardrums.

The sound reverberated around the small space, and I lowered my gun incrementally, turning to Roman. But he had not shot Aryus.

I turned to Logan and saw her gun drop to her side. She met my gaze, and then my eyes traveled down to her chest.

A sticky wet spot had appeared on the front of her black turtleneck.

Confusion came first, followed by a sick feeling in my throat.

"No!" I yelled, whipping around behind me, gun poised.

Mariah was standing in the doorway holding a handgun, her face devoid of all emotion.

"Do you think I'm so stupid I didn't know about Jared?" she snarled. "Do you think I don't know when I'm being *fucked* with?"

"So you helped him?" I spat.

"I should have been smarter. You can't trust anyone. Only —"

I didn't hear the rest of what she said — just the blast of my own rifle.

With her last hateful words still lingering on her lips, Mariah fell backward and slumped against the far wall.

There was another shot. Aryus staggered back against the high glass table, knocking it to the floor.

The table shattered into a million pieces over the white marble floor and the snowy rug.

Roman had placed a bullet in Aryus's forehead, right between the eyes.

Logan staggered and fell to her knees, and I grabbed her around the shoulders to slow her fall.

She collapsed onto the white carpet, and I pushed my hands against her wound, trying to stop the flow of blood. She grimaced in pain, but I kept my hands over the hole in her chest.

"Oh my god . . . Logan!"

"She shot me," Logan mused. "I can't believe that bitch shot me."

"It's okay. It's okay." My heart was pounding so loudly, I couldn't hear anything except her voice and the rush of blood in my ears.

"Haven . . . I'm hit . . ."

"I know. It's okay."

"I . . ." She stopped, looking around in confusion.

"Logan . . . Logan! Stay with me."

She sucked in a shaky breath, trying to smile, but tears just filled her eyes.

"Logan, come on . . ."

"I don't think I'm going to make it." She sounded vaguely surprised, disappointed.

"You have to!" I cried, my voice breaking. "Don't give her the satisfaction."

"I won't," she gurgled. "No . . . Mariah did what she had to do."

I shook my head, tears clouding my vision. "W-What do

you mean?"

Logan tried to swallow, but it looked painful. "It doesn't matter."

I stared at her. She couldn't be hurt — not Logan. Logan couldn't die.

Her golden hair was fanned out behind her like sunshine, and her bright green eyes were glassy with tears. She was invincible.

"Don't tell Greyson, but . . ." She paused, and I gripped her arm, squeezing tightly.

"Tell Greyson what?"

"At least this way . . . I get to see Max again."

A wet sob escaped my lips, but I didn't feel anything. I was numb with shock.

"Logan . . . Max would want you *here*."

My voice sounded as though I was pleading with her to stay, and maybe I was.

She shook her head slightly, but it cost her too much effort. She closed her eyes. "No . . . Max wanted to *be* here. He should be here."

"But your parents . . . and Sebastian."

Her eyes opened hazily. "Will you find them for me?" she asked, hope lighting her face. "If you know they're all right, then I'll know they're all right."

I didn't know what that meant. She wasn't making sense, and her warm blood was gushing between my fingers, spilling out onto the carpet. I wanted to pour it back into her and put her back together again, but I couldn't fix this.

"Haven . . . I'm so glad I got to know you." Logan's eyes were lidded, barely staying open. "You're my best friend."

I sobbed openly just then, letting my head fall toward my chest. "I can't do this without you."

"Sure you can. Don't be sad for me." She swallowed laboriously. "We did it."

I nodded, pushing my hands into her wound harder, desperate to stop the bleeding. But her eyes were closing now. Her face was no longer strained in agony.

Her perfect lips relaxed, as though in sleep, and I felt her slip away.

I stared at her for a long moment, waiting for her to speak again, but her lips were frozen. She wouldn't laugh or smile or talk to me again.

I looked up at Roman and was startled to see he had tears in his eyes.

He wiped his face on his sleeve, sniffing loudly. He let out an agonized yell as I'd never heard, shooting at Aryus's motionless body again. It twitched where the bullet hit him, but he stayed like that.

"He's ruined *everything*," he spat, a low waver in his voice.

I could barely understand what he was saying. There was an odd ringing in my ears.

Logan was dead.

I couldn't fathom it. Logan — the sharpshooter who saved up her nail polish after the Collapse and read trashy romance novels and kissed my friends. She was gone. It was as though a light had gone out in the room.

Wordlessly, I stood and crossed to the cabinet fitted seamlessly into Aryus's wall and pushed against it. A drawer slid out, revealing six gleaming syringes filled with clear liquid — so harmless looking, yet so potent.

Roman was still yelling, his face red and hot with anger. I

didn't even hear what he was saying.

I grabbed his flailing arm, and he physically flinched when I touched him. My hands were red with Logan's blood.

I removed the cap, tested the syringe as Amory had taught me, and plunged the needle into Roman's arm.

When I had finished, he was blinking in disbelief. He'd stopped yelling, and his shoulders slumped forward as if the silence took a physical toll on him.

Thinking of the value of these five syringes — with the power to save five people's lives — I scooped them out of the tray and handed them to Roman. He looked at them for a moment and then nodded, shoving them into his coat pocket.

I looked back at Logan lying on the carpet, so still and peaceful, like a sleeping angel.

Now that it was quiet, I could hear commotion outside over the sound of Aryus's helicopter. There was a narrow spiral staircase along the wall, and I followed Roman up the clanking stairs. He pushed open the hatch on the ceiling, and we stuck our heads out of the top of the building.

I peered over the edge. Aryus had not exaggerated. There was a crowd of carriers moving down the block. A thin column of PMC officers was poised in front of the Infinity Building trying to subdue them, but I knew it was futile. There had to be more than five hundred carriers and only a hundred officers. Even if they managed to mow down some of the carriers, they would be overwhelmed by sheer force.

I looked around for Roman, but he had disappeared. I called out for him, but there was no answer. I knew I should return to Aryus's chamber, but I couldn't stand to see Logan's lifeless body again.

Amory, I thought suddenly. I couldn't lose him, too. He and Greyson were waiting for us. We had to move.

But then Roman appeared again, dragging something — someone — through the hatch with his uninjured arm.

"No!" I cried, horrified when he hauled Aryus's limp form through the hatch. "What are you doing?"

"This has to happen, Haven."

The disgust churned in my stomach when I realized what he was suggesting.

"That's barbaric, Roman."

"It's the only way this will ever end."

I shook my head.

"Haven! If we leave him in here, who do you think will find him next? World Corp will just pretend that he's still alive."

"It doesn't matter."

"It *does* matter. He's the symbol of all of this. People need to see he's gone, or they'll never believe it's over. They need to understand they've lost."

I couldn't argue. I knew he was right. World Corp would definitely try to cover up Aryus's death. He was the most powerful man in the world.

Roman could see from my face that I'd given in. Without another word, he hoisted Aryus over his beefy shoulder, wincing in pain as he moved his bleeding arm, and stepped toward the ledge.

The carriers had reached the teetering chain of officers. I could almost feel Roman's satisfaction wafting over me. He wanted the carriers to rip Aryus's body to shreds. Even I couldn't argue that it had some poetic justice.

With a grunt like a shot putter, Roman launched Aryus over the ledge, and I watched him sail toward the ground in a flash of white. I looked away, not wanting to see him hit the pavement.

"We have to go," I said. "We have to get Amory and Greyson."

Now that the job was done, all I could feel was terror for them.

Roman was surprisingly gentle as he helped me down from the roof. He'd covered Logan's body with one of Aryus's fluffy white blankets, and I marveled at the thoughtfulness of this gesture.

"I don't want to leave her here," I choked.

"We don't have a choice," said Roman. "Besides, Logan's not in there anymore."

To anyone else, this might have sounded harsh, but Roman's voice was softer than usual, and he was right. Logan was never one for this world. She was too good.

I knelt briefly beside Logan's body and touched a single lock of blond hair that had escaped her ponytail.

"I'll take care of them," I whispered, pulling the blanket over her still face.

I stood, fighting the tears that threatened to burst forth, and followed Roman back down the spiral hallway. He punched the elevator button furiously, but the doors wouldn't open. I remembered that all the elevators were controlled from the desk in the lobby. The rover with the camera was down, and even if Greyson and Amory were all right, they wouldn't be able to see us leaving Aryus's chamber and coming back down the hall.

Following the smooth wall opposite the bubbling fountain, we located a door to the emergency staircase and pushed.

It took forever to wind our way down through the building, and by the time we reached the bottom, I was dizzy and out of breath.

Roman shoved against the door, pulling his gun out of his waistband, but the lobby was deserted.

"Greyson!" I called. My voice echoed off the rounded walls, and the emptiness made me feel more alone than ever. I'd lost Logan already; I didn't think I'd be able to stand it if I'd lost Greyson and Amory, too.

I ran to the center of the room where we'd left them behind the desk. There was only a pool of blood, smeared by footprints and someone being dragged away. Whether the footprints belonged to Greyson or PMC, I couldn't tell.

"Greyson!"

Only my own voice answered back. Roman sighed beside me, and I felt the surprising weight of his hand on my good shoulder.

"We'll find them," he said.

"No we won't," I said with a sniff. "They're gone."

"Ready to give up on me so quick?"

I snapped my head around toward the sound of Greyson's voice, hope flooding my chest.

His head was sticking out of a door fitted seamlessly into the titanium wall, floating like a ghost.

"Oh my god!" I cried, sprinting toward him.

He stepped out into the lobby, nearly falling back against the wall as I threw my good arm around him.

"Where's Amory?" I asked anxiously, pulling back to examine Greyson for injuries.

"He's fine." It was just like Greyson to understand instinctively what I *really* wanted to know. I looked around him and saw Amory's feet resting against a huge stack of paper towels.

"It's a janitorial closet," said Greyson. "I moved him in here to hide, and I found a first aid kit. I got the bleeding to stop, but he needs to see Shriver right away."

Greyson was looking around me at Roman, his eyes scanning the lobby anxiously.

My heart sank when I realized who he was looking for. I didn't want him to ask. I didn't think I could handle it.

"Where's Logan?" The anxiety in his voice tore at my heart.

I looked away, unable to see his face fall when I told him. "She got shot," I choked. "By Mariah."

Greyson's gaze flickered, and a shudder rolled through him. "What?"

He didn't want to put this information together with Logan's absence. He didn't want to face the truth.

"No!" said Greyson, tears filling his eyes.

I gripped his arms tightly, but he jerked around, shaking his head in disbelief.

I didn't say anything. Tears were streaming down my face. I looked at him, willing him to accept what had happened. I couldn't take the denial.

He yanked out of my grasp and flung himself away from me. "No! She can't be *gone!*"

I didn't know what to say. I never did when Greyson was hurting. His pain had a way of mixing with my own grief and compounding it.

He spun away, pressing the heels of his hands against his eyes — hard — as if trying to stop the tide of despair.

"We shouldn't have believed her," I said. "Mariah tricked

us."

The weight of responsibility hit me like a ton of bricks. If we had just killed Mariah as she turned to leave, Logan would still be alive.

But then I realized Mariah must have intended to leave when she had heard her brother had been killed. She had only returned because she knew she had nowhere else to go.

"We have to get out of here," said Roman. I noticed his voice had changed since we'd lost Logan. Everything he said was softer, as though her death had ripped away his usual hard exterior. "Carriers are storming the city. We'll be trapped here if we don't move."

"I'll get the car," said Greyson, his voice husky.

I didn't want him going out there alone, but I couldn't look at him. Roman seemed to read my mind and followed him outside, reloading his gun.

When they disappeared from sight, I ducked into the closet to check on Amory. He was covered in blood and too pale, but he was breathing. His dark lashes were fanned out, throwing shadows over his cheeks as he slept.

As I reached out and ran my thumb over his scruffy jaw, I was glad he was unconscious. I didn't think I could bear to explain Logan's death again.

After a moment, his eyes opened lazily, and he smiled up at me.

"Hey."

"Hey," I said, unable to hold back a weak smile.

"I got shot," he said, as though he needed to bring me up to speed. "It hurts like a bitch."

"I know. You took a bullet for me."

He shrugged, wincing. "I'd do it all again."

I squeezed his hand. "Just hang in there, okay? We're going home."

As I said those words, my heart sank a little because I had no idea where "home" was anymore. I forced myself not to think of the future — only about getting Amory to Shriver and getting us out of this city.

A few minutes passed with Amory slipping in and out of consciousness, and I heard the rumble of an SUV.

I flew out of the closet and ran outside. The Xterra was blazing toward the building through a huge swarm of carriers, mowing down any that crossed in its path.

Roman was white-knuckling the steering wheel, and Greyson looked as though he might be sick. I realized Roman wasn't hitting the carriers on purpose — there was just no other way to get through the huge mob.

He stopped the car, parking parallel to the marble stairs, and Greyson jumped out and ran toward me. The look on his face sent a shiver down my back: sheer ruthless determination devoid of emotion.

Greyson was shutting down.

I followed him back inside. Without a word, he lifted Amory from behind the shoulders, and I grabbed his feet. Amory awoke, wincing in pain as we shifted him, and I forced myself not to look at his face. Roman was standing outside the SUV, fending off encroaching carriers with his fists.

Two stray carriers staggered toward me, and I dropped Amory's feet for a moment.

My elbow jutted out and connected with the nearest carrier's jaw. He groaned, and I stomped my boot down above his knee cap, bringing him to the ground. My arm flew out on its own again, my fist striking the second carrier. She wailed, and I grabbed her by the shoulders so I could lodge my knee in her gut.

Greyson was staggering under Amory's weight, so I pushed the carrier aside and ran to help him hoist him into the backseat.

Greyson jumped in the car, and I called out to Roman.

He was no longer fighting, but five more carriers were ambling up the marble steps toward him.

"Roman!" I yelled.

He was in a daze.

"Roman!" I called again. He didn't move.

I grabbed the rifle lying across the front seat and turned it on the carriers. The kickback stung my shoulder, and Roman seemed to come back to life. He kicked one of the carriers out of the way and threw out his fist to take out another. Then he climbed into the driver's seat as I picked off the last two, his big hands shaking as he pulled on his seatbelt.

I dropped the gun and jumped in, feeling the bile rise up in my throat. I didn't have the stomach for killing anymore.

"I have to fix this," Roman groaned, putting the vehicle into reverse and pulling out around the dead carriers.

"What?"

I wanted to be patient — sensitive to the agony he must be feeling — but we needed to forget about hitting carriers and get the hell out of here.

"All this time I've been hating *them*." Roman nodded toward a carrier that was bent over a dead officer, tearing at his jugular. "When I should have been trying to stop Aryus."

I glanced over at him and was startled to see a muscle working in his jaw as though he might cry.

I looked away. I couldn't think about Logan, all the

The Last Uprising

people we'd killed, or all the people I would *still* kill just to get my friends to safety.

"You did stop him," I said quietly.

Roman shook his head, reaching into his pocket to pull out the extra syringes. "It's not enough."

"No," I sighed, staring down at my blood-soaked sleeves. "It's never enough."

Chapter Thirty

After the last base fell, it wasn't difficult to find the rest of the rebels.

They had taken over an enormous hotel far enough removed from the fighting to shelter the injured rebels and refugees who had fled the communes. There were guards stationed all around the block, fending off stray carriers that had wandered from the horde.

When Roman pulled up to the circle drive, two rebels toting a stretcher appeared to help us extricate Amory from the car. He was barely conscious by the time they lifted him out of the backseat, and I worried that the move had been too much for him.

We followed the men into the hotel lobby, and my eyes settled on an unusual sight. Rebels were sitting with escaped commune dwellers. People in white and black were bunched together between potted plants on the green loveseats, shaking, sobbing, laughing, and holding one another. They had tracked blood and dirt all over the polished parquet floor. The bewildered hotel staff were flitting around with carafes of hot coffee, setting out trays of bagels and cream cheese, and discreetly trying to mop up the foyer.

We followed Amory's stretcher into the grand ballroom, where twenty or so rollaway beds had been lined up to form a hospital ward. Most were already occupied by injured rebels, and Shriver was flitting from bed to bed, looking harried but completely in her element.

Doctor Carson was also bent over a bed, and it warmed my heart to see Shriver sharing the space with him. Despite their differences, they were fighting for the same thing.

When Shriver spotted us, a smile broke over her face. "I can't believe it," she said, coming toward us. "I never thought you'd make it. Honestly."

"Thanks for the vote of confidence," grumbled Roman. I knew the cure had to be taking hold because he looked a little nauseated.

"Amory's hurt," I said. "He's been shot. Actually, most of us have been shot."

"Where's Logan?" she asked.

I swallowed. "She didn't make it."

Instantly, Shriver dropped her veil of cool efficiency, and she directed the men with the stretcher toward a table surrounded by a decorative bamboo partition.

I refused to leave Amory's side as Shriver removed his bandages and extracted the bullet fragments. At one point, Amory passed out from the pain, but I held his hand and listened for the *ding* of metal on metal as the fragments hit Shriver's tray.

Roman watched the operation slumped in an armchair, and Doctor Carson came over to treat his gunshot wound. I caught Shriver shooting Roman concerned looks. She didn't know he had taken the cure, but it was written all over his face. He had witnessed Logan's terrible recovery, and I knew he was anticipating the weeks or months of fever and sickness and possible loss of motor function.

After an hour, he fell asleep, his hand curled in his pocket with the extra syringes. I was grateful for the cure, not just because Roman wouldn't turn, but because he now had a purpose that would carry him through the months to come.

Doctor Carson insisted on cleaning my wound, and once Amory had passed out from the painkillers, I looked around for Greyson. He was nowhere in sight.

I asked the Canadian teenager at the front desk, who told me he had given Greyson a room. When a new wave of rebels staggered through the front door and distracted the boy, I swiped the master key and went upstairs.

The hotel was eerily quiet away from the chaos of the lobby and ballroom. I found Greyson's room and knocked softly on the door. He didn't answer.

Fitting the key card into the lock, I tried to think what I would say to him, but there was nothing I *could* say. There were no words for what had happened.

The door swung open. It was dark inside the room, except for the light coming through the open curtains. The room had a window that went nearly all the way from the floor to the ceiling, and Greyson was lying in bed on top of the covers, staring out at the night sky.

I didn't blame him. I didn't like the room's oppressively low ceiling, the nondescript walls, or the pristine burgundy carpet. After months of camping outdoors and living on the farm, the inside of a hotel felt fake — too clean.

I pulled back the covers and lay down beside him, watching a lone car speeding down the road. It was strange how few of the skyscrapers were lit up. Most had been overtaken by the PMC, and now they stood empty.

"I'm sorry," I whispered, not knowing what else to say.

"I should have been there, Haven," he mumbled.

"No. There was nothing you could have done."

"How did it *happen*?" His voice was overly accusatory, but I shoved down my guilt.

"It was Mariah," I said.

I explained how she had been guarding Aryus's chamber — how she had turned on him, only to return moments later to kill us.

"So she *lied*?" Greyson asked when I had finished. His voice was muffled and watery, and I knew he was crying.

"No," I said honestly. "I really don't think she was lying at all. We could have easily killed Aryus the second we walked through the door. He wasn't armed.

"I think she realized she had been betrayed but had nowhere else to go. She couldn't trust the rebels, the PMC, or Aryus, but she probably believed the rebels would lose, and she wanted to align herself with power."

Greyson shifted to stare at the ceiling, and I watched a lone tear slide down the side of his face.

"Do you think she loved me?"

"Yes," I said automatically.

It didn't feel like a lie — even after what Logan had said right before she died. I truly believed that if Logan had lived, she and Greyson would have been together.

Greyson nodded, drawing in a shaky breath. "God, she was impossible sometimes."

I smiled, thinking of Logan arguing with Greyson just to get a rise out of him. "She was."

"I'm going to miss her so much. I can't believe she's gone."

"I know."

I stayed with Greyson for a long while, listening to the sound of his breathing and squeezing his hand when he cried. Taking part in Greyson's pain was exhausting, but it gave me a purpose. I couldn't stop to think, because when I did, I knew I would fall apart.

The Last Uprising

For the next week, I slept very little. I shuffled from bedside to bedside, administering Amory's pain medication and forcing Greyson to eat. I watched the rebels draw out the last remaining PMC officers from Greyson's window, and more commune refugees showed up.

They were pale and broken, and they brought news of the revolution. The carriers had been contained to one quadrant of the city. Ida was evacuating the last communes in the region and working with the Canadian government to grant them safety until they could return to the states.

I listened to the staticky radio in the hotel lobby, and I knew the rebels from the west were traveling to Sector X to drive out the last of the PMC there.

One evening, I was on the verge of dozing off in my favorite chair in the lobby, enjoying the cool, rainy breeze sneaking in through the sliding glass door.

I heard a voice calling me from a distant place in my memory — a home that smelled like summer.

I opened my eyes and saw the back of a woman standing at the front desk. She was clearly a refugee from the communes, but she was wearing a gray raincoat over the telltale white scrubs. She had a flimsy backpack slung over one shoulder, and the lanky little girl next to her had her elbows resting on the counter, watching the young desk attendant sort out the room keys.

As the woman turned, I caught a good look at the messy curls that framed her face and those warm brown eyes that were so familiar.

The girl was unfairly tan, considering it was early spring, with a long curly ponytail and huge chocolate eyes.

"Mrs. Frey?" I blurted.

The woman turned cautiously, and from the man's confused look and her panic, I knew instantly she had used

The Last Uprising

an alias to book a room. She studied me for a long second, her brain working to connect two very separate worlds.

"Oh my god. Haven?"

Before I knew what I was doing, I was out of the chair and launching myself into her arms.

I didn't think about how I must look — tangled hair, borrowed clothes, and bedraggled from days without sleep — but she didn't seem to notice. Her arms held me tightly with the gentle care only a mother can manage.

When I pulled away, she seemed unsurprised to see me in rebel black, and her eyes filled with tears.

"I know you," said the girl with a voice like a bell.

"I know you, too," I said.

"You're Haven . . . Greyson's friend."

"That's right, Dani."

Mrs. Frey looked absolutely beside herself. She smiled weakly and let out two full breaths before asking the question I knew she had been dreading the answer to.

"Is he . . . Is he *alive*?" She spoke the word quietly, as though Dani's eleven-year-old ears couldn't hear them if she whispered.

"Yes!" I said, laughing with relief. "He's alive."

The look on her face was enough to make it all worth it — the revolution, killing Aryus, losing a part of myself in the process. For once, I did not have to deliver the news that a loved one was dead. I got to bring Greyson back to his mother and sister.

"Do you know where I can find him?"

I laughed again, the grin almost hurting as it stretched muscles in my face that I hadn't used for weeks. "Yes! He's here."

Suddenly, Mrs. Frey's look of joy was replaced by a quiet fear. After all this time, she was so close, and she probably didn't want to let herself hope.

I marveled at how much she resembled Greyson. Their eyes were identical: loving but guarded. She had his unruly curls and caramel skin. An older Dani could have been his twin.

"Why don't you go get settled," I said, thinking of Greyson lying in the dark, completely dead to the world.

I couldn't let his mother see him like that. Not after nearly a year apart. "I'll bring him to your room in a few minutes."

She nodded, wiping the tears that threatened to spill over with a shaky hand. Dani was jumping up and down, nearly pulling her mom's arm out of its socket in her excitement.

I left them in the lobby and tore up the stairs to Greyson's room. I shoved the key in the slot and barged in without knocking.

Greyson was still right where I'd left him: lying on his bed fully clothed, staring up at the ceiling.

"Get up!" I nearly shouted.

He turned his head to face me, intrigued by my breathless voice and the excitement on my face.

"Hurry!" I yelled, springing onto his bed and jostling him.

He rubbed his eyes lethargically, hair sticking up in the back.

I grabbed his arm and pulled him out of bed.

"Get in the shower! You won't believe who's here!"

He stood there, arms hanging limply at his sides, and I

wanted to hit him. Yes, I knew he was grieving, and my heart broke for him every time I looked in those eyes. But he wasn't the only one who had lost Logan — just the only one who seemed to have died right along with her.

His look of emptiness turned to irritation when he caught me staring at him, and he gave a heavy shrug and slumped back down on the bed.

"Go away, Haven. I don't want to see anybody."

"Yes, you do," I said, unable to rein in my enthusiasm.

"No."

"Greyson, your mom and Dani are here."

He looked up at me, a wrinkle appearing between his brows. "Shut up."

"Really. I was just sitting in the lobby, and they walked right in the front door."

"I said *shut up*, Haven!"

His voice was angrier than I'd ever heard it, and I took a step back, bumping into the wall.

"I know you're desperate to get me up and at 'em so you can stop thinking about Logan, but that's just about the shittiest thing you've *ever* done."

His words felt like a slap. Without thinking, without pausing to explain, my fist flew out and decked him across the face. He lurched backward, smacking his head against the fake hotel headboard, and looked up at me.

What was that gleam in his eye? Satisfaction? Amusement?

"I'm being serious. Your mom and Dani are getting settled in their room right now. I told them you'd come see them in a few minutes. But I won't bring you to them like this. You look like shit."

"Are they really here?" he asked in a scratchy voice.

"Yes."

He tried to smile, but his shoulders sagged in defeat. He knew he'd been a ghost for the last week. He'd only eaten the food I'd shoved under his nose, and judging by the rank mustiness of the room, he hadn't so much as showered since we'd been here.

"I'm sorry I hit you," I said. "But you have got to pull it together."

He sighed, and I continued. "We all lost her, Greyson. But Logan would kick your ass if she saw you moping around like this. This isn't grieving. This is you wishing you were dead, too. She wouldn't want this for you. She *told* me."

Greyson pulled in a shaky breath. "Yeah . . . that sounds like her."

He sagged against the headboard, his shoulders drawn in so tight that he looked like a little kid. I sank down beside him and put an arm around him.

Then the sobs came — horrible, dry sobs — and I realized how much Greyson had changed since he was taken from Columbia. Now the revolution was nearly over, and he had nothing to redirect his focus. He had suffered as much as I had, and he was broken.

But now his mom and Dani needed him.

I let him cry for a few more minutes, stroking his messy hair, and then I shoved him in the bathroom and went to round up some clean clothes from the donation bin in the lobby. They wouldn't be his clothes, but at least they would be clean.

I fished out a well-worn pair of jeans and a light-blue T-shirt I thought he'd look good in. Then I waited outside the bathroom while he fussed over his clothes and his overgrown, shaggy hair. I called through the door that he should shave, and he muttered an irritated stream of words that sounded like reluctant agreement.

When he finally emerged, I swallowed down the urge to tell him how handsome he looked. There wasn't much to be done to hide the dark shadows under his eyes or the strain to his smile, but he was clean-shaven, dressed, and up and about with a new purpose.

Secretly, I smiled because I knew Logan would wolf-whistle and cock her head to the side in the flirty way she always did.

I steered him down the hallway to the correct room and knocked softly.

The door flew open almost instantly, and Mrs. Frey's eyes filled with tears.

Before she could close the small distance between them, Dani flew into Greyson's chest like a cannon. He looked good-naturedly winded in a big-brother sort of way, and his mom reached forward to wrap her arms around him.

They stood like that for a while: Dani's skinny arms wrapped around Greyson's waist, and his mother enveloping them both, stroking Greyson's hair and sobbing quietly.

I tiptoed down the hallway to leave them on their own. Greyson was in good hands now.

I let myself into Amory's room and was surprised to find him sitting up in bed, leafing through a John Grisham novel. He jumped a little when he heard me come in but gave a small smile. There was an odd strain to the corners of his mouth I'd never seen before, and a wave of dread washed over me.

"Shriver brought me this when she came to check on my wound," he said, holding up the book. "She also said that painkillers are being rationed, so she can no longer allow my 'recreational use' of oxycodone now that I'm starting to recover."

I laughed. "That sounds like Shriver."

"She also told me what happened to Logan," he said quietly. "How she died."

My breath caught in my chest. "I'm sorry. I should have been the one to tell you."

Amory sighed. "It's okay. I've been really out of it."

I gave a shaky nod and sank down on the edge of his bed. Amory's eyebrows drew together, and he held out his good arm expectantly. "It wasn't your fault."

I climbed gratefully over to him, settling in the crook of his arm and breathing in the warm, woodsy smell of him. Somehow, the hospital antiseptic and the stale, smoky odor of the hotel room could not mask his true smell.

Maybe I didn't have the right to be happy after everything that had happened, but in that moment, I was so thankful for him. I squeezed him tighter and buried my face in his good shoulder, trying to memorize every curve of his chest.

Sometimes I didn't feel as though I deserved Amory.

"What is it?" he asked.

"I thought you would blame me. I know I do."

"What?" His grip tightened around me. "No. No, of course not. Not ever."

"I'm sorry I didn't tell you right away. I just . . . I-I should never have trusted Mariah. All she's ever done is lie, and in the end, she even lied to herself. I believed her, and I shouldn't have."

"No. Haven, no." He gave me a little shake. "Look at it this way: Logan knew her better than anyone, but Logan believed her."

I shook my head, fighting the tears threatening to burst. "It doesn't matter. Logan's gone now." I drew in a ragged breath. "I won't ever see her again."

Then, strangely, I felt a rumble of laughter.

It started low in Amory's chest and burst forth from his lips. He squeezed me as his chest shook, and I jerked around in his arms, worried that he'd completely lost his mind.

"*What?*"

"I'm sorry. I blame the painkillers for the insensitive laughter, but . . ." Amory's eyes crinkled, and I could tell this smile was real. "Sorry, I just don't believe that for a second."

I must have looked confused, because Amory continued. "Logan was so . . . feisty. I think I'll probably see her all the time. Even when she was alive, it was like she was in my head . . . like my annoying, violent conscience.

"Any time I would pick out something to wear, I'd hear Logan making some snide remark. When I'd shoot, I could practically hear her scoffing behind me like *she* could do better. It's like she was arguing with me before I even made a decision."

Amory was smiling, and I realized I was, too. He was right. Logan wouldn't fade away that easily. She refused to be ignored.

We sat like that for a while, both of us remembering Logan. We talked about her and Godfrey and Kinsley, and I finally let myself cry. Amory didn't mind that my tears soaked the shoulder of his T-shirt. He just held me tighter.

I told him about Greyson's mom and sister, and we speculated about what Ida might be doing and how long we thought the revolution would last.

It felt good to talk to him. I needed Amory now more than ever. After absorbing Greyson's grief all week, I needed someone to absorb some of mine.

Soon I felt the exhaustion taking hold, lulled by the steady fall of rain against the window and the warmth of Amory's arms around me.

Before I drifted off, I remembered I still had a promise to fulfill. I had no idea how I would find Logan's family after the New Northern Territory fell. They would be refugees, and it was possible they'd be staying under some alias as Greyson's mom had been.

I found I didn't care how difficult it was or how long it would take. We would find them — at least we had to try.

With or without the revolution, I needed something to fight for.

Epilogue

Three months later.

The farmhouse was empty for the first time in weeks. We'd spent the spring rebuilding, and the farm was once again home to former rebels and commune dwellers passing through. People were migrating back to the states — returning to their former homes to rebuild their lives.

I was making lunch for Greyson and Amory, who'd been working to fix the flower bed in front of the porch, the last remaining indication that the farm had been bombed.

As I shoved the lunch meat and mayonnaise back into the fridge, my thumb brushed the school picture of a little boy with bright blond hair and vibrant green eyes.

Eight years old with skinned knees and an obsession with dinosaurs, Sebastian was a spitting image of Logan. Even the way he moved — graceful, confident, and hell on wheels — made my heart hurt remembering her.

It had been my mission to find Logan's family and tell them that her last thoughts had been to make sure they were safe. But now that I'd found them, putting their lives back together in Logan's childhood home, I was faced with the reality that the revolution was finally over.

"You're deep in thought," said Amory.

I jumped. He was leaning against the doorframe wearing shorts and a T-shirt that was soaked with sweat. His hair was

The Last Uprising

a little longer than it had been during the revolution, and it stuck to his damp forehead and neck. Even sweaty, he was beautiful.

"Just thinking about what happens when Ida comes back . . . after everything is settled."

Ida had been busy helping refugees in the New Northern Territory, and Shriver and Roman had been away for a month curing the infected and rounding up the carriers who'd already turned. Tonight, they were all returning to the farm.

"Everything's going to be different now." I was trying to sound casual, but Amory heard the panic in my voice.

His eyebrows came together in concern, and he crossed the room to close the space between us. He drew me into him with a hand on my waist and buried his face in my neck.

"Hey, don't worry."

I leaned against him and felt myself relax a little. I couldn't go back to my old life, where I'd be forced to face everything that had happened in the last year.

"Whatever happens . . . we'll stay together," Amory whispered, his warm breath tickling my neck.

My heart flipped over twice. He hadn't said that before.

He drew in a shaky breath. "If you want me, I mean."

I pushed him away a little so I could see his face. "Of course I do."

His gray eyes warmed as he smiled, and I felt the heat burning low in my stomach, spreading to all my extremities. He cupped his hands around my neck, tilting my head back so his warm lips could reach the spot where my pulse was pushing against my skin.

"Whoa. Please contain that," said Greyson from the

doorway.

We sprang apart like magnets, and Greyson inched between us to grab one of the sandwiches. He stuffed it in his mouth and fumbled in the fridge for a bottle of water.

"Come on," he said through a mouthful of mayo. "Ida will be here soon."

I scooped up the rest of the sandwiches and followed him outside. Taking in the view of my vegetable crops, the chickens pecking lazily at the dirt, and the freshly transplanted impatiens in the flower bed, I had to admit that we had done a pretty good job returning the farm to its former glory. It was easy to forget that the rest of the country was still struggling, people had been displaced, and entire cities had been reduced to rubble.

We walked over to the spot in the yard overlooking the fields, and Greyson flung himself down in the grass. I blushed and avoided Amory's gaze when I recalled our last encounter here. There was little need for a nightly carrier watch anymore, but whenever I couldn't sleep, I'd often find Amory out here sitting in the spot where I'd first told him I remembered him.

"What do you suppose will happen now?" Greyson asked. He was staring off across the field, but I could tell there was some weight to his question.

"I don't know," I said honestly. "But I don't want to go back. I can't just go to school and pretend everything's fine."

Greyson looked at me quickly. I expected to see surprise on his face, but his expression mirrored the way I felt. "I know what you mean."

Amory cleared his throat, and I knew it was time to change the subject.

We rarely talked about what would happen when the dust settled. The last three months had been complete chaos as

The Last Uprising

the U.S. government found its footing and rounded up anyone who had taken part in the PMC's atrocities.

Amory's father was being tried for treason and crimes against humanity. He would likely spend the rest of his life in prison. Amory said it was what his father deserved, and maybe it was, but I still knew it bothered him.

A crunch of gravel stole my attention, and the three of us jumped to our feet and craned our necks to get the first look at Ida's dirty turquoise pickup truck. Through the windshield, I saw her eyes grow wide with excitement as they landed on us, and she swerved to a stop and jumped out of the car with a motherly squeal.

Even in June, she still wore one of her long, sweeping skirts under a flowing orange tunic. Her waist-length blond hair was nearly pure white from the sun.

"It's so good to see you," I said as she crushed me against her chest.

"Oh my goodness! You look more beautiful than ever."

She pulled Amory and Greyson into her, and the sunburnt lines on her face rumpled with happiness.

When she pulled away, I watched her take in the new barn, the roof we'd repaired, and the fresh black dirt in the flower bed. Her eyes filled with tears.

"It's not quite back to normal yet," I said nervously. "We did the best we could to make repairs, but the barn and the guest house were both completely destroyed in the bombing."

She turned and fixed me with a watery stare. "I couldn't have done it better myself."

Later that night, Amory and Ida prepared a celebratory feast.

It made my heart swell to see them tripping over each

other in the tiny kitchen. The rolls were a little burnt, and the green beans were mushy, but sitting at the dining room table with Amory to my left and Greyson and Ida across from me, I didn't think I'd ever tasted anything better.

I had just put a pot of coffee on when I saw the flash of headlights from the kitchen window. Ida squealed and got up from the table to greet Roman and Shriver.

I didn't know why, but I was nervous to see them — maybe because once they were back, reality would set in. Amory appeared behind me and put a reassuring arm around my shoulders, pulling me toward the hallway to greet them.

Roman was towering over Shriver in the doorway. I'd forgotten how massive he was, but judging by how his T-shirt hung off his frame, he'd lost a lot of weight during his recovery.

His arms bore several new scars, but his eyes had returned to their normal color. They met mine and Amory's over Ida's head, and he nodded to us, the corners of his mouth lifting slightly.

Amory stiffened next to me, and I wanted to laugh. It was the friendliest greeting we'd ever gotten from Roman.

He allowed Ida to steer him into his usual chair in the dining room and interrogate him about what he and Shriver had been up to.

They'd been hunting down carriers Van Helsing–style. Only, instead of killing them, they were curing the ones they could. Those who were beyond saving were relocated to the North Cascades National Park, where nearly eight hundred miles of wilderness and plenty of natural predators could, in theory, keep them contained.

Something about the way Roman indulged Ida's curiosity made me realize how much he'd changed. He was no longer moody and withdrawn. I realized he was grateful to be alive.

Occasionally, Shriver would smile up at him as though they shared a private joke, and he threw his head back to laugh when she finished a funny story. A full-body laugh from Roman was something I'd never seen, and it made me inexplicably happy.

Roman talked about wanting to join the military when it was all over so he could help round up PMC who were still in hiding, and I cringed internally as the discussion turned to planning.

"What about you, Haven?" Shriver asked.

My faced burned. I didn't want to say I didn't have a plan. It felt like admitting I wasn't strong enough to face real life.

There was a long, awkward pause, and I could feel Amory's eyes on me. But then, like always, Ida came to the rescue.

"Actually, I was hoping Haven might help me with something," she said. "And Greyson and Amory, if they're up for it."

"What is it?" I asked, my stomach filling with dread. I didn't want to go back to the New Northern Territory to help the refugees. I didn't want to be anywhere near the border.

"I was hoping we might keep the farm open as a safe house for a while longer."

Her voice was casual, as if she were merely voicing a passing thought, but my heart fluttered with hope.

"There are still so many displaced commune dwellers who will need to make their way back to their homes. I'd like to help them if we could, but I'll understand if —"

"I'd love to," I said.

"Me too," said Greyson through a mouthful of food.

The Last Uprising

"Count me in," said Amory, reaching for my hand under the table. My chest filled with warmth, and I returned his gentle pressure with a squeeze.

Ida beamed. "Wonderful! I knew I could count on you three."

As Amory held my hand, I allowed myself to soak up Ida's words.

I didn't have to leave. I could stay at the farm with Amory and Greyson.

I fought back the tears that threatened to make an appearance. It was as if Ida had sensed without ever asking what I wanted most of all: a home.

As Ida poured everyone a second cup of coffee, Roman leaned in briefly and touched his lips to Shriver's brow. I watched Amory and Greyson exchange a look of shock, and Greyson put his cup to his lips to hide the grin that was spreading across his face.

Amory's fingers were tracing soothing circles on my knee, and I resisted the urge to knock over my chair and drag him upstairs.

Usually, all I wanted was him. With Amory, I didn't have to pretend everything was all right. We understood each other perfectly. But tonight, everything felt as though it was all right, and I wanted to soak it in just a little bit longer — all of us, here, together.

I didn't know what next year would be like, or even tomorrow. I found I didn't care. The only things that mattered had fallen into place, and that was good enough for me.

Finally, everyone I loved was safe.

Enjoy this book?

You can connect with the author at www.tarahbenner.com to stay up-to-date on the latest from Tarah Benner.

Printed in Great Britain
by Amazon